The Butterfly Girl

ALSO BY TANIA CROSSE

DEVONSHIRE SAGAS
Book 1: The Harbourmaster's Daughter
Book 2: The River Girl
Book 3: The Gunpowder Girl
Book 4: The Quarry Girl
Book 5: The Railway Girl
Book 6: The Wheelwright Girl
Book 7: The Ambulance Girl
Book 8: The Dartmoor Girl
Book 9: The Girl At Holly Cottage
Book 10: The Convent Girl
Book 11: The Butterfly Girl

THE BUTTERFLY *Girl*

TANIA CROSSE

Devonshire Sagas Book 11

Joffe Books, London
www.joffebooks.com

First published in Great Britain in 2025

© Tania Crosse

This book is a work of fiction. Names, characters, businesses, organizations, places and events are either the product of the author's imagination or are used fictitiously. Any resemblance to actual persons, living or dead, events or locales is entirely coincidental.
The spelling used is British English except where fidelity to the author's rendering of accent or dialect supersedes this.
The right of Tania Crosse to be identified as author of this work has been asserted in accordance with the Copyright, Designs and Patents Act 1988.

No part of this book may be used or reproduced in any manner for the purpose of training artificial intelligence technologies or systems. In accordance with Article 4(3) of the Digital Single Market Directive 2019/790, Joffe Books expressly reserves this work from the text and data mining exception.

Cover art by Jarmila Takač
Cover figure by Richard Jenkins Photography

ISBN: 978-1-83526-951-0

*In memory of the little ones who were killed
in the Maternity Unit at Plymouth's City Hospital
during the bombing raid of 21 March 1941*

*And as always for my dear husband whose love
and understanding know no bounds.
We've travelled the road together for over fifty years
and every step has brought me joy.*

CHAPTER ONE

Plymouth, March 1941

It happened in the blink of an eye.

The haunting wail of the siren suddenly rolled out across the city, sending sparks of horror down every spine. After the deadly attack the previous night that had been hell on earth and by far the heaviest raid Plymouth had experienced so far, the idea of another horrific bombing didn't bear thinking about. But it seemed they could be in for it again. For an instant, everyone froze into a macabre tableau, breath held in eerie silence as they listened. Praying they were mistaken.

But there it came again, that deathly moan that struck an icy chill into every heart. All at once, the scene sprang back to life, almost as if a film reel had become momentarily stuck in its projector before freeing itself and spinning on. But this was no film. This was real.

'Right. You all know what to do,' Sister Atkins said calmly and efficiently as her eyes swept around the ward in the City Hospital's brand-new maternity block.

The nurses hurried off in all directions. Probationer nurse Philippa Luscombe strode swiftly towards the sluice room where two trolleys, equipped with sterilised enamel washbowls, stood ready and waiting. In a trice, her new friend, probationer nurse Stephanie Chappel, was by her side. While Sister Atkins went to supervise the transferring of the new-born babies from the nursery area of the children's ward down to the relative safety of the basement, Philippa and Stephanie wheeled the trolleys at breakneck speed into the ward. Philippa's heart was thudding in her chest, her whole body shaking, but she had a job to do. These mothers were relying on her.

Out of the corner of her eye, she saw those women who'd been delivered of their babies several days before, and who had therefore been moved to the far end of the ward, being helped out of bed by student midwives. Considered able to walk in an emergency, they'd be assisted down to the basement. Stephanie dashed with her trolley to the central section of the ward, just as they'd practised, while Philippa dealt with the patients in the beds nearest the doors. The first was an ashen-faced girl, no older than Philippa herself, who'd given birth only that afternoon after a difficult labour. She was pale and weak, her eyes huge with fear in her pinched face. With an intravenous drip in her arm, there was no way she could even seek protection by getting under the bed.

Philippa turned on her what she hoped was a reassuring smile. 'Put this on your head,' she instructed, handing her one of the bowls. Though what good it could do if it came to it, she really didn't know.

The girl took it in silence, her eyes swivelling skyward as the siren continued to blare across the darkened city, its unearthly cry rising in wave upon wave of ghoulish moans until it stopped abruptly. Then came the all too familiar drone of planes filling the sky, and the dull rattle of anti-aircraft guns. Philippa would have liked to offer the girl some comfort, but there was no time.

She turned to the patient in the next bed, a rotund woman who'd delivered her seventh child the previous day as easily as shelling a pea.

'Give it yere, my flower,' she beamed, grabbing a second bowl from Philippa's grasp and plonking it on her head. 'There, rather fetching, don't you think?' she joked. 'Makes us look like Mae West, I shouldn't wonder. *Come up and see me some time*,' she mimicked, her mouth pouting seductively.

At any other time, Philippa would have chuckled, but now a wry grimace flickered over her face as she turned away. Quite a character was Mrs Chollacott. But underneath, she knew she was probably just as terrified as the rest of them.

Philippa scooted back to the trolley in the middle of the ward to distribute more of the metal bowls. It was forbidden to run except in the case of fire or cardiac arrest. There was nothing about air raids in the rules. And in this instance, Philippa was prepared to break any rule she deemed necessary.

It was as she reached for the next item of improvised head protection that it happened. A shrieking scream somewhere in the sky above the building drew her gaze towards the ceiling. A dart of fear. And in that instant she somehow knew that one was for them.

Less than a split second later, a blinding flash pierced the gloom of the dimly lit ward at the same time as a mighty explosion hammered into Philippa's ears and roared through her entire being. The force of the blast rippled through her body, lifting her off her feet and hurling her backwards across the ward as if she were a rag doll. Her back slammed against the wall, completely winding her, flinging her head back so that her skull cracked against the painted brickwork. Her vision darkened with black stars but she was unaware of any pain as the force of the impact then threw her forward. She knew she was falling and instinctively thrust out her hands to save herself, heard the crack and a fire burned into her wrist.

She landed with a thud, pinned to the floor, shocked, blinded, unable to move. Could hear the terrifying clatter as masonry and twisted iron girders crashed downwards around her, the groan and cracking as more plaster and splintering wood strained and gave way. The air was a sudden smog of choking dust, sticking to her nose and her lips. Women were crying out, screaming in terror, the horrifying sounds filling her head, resounding like thunder. She must get to her feet, help whoever she could. She was a nurse. It was her duty. But just as she tried to scrape herself from the floor, something landed across her, knocking the breath from her lungs. She tried to heave herself upwards, but everything started to fade. She couldn't . . . Was slipping away into nothingness and was lost in oblivion.

***

Where am I?

She could hear voices all around her, calm and yet muffled so that she couldn't make out what they were saying. It was as if she had cotton wool in her ears. Or as if she was under water. Her head was full of a whooshing, gurgling sound. She wanted to call out, to find out what was happening, but nothing in her wanted to work. She felt as if her body was weighted down, leaden. She couldn't even open her eyes.

She remembered the sudden flare of brilliant, dazzling light, a bit like in a thunderstorm. There'd been a deafening crash, too, like thunder exploding overhead. But she couldn't recall anything else.

And yet it was quite a pleasant sensation if she didn't try to think. As if she was floating on a calm and gentle sea. She felt relaxed and comfortable. Perhaps she wouldn't try to think anymore. Wouldn't try to remember. She'd just allow herself to sink slowly beneath those lapping waves, to a place where it felt warm and peaceful . . .

***

It was the smell she recognised first. A distinctive mixture of carbolic soap, Dettol and whatever else that had become so familiar to her. She was on a hospital ward, and she was a nurse. Or at least, a probationer nurse. Except that now it seemed she was a patient, lying in a bed and listening to the sounds of low voices, screens being moved and padding feet. She didn't feel any pain, but was gently drifting like a floating feather, as if she were lying in a soft cradle that was rocking in the breeze.

Although her eyes didn't want to open, she could tell it was daylight now, banishing all those dreadful fears of the night. She wasn't sure how she'd got here, but she was certain something awful had happened. But she knew she was being looked after and she felt content and safe. Everything would be all right, and she was lulled in a sense of calm and security so deep that she was happy to let it wash over her and send her back to sleep. She would find out the truth when it was time to wake up. For now, all was well and she could surrender to slumber again.

***

'Oh, come on, Pippa, you must wake up!'

She knew that voice at once. The words came, urgent and imploring, as if they were echoing through a dense fog, but it was definitely her new friend, Steph. The memory was all a bit hazy, but she recalled how they'd met on their first day at the hospital. Pippa was so excited. She'd wanted to train as a nurse for as long as she could remember. She'd liked the look of Steph as soon as she'd seen her, and had been delighted when they'd been put to share a room together.

Oh, how she desperately wanted to respond to her now, but her lips wouldn't move. What was wrong with her that she seemed cut off from the outside world?

'Come on, Pippa,' she heard Steph continue, her tone softer now. 'Rusty and me, we want you to make a foursome with us with another airman at the base and—'

'Probationer Nurse Whoever-you-are, what do you think you're doing? You know nurses are only allowed to address each other by their surnames, and you're not allowed to fraternise with the patients.'

The reply was almost instant. 'Well, just now I'm a visitor, visiting a friend in hospital, so neither of those rules apply.'

The words raced through Pippa's head. She would have gasped in horror if she'd been capable. From somewhere deep down, she knew it wouldn't be the first time Steph's outspoken tongue had got her into trouble, and she'd certainly be for it now!

'While you're in uniform and on my ward, *both* those rules apply,' the other voice reprimanded sternly.

'Would you like me to take my uniform off, then, and stand here in my underwear?'

Oh, Lordy love. Pippa didn't know whether to feel horrified or amused. But the harsh voice caught her attention again.

'Well, I've never heard such insolence. What's your name? I shall be reporting you to Sister Tutor.'

'Go ahead. I'm Nurse Chappel, and right now, Pippa's health is the only thing I care about. We've been taught that talking to a patient with concussion is the best way to bring them round, like, and that's just what I'm doing.'

'Not now you're not. And it isn't even visiting time. Now leave my ward *at once!*'

'All right, I will. But only because I don't want to upset Pippa if she can hear us. But I'll be back. *In my civvies.*' Pippa heard the sharp sarcasm in Steph's final words. And then she felt soft breath against her cheek as her friend whispered in her ear, 'Rotten cow. She'd better be looking after you properly. And I'll be back as soon as I can.'

All Pippa heard then was fading footfall and the sister huffing at the bottom of her bed, before the muted sounds of the ward engulfed her brain again. Things were becoming clearer now, and she was able to work out which ward she must be on. Women's Medical, under the eagle eyes of Sister Pudifoot. She and Steph hadn't encountered her before, but the sister had the reputation of a tartar.

After three solid months of lectures and practical training, Steph and Pippa had finally been allowed on the wards. She, Steph and Ruby Saundercock had been allocated to Men's Surgical. After another three months, she and Steph had been picked for a stint on the coveted maternity unit, reward for being the highest achieving probationers of that intake. Ruby hadn't been best pleased about that, Pippa remembered, and she'd tried to pacify her by saying it was probably only because they were very short-staffed and didn't have enough student midwives to go round. After all, you couldn't start specialising in midwifery proper until you'd completed your three years nurses' training, and it wasn't everybody who stayed the course.

Ah, the brand-new maternity block. Pippa had loved it from the very first day. A soft sigh whispered from her lungs as things began to fall into place, a bit like an ethereal jigsaw. Neither she nor Steph had witnessed an actual birth yet, but they'd learnt how to make up bottles of Cow and Gate and feed the babies, bath them and change their nappies. The dear little things were so sweet and vulnerable, their heads smelling so clean and pure as you held them against your shoulder to wind them. And then there were their mothers who came in all shapes and sizes, some experienced, others novices. Pippa remembered one young girl no older than herself who'd had a difficult time . . .

She breathed in a sudden, deep, horrified gasp that made her feel dizzy as the terrifying memory flooded back. The drone of the aircraft overhead, the blinding flash of light, the deafening explosion that had hurled her across the ward, the noise that had blasted into her head, fear you could taste as screams and dust filled the air. *Oh, dear God!* Terror slashed through her heart and she opened her eyes wide and she sat up in bed, ignoring the pain in her chest as her head swam.

The ward shuddered into focus. All was calm and peaceful, women lying quietly in two regimented rows of beds, and two nurses smoothing the sheets over a patient in a bed near the door. Pippa caught her breath. Had she imagined that horrific scene? Her head ached and she felt so confused, but she was lying in a hospital bed and in pain. No. Her mind wasn't playing tricks. It had happened.

'Ah, there you are, Nurse Luscombe, back with us I see.' Sister Pudifoot's efficient voice made Pippa blink hard. 'Good. You've had a nasty concussion, so let's lie you back on the pillows. You have badly bruised ribs, though not broken, but you do have a fractured wrist.'

Pippa barely had time to glance down at the plaster cast around her right arm before the sister was supporting her in the way they'd been taught in the lectures, and was easing her backwards. Oh, yes, her ribs did hurt and she was happy to sink back into the comfort of the sea of pillows. But . . .

'The maternity ward?' she demanded in alarm as Sister Pudifoot tucked her in.

She saw the woman's face stiffen. 'No need to worry about that now,' she replied crisply. 'You just concentrate on getting yourself better.'

Her face cracked into the fleetest of smiles before she turned and walked swiftly down the ward, leaving Pippa bewildered. But no. She knew something appalling had happened. The maternity block had been hit, she was sure of it. But how badly? Was she the only one hurt?

She groaned, biting her lip. She'd have to wait until Steph came to see her again. And would she tell her the truth? It was all so awful! And what good could she do with one arm in plaster? Absolutely nothing.

She gritted her teeth as tears of sadness and frustration welled up in her eyes. But she mustn't cry. She was determined not to give in, no matter what.

CHAPTER TWO

'Oh, my poor darling girl!'

'Oh, Mum, it's good to see you!' Pippa cried as a wave of panic rushed through her. 'But is Dad okay?'

'Yes, he's fine. But look at you, my poor cheel!'

'Really, Mum, it's all right.' Pippa tried to pacify her mother as she saw the worried expression on her face. 'Only please don't try to hug me. It hurts too much.'

'Well, then, it isn't all right, is it?' Adeline Luscombe moaned, looking as if she might burst into tears. 'And not letting me see you until now is quite ridiculous.'

'Well, visiting is only once a week, so they were only keeping to the rules.'

'And don't they think patients get better quicker when they can see their friends and family? Or at least feel better for having seen them?'

Pippa could see her mother was shaking with emotion, and gave a wry smile. 'As it happens, I agree with you, but the theory is that it's too disruptive and could interfere with patients' treatment.'

'Poppycock! I don't see much actual treatment going on now. And look at you. Propped up on pillows just waiting to get better. How much treatment is that? And knowing you, I bet you're bored stiff, doing nothing.'

'Ah, well that's not quite true,' Pippa grinned back. 'Steph sent me in my Baillière's. You see?' she said, pointing to two small red text books on her bedside cabinet. '*Aids to Practical Nursing* and *Aids to Anatomy and Physiology*. Now that my headaches have stopped, I'm doing some studying so I'm not wasting my time.'

'Well, you make sure you don't overdo it,' Adeline frowned. 'And how can you manage to turn the pages? Your fingers scarcely stick out from the plaster on that hand.'

'It doesn't take much to turn a page, Mum. Why don't you come round this side and then you can hold my other hand?'

'Oh, yes! I just want to hold you and make you better!'

'Nurse!' Pippa called to a young girl in a pale blue check uniform who happened to be passing the bottom of the bed. 'Please could you bring a chair for my mother?'

'That were very brave of you, my love,' Adeline said in a timid voice as the chair appeared beside her.

Pippa lowered her voice. 'Actually, this is Geraldine, in the same intake as me, only we're not supposed to acknowledge the fact. Thank you, Nurse,' she said a little louder now, and exchanged winks with her colleague. 'Now tell me, Mum. How are you? You must've been petrified during those raids. And where's Dad?'

'He's sorry he couldn't come, too,' Adeline replied, settling herself in the chair and taking her daughter's hand. 'But he's still at the office. Building's so badly damaged, they're in the process of moving out to new premises Mutley way.'

'Sorry to hear that. But we're only allowed one visitor at a time, anyway, so one of you would've had to wait outside and then swap over.'

'Just as well, then. Though I wouldn't have minded someone with me trying to get across the city. Or at least what's left of it.' Adeline let out a deep sigh and shook her head. 'I know we've had raids afore, like, but those two a week ago were something else. The whole city centre's been flattened, either bombed or burnt to the ground. That first night, Spooners and the Royal Hotel had the worst fires. Just burnt-out shells now. I were terrified with your dad being out on his ARP duties. And then the second night, well . . . I can tell you, they finished off what they'd started the night afore. Half of Union Street's gone, too. And I don't need to tell you about the hospital. When we heard about the maternity block being hit, we thought we'd lost you. And all those poor babies!'

Pippa watched her mother's face crumple as she pulled Pippa's hand up to her cheek, a torrent of tears suddenly flowing from her screwed up eyes and dripping down over their joined fingers. Pippa's heart squeezed. Her mum had always been the nervy type and this war wasn't helping. But what was that she'd said about *all those poor babies*?

Pippa's pulse ratcheted up in her chest. She could see her mother was trembling and so she didn't want to press the matter. But . . . what had really happened? It seemed that no one wanted to tell her.

'How's your knitting going?' Pippa reluctantly changed the subject. She really didn't like seeing her mother so upset and hoped that mention of her hobby might distract her. 'And the pig club?'

Adeline gave a giant sniff. 'Well, I could see I weren't going to have enough of the blue to finish the jumper for little Timmy next door, but Mrs Hodges down the road had a bit of grey going spare. So I worked in a grey diamond pattern down the front and it were just enough. Looks super, too.'

'I bet it does.' Pippa gave a beaming smile. 'You're so clever at knitting. I could never get the hang of it myself.'

'Not for want of my trying to teach you,' her mother chuckled, her tears drying now. 'But you're so clever in other ways. Scholarship to the grammar school in the end, and now look at you! So proud of you we are, your dad and me.'

Pippa grunted in reply. 'I've only ever done what came naturally, like. And I really am loving my nursing training. But you were going to tell me about the pig club?' she prompted, not wanting the conversation to revert back to the hospital.

'Oh, well, we've had some fun and games there.' Adeline nodded her head in amusement. 'You know how we all take our scraps down to the pen. Well, someone didn't shut the gate proper like, and Percy pushed his way out. First I heard were when there were screams coming from over the road. A pig on the loose, and one as big as Percy, can be quite frightening. Mrs Harper had a string bag full of veg from the market and were trying to open her front door when Percy toddles up and pushes his snout into her shopping. Quite forceful he can be, and she were petrified, poor soul. So a few of us went out, and Mrs Hodges went to the shed to get the boards and between us all, we managed to persuade Percy back to his pen. But it took the best part of an hour. Didn't seem very funny at the time, but looking back, it must've been quite a sight!'

'Yes, I can imagine!' Pippa giggled, thinking of dumpy Mrs Hodges waddling along while trying to push an obstreperous Percy along with a pig board.

She could see her mum was laughing now, too, and she relaxed back against the pillows. She hadn't realised that her neck muscles had tensed up causing a niggling ache in her head, and she didn't want that coming back fiercely again. But now her mother seemed recovered from her outburst of emotion, she felt they could chat normally again.

'So, how long d'you reckon they'll keep you in here?' Adeline asked next.

Pippa puffed out her cheeks. 'I don't really know. My wrist will be in plaster another four of five weeks, so I'll be no good on the wards. My ribs are bruised, not broken, and the effects of the concussion have pretty well gone, although I'll have to take things easy for a while. So I'm guessing another week or so, and then it'll be back to the nurses' home, just attending lectures when I feel up to it, I suppose. At least I'll have plenty of folk around to look after me!' she managed to joke, seeing her mother's downcast expression.

'Well, you make sure you take care,' Adeline insisted.

'I will. Better to be careful now and make a full recovery, rather than push myself and take longer. Oh, is it that time already?'

The probationer nurse, Geraldine, was walking up the ward, ringing the bell to announce the end of visiting hour, and there was a general scraping of chairs as people stood up and were saying their fond farewells.

'Well, that hour went proper quickly,' Adeline complained, getting to her feet. 'I'll be in to see you again next week if you're still in here. Or if you're back in the nurses' home, maybe I can see you there.'

'If I'm no longer in here, I'll ask Sister Tutor permission to use the phone and give you a ring to let you know. She's really nice, is Sister Tutor, and very understanding. Much more so than Sister Pudifoot who's in charge of this ward. Right dragon she is, so you'd best be off afore she flies down the ward breathing fire all over you!'

Adeline bent over to kiss her daughter's forehead. 'Bye, bye, then, love.'

'Bye, Mum. Take care out there and give Dad a kiss from me.'

Pippa watched as her mother walked down the ward, then turned to give a final wave before disappearing out of the doors. Pippa let out as deep a sigh as her ribs allowed, and sank back into the pillows. It was lovely to see her mum and she appreciated her coming across the devastated city, but she felt surprisingly tired now, and was happy she was in bed. It would be a cup of tea and a Rich Tea biscuit soon, a quick tea of sandwiches and plain cake having been squeezed in before visiting began at five thirty. Then it wouldn't be long before lights out, and the hours of darkness would begin. Pippa just prayed there wouldn't be another raid. Memories of the night she'd been injured kept flashing through her brain at the most unexpected times. She certainly didn't want to go through that again.

She wondered once more exactly what had happened. The maternity block had been hit, that was obvious. But how badly? There'd been the noise and the dust and the screaming. Had she been the only one hurt? There was nobody else on this ward that she recognised from Maternity and who could've been injured. But what was it her mother had said? *All those poor babies*? A groan rumbled deep in Pippa's chest. It might be dreadful news, but she felt she needed to know.

It was just like everything else, really. As nurses, their lives were so contained within the hospital, their days so full of work and study with little contact with the outside world, that sometimes they had no more than a vague idea of what was going on. But when there were raids on Plymouth, they couldn't help but be involved, holding their breath as incendiaries and explosives rained down on the city. They even had a rota for fire watching up on the roof.

Thinking back as she lay in bed, Pippa reckoned that the last full night she remembered must have been the twentieth of March which had been by far the worst raid to date. Had Hitler known that the king and queen were visiting that afternoon and hoped to catch them in the attack? If so, he had failed as the Luftwaffe had arrived too late. But if the raids over the previous months hadn't been bad enough, the one that night was cataclysmic. As Adeline had said, savage infernos had blazed all over the city so that the sky itself had seemed on fire, lighting the way for the bombers. Even at the hospital, you couldn't ignore it. Sitting exposed at the top of a hill to the north-east of the city, the hospital was a sitting target and had been hit in a raid back in January, killing a young girl patient and wreaking extensive damage. So, when wave upon wave of planes swooped across the March sky, Pippa had exchanged frightened glances with Steph, but they had to carry on almost as if nothing was happening.

But it was, and every jaw had been clenched in fear. The noise of aircraft, ack-ack guns and explosions had been deafening, the floor shaking beneath their feet and the insidious stench of cordite, smoke and aircraft fumes seeping in through the closed windows. They'd gone off official duty at nine o'clock as usual, but instead of going to bed, it was an unwritten rule that in a raid, they should go to Casualty to see if there was anything they could do to help as the injured rolled in. Besides, it was unlikely they'd manage to get any sleep anyway.

The scene that had met their eyes had been shocking, the injured crammed into every corner. Adrenaline had circled Pippa's body as between them, she and Steph and a number of other volunteer nursing staff had applied bandages and pressure pads, cleaned minor cuts and offered comfort to the less badly wounded, leaving doctors and more senior nurses to cope with the more serious cases. Pippa's stomach roiled as she remembered some of the appalling injuries she'd seen that night, blood everywhere, people crying out in pain, dreadful burns, blackened faces, absolute chaos as the ward overflowed with more and more victims, some being rushed to Theatre, others being taken up to wards that were already full to capacity and had beds and trolleys parked in a new row down the middle.

And then there were those who were taken straight to the morgue.

Pippa sighed as she recalled how little relief there'd been when the raid had stopped in the early hours of the following morning. The various rescue services kept on bringing in the dead and wounded, innocent civilians, service personnel and all branches of Civil Defence. Pippa and Steph and all the other off-duty staff had finally been chivvied away about three o'clock to grab a few hours' sleep before going back on duty on their normal wards at seven thirty. Needless to say exhausted though they were, nobody had slept a wink. Everything had been going round and round in Pippa's head, her heart fluttering as she'd thought of her timid mother alone in the Anderson shelter in the garden, with only the cat for company, and her father out in the thick of it in his work as an ARP warden. Pray God . . .

It was clear the raid had been unimaginably devastating. They'd learnt next day that hundreds of homes and businesses had been destroyed, much of the city centre obliterated, and heaven knew how many people had been killed or injured. The City wasn't the only hospital in Plymouth to have been inundated with victims. The extent of the devastation had been incomprehensible, and Pippa remembered how the peace and quiet on the maternity ward had somehow seemed incongruous after the crazy to-ing and fro-ing in all other parts of the hospital she'd been part of during the night. All other wards were still chock-a-block, some patients recovering from treatment or hasty operations, while others were still waiting to go to Theatre. Doctors, surgeons and nursing staff had been at breaking point, and it was still going on the next day.

Pippa squeezed her eyes shut as she tried to block out the horrendous details, but as she'd emerged from the concussion, the memories had kept leaping into her head. By the end of the following day on the maternity ward, she'd been dead on her feet and couldn't wait for the shift to end at nine o'clock, and hopefully she'd get some sleep that night. When the air-raid siren had gone off, her heart had sunk at the same time as adrenaline had pumped through her body. And then it had happened.

She vaguely remembered being lifted from her feet and thrown across the ward, but after that, it was one great blur. She knew something horrendous had happened, but she needed to know the details. She was so much a part of it that she felt a piece of her was missing. If only someone would tell her.

'I know you're not asleep because your face is all screwed up, like.'

Pippa's eyes sprang open and delighted surprise lit up her face. 'Steph! How on earth did you get in here? Visiting's finished and—'

'I've just confirmed a late pass with Matron, and who should be going in to see her next but Sister Pudifoot. So I slipped down here quickly to see if I could sneak in, but just for a few minutes afore she comes back. And then I'm off to see Rusty.'

'Yes, I can see you're dressed up to the nines,' Pippa giggled, eyeing up her friend's fitted green coat and the matching hat set at a jaunty angle on her halo of auburn hair. 'But I'm surprised Matron let you have a late pass after you came to see me afore and had that barny with the dreaded sister! I know I wasn't properly conscious but I could hear what was going on.'

'Really? Then you'll know the old cow reported me to Sister Tutor, but I turned on the tears about you and *she* just told me never to let it happen again. I don't think she even told Matron. So now I'm off to trip the light fantastic with Rusty or whatever we decide to do.'

'Well, have a great time but do be careful. Don't take any chances.'

'What, me?' Steph blinked her eyes wide with mock innocence. 'I won't, but I wanted to see you're all right afore I went, otherwise I couldn't enjoy myself proper like.'

'Well, I'm doing fine, only . . .'

Steph tipped her head. 'Only what?'

Pippa sucked in her bottom lip. 'I need to know what happened that night when the maternity block was hit. Nobody will tell me. But Mum visited earlier and she mentioned something about *all those poor babies*. So . . . what did happen?'

She watched as her friend's face drained of its colour behind the powder and rouge she'd applied. Steph's eyes met hers and she could see the sadness in them.

'D'you . . . not remember?' Steph's forehead pleated in earnest. 'Do you really want to know? And if I tell you, you won't let on it was me? But I suppose you'll find out eventually. It was pretty awful, mind.'

Pippa could feel her heart thrumming in her chest, but she nodded in reply.

'Well,' Steph hesitated, 'you're right that the maternity block got a direct hit. On the children's ward. It was utterly destroyed. There . . . there weren't many survivors. About twenty babies and young kiddies were lost, that lovely staff midwife and five nurses, some of them younger than us. And one mother, the one nearest the door who'd had a bad time of it, poor soul, if you remember. Just a young cheel herself, she was. You were standing at the bottom of her bed between her and that Mrs Chollacott when it happened. I think the blast must've lifted you off your feet. I didn't really see because I was further down the ward. Escaped with just cuts and bruises did Mrs Chollacott and the rest of them.'

Horror flushed through Pippa's body and she shuddered. Perhaps people had been right to try and hide the truth from her. She could feel emotion welling up inside her, moisture trembling on her eyelashes. Tears glistened in Steph's eyes, too, but then she sniffed hard and straightened her shoulders.

'I'd better go afore the witch gets back and catches me. And . . . I hope you don't think badly of me going off to enjoy myself when . . . well, you know.'

Pippa shook her head. 'No, of course not. I know it's hard for you to find times when you and Rusty are both off duty. So you have a lovely time. It won't change what happened.'

Steph nodded wistfully and then, with a little wave, scooted off down the ward before Sister Pudifoot returned. Pippa watched her go, but the moment her friend had disappeared through the doors, her heart felt leaden again. All those poor babies, indeed. And all those poor mothers who'd just given birth and had their new-borns ripped away from them so cruelly. That young girl who'd seemed so terrified, the nursing staff, the midwife who'd been so kind to them as students, explaining everything with such patience. It was all so awful.

She tried to bite back her tears but she couldn't stop them and they flowed down her cheeks unchecked. Misery engulfed her like a black cloud. Just so many had died or been injured, and now those innocent children . . . She'd wanted to train as a nurse to make a difference but now she just felt so helpless. Even if she hadn't been lying in bed recovering herself, what good could she really do? She couldn't stop this terrible war. And who knew what would happen next?

She just closed her eyes and wanted it all to go away.

CHAPTER THREE

'Well, young lady, I think it's time you were discharged, don't you?' The doctor looked up from consulting the charts on the clipboard at the foot of Pippa's bed, and beamed at her. 'You've made an excellent recovery with no unwanted complications, so you're fit to go home. Which is . . . ?' Before Pippa had a chance to enlighten him, his eyes travelled swiftly to the top of the page and his eyebrows lifted. 'Ah, I see you're one of us. Well, Nurse, I'll have a word with Sister Tutor and see what can be arranged.'

Pippa took in a breath — much deeper now that her bruised ribs were almost healed — and let out a sigh of relief. 'Thank you, Doctor.'

'Don't thank me. It's the nursing staff who've looked after you. But I don't need to tell you that. Now, I'm not envisaging anything at this stage, but if you do notice any post-concussion symptoms, do seek medical advice. I imagine I don't need to tell you what they are. And good luck with your training. I'll look forward to having you on my wards when the time comes.'

He nodded sharply and hanging the board back over the bottom of the bedstead, moved on to the next patient. Pippa relaxed back against her pillows, a smile creeping on to her face. It would be so good to get away from Sister Pudifoot and the boredom of lying in bed. There was a limit to the amount of studying you could do, and conversation with the other patients was frowned upon. Besides, in order to relieve pressure on the surgical wards, many of them had been brought in to recuperate from their injuries or operations, and they weren't up to chatting. All the beds had been moved closer to each other so that more could be squeezed in. There were even a couple parked lengthways down the middle of the ward. But, although the ward was overcrowded and the nursing staff run off their feet, an atmosphere of calm efficiency still reigned. Much as she disliked the woman, Pippa had to hand it to Sister Pudifoot that she coped as if nothing out of the ordinary was going on.

Well, sooner or later, Pippa knew that she was going to find out what it was like to work under the tyrant. Under the rotation scheme, her three years' nursing training would involve stints on most wards, and she was determined to learn from her superiors, including Sister Pudifoot. For a while, though, she wouldn't be working on any ward at all. Until her wrist was out of plaster, she could do nothing to help. She felt so useless when there were so many injured from those two horrific raids, worse than anything the city had suffered before. As luck would have it, Hitler hadn't seen fit to send the Luftwaffe again. Yet. But who knew when that might change? Every night after lights out and the ward was plunged into darkness save for the dim glow of the night lamp on the nurses' desk in the middle of the ward, there was a tense silence as everyone strained their ears to catch what they most definitely didn't want to hear — the wailing of the air-raid sirens.

Pippa picked up her copy of *Aids to Practical Nursing* and flicked through the pages. But she couldn't settle to any studying and letting the book fall into her lap, she closed her eyes. But the instant she did so, unwanted images flashed across her mind. She just couldn't stop thinking about the tiny babies she'd fed and changed and held against her. Now they were all gone, their chance of life snatched away from them. She just prayed they'd been killed outright and hadn't suffered. But who knew? Sometimes it took rescue workers days to dig out bodies — days when she'd been lying unconscious in a comfortable bed — and some of those poor little mites could have ... Oh, it was unbearable. And if she couldn't get it out of her head, just think what their mothers must be going through. To have carried a child for nine months, gone through the throes of childbirth, only to have their beloved new-born torn away so cruelly just a few days — or in some cases, hours — later. It was unimaginable.

Pippa felt rage bubble up inside her, but she could no more bring them back to life than she could fly to the moon. How she hated that Hitler! If only she could get her hands on him. But doubtless millions of people felt the same way, even though the chances of doing so were so ... well, nil. They just all had to keep going until this dreadful war was over. In the meantime, she'd just have to do what she could to help. As soon as she was able, of course. For now, it was so frustrating, and she released a sigh of anger and exasperation.

'Oh dear, that sounded heartfelt.'

Pippa opened her eyes and looked up into the concerned face of Sister Tutor Amanda Honeywell. A tall, strong woman in her fifties, at a guess. With the ribbons of her cap tied under her chin, her sharp eyes and straight back, Pippa thought she looked more like a Victorian workhouse matron than the caring teacher she knew her to be. Nothing got past her but she was fair and understanding provided you did your best, and Pippa had liked her from the word go.

'Good morning, Sister Tutor,' she replied. 'I was just thinking about all those poor babies and their mothers. And all the nursing staff, of course.'

Sister Tutor's head bobbed up and down. 'Yes, a terrible business. I don't think any of us will ever forget it. But we must be thankful that you survived. That was partly due to your friend, Nurse Chappel, who was first on the scene pulling the debris off you.'

'Really? She didn't mention that when she came to see me.'

'Yes,' Sister Tutor nodded. 'And it was she who noticed your wrist was at a strange angle so we were able to reduce the fracture and get it plastered up in record time so you shouldn't have any problems with it afterwards.'

'Goodness, I must thank her when I see her next. Which should be soon because the doctor's discharging me.'

'Ah, yes. That's what I've come to see you about. Now, obviously you can't do any work on the wards for a few more weeks. You could just study in your room and attend lectures, but there'll be a lot you can't do properly for yourself, making your bed and so forth. Even washing and dressing yourself will need help. So, to be honest, you'll be quite a hindrance to others, and I also believe you would benefit from further convalescence. So I've taken the liberty of ringing your mother and she's coming to take you home tomorrow as I didn't want you travelling alone as yet.'

'Oh.' Pippa's voice landed at her feet. 'It'd be lovely to spend some time at home, but what about my studies? I wouldn't want to be put back.'

'You won't be, my dear.' Sister Tutor gave a reassuring smile. 'You're one of the brightest students we've ever had, as is Nurse Chappel despite her forthright personality, shall we say. You'll soon catch up and I'll allow you to copy up her lecture notes on your return. And with your training spread over three years, everything will be repeated several times so you've no need to worry. You're a conscientious girl and have the makings of an excellent nurse.'

'Thank you, Sister. But how . . . ?'

'Nurse Chappel will be in soon to help you get dressed and then go back with you to your room and you can spend the rest of the day literally finding your feet as you've been in bed for so long. She'll also help you to pack the essentials in a small bag. Your mother tells me you left sufficient clothing at home so you won't need a suitcase.'

'I did, yes. So thank you, Sister, for arranging everything.'

Sister Tutor smiled. 'The welfare of my students is most important to me. And it made it easier with your parents having a telephone. And just as well all the lines have been restored after those raids. Now, I must get on, and I'll look forward to seeing you back here in a few weeks' time.'

Pippa nodded her thanks and watched as Sister Tutor marched off down the ward. Well, she supposed a little time back home would be nice, especially for her mum who she knew missed her dreadfully. Oh, she hadn't asked if she'd still receive her meagre wages . . . Not that it really mattered. Her dad had a good job in insurance. That was how they could afford to have a telephone installed, although it did mean that some of their less well-off neighbours would sometimes send messages through it and they had to act as go-betweens. But it was a pleasant area where they lived and they really didn't mind helping out the community around them.

Well, then, she thought, if Steph was coming soon, she might as well start getting herself organised. She flung back the bedcovers with her left hand and swung her legs over the side. She'd been allowed to walk unaccompanied to the bathroom for several days now but it would be great to have total freedom again. Opening the bedside cabinet, she began taking out her few possessions, her textbooks, toothbrush that Steph had fetched for her, and some magazines, also courtesy of her friend. They weren't her cup of tea. She'd have preferred a good novel, but it was so good of Steph to send things in for her, she didn't like to ask for more. There wasn't much else, so once she'd piled everything at the bottom of the bed, she climbed back in between the sheets.

So, she was going back home for a while. It would be welcome, she had to admit. She'd been away for seven months now, and although she'd managed a couple of fleeting visits on her full days off, she did miss home. And she did worry about her mum's nerves, especially with the raids getting so very much worse.

A sudden rumpus at the far end of the ward drew her attention to the doors. Oh, dear. There was Steph with a pile of clothes in her arms arguing with Sister Pudifoot.

'Afore you say any more, Sister, I have permission from Sister Tutor to bring some of Nurse Luscombe's clothes over and to help her get dressed and then take her back to the nurses' home. So, if you wouldn't mind . . .'

Even from that distance, Pippa saw Sister Pudifoot huff up her shoulders and walk away with an annoyed shake of her head. Well, she couldn't argue with that, and Steph had been polite enough. Well, reasonably so. And Pippa couldn't resist smiling to herself as she slid out of bed again.

Steph was beaming as she came up to her and dropped the pile of clothes on the bed. 'You know what's happening, then? You must be pleased to be getting out of here. I'll just get some screens and then we'll have you dressed. I've brought that big floppy jumper of yours as it should go over the plaster cast. We might be into April now, but it's still pretty chilly out there and I don't want you catching a chill.'

'Thanks, Steph. Really good of you.'

'Don't thank me. Sister Tutor told me to. Not that I wouldn't have done it anyway. I did clean your shoes for you, mind. I took them away when you were rescued so they wouldn't get lost.'

'You're a real pal. And Sister Tutor told me how you were the first to get to me after the . . . well, you know.'

Steph gave a casual shrug. 'You're my mate. You'd have done the same for me. Now let's get some screens.'

Ten minutes later, Pippa was dressed and ready to go. It had actually been harder than she'd thought, so Sister Tutor had been right. Attaching her stockings to her suspenders was the hardest bit, and Steph had chosen a short-sleeved blouse that she could just about fit the plaster cast through. Tying the laces on her shoes wasn't that easy, either.

'Thank you for everything, Sister,' she said as she walked down the ward and passed the dreaded Sister Pudifoot. The woman flicked her a reluctant smile, then glared at Steph who was walking just behind with Pippa's other bits and pieces in a string bag.

A few moments later when they were outside and out of earshot, they both burst out laughing.

'Oh, dear, I think you've made an enemy there!' Pippa giggled. 'She's going to give you merry hell, like, when it's your turn to be on her ward.'

'No, she won't, because I shall be an exemplary student and she won't have a sausage to reprimand me for.' Steph lifted her chin imperiously, making Pippa chuckle even more.

They were still laughing when they'd come down in the lift and reached the outside of the building. To get to the nurses' home — or nurses' accommodation more like as the student nurses were housed in the converted wards of another block — they had to cross over a wide tarmacadam area at the back of the hospital.

As they turned a corner, the noise of heavy machinery and other crashing and banging suddenly caught Pippa's attention and she turned her head. Stopping in her tracks, her heart started thumping. Where the beautiful, pristine new maternity block had once stood, half of it was now a mountain of rubble. Bulldozers were scraping up the debris of bricks and plaster and depositing it into waiting lorries. A bit further along, some men were sorting through further piles of wreckage. Two of them dragged out a mangled iron bedstead and hurled it onto another pile of twisted metal next to a heap of mattresses. Pippa felt the strength drain out of her as a jumble of wood came into view next, among it a twisted baby's cot. The breath caught in her throat and she almost stumbled.

'Hey, you all right?' Steph caught her arm to steady her.

Pippa nodded and took a calming breath. 'Yes. It was just seeing . . .' She jabbed her head towards the scene of destruction.

Steph's voice was low and compassionate, her usual ebullience missing for once. 'Yes, I know. It'll be better once it's cleared and we don't have the daily reminder. Wouldn't surprise me if they decide what's left of the building is unsafe and they knock the whole lot down. But come on. Let's get you back.'

Pippa gratefully held on to Steph's arm as they crossed to the other building and went in through the front doors. The student nurses' accommodation was on the ground level and in the semi-basement, and Pippa stepped carefully down the stairs. The wards had been divided into twin rooms by stud walls, offering some degree of privacy, although you could easily hear what was going on in the next room. Pippa was so glad that she'd been put to share with Steph. She could tell from the start that she was going to be fun to be with, yet utterly dedicated to her work.

She sat down on her bed with a sigh of relief, surprised at how the short walk had tired her. Then she noticed her uniform was neatly laid beside her, laundered and looking as good as new.

'Is this my spare or the one—'

'The one you were wearing, yes. It had a tear near the hem at the back, but I mended it for you, and then just sent it to the laundry. The stockings you were wearing had had it, mind.'

'Oh, Steph, you've been so good to me.' Love for her friend warmed her heart and she felt a lump swelling in her throat. 'Maybe one day I can repay you.'

'Just as long as it's not because I've been blown up, too!' Steph grinned.

'Of course not! But I thought I was going to have to buy a new uniform, so you've saved me that.'

Steph winked. 'Watch it or my halo will get too big to go through the door, like.'

'Never.' Pippa smiled back. 'I'm sure Sister Pudifoot will see to that.'

'What, the dragon from hell?'

Pippa laughed, then winced as it caught her ribs. 'Don't make me laugh, it hurts too much.'

Steph's expression became serious. 'You'll need to take things easy for a bit so it was a good idea of Sister Tutor's to send you home for a while.'

'Yes, it was, and I'm quite looking forward to it. But . . .' A cloud descended over Pippa's thoughts. 'What happened to all the mothers who survived? I've been wondering . . .'

'Transferred to other hospitals around until they're recovered. Physically, that is. God knows how they'll ever get over it mentally.' Steph shook her head sadly. 'But they're hastily converting a big house out in the country near Modbury to act as the new maternity hospital for Plymouth. Flete House it's called. Huge aristocratic pile, more like a castle so they say.'

Pippa raised her eyebrows. 'Oh, well, at least mothers and babies should be safer there in the future. Let's just hope there's no more raids in the meantime.'

'They say there's not much left of Plymouth for Hitler to bomb,' Steph told her, chewing on her bottom lip. 'Saw some of it myself when I went to meet Rusty. I was so shocked, like, that we just went into a café down by the harbour and talked for a couple of hours afore it was time for both of us to go back. But folk are so frightened, lots of them are going up on to the moor at night by whatever means they can, just in case.'

'Well, who can blame them for that?'

'Exactly. But if I don't get back on the ward, they'll have my guts for garters. I'm off duty this evening, mind, and there's no lecture so we can have our evening meal together in the dining hall. And you can give me your phone number in case I'm going insane and need someone proper to talk to!'

'Yes, all right,' Pippa chuckled. 'But it'll be nice to eat together tonight. And I can catch up with anyone else who's around, too.'

'Hopefully Ruby will have gotten over her jealousy at not being chosen for the maternity ward by now, at any rate. She might've been killed along with the other nurses if she had. But I must go. See you later, cheel!'

Pippa gave a wistful smile as Steph left the room. Once she'd gone, it seemed so horribly quiet. And Steph had left her with a sobering thought. Any of them could have been killed that night. Any part of the hospital could have been hit, it was such a large building in a prominent position. She knew she'd been lucky to have survived when the young girl in the bed she was standing by hadn't. It was all in the lap of the gods. She just prayed that she wouldn't come so close to death again.

CHAPTER FOUR

Pippa perched on the low wall outside the hospital gates, enjoying the spring sunshine as she waited for her mother. She was glad of the gentle warmth as her coat wasn't done up properly. The plaster cast wouldn't fit through the sleeve, and to make her arm more comfortable for her journey home, Steph had made her a sling out of a scarf so there was a bulge beneath her coat and only the top button could be fastened. It stopped the garment slipping from her shoulders, but the rest of it flapped open. If it hadn't been such a pleasant day, she could have been quite chilly. But as it was, she felt relieved and happy to be outside the confines of the hospital and was relishing the sense of freedom.

Well, it had certainly been a strange experience, she mused, being a patient on a ward rather than a member of the nursing staff. But maybe she could learn from it. Perhaps in the future when she was further up the hierarchy, a sister even, she could try and bring about some changes on her own ward, at least. She was sure her mum had been right. Patients would feel a lot better in themselves — and possibly hasten their recovery even — if they were able to receive visitors more often and if the ward rules were less regimented.

That would be years ahead, mind. She might not even stay the course. Many didn't, although she was pretty determined that she would be among those who became fully qualified. She felt so frustrated. Look at the frequent passers-by who were turning in at the hospital gates. She wanted to help them. To make a difference.

Glancing along the pavement, was that her mum coming now? She couldn't quite see between the other pedestrians, but then, yes, she recognised the harassed and nervous way Adeline was walking along the unfamiliar road. Reluctantly leaving her nice warm spot on the wall, Pippa stood up so that her mum could spot her more easily.

Adeline's face at once brightened when she caught sight of her daughter. Though Pippa's dad earned a decent wage and they were well able to afford it, her mum had never been one to keep up with fashion. Her coat, though tailored at the waist, reached half way down her calves and her hat was more of the cloche style fashionable after the last war. It all added to the timid mouse impression, and Pippa's heart went out to her.

'Hello, Mum!' she called, and Adeline was happy to give her a bit of a hug.

'Oh, dear, I think your cast got in the way,' she laughed nervously. 'Must be nice for you to be outside again, mind.'

'Yes, it is. But how was the journey today?'

'Oh, much better. The buses are running properly again. The city centre's a mess but at least the roads are mainly clear again. I just wish there were a direct route home instead of having to go into the centre to change buses. But,' she lowered her voice to a confidential whisper as she bent over slightly, 'd'you think they'd mind if I popped inside to use the lavvy? Proper bursting, I am.'

'No, of course not, Mum. I'll go on sunning myself.'

A smile lingered on Pippa's face as she watched her mother scuttle inside the hospital building. Her poor mum had always been tremendously shy. It was a wonder she'd ever got married, but Neil had been the boy next door and they'd grown up together. Her dad was a lovely fellow, and Pippa could never have wished for better parents.

'Ooph, that's better.' Her mum's voice broke into her reverie. 'Now, then, I'll take that bag so you don't have to carry it.'

'No, it's all right. I've got one good arm, you know, Mum.'

'No, I insist. Now, have you got everything? Identity card, ration book — I'll need that to register you in our local shops as you're staying a few weeks.'

'Yes, of course, Mum. I got it from Sister Tutor this morning. And I've got my gas mask, see?'

'Not that Hitler needs to gas us after bombing the city to kingdom come,' Adeline muttered. 'You'll see some of it on the way. Mortal dreadful, it is.'

Pippa could sense her mother drifting into anxiety and quickly linked her good arm through hers. 'Come on, let's enjoy the walk to the bus stop and hope one comes along soon.'

'Should be the same one coming back as I came on. If I didn't take too long going to the lav, that is. Goes up to Mount Gold Hospital, then turns round and comes back.'

'That's right. Oh, look! Come on, it's coming now. Don't want to miss it.'

They hurried forward but there was no need for them to run. There was quite a queue at the bus stop and they joined it at the back. Nobody got off. Pippa could see a few passengers through the windows, but there was plenty of room and her mother waved her in to sit by the window.

Though she felt so frustrated and wished it wasn't because of her broken arm, Pippa had to admit it was a delightful change to be outside the hospital. Trees were coming into leaf and there were flashes of vibrant yellow daffodils in front gardens which lifted her heart. But as they came down Lipson Road, they passed one or two bombed out buildings, and Pippa's heart lurched. The nearer they got to the city centre, the worse it became. In Ebrington Street, they passed the ruins of both the Palladium and Cinedrome cinemas, and when they turned into Old Town Street, Pippa couldn't help but gasp.

It was almost unrecognisable. Woolworths and several other neighbouring stores had their shop fronts blown out and there were mountains of rubble and other debris piled up at the side of the road, still waiting to be taken away. The road itself was clear although there was a shallow crater the bus had to slow to a crawl in order to negotiate. Several buildings were just blackened shells, completely burnt out where before they had been thriving shops and offices. Gaping holes where three-storey establishments had once stood, smashed bricks and roof tiles, huge rafters splintered into what resembled giant matchsticks, the twisted metal frame that had been at the core of maybe a shop or some sort of business. Remains of edifices that now looked like skeletons. Blind. Sightless, their hearts gone.

Pippa was too shocked to speak and glanced at her mum seated next to her, but Adeline's face was stiff. She'd seen it before and perhaps was trying to blank it from her mind. Pippa couldn't blame her. It was horrific.

The bus finally reached its stop in Guildhall Square. Pippa queued down the aisle with the other passengers waiting to get off, but as she alighted and glanced around, she was stunned into silence. Opposite, the massive department store of Spooners with its vast showrooms must have blazed from floor to roof, and she could see that the popular shopping thoroughfare of Bedford Street, where she'd often enjoyed shopping expeditions with her friends, was a heap of ruins. Further along the square, the new Post Office, County Court offices and other buildings had been destroyed. Then, as she slowly turned round, the lovely Guildhall behind her was nothing more than a burnt-out shell.

She met her mother's gaze and could see tears sparkling in her eyes. Plymouth's heart was bleeding. Pippa knew it was bad, but this was indescribable. It was said over three hundred people had been killed in those two nights of the heaviest raids. She'd seen some of the bodies herself at the hospital. Many survivors from those two appalling nights in March and also previous raids had life-changing injuries, horrendous burns. It was apocalyptic and the destruction before her eyes hammered it home.

'There's worse,' Adeline mumbled, and scuttled forward, shoulders hunched, towards the other bus stop round the corner where they'd pick up the bus that would take them home.

Pippa gulped, and a surge of desperation, anger and hate washed through her in a tidal wave. As if she hadn't seen enough, beloved St Andrew's Church had been burnt out from end to end. Roofless, windowless, only the walls, wrecked and unearthly, remained, guarded by the tower at the west end, thankfully still standing, solid and symbolic, somehow reflecting the resilience of the people of Plymouth in the face of such devastation. Pippa wanted to cry out in an agony of frustration, to undo all that had been done, to lash out at . . . at what? Dear Lord, she felt so helpless, but surely everyone in the city, in all the cities in the country that had been targeted, must feel the same. So, she gritted her teeth, and shocked to the core, followed her mum round to the far side of the ruined Mother Church to the other bus stop.

It felt incongruous and unreal, standing in the spot where she'd waited countless times in her life. The sun was shining and it felt as if everything should be the same, and yet it was totally different. A certain tang of burning still lingered in the air, even though those dreadful raids had occurred ten days ago. The droning and exhaust fumes of bulldozers wafted across the road, the rumble and crash of debris being shifted, dust billowing in clouds.

A sudden distant explosion made Pippa jump, jarring her ribs slightly, and she stifled a wince. She didn't want her mum fussing over her, but when she glanced to her side, Adeline was crouched on the pavement, hands over her head. Pippa stared at her in bewilderment. She wanted to bend down and comfort her, but her ribs were starting to ache after the journey.

'All right, my flower. They'm just blowing up unsafe buildings. 'Tis perfectly safe.'

Pippa was so grateful to the stranger who'd put a gentle arm around her mother's shoulders. But that's how it was, everyone helping everyone else. With the stranger's help, Adeline was straightening up, her pale face flushing with embarrassment.

'How silly of me,' she muttered, and Pippa felt so sorry for her. The last thing her mum would ever want was to draw attention to herself.

'After what us has all been through, 'tis no wonder. Us must all help each other,' the woman insisted, bobbing her head up and down. 'And I see this poor cheel has been in the wars, too,' she concluded, with a lift at the end of her words as if she was expecting an explanation.

Pippa didn't feel like engaging in conversation, so nodded with a rueful smile. 'Thank you. Mum will be all right now. Here comes the bus.'

She was grateful as the Number Eight trundled to a stop and they climbed on board. Fortunately, the kind woman went further down the aisle, saving Adeline any further embarrassment, but the incident made Pippa even more concerned about her mum. She did worry about her being alone while her dad was out at work, and then performing his ARP duties during the raids. They had no immediate family nearby, so while Pippa was staying at home, she must try to make other arrangements for her mother for when she eventually went back to nursing.

The bus followed its familiar route out of the city centre, and to Pippa's relief, the further they went, the less evidence there was of the destruction the raids had wreaked. By the time they reached their stop near Devonport Railway Station, everywhere appeared unchanged, as if the horrific scenes they'd left behind were but a vision. It was a ten-minute walk to their house in a pleasant terrace of small houses with well-tended front gardens, all so familiar, and that in itself made Pippa feel uneasy. Would it last?

Adeline let them inside, and Pippa was met by the scent of lavender polish and fresh baking. She sensed her mum must have caught the smile that flickered across her face.

'Saved up our fat rations and made you a cake special, like,' Adeline beamed. 'You go and sit down in the sitting room and I'll bring it in with a nice cup of tea. I've made some spam sandwiches for our lunch as well.'

Pippa didn't need telling twice. She was surprised how tired she felt after a journey that once would have been so easy. It was good to be home, though, and she sank back into one of the comfortable armchairs.

'So, what's the news on Percy Pig?' she asked when Adeline bustled in with a tray neatly set with an embroidered tray cloth and the necessary items of bone china. 'Oh, you're using the best tea set?'

'Well, I thought we'd make this a special occasion, like. Not often our clever nurse daughter gets the chance to come home.' Adeline sat down and began pouring the tea. 'As for Percy Pig, he is no more. The butcher said he were as big as he were likely to get for his breed, so he turned him into joints and sausages and bacon and ham and so forth for us. We came to an agreement whereby he could keep some of it to sell in his shop in exchange for his services. You know we had to give up our meat rations for the pig club? But as you're only here for a few weeks, you needn't be involved so you can still get your rations,' Adeline winked. 'I must say it'd be nice to have something other than pork meat, if you wouldn't mind sharing?'

'No, of course not, Mum.'

'That's my girl. Depending on what's available, of course.' There was a tap on the door. 'Oh, I wonder who that could be? Probably nosey Mrs Hodges, the old busybody. I expect she were twitching her curtains, looking out for us.'

'Did you tell her I was coming home, then?'

'Well, yes, I suppose I did.' Adeline pulled a wry face as she got to her feet. 'I were so excited about it. Won't be a jiffy.'

Pippa sighed as her mother left the room. She could have done without seeing Mrs Hodges straight away, but the woman meant well. You just had to be careful you didn't say too much or it'd be all over the district by tea time.

'Don't you get up on my account, cheel,' Mrs Hodges instructed as she trotted into the room and plonked herself down in one of the armchairs. 'You poor soul. I hear you were in the thick of it. Oh, that cake looks good. Mind if I have a slice?'

Pippa said nothing and watched as their neighbour helped herself without waiting for an answer. She really didn't want to relate to the woman how awful it had been at the hospital both the first night when they'd been flooded with the mangled victims of that horrendously brutal raid, and then the bombing of the maternity block the following night. It was impossible to put into words the horror of what she'd witnessed. Better to say nothing at all.

'I hear Percy Pig is now gracing our tables,' she said instead. 'It was so good of you to organise it all.'

'Not at all.' Mrs Hodges glowed with pride. 'Living on the corner, I have the biggest garden so there's ample room to make a pen in front of the old shed to act as a sty, and it means people can just pop their scraps in the bins over the fence. As an upright citizen, it's the least I can do for the war effort.'

'And what'll you do next, Mrs Hodges?' Pippa enquired, trying to look innocent while hiding a mocking smile.

'Well, that's just what I've come to tell you!' Mrs Hodges put down her empty plate and hiked up her ample bosom. 'My farmer cousin up on Dartmoor has another little piglet for us. Fully weaned, and will be arriving in the next few days.'

'Oh, well done.'

'That's all I came to tell you,' Mrs Hodges preened, standing up now she'd finished her cake. 'Now you take care, and don't let what that Lord Haw Haw's been saying worry you.

That it'll be Devonport's turn next. After his latest efforts, that Hitler can't have any bombs left.'

Pippa could have throttled the woman as she watched her mother's face turn white. Devonport. Their end of the city, that had so far escaped the worst of the attacks — but it housed the Royal Naval Dockyard and was home to about a third of the entire Royal Naval Fleet... Surely, they didn't need that treacherous Lord Haw Haw to tell them it would be in Hitler's sights?

As her mother went to see Mrs Hodges out of the front door, the next mouthful of cake stuck in Pippa's throat.

***

'Oh, it's good to have our little girl back home for a while.' Later that evening, Neil Luscombe smiled lovingly across at his daughter when Adeline had left the dining room, carrying the tray of used plates and cutlery out to the kitchen. 'I just wish it wasn't because you'd been hurt. It must've been awful for you.'

His expression had become serious now and he leaned forward across the table. Pippa chewed on her bottom lip and flicked her eyes towards the door to make sure her mum wasn't coming back in. But she could hear her running water into the washing-up bowl.

'To be honest, Dad, it happened so quickly, I hardly knew what was going on,' she said, keeping her voice low. 'And then I was unconscious for a few days. At least, sometimes I was vaguely aware of things going on around me, but I wasn't in any real pain. Just my ribs are still sore but it's not that bad. No,' she confided, thankful for the clattering of plates coming from the kitchen.

She didn't want to upset her fragile mother by talking about it to her, but it would be a release to open up to her dad. 'It was finding out about all the babies and little children that were killed,' she went on, her voice faltering. 'And the young mother. I'd nursed them all, you see, so it was the personal connection. And I was getting to know the nursing staff who died, too, some even younger than me. And the night afore, when we went off duty, we went down to Casualty to help in whatever way we could. What we saw . . .' She broke off, shaking her head. 'It was . . .'

'Horrific. Unspeakable.' Neil's voice was a cracked whisper. 'I thought I'd seen enough in the first war, and I never expected my little girl . . . You and I have seen things no man or woman should ever have to. It's why . . . I just wanted to say, we should keep things from your mother as much as possible. You know what a bag of nerves she is.'

'Yes, of course. I try not to remember it all myself.'

Neil nodded and then getting to his feet, came round to her side of the table. Pippa instinctively stood up and let her father embrace her in a hug that spoke far louder than words. 'To think that you and I should share such things,' he mumbled into her hair, and she felt a bank of emotion rolling through her.

Before they could pull apart, the dreaded sound moaned out across the city and they stood back, staring at each other in annoyed desperation. *Oh, no. Not again. God save us.*

Neil's face twisted in a wry smile. 'I'm not officially on duty tonight, but when there's a raid . . .' He lifted an eyebrow and then rushed upstairs.

'Oh, my God.' Adeline appeared in the doorway, her face white. 'You'd think he'd leave us alone—'

'Come on, Mum. Down the shelter. It'll be all right. Everything's down there, I assume? Just need our gas masks and the tin box with our papers in.'

'They're in the string bag with the thermos flasks. I've just filled those with hot water like I do every night. Just in case, like. Oh, but where's Willow?' Adeline's voice was a panicking squeak. 'Where is she? Have you seen her?'

'She was in the sitting room afore we came in here to eat.'

Adeline dashed from the room. Pippa followed her out into the hall where she reappeared a moment later, clutching the cat, just as Neil nimbly descended the stairs in his ARP uniform.

'You two girls look after yourselves and get down the shelter quick, like.'

'You be careful, too, love!' Adeline squealed, freeing one arm to cling desperately on to him and almost squashing the cat between them.

Pippa and her father exchanged glances over her head, and Pippa gently took her arm, leading her out of the back door and into the garden. She could hear her mum almost sobbing in fear but when Willow started wriggling in indignation, Adeline held her even more tightly. Pippa gave a sigh of relief. At least the cat was distracting her mother from her fear.

There was still a glimmer of light in the sky, just enough to see their way without a torch. Pippa wrinkled her nose as they went down the steps into the shelter buried beneath the ground. After the long winter, it smelled horribly of damp earth. Her father had built staging and covered it in lino, with two raised bunk beds on one side and a table and chairs on the other. Pippa closed the door and pulled the blackout curtains across while her mother lit the candle on the table, its dim flicker casting lurid shadows on the corrugated iron ceiling. Pippa shuddered. It was like being buried alive, and she wondered just how much protection the shelter would really offer — not that she'd voice such a thought to her mum.

'Let's have a cuppa, shall we?' she said brightly. 'I could really do with one.'

'Good idea. There's enough hot water in the flasks to last the whole night. If need be,' Adeline concluded with a grimace.

Pippa watched as her mother spooned some tea leaves into an old teapot and poured on some hot water from one of the flasks. Very soon they were sipping tea and nibbling at the biscuits Adeline kept in a tin on the table. The siren had stopped which meant . . . Pippa was trying to act casually and not let her fear show, and when she heard distant thuds, she tried to ignore them and keep up a normal conversation.

'How's Mrs Harper now? Recovered from being attacked by Percy?'

'Oh, yes. And mortal happy to be eating him off her plate, no doubt.'

'And how about your knitting? What are you making now? I hope little Timmy next door appreciated the jumper you made him, or at least his mum did. I must pop round and see them in the morning.' *Provided we're all still here*, she thought grimly. Not that she'd say so.

And then, remarkably after such a short time, a high-pitched steady wail echoed through the walls of the shelter. Pippa met her mother's surprised — and relieved — stare. The all-clear. Not so bad a raid after all. Although sometimes the bombers returned and you could go down to the shelter and back up again several times in one night.

Five minutes later, they were back indoors, and not long after that, Neil came back home and flopped down in a chair.

'Just a few of them tonight, and six were shot down, two of them out over the sea,' he said grimly. 'Hopefully the others won't be back, but you never know. Not a great home coming for you, my flower,' he told Pippa. 'I suggest we all go to bed and try and get some shut-eye now, just in case.'

Pippa nodded in agreement. She felt exhausted and couldn't wait to get some sleep, back in her own bed. But would she able to relax enough to drop off after what had happened? She just prayed the raiders didn't return as she really didn't think she could face going down the shelter again. No wonder her mum's nerves were in such a state. But what other choice did they have?

CHAPTER FIVE

'You weren't long next door, my flower?'

Adeline's voice lifted into a question as she glanced up from scrubbing some carrots. At one time she would have peeled them, but every morsel of food counted nowadays.

'No, I wasn't. Ivy's busy packing some suitcases. She and the children are going to live with her sister. Up on the moor near Horrabridge, apparently.'

Adeline breathed out a heavy sigh. 'Well, who can blame her? I'll miss her, mind. And I hope she's packed that woolly jumper I just knitted for Timmy.'

'Oh, he's wearing it. Loves it so much, he won't take it off, so Ivy says,' Pippa chuckled. But then the amusement faded from her voice. 'You know, Mum, I think we should maybe try and find somewhere for you to stay. People are opening their doors—'

'What, and leave your dad? I vowed to love him for better or for worse.'

Pippa knew she had to tread carefully. 'But this is different, Mum. It wouldn't mean you loved him any less. And I think he'd feel happier. When he's on duty, I'm sure it'd be better for him not to be worrying about you at the same time.'

'We-ell.' Adeline hesitated and Pippa had her fingers crossed that perhaps she'd sown a seed in her mother's mind. 'Maybe I'll think about it. But where would I go? I don't know anyone I could stay with.'

'We could look into that. People are offering—'

'Not sure I'd like staying with a stranger. Besides, Hitler's already done for Plymouth. And our lads soon saw off those few raiders last night.'

'Maybe they did. But there's bound to be a next time, you know.' Pippa didn't want to say what was really on her mind. That what that traitor Lord Haw Haw was saying was likely true. That Hitler would be back to destroy Devonport soon, and where they lived wasn't that far away. And it wouldn't be a minor attack. Hitler would throw everything he could at it.

'Well, think about it, Mum. Seriously,' she said, not wanting to frighten her mother too much. 'But for now, I'm going to sit in the garden while the sun's out and do a bit of studying. It's really warm on the bench in that sheltered spot.'

'I might come and join you and do some knitting,' Adeline smiled. 'You go out and I'll come when I've finished doing this.'

Pippa sighed as she picked up one of her text books and headed to the back door. Her mother was clearly relieved to have changed the subject. Pippa just prayed that she really would give her suggestion some serious thought.

* * *

'Ivy's taken the children to live with her sister near Horrabridge,' Pippa told her father over their evening meal, trying to introduce the subject gently. 'They called round to say goodbye just afore lunch and then were catching an afternoon train.'

'Ah.' Neil nodded slowly as he speared a cube of Percy on to his fork, Adeline having made a stew with plenty of vegetables to eke out the meat. 'Lots of people are doing the same, you know. And those who haven't got friends or family to stay with or who can't leave the place during the day are finding their way up on to the moor at night by whatever means they can. Train, bus, in the back of lorries and vans, bicycle. Even on foot some of them, they're so desperate. I've seen them myself when I've been on duty. Terrible sight.'

'Yes, well, I was wondering whether Mum shouldn't be considering it,' Pippa put in, mentally crossing her fingers. 'I know we don't know anyone personally she could stay with—'

'And who'd get your meals and do your washing, like?' her mother cut in. 'No, I'm not going anywhere.'

Pippa's heart sank. She'd hoped her mum might have had second thoughts during the day, especially after Ivy's visit, but evidently not. But then her father put down his knife and fork with deliberate precision.

'Well, now,' he said calmly and firmly, just as if he was discussing insurance with a client. 'The raids are invariably at night, so you can do all you need to during the day, and then travel up with everyone else every evening. I'll make some enquiries and look into it. On the nights when I'm not on duty, I'll come with you, at least until you get used to it. And it'd be good for Pip to go, too, while she's staying here. She's been through enough already.'

He pulled in his chin and raised his eyebrows in an expression that said *you know I'm right*. Pippa glanced at her mother who merely lowered her eyes to her plate. It seemed strange that her nervous, timid mother wasn't keen to get away from the danger, but perhaps just thinking about it was upsetting her and she wanted to brush it under the carpet. Or was it really the fact that she didn't want to feel she was too far away from her husband? That the house they had lived in all their married life was so familiar that it brought her comfort even if staying there could be putting her at risk? Perhaps if Pippa declared that she was going anyway, it might make her mum decide to go with her. But if she didn't, would Pippa really want to feel she was abandoning her? It was all too much, and

Pippa prayed for all she was worth that the raids that seemed inevitable simply didn't come.

* * *

'Well, that was a night we could all have done without.' Pippa's father stretched out his arms as his mouth opened in a huge yawn. 'You two up and down to the Andie, and me coming up the front path when I had to keep turning round and going back again.'

'You're overdoing things, Neil,' Adeline scolded him as she carefully scooped tea into the pot. 'You weren't officially on duty and yet you still went out. You're not as young as you were, you know.'

'Well, I just feel I have to.' Neil pulled an awkward face. 'And let's face it, I wouldn't have got any more sleep if I'd been here. Three alerts in one night's exhausting for everyone. But at least we got a few hours' kip in the end.'

Pippa stifled a yawn of her own as she used her left hand to lift a slice of toast with a scraping of butter to her mouth. At least the raids hadn't come to much. News had travelled through the ARP wardens' grapevine that although hundreds of incendiaries had been dropped to the north and east of the city, all had been extinguished before any significant fires could take hold. There'd been hardly any high explosives, though they'd heard a few distant thuds.

'Mum's right, though,' she ventured when she'd swallowed the mouthful of toast. 'You shouldn't do more than your three nights a week. It's enough.'

'Well, I'll stop doing extra duty if your mother agrees to take herself out of danger every night.' Pippa noticed he met her mother's gaze with a challenging stare. 'Thousands are doing it so she'd have plenty of company. Tavistock's already bursting at the seams with evacuees but people there are still offering shelter to strangers. And they're opening schools and churches and halls and what have you there, too.'

Pippa was listening with interest. She loved the old market town of Tavistock, snuggling on the western edge of Dartmoor. She often thought it would be a wonderful place to live, away from the hustle and bustle of Plymouth. It had the added attraction just now of being a relatively safe place to be.

'Sounds like an excellent idea to me, Mum,' she said optimistically. 'Why don't we give it a go and catch the train up tonight?'

'I'm not kipping down on the floor among a load of strangers.' Adeline's tone was fierce and yet Pippa detected a quiver in her words. 'Besides, it's been a whole week since Hitler's last effort and that were pretty pathetic and all. So maybe he's losing interest in Plymouth after all.'

'Then why's the government finally listening to the local authorities and planning an official evacuation for those that haven't got the wherewithal to do so privately? Mind you, it's a case of bolting the stable door, and if they don't get on with it quickly, it could be too late for whatever's to come!'

Pippa blinked at her father who was usually such a mild-mannered man, and saw him glare at her mum before giving an exasperated sigh.

'Well, I'm off to work,' he announced crossly. 'I want you to be sensible about this, Ade. I'm not on duty tonight so I'd come with you. Just think of Pippa if you won't think of yourself.'

With that, he pulled his suit jacket on over his waistcoat, picked up his briefcase and his gas-mask box that was hanging on the back of the kitchen door, and made his way out into the hall. A moment later, Pippa heard the front door close none too gently and she turned to her mother, her pulse jumping nervously.

'Really, Mum, we ought to give it a go.'

She ruched her forehead into the most pleading expression she could muster, and watched her mother's face soften.

'All right, I'll think about it,' she agreed. 'But right now I need to go and do some shopping. Just hope I don't have to queue for too long.'

'I'll come with you if you like.'

'No, you stay here and put your feet up. Maybe have a little nod to make up for last night.'

The idea of catching up on some sleep was certainly appealing. The constant to-ing and fro-ing to the Anderson shelter had made Pippa's ribs ache again, so wallowing in the comfort of a proper bed would be just the ticket. As she was still in her dressing gown, she wouldn't even have to get changed.

'Okay, Mum, I will. In fact, I think I'll go back to bed.'

'You have a nice sleep then, my flower.'

Pippa stood up and made for the door but as she passed her mother, Adeline took her hand. 'I will think on what you and your father are saying, I promise,' she smiled.

Pippa nodded, hoping her mum really would consider their proposal. Not that she particularly fancied communal sleeping arrangements either, but it was better than being blown to pieces. She'd had enough of that, and once she was back at the hospital, she'd be in more danger again. But that wouldn't be for another three weeks. It would be a relief to feel safe for that time, particularly if it got her mother into the habit of a nightly trek out of the city, too.

Oh, this war had such a lot to answer for!

***

Pippa woke to the shrill ringing of the telephone down in the hall. She dragged herself from sleep, willing her mother to answer it. She had no idea what the time was, so maybe she hadn't slept for that long and Adeline had been delayed. After all, you never knew how long you might need to queue for something nowadays.

She hurried down the stairs, nonetheless concentrating on each step. It wouldn't do to go hurtling to the bottom and do herself some further damage. She lifted up the receiver with her left hand, which felt really peculiar.

'Hello?'

She waited while there were various clicks at the other end of the line. Someone was calling from a public phone box, then. She wondered who it could be.

'Can I speak to Pippa, please?' a familiar voice said.

'Yes, it's me. Is that you, Steph?' Pippa bubbled with excitement. 'How are you?'

'No time for that now. I'm in a call box. Someone's just asked me to swap, so I'm off duty this morning and there's no lecture. So fancy meeting me on the Hoe, like?'

'Oh, well, yes!' Pippa was taken by surprise, but it was a great idea. Much as she loved her parents, a break would be most welcome. It was another pleasant spring day and a walk along the Hoe would be just what she needed. 'What time?'

'As soon as either of us can get there. Meet you at Smeaton's Tower?'

'Yes, sounds perfect.'

'I'm going to ring the base and try and find out if Rusty's off duty, too. Oh, the pips are going. See you soon then.'

The line crackled and went dead. Pippa replaced the receiver in its cradle and sat down on the bottom stair for a moment to catch her breath. A morning off duty meant you had to be back on the ward at half past one sharp, or your life wouldn't be worth living. So she'd better get a move on.

She popped her head round the sitting-room door. The clock on the mantelpiece was showing a quarter to ten, so she'd only had about an hour's extra sleep, but she felt refreshed and the unexpected anticipation of seeing her friend again was filling her with energy. She didn't know how long her mother would be so she'd have to leave her a note. She could just about hold a pen in her right hand and as long as it was legible, it didn't matter if it was a bit of a scrawl. Getting washed and dressed might be a bit of a struggle ... Her mum had been helping her, but she was sure she could manage to make herself respectable. And after last night's trauma, it would just be wonderful to get out and get some sea air in her lungs.

She turned back to the stairs, but as she did so, she heard the key turn in the front door and in came Adeline.

'What, you up already? Couldn't you get back to sleep?'

'Yes, I did. Slept like a log but the phone woke me up. It was my friend from the hospital, Steph. Got some off-duty time and wants me to meet her on the Hoe as soon as I can get there.'

She could feel happiness glowing from her cheeks and she hopped up and down around her mother.

'Well, we'd better get you presentable, then,' Adeline beamed back. 'It'll be good for you to get out for a while. I'll just put this shopping in the kitchen and I'll be up to help you.'

Pippa trotted up the stairs, her heart light. If she were honest, she hoped Rusty couldn't join them. She'd met him a few times and he was a pleasant enough fellow. Steph had known him for a year or so, ever since some members of the Royal Australian Air Force had got delayed waiting to collect some planes from the Mount Batten Air Base and had ended up staying there. But she mustn't be selfish. Steph had little enough opportunity to see Rusty, and Pippa had never felt like a gooseberry on the odd occasion when the three of them had been together.

She pushed open the door to her bedroom. Now what should she wear — or more to the point, what could she get into with her plaster cast? She sat down on the edge of the bed and gave a wry grunt. What did it matter what she wore? She was alive, and that was all that counted.

CHAPTER SIX

Pippa tried not to look out of the window as the bus trundled back into Plymouth city centre. It was just too awful to see what had been such a vibrant metropolis ravaged by such destruction. But when she stepped on to the pavement beside the ruins of St Andrew's Church, she knew it would be impossible to find her way without looking around her.

In the eight days since she'd stood there with her mother, she could see that work had been going on apace to clear the mountains of rubble, twisted metal and burnt timbers that were strewn everywhere. It was clear now that although the inside of the church was completely gone, the blackened walls looked to be intact. The beautiful Guildhall shared the same fate, but would either building be salvageable? Across the square, there was no such luck. Some of the buildings were nothing but crumbled ruins.

She turned her back on the distressing sight and made her way towards the open expanse of the Hoe, keeping her fingers crossed that the extensive lawns sloping down to the sea hadn't been hit. She passed the area where the corporation had dug up the grass to make way for a vast allotment. Some men were busy planting out seedlings of some sort, making

Pippa smile. Her dad had trays of similar greenery ready in the greenhouse. Her mum hadn't been too pleased when more of the garden was being taken up by his expanding vegetable plot, but everyone had to *dig for victory*. There was even a small vegetable garden in the hospital grounds.

Pippa hurried up the slight incline towards the gentle brow beside the Royal Navy Memorial where the panorama of the sea suddenly opened up to view. The sight always filled her with a sense of pleasure and freedom. She held her breath in case some of the landmarks had been destroyed but the various statues along the seafront remained standing in all their majesty, including the old lighthouse of Smeaton's Tower. She noticed there were numerous patches of scorched grass, evidence of incendiary bombs that had thankfully been extinguished or burnt themselves out.

But she was here to meet up with her friend and ignoring the reminder of the raids that had decimated the city, she hastened towards the tower. She could see a girl who from that distance looked like Steph, but she was accompanied by not one but two men in uniform. Was it her? As Pippa drew nearer, she could see that it was. She recognised one of the men as Rusty, but didn't know who the other one was.

Steph waved frantically when she saw her and rushed over to give her a hug.

'Pippa, how are you?' she cried, standing back and holding her at arms' length.

'Hope I haven't changed much in just over a week.' Pippa felt herself flush with embarrassment at Steph's enthusiasm in front of the two men.

'Well, you look much better. You were so pale afore. Oh, now let me introduce you.' Steph was clearly brimming with exuberance. 'Rusty you know. But this is his friend, Flying Officer Jack Hastings.'

'Hello, Rusty. Nice to see you again.'

The young man grinned at her, yet there was concern in the chestnut eyes that danced below his thick, auburn eyebrows. 'Glad to see you're okay, Philippa. Must have been one hell of a shock.'

Pippa gave a rueful shrug. 'To be honest, it happened so quickly, like, I didn't really know much about it. I was lucky. Not like . . .'

Her voice cracked, and there was a moment when she and Steph exchanged a glance that spoke louder than words. In that second of shared grief, Pippa wondered what exactly Steph had seen that night. Though she'd hardly witnessed anything herself, she kept having visions of what it must have been like as the rescue teams searched through the rubble, discovering those tiny, broken bodies. It must have been hell itself.

Rusty must have sensed the sorrow between them, and neatly stepped in.

'As Steph said, this is my mate, Jack. On the same shifts, so I thought he might as well come along rather than putting his feet up and twiddling his thumbs.'

'Yes, of course.' A good chap was Rusty, and Pippa could see why Steph liked him. She turned now to Jack who she thought must be feeling a bit of an outsider. 'Hello, Jack. Pleased to meet you.'

'G'day, miss.' Jack swept off his cap, revealing a shock of straw-blond hair on the top of his head that was cropped short at the sides like most service personnel. 'Steph said you were a beauty.'

He held out his hand. Pippa felt obliged to take it even though she wasn't sure about his direct manner. As she did so, she noticed the single gold braid above the cuff of his jacket. The dark blue Royal Australian Air Force uniform was striking, and Jack was a handsome specimen but whether or not Pippa would come to like him was another matter. Besides, all she'd been interested in for years was a career in nursing where men were actively discouraged.

'I don't feel very beautiful now with this,' she replied, waving her plaster cast in the air. She didn't add that although her hair had been shampooed once in the hospital to remove all the dust and grime from the explosion, it hadn't been washed since and was feeling lank and greasy. Her mother was going to do it again for her that very day, but there hadn't been time if she was to meet Steph at such short notice, so she'd bundled her hair up under her hat for her instead.

'Steph has told us all about what happened. But I'm glad you're okay now.'

Pippa was somewhat relieved to detect genuine sympathy in Jack's tone and smiled back. 'Yes. It's nice to be spending some time back with my mum and dad, but I am missing being at the hospital. So I need to hear all about what's been going on, Steph.'

'Not much to tell,' Steph shrugged. 'Me and Ruby Saundercock and a couple of others have been put on Men's Medical. Mainly old men with bronchitis or pneumonia, coughing all over the place, or heart problems. Nobody young and handsome, unfortunately.'

'Just as well!' Rusty joked. 'Don't want anyone stealing my girl.'

'Oh, you!' Steph giggled, pushing his arm playfully.

Pippa chuckled as she watched them. She noticed Jack raise an amused eyebrow. Did he feel a bit of a gooseberry, as she did? The only thing for it was to try and open up a conversation.

'What about you, Jack?' she asked. 'Did you come over here right at the start to collect those planes and got stuck here like Rusty? Or have you arrived more recently, like? Rusty hadn't really mentioned you afore.'

If Pippa wasn't mistaken, a darkness came over Jack's expression. 'No, I came over here with Rusty to collect those Sunderlands. But like you said, we were waiting so long because of production delays that we were still here when the RAF moved out of Mount Batten and we were moved in.'

'And you ended up staying.'

'That's right. Number Ten Squadron became an operational unit last February. Patrolling the Bay of Biscay and out over the Atlantic as part of Coastal Command. That's how Rusty and me became mates.'

Pippa nodded, glancing across the Cattewater to the air base. As usual, there were several gigantic Sunderland flying boats anchored in the sea around it. At the moment, all was quiet, but it always amazed her how the huge seaplanes managed to get airborne. But the work they did was both vital and dangerous. Not only did they perform reconnaissance and destroy German U-boats trying to pick off Allied convoys from America, but they landed on the water to rescue survivors of sunken merchantmen. Pippa shuddered. These two young men were among many Australians putting their lives at risk to help the Motherland. Often they didn't return from their missions. She just prayed for Steph's sake that Rusty was never among them. Or Jack, now that she'd met him.

'And then Rusty and I met at one of the open-air dances here on the Hoe last spring,' Steph threw in, her thoughts clearly not taking the same track as Pippa's. 'But you know that.'

'Not much of a dancer, me,' Jack explained almost apologetically. 'Stayed on the base most of the time.'

Thinking of the wonderful dances by the bandstand, Pippa managed to shake off her earlier morose thoughts. 'Steph and I only met in September when we started at the hospital and we're not left a lot of time for socialising, like. I've only met Rusty a few times and I don't think he's mentioned you afore.'

She frowned as she caught a dark expression passing between the two airmen. 'No reason why he should. And I have been out of action for a while,' Jack murmured.

'Oh, yes?' At first Pippa hadn't been sure of this somewhat brash Australian, but now she felt full of concern. 'Why was that, may I ask?'

Jack dipped his head. 'You must remember the big air raid back in November?'

'When the oil tanks on Mount Batten were hit and blazed for days on end?' Pippa's eyes widened at the memory. 'I don't think anyone will ever forget that. It was like Dante's inferno, our worst raid to date at the time. They reckoned there were over a hundred aircraft in the attack. There was a thick, black oily cloud over the city for over a week. And those two firemen who were killed trying to put it out . . . It was awful. I remember Steph being beside herself with worry over Rusty.'

'Well, she was right to be. One of the hangars was hit and caught fire, too. I was . . . Let's just say if it hadn't been for Rusty, I'd have burnt to death. He saved my life that night. But I was hospitalised afterwards and I've only been back on duty the last few weeks.'

Pippa felt a spike of horror ripple through her. What she'd been through was nothing compared to that. She saw Jack's hands shake as he drew out a cigarette case from his inner breast pocket. It was only then that she noticed the twisted red skin on the back of his left hand disappearing beneath his cuff, and wondered how far his burns had extended. Thankfully his face had escaped, but his injuries must have been bad enough to take three months or so to heal.

Pippa wasn't sure what to say, so was relieved when Steph piped up, 'What? You were a real hero that night, Rusty, and you never said!'

'I only did what—'

Rusty didn't have time to finish his sentence before he was crushed in the bearhug that Steph gave him, making them all laugh. It was enough to ease the tension and Jack offered round his cigarettes.

'No, thanks,' Pippa declined. 'I don't.'

'I'll have one, though. To celebrate!' Steph grinned, helping herself.

'But you don't smoke, either,' Pippa frowned.

'Well, perhaps I should start.'

Pippa shook her head. There'd be no stopping Steph if she'd made up her mind. A minute later, Steph was coughing like a donkey and the young airmen were laughing at her.

'Oh, perhaps I won't,' she gasped, and handed the cigarette to Rusty who was happy to take a puff and blow smoke into the air.

'Just as well,' Pippa told her. 'You'd be hauled over the coals if Sister Tutor were to smell cigarette smoke from you. Now you haven't got a lot of time, so shall we wander along a way?'

They all fell into step beside each other, walking across the wide expanse of grass. Pippa was sad to see that the bandstand had been demolished, its pretty ironwork taken for scrap, she imagined. The handsome belvedere where you could sit and look out over the sea while being protected from the elements, had also been damaged although not beyond repair. Worst of all, the pier where Pippa had enjoyed herself all her life, listening to concerts, enjoying a tea dance, playing in the penny arcade or just relishing the sensation of walking out over the sea, was nothing but a framework of mangled steel girders with everything else reduced to ashes that had been washed away by the tides. As one, they came to a halt, contemplating the sorry sight.

'I wonder if they'll ever rebuild it?' Steph murmured. 'Be a pity if it was lost forever.'

Pippa gave a rueful nod. 'Yes, it would. But I suppose there'll be more important things to do. Once the war's over. Whenever that'll be.'

'Well, I don't want to waste my precious few hours being morose.'

'You started it,' Rusty teased.

'All right,' Steph grinned back. 'Let's sit on the grass for a while if it's not too damp. One thing Hitler's bombs can't change is the view out over the sea.'

That was true, Pippa thought to herself. But ever since the war had started, there'd been far more naval activity in the Sound. So, as they sat in the spring sunshine, gazing out over the water, the war was niggling away at the back of her mind.

'So, tell us about Australia,' she suggested, trying to divert her own thoughts. 'Are there as many koala bears and kangaroos — and whatever the smaller ones are called — as we're led to believe?'

'Roos, yeah,' Jack told her. 'All over the flipping place. Away from the cities, that is. Bloody dangerous. Breed like flaming rabbits. Wallabies are almost as bad. But koalas you usually have to spot up a tree. And they're not bears. They're marsupials, too.'

'Oh, I see. So, d'you live in a city or in the country, like?'

They sat for an hour or so, chatting, laughing, Rusty and Jack smoking a few cigarettes as they talked about their homeland. Pippa wasn't sure about Jack. Why did he have to use such language? But despite his brashness, it seemed to her that he was the one who missed home the most. Sounded awful to her, mind. All those poisonous spiders and snakes! She shuddered at the thought.

'I'd love to visit one day.' Steph utterly surprised her with an outburst of enthusiasm. 'Don't suppose I ever will, mind.'

'Don't see why not,' Rusty shrugged casually. 'After the war, of course.'

Steph sighed deeply. 'So many things will be *after the war*. Hitler's taken over most of Europe and we're living in fear of invasion. Strikes me we haven't seen the worst of it yet. And I'll have a war of my own with the ward sister if I don't make a move and get back on duty on time.' She jumped up, brushing down her skirt. 'It's been lovely catching up with you all. Don't know when it'll be possible again, mind.'

She put out a hand and helping Pippa to her feet, gave her a hug.

'Well, I'll see you back at the hospital in three weeks,' Pippa reminded her, 'if not afore.'

'And give us a call next time you're off duty,' Rusty instructed her.

'It's not that easy. We're only allowed to use the phone in exceptional circumstances so I can't ring until I get out to a phone box. Lucky you're more easy-going at the base.'

'We're Aussies, so what d'you expect?' Rusty grinned, giving Steph a kiss on the cheek. 'See you both some time, then!'

'Yes, bye!' the girls chorused as the two young men began walking back towards where the ferry would take them back to the base. Pippa watched them go. It had been a pleasant enough outing. She didn't have anything else to do anyway, did she? But she wouldn't be in any hurry to do it again.

'Come on.' Steph dragged her from her thoughts. 'Let's get back to the bus stop. Yours is just round the corner from mine, isn't it?'

'Yes, but it's such a lovely day, I think I'll walk home.'

Steph frowned. 'You sure you're up to it?'

'Don't you start!' Pippa groaned. 'I'm absolutely fine, but Mum's treating me like an invalid. I just can't use my arm to do much, that's all. I'll walk up Lockyer Street with you, but I'll be going the opposite way at the top.'

'Okay.' Steph linked arms with her as they walked up the street. Pippa was horrified to see that a couple of houses in the grand terrace had been badly damaged, and that the YMCA and the nurses' home of the Prince of Wales Hospital had been destroyed. It just felt as if death and destruction were everywhere. It was inescapable.

'I'll give you a call when I'm off duty next and there's no lecture,' Steph said as they came to a halt at the top of the street. 'I should be due a whole day next week or the week after.'

'I'm sure you'd rather spend it alone with Rusty if you can.' Gosh, did that sound diplomatic enough?

But Steph had seen through her. 'I take it you weren't impressed with Jack, then?'

'Not really, if I'm honest.' Pippa felt she had to come clean. 'But I'm not interested in having a man in my life anyway.'

'Well, take care of yourself, Miss Prim and Proper,' Steph joked, and waved as she hurried away.

Pippa stood for a moment, shaking her head at Steph's back. She was a one! Fun to be with and apparently scatter-brained, so how she managed to come joint top in all their tests, Pippa didn't know.

She was still chuckling as she turned into Union Street. The bus route would have taken her via King Street, but from where she was, it was more direct to go this way before turning up the long road home. Buildings were destroyed everywhere, and her chuckles turned to horrified gasps. Union Street was almost unrecognisable. The New Empire cinema was gone, and parts of the street had been blasted away. She should have known not to come this way, and not to be on foot when you were forced to look around you to see where you were going. There was still debris everywhere and you had to be careful if you didn't want to trip over some piece of broken brick, splintered wood or even some household item that had found its way on to the pavement. It almost seemed unbelievable, an alien landscape, and yet Pippa knew only too well it was for real.

She passed under the railway bridge. By some miracle, the Luftwaffe had missed the tracks throughout the city even if it had been obvious they were a target. Just past Millbay Station, lines ran down to the docks. It would have been a huge blow if they'd been hit.

Oh, now. Pippa suddenly remembered she'd be passing by where her old school friends lived. It would be lovely to call in on them and have a catch-up . . .

But oh, *good God*. As she neared Janet's Tea Rooms where they'd lived and worked, there was a great, gaping hole. The entire front of the building was gone. The site had been partially cleared, leaving the back of the building tottering and shored up by timbers to make it safe until it could be demolished.

Pippa stood, rooted to the spot, her heart jumping in her chest. What had happened to her friends? If they'd been inside, they wouldn't have stood a chance. She couldn't move, her muscles frozen rigid as something like ice trickled through her veins.

'Did you know them, miss?' a voice said at her elbow.

She gulped, her throat closed up so that she couldn't speak. She barely managed a nod.

'I be so sorry, cheel, but they was all killed.'

A hand, belonging to the same person who'd spoken probably, rubbed her arm, and then she was alone again. The horror of it seeped into her bones. Oh, no, it mustn't, couldn't be. She wouldn't let it.

'Hello!' a voice that sounded familiar cut into her shock. 'It be Nurse Luscombe, in it? Well, fancy meeting you yere.'

Pippa turned, dazed, and looked into the round face of Mrs Chollacott. She'd recognise her anywhere. There was something so homely about the woman that she felt strangely comforted by her mere presence.

'Yes, it is,' she managed to reply. But poor Mrs Chollacott might have lost . . . Then it dawned on her that she was pushing a pram. So perhaps . . .

'I be so pleased to see you, my flower. Looked like you was proper poorly when they pulled you out. Right next to me, you was. I saw the blast blow you across the room. If I hadn't been tucked up in bed, I reckon as I'd have been as well. But that poor cheel in the bed next to me, she must've been killed.'

Pippa lowered her eyes and nodded. She'd been trying so hard to forget, but things would always come back to you, wouldn't they? And now her old school friends, too.

'And . . . what about you?' she managed to ask in a faltering whisper.

'Me? Oh, just a few cuts and bruises. And I were one of the lucky ones. My little angel survived. Lucy we've called her. As near to lucky as we could get.' Pippa recalled that Mrs Chollacott was usually full of the joys of spring, but now the woman's voice had softened with emotion. 'Take a look at her.'

Pippa was flooded with relief. Lucy Chollacott must have been one of the few babies who survived. Pippa peered into the pram at the little bundle wrapped up safely and fast asleep. A little miracle. Tears welled up in Pippa's eyes. It was all too much.

'She's beautiful,' she murmured.

'Always are at that age,' Mrs Chollacott chuckled, and Pippa could hear the pride in her voice. 'Come a year and she'll be crawling around and into everything, and I'll be needing eyes in the back of my head! Don't I know it with all my others.'

Yes, of course. Pippa remembered now that this was Mrs Chollacott's seventh. 'Where are the others now?' she asked, the conversation helping her to put to the back of her mind what she'd just discovered.

'Well, the eldest's in the Merchant Navy, and the next one works with his dad on the railways. Susie'll be leaving school in the summer, but it's Easter holidays so she and Sharon — that's the next one down — they'm looking after the others while I see what I can get in the shops. First time I've been out on my own since having the babby. Then tonight after we've eaten, we'm catching the train to their grandparents in Tavistock to spend the night. Don't feel it's fair to stay with them during the day. They've got the place to run and the chiller are a bit too much for them. But at least we'll feel safe at night.'

Pippa gave a wistful smile. 'I wish my mum would do that. Leave the city at night. I've been trying, but I can't persuade her. She doesn't like the idea of sleeping on the floor with a load of strangers in a hall or something. Yet she's terrified when my dad's out on ARP duty.'

'Oh, well.' Mrs Chollacott's chubby face split into a beaming smile. 'My in-laws have a big enough place. It's actually a boarding house. I be sure they could squeeze in one more even if your mum had to sleep in a chair or on a settee. I'll ask them tonight and you give me a ring tomorrow. Look, here's my number.' She delved into her handbag and pulled out a scrappy piece of paper and a pencil whose end had been chewed to a jagged point. 'There. Now please don't hesitate. I'll be waiting for your call. And, by the way, the name's Beatrice. Or Bea as everyone calls us.'

'Oh, right.' Pippa was so overwhelmed it took her a moment to gather her thoughts as Beatrice handed her the scrap of paper. 'And I'm Philippa, but everyone calls me Pippa.'

'Right then, Pippa. Well, I'd best get on afore all the food's gone from the shops. So perhaps I'll see you tomorrow night.'

'Yes. And thank you so much.'

'Not at all. Got to stick together against flaming Hitler, haven't us?'

Pippa watched as the woman wheeled the pram away down the street to find some of the shops that hadn't been destroyed. How kind. Pippa felt herself overspilling with gratitude and admiration. Mrs Chollacott, Bea, was the salt of the earth. A humble heroine in Pippa's eyes.

She just hoped her mum would agree to the proposal. After discovering the horror of what had happened to her old school friends, she couldn't bear the thought of the same thing happening to her own family.

CHAPTER SEVEN

'Oh, no!' Adeline wailed as she stood on the landing in her dressing gown, her hair in curlers under a net. 'I hadn't even got into bed.'

'No, nor had I, Mum.' Pippa was scared enough herself, but she had to take care of her mother, didn't she? 'Come on. Let's get down the shelter. Have we got everything? Gas masks, torch, the string bag with the tin and the flasks?'

'All ready by the back door.' Adeline gave a huge sigh as they hurried down the stairs. 'I do wish your father weren't on duty tonight.'

'Well, you know he'd probably have gone out anyway once the siren went.'

They'd reached the back door now. Pippa slung the two gas-mask boxes over her shoulder and picked up the bag with her free hand. Willow was meowing at their feet and Pippa watched as her mother turned off the light before drawing back the heavy blackout curtain over the back door. The room was plunged into darkness and Pippa heard Willow protesting as her mother picked her up. As she waited for her eyes to adjust, she expected to hear the click as her mum turned the key in the lock, but none came.

'Mum?' she questioned.

There was a pause, then her mother's distressed squeal came to her through the gloom. 'I really don't think I can do this again,' she squeaked desperately. 'I can't bear another night down that awful shelter.'

Pippa gritted her teeth in exasperation. Why hadn't her mother listened to her pleas to go with Mrs Chollacott? But she couldn't really be cross with her, could she, she sounded so torn with anguish? But what could she do just now, this minute?

'Look, Mum, I know it's horrible, but we've got to.'

'No-o!' Adeline's cry was almost demented. 'I can't!'

Oh, Lord. Pippa glanced round in frustration as her eyes adjusted to the murk. Think, think! How on earth could she persuade her mum, and quickly? And then another idea hit her.

'All right. But at least let's get in the cupboard under the stairs. They say it's the safest place.'

Not as safe as the Andie, she knew, but it should shelter them from any flying debris. And after all, if you got a direct hit, your chips would be up in an Andie, too.

'Oh, yes,' her mother mumbled, relief echoing in her voice. 'There's a little ledge in there. We could take everything off and use it as a seat.'

'All right. I'll grab a couple of mugs and the teapot.'

'Don't forget the tea caddy.'

No, of course not. Though it took her two trips, fumbling in the shadows with her one hand. But at least her mother seemed to be in control of herself again and soon they were squeezed together on the ledge with the underneath of the stairs sloping just above their heads. To be frank, Pippa felt they'd be far more comfortable in the Andie where they could lie down and maybe even get some sleep. But if it made her mum feel happier . . .

They waited. All went quiet. The siren had stopped. And then the hum of aircraft, like hundreds of bees, in the distance at first, then getting louder. The boom of ack-ack guns, the dull thud as their shells exploded. Pippa imagined the barrage balloons soaring into the sky all over the city, the one on Mount Batten protecting the airbase.

The flasks began to rattle against each other. Gently at first, then harder and harder. Pippa heard her mother draw in a shaky breath and silently she moved the flasks apart. She might not have bothered. The drone overhead was growing louder, the whirring sound becoming a rumble. A distant crash made the ground tremble. Pippa stifled a gasp. For a second, she was back on Maternity, waiting . . .

Her eyes swivelled upwards as the vibrations grew stronger. The familiar scream as an aircraft dived. Oh, no. The next moment a thunderous boom. The house around them shook, and Pippa instinctively ducked. Felt her mother grab her hand so tightly.

'Phew, that was close,' she breathed again.

'I hope your dad's all right.' Her mother's voice was a terrified whisper.

'Mmm.' What could Pippa say? She, too, prayed that her father was safe out there. His main job was to make sure there were no cracks of light showing anywhere and that everyone had taken shelter once the siren had gone. It was hard to say if he was in any more danger than anyone else, but you never knew.

Time passed with neither Pippa nor her mother uttering a word as they sat in the dark, too scared to speak but with Adeline disguising a low moaning. They could hear more bombs falling, some relatively near, others much further away, but always the vibration of planes. Was it over? Were they coming back? And then suddenly, the distinctive roar of an aircraft engine swooping low overhead. No time to think. A mighty explosion shattered their eardrums.

A cry of terror. Was it Pippa's or her mum's? The house seemed to lift and they were knocked off the ledge. Tinkling of broken glass, groan of straining timbers. Listening to everything falling. And then all went quiet.

Pippa suddenly realised that she was holding her breath. So, she was still alive. She began to breathe again. Even though she'd been tipped on to the floor with her mother almost on top of her, she wasn't hurt and the cupboard was still standing around them.

'Mum?' she said urgently. 'You all right?'

'Yes.' Adeline's words were barely audible. 'And you? I'm squashing you. Let me just shift back. You don't think the house . . . ?'

'No, Mum. It was close but if we'd been hit, it would have been even louder than that, believe me,' Pippa assured her as the memory of that night at the hospital sprang into her brain. Mind you, she was shaking like a leaf herself. Just to be sure, she'd better check.

She shuffled forward to the little door, her heart pounding, and opened it a fraction. Just in case. She glanced around. Difficult to see in the dark, but . . .

She drew in a gasp. Then quietly, moving as silently as she could, she pulled the door shut.

'Mum,' she whispered, pulse exploding in her ears. 'Mum, keep very, very still. There's a German with a rifle standing by the window.'

She heard her mother snatch in her breath. For a moment, the world stood still. 'Are you sure?' Adeline's whisper was hardly more than a breath.

'Yes. Take a look yourself.'

There wasn't a sound, but she felt her mother edge forward. She couldn't even have opened the door, but must have peered through the narrow gap at its edge. Pippa felt her wriggle back, her breath against her ear as she mouthed, 'Yes, you're right. But I thought as they were going to ring the church bells if we were invaded.'

'Perhaps they don't know yet,' Pippa mouthed back, absolutely terrified. 'Perhaps it's just a few of them and they parachuted in under cover of the raid.'

'Oh, Lordy! What should we do?'

'Nothing. Just sit here in silence. He's bound to go away. And when he does, we can ring the police.'

Crikey. Could they really sit there in this tiny, cramped space, without moving, for however long it took? Would he come right into the house? Open the door and find them? *Shoot* them? Pippa felt terror surge through her.

They waited. Hardly daring to breathe. Muscles starting to cramp. Grasping each other's hands tightly. Pippa could feel her heartbeat racing. No sound from outside. He must still be there.

Minutes, hours maybe, dragged past. They shuddered as other bombs exploded at a distance. Force themselves not to move. Legs going numb from crouching on the ledge. Mouths dry and parched from fear. And then, when Pippa felt neither of them could stand another minute and they'd sooner risk being shot, the all-clear sounded, its long, steady moan such a relief they could have cried.

But what of the German soldier?

'He still there?' Adeline's whisper trembled.

'I'll look.'

Pippa inched forward, every muscle stiff and protesting. She squinted through the gap. He was still there. Like them, he hadn't moved. She frowned. It must have been hours. That seemed just so odd. Why should he . . . ? Holding her breath, she opened the door just a crack. Still he didn't move. And then, he looked different. Slowly, her hand trembling, she pushed the door wider. And wider. Then right open.

She slid outside, springing to her feet and her head thrown back in a gale of hysterical laughter.

'Oh, Mum, it's okay! You can come out!' she spluttered, doubling over in frenzied relief. 'It was the blackout curtain! The windows got blown out and it ripped the curtain, and from where we were it looked like a German but it wasn't at all! Come and look!'

An instant later, Adeline was by her side. A faint glimmer from outside showed her that Pippa was right. They jumped up and down, holding each other as their pent-up emotions dropped away and the pure joy of relief filled them instead.

'Be careful!' Pippa warned as she felt something crunch beneath her foot. 'There's broken glass on the floor.'

'Oh, no—'

'Don't worry. There might be a bit of clearing up to do, like, but we can't do it until daylight and we can see proper, like.'

'Oh, God, I hope your dad's okay!' Adeline's voice rang with terror. 'That bomb must've been quite close and his patch is only two streets away!'

'Mum, I'm sure he'll be fine.' Pippa squeezed her mother's arm, hoping she sounded a deal more confident than she felt. It was all she could think of, too, but no more than a second or two later, the front door opened and Neil hurried in.

'You two all right?' he asked at once, and suddenly nothing else mattered as the three of them held each other close.

'Bit of clearing up to do, and the window will need boarding up, but now our German's gone—'

'What?' Neil was so aghast that mother and daughter burst out laughing again as they explained what had happened. It was a release of the tension the night had brought them, but Neil wasn't so amused. 'Well, that settles it. Tonight's raid has proved that Hitler's not finished with us yet. And it was more our end of the city, so Devonport's in his sights. So you're going with that Mrs Chollacott tonight, and I'll brook no argument. As it happens, I'm not on duty tonight, so I'll come with you.'

'Yes.' Adeline's voice was level now. 'With there not having been a raid for another week, I were kidding myself it were over. But this were too close for comfort. So later on, if you can give your Mrs Chollacott a call, Pippa, love. But we'll go anyway, even if she can't help us.'

Pippa nodded, swamped with relief. Thank goodness. At last!

***

'There she is, by the clock, just like she said.'

Having bought their tickets, Pippa and her parents came out of the booking office and on to the platform at North Road Station. The place was packed with people wanting to escape for the night, just like themselves. Miraculously, the Luftwaffe's attempts to bomb the all-important railway lines had failed, so at least the easiest way out of the city was still possible.

Pippa eased her way through the crowd. Every time she said *'Excuse me'* and people saw the plaster cast on her arm — which she'd deliberately worn in a sling to make it more visible — they immediately moved aside to let her through.

'Mrs Chollacott!' she called.

The good woman at once looked round and gave her beaming smile. 'Pippa! You made it! And these must be your parents?'

'Yes, my mum and dad, Adeline and Neil,' Pippa introduced them.

'How do? I'd shake your hands but they'm rather full with this one.' Bea Chollacott's jolly face lit up with pride as she jiggled baby Lucy in her arms. 'Now these be my eldest two girls, Susie and Sharon, and these two little tackers be Norman and Bernard.'

Pippa nodded at the two girls, both the image of their mother and clearly used to keeping their younger brothers in check. The elder of the boys was plainly fed up with waiting on the crowded platform, jigging about while Susie held on to him tightly. But the other child, about three years old Pippa would have guessed, was more placid and stood quietly with his thumb in his mouth.

'I want to see Daddy!' Norman demanded, wriggling from Susie's grasp.

'Don't be silly,' Susie retorted. 'Look how busy the station is. He's got to look after all these people.'

'Well, you'm in luck as it happens,' his mother told him. 'He be coming down the platform now.'

Pippa turned and saw a tall, thin man in a railway uniform making his way down the platform, instructing people to stand back as the train was arriving. To her surprise, his cap bore the extra insignia of senior staff. She hadn't expected the husband of someone like Bea to hold such a high rank. His face spread into a grin when he saw his family, and he edged his way through to them.

'Daddy!' Norman cried, but Mr Chollacott wagged a finger at him.

'I can't stop. Now you be a good boy for your mam tonight.'

'These be the people I told you about, Len.'

'Pleased to meet you.' Len Chollacott raised his finger to his cap. 'But must be off.' He moved on up the platform. His wife watched him go then bobbed her head at Pippa and her parents.

'Sub-station Master,' she explained almost majestically. 'Our Ernie works on the railway, too, but much lower down, of course. At least it means he'll never be conscripted,' she added, lowering her voice wistfully. 'Not like our Duncan. Well, he won't be conscripted cuz he be in the Merchant Navy. But they'm in more danger than the Royal Navy or so they say.'

Pippa couldn't think what to say to that. Any mother would be out of her mind with worry yet, on the whole, Bea Chollacott hid her anxiety well. But Pippa and her parents were saved having to think of a reply as just then, there was a deep rumbling and a massive steam engine rolled into the station and the carriages drew up alongside the platform. Doors banged open and a few passengers alighted, but mainly the crowd surged forward and everyone scrambled to get aboard, despite the bellowing voices of the railway staff telling them to keep back. Pippa and her parents found themselves squeezed into a compartment with the Chollacott family and several other travellers, the two little boys sitting on their sisters' laps to fit everyone in.

Little Norman turned out to be an irrepressible chatterbox. As the train chugged out of the station, he pressed his nose up against the window and gave an almost non-stop commentary so that nobody else needed to think of anything to say. A couple of their companions got off at Yelverton, and when they stopped at Horrabridge, Pippa thought of their next-door neighbour, Ivy, but soon they were flying over the Magpie Viaduct and then through the tunnel to Tavistock.

It was good to breathe in some fresh air again as they walked down the hill and across the bridge into the town centre. Baby Lucy was starting to complain and Bea was looking a little flustered for once, Pippa thought.

'Ooph, not far now, thank goodness' Bea announced. 'My arms be aching summat rotten, like.'

'Shall I take her for you?' Adeline offered. Pippa smiled to herself. Her mum loved babies.

'That's kind of you but she'd grizzle even more with a stranger. Nearly there and I can feed and change her.'

Pippa was all eyes as they trooped along past the church and down a long, straight road. She'd always liked Tavistock on the odd occasion she'd been there and wondered where they'd be staying. Bea had said it was a boarding house so it must be a reasonable size. The road they were walking down was a wide avenue lined with grand Victorian terraces, which eventually gave way on one side to a vast area of parkland. Surely they must turn off one of the side streets soon. But then, to Pippa's amazement, the children marched up the front path to one of the opulent villas overlooking the park. Pippa couldn't believe her eyes. This wasn't what she'd expected at all!

She glanced at her mother whose face was a picture of surprise and pleasure. Pippa's heart did a little dance. It looked as if everything was going to be all right after all.

CHAPTER EIGHT

'Ah, good evening, ladies. Do come in.' Don Chollacott's pale eyes twinkled as he opened the front door a week later. 'We were beginning to think you'd decided not to come tonight. Beatrice has been here with the children for about an hour.'

'To be honest, we were wondering whether to come or not,' Adeline confessed, stepping across the threshold. 'What with there not having been a raid for a whole week, like.'

Pippa shot Don a knowing look and rolled her eyes. 'Mum might've been wondering, but I certainly wasn't. Only another couple of weeks and this wretched plaster will be coming off and I'll be back at the hospital. And by then, I want Mum to be so much in the habit of coming here every night that she doesn't even think about it. We caught the train from Devonport this evening as it's closer for us, but that route does take a bit longer."

'Of course.' Don nodded as he shut the door behind them. 'I remember when the London and South West Railway was built as a rival to the GWR line. I was just a tacker, and it was so exciting watching the first trains going over the viaduct in Bannawell Street, craning my neck to see those great monsters lumbering past way above my head. Aaah.' He sighed, and for a moment seemed lost in his childhood memories before shaking himself back to the present. 'Well, we're about to eat if you'd like to join us?'

'That's very kind,' Pippa told him, 'but we can't keep eating your food. So we ate afore we came out. Another reason why we're a bit late. And also Dad's on duty tonight so Mum wanted him to have a good meal first, like.'

'I've brought some pork belly from our pig club,' Adeline added, delving into her bag. 'And Pippa's donated some stewing steak from her meat ration to put in the pot for tomorrow. It'll help to make up for the meals we've had here. You've been so kind to us.'

'Not at all.' Don looked abashed. 'All got to stick together. And proper stewing steak will be nice. Just scrag end tonight.'

'And there's some tea, some sugar and some butter.'

'That's proper kind of you,' the elderly man thanked her. 'I'll just take them down to the kitchen. You go on in.'

Pippa watched him turn to the narrow steps that led down to the basement, while her mother crossed to the grand staircase that twisted its way to the two upper storeys.

'Just going to use the lav,' Adeline whispered, hanging her coat on one of the array of hooks on the wall. 'Let me hang your coat up for you, too.'

It only took a second for Pippa to slip off her coat that was only draped over her right shoulder because of the plaster cast. She handed it to her mother, then braced herself to enter the living-cum-dining room from which she could already hear a babble of noisy chatter. The dining room on the opposite side of the entrance hall had become a bedroom for Beatrice and the children, with a sofa that opened into a double put-you-up, a camp bed each for the girls and another that the two little boys shared, sleeping end to end, plus a cot for baby Lucy. It was all very cramped, especially on the odd occasion that Len was able to join them. And if Ernie, Beatrice's second eldest son, spent the night at his grandparents' house, too, he had to sleep on a couch in the other room. Pippa knew her mother felt guilty, as did she, at having taken up the only other spare bedroom in the house. But she knew she wouldn't rest easy unless she knew for certain her mother would come here every night once she herself had returned to life at the hospital.

'Pippa!'

The two little boys, Norman and Bernard, jumped down from the table and ran to hug her the moment she entered the room.

'Oi, you two tackers!' Bea berated them. 'Who said you could get down from the table? Proper bad manners that be. Get back up yere this instant!'

Two little faces fell as they did as they were told. 'Sorry, Mam.'

'Eat up nicely and I'll give you a game of Snakes and Ladders afore you go to bed.'

'Would you? Oh, thanks, Pippa!'

'But only if you eat every morsel and are well behaved,' she reminded them.

'You and your mum eating with us?' Sylvie Chollacott asked, beaming across the table as she ladled out a delicious smelling stew.

'No, thanks, we've eaten,' Pippa explained again. 'But we've brought some rations to contribute to the pot. Don's just taking them down to the kitchen and Mum's just coming. Sorry, evening everyone!'

There were so many replies as she glanced around at everyone seated at the long table towards the rear of the room. The elderly spinster twins, Miss Polly and Miss Primrose, both as scatty as each other, shared the large bedroom on the second floor. Now they nodded at her in unison. Then there was young Arthur Bell, a junior bank clerk, who rented the box room next to theirs. A middle-aged couple, Mr and Mrs Robbins, had for many years occupied the double room on the first floor, opposite Don and Sylvie's room and next to the smaller room Pippa and her mother shared, squeezing in her father as well on the nights he wasn't on ARP duty. With everyone seated around the table, together with Beatrice's brood, it made for a friendly if chaotic atmosphere.

Pippa and her mother went to sit at the other end of the room where a sofa and armchairs were shoe-horned in to form a relaxing area for the house guests. It was the largest room in the house, reaching from back to front of the entire building. Fortunately, a long, glass-enclosed veranda, its windows criss-crossed with anti-blast tape — as were all the windows in the house — ran across the front of the house, providing an additional seating area overlooking the front garden and the park on the opposite side of the broad road.

When the meal was over, Adeline, Beatrice and the two girls helped Don and Sylvie clear the table and take everything downstairs to the kitchen in the semi-basement to be washed up and put away. As promised, Pippa played a game of Snakes and Ladders with Norman and Bernard before Bea put them to bed and then brought a wailing Lucy into the room.

'I don't know,' she said with a fond smile. 'I get they two tackers off to bed and then this one wakes up wanting her feed. I'll take her up to your room to do the necessary, if that's okay, Sylvie.'

Her elderly mother-in-law nodded her agreement. 'And I'll come up shortly and we can discuss what we were talking about earlier.'

Pippa wondered what that was about, but it was none of her business so she went to join her mother, Mr and Mrs Robbins and the lady spinsters in a game of cards. She'd learnt that Miss Polly and Miss Primrose could be quite amusing without realising it, and it would help keep her mother from worrying too much over her father.

They'd just come to the end of a round when Bea came back into the room carrying an alert and satisfied baby, closely followed by Sylvie. Beatrice settled on the sofa, rocking Lucy in her arms, while Sylvie stood behind them, gazing down lovingly on her granddaughter before lifting her head and attracting everybody's attention.

'If I can just interrupt a moment,' she began, 'we have an announcement to make. It's just getting too much for Bea to bring the children here every night. School's about to start again after the Easter holidays and it'll be difficult to get them back in time for class every day, and poor Bea's worn out. So from now on, they'll be staying here full-time. You girls will go to school here in Tavistock,' Sylvie explained, looking across at Susie and Sharon, 'as will Norman. It'll only be for the duration, but they'll all be much safer as well this way.'

'Oh, but what about our school friends?' Sharon piped up.

'It makes sense, silly,' Susie reprimanded her. 'Poor Mam's worn to a frazzle, and lots of our friends'll be doing summat similar if they've got somewhere to go. We can meet up with them again after the war.'

'I suppose so,' Sharon pouted.

'Yes, and we'll soon make new friends here.'

'We'll leave the little ones yere with Grammar and Granfer the next few days,' Beatrice told them. 'Lucy yere can have a bottle while I'm gone, cuz you girls and me will go home to fetch more clothes and what have you. But now it's off to bed for you, too. Go quietly so as not to wake your brothers.'

'All right,' Sharon grunted. 'But it will only be for the duration?'

'Of course. Couldn't expect everyone to put up with the tackers indefinitely, could we? Now off you go.'

A general babble of discussion broke out over the prospect of having the entire family to stay. Miss Polly and Miss Primrose in particular, were delighted as they doted on their landlord's and landlady's offspring. Mr and Mrs Robbins, however, seemed less enthusiastic, but it was only *for the duration*, Pippa considered. She bit her lip. Those words that were on everybody's tongue held a deep irony. It was always acceptable if you had to put up with some privation for just that length of time, but who knew how long that would actually be? And what if Britain was invaded? But then there would be greater worries than having a slightly rowdy family to share your home with.

'And why don't you consider doing the same, Adeline?' Don was saying now. 'You'd be more than welcome. Once Pippa here goes back to the hospital, you'll be travelling back and forth on your own most of the time, and it'd save that. And of course, your husband can join you at any time. To be honest, it would suit us well, as we could do with an extra pair of hands with so many more people living here.'

That would be wonderful, Pippa thought to herself. But her hopes shattered into pieces when she caught the expression on her mother's face.

'That's very kind, but I couldn't possibly leave Neil to fend for himself the rest of the time. And there's the cat to feed—'

'Cat? Well, bring it here. I'm sure—'

'No, my mind's made up. I'll not abandon Neil for anything.'

'But, Mum, you wouldn't be abandoning—'

'Thank you all the same, but no.' Adeline was firm. 'Now whose turn is it to deal? Miss Polly?'

Pippa shot Don a grateful glance but then breathed out a sigh of exasperation. If only her mother would give in, she'd feel a lot happier.

With the excitement of Sylvie's announcement over, the level of conversation dropped back to normal as everyone sat around the one coal fire in the house. Pippa decided not to join in the new round of cards and instead drifted out into the quiet of the veranda. Dusk was closing in fast. The blackout blinds inside were securely fastened, so with no streetlamps lit outside, the veranda was in complete shadow. Alone with her thoughts, Pippa reflected on the recent conversation. If only her mum would reconsider Don's proposal.

The front door clicked and Pippa turned to see a black silhouette emerge from the house. She recognised the shape at once and her mouth curved into a wry smile, though she doubted Don could see it in the gloom.

'For a house so near the centre of town, it's a nice view, isn't it?' he mused, coming to stand by her side. 'It was Sylvie's parents' place, you know. But when she inherited it, we couldn't afford the upkeep. I don't think I've ever told you, but I was gassed in the first war, you see.'

Pippa gave an involuntary shiver. So many had been through all that, and now here they were again. 'Goodness, I didn't know,' she said. 'I'm so sorry. It must've been awful.'

'Well, it meant I couldn't do a proper day's work so we had no income, only my army pension which wasn't enough for a place this size. Leonard was at the grammar school, but when he left and the war was over, he was just passionate about going to work on the railway. Not what we'd envisaged for him, but it was what he wanted, even if he had to start at the bottom and earn so little at first. Look at him now, though. Sub-station master of a big and important station.' He paused for a moment, and Pippa could hear the pride in his voice before he went on, 'And then he met dear Bea. We weren't sure of her at first, what with her coming from a different background. But we soon saw her heart of gold and why Leonard fell in love with her, and now we wouldn't have it any other way. But he soon had a family of his own to support, and it was then that Sylvie had the idea of turning the place into a boarding house, and we've never looked back.'

Pippa listened to him with great interest. Well, that answered many of the questions she'd wanted to ask but hadn't done for fear of making it seem as if she was prying. She nodded as she peered into the deepening darkness outside.

'It certainly seems a very happy place, like one big family,' she replied. 'I do wish Mum would take you up on your kind offer, but she seems adamant that she won't. She relies on Dad far too much, and personally, I'd love to live here with this lovely view over the park. Well, a lovely view in the daytime at any rate,' she added ruefully, staring across at the inky blackness at the far side of the road.

'It's called the Meadows,' Don informed her. 'Did you know the old Tavistock Canal runs through it? Goes all the way down to the old copper port at Morwellham on the

Tamar. Stops just short of it now, though, since they diverted the water down the steep hill into a hydro-electric power station.'

'Really? That's interesting. I must take myself for a walk in the park, or the Meadows should I say, tomorrow morning afore we go back home. Actually, now that you mention it, I can see what must be moonlight reflecting on the water. And . . . there's something moving. In fact, I can see . . .'

'Yes, people like you, who've come from Plymouth to escape the raids. Those that can't get into the schools and church halls and what have you are camping out over there. It's heartbreaking. And yes, that's moonlight on the water. It's by no means a full moon, but the sky's as clear as a bell.' Don's voice hardened with bitterness. 'And it's really still. Unfortunately, you know what that could mean, don't you?'

Pippa nodded grimly. Yes, of course. A raid. It was perfect weather for it.

'I think I'll go outside to gaze up at the stars,' she said. It would stop her thinking about a raid, anyway. 'I don't get the chance very often. Might as well observe the beauty of nature, even if it could be a bad omen.'

'Be careful on the steps in the dark,' Don warned her. 'But I'll join you if you don't mind. Enjoy a bit of stargazing myself. I'll fetch both our coats. It might be April but it's still chilly at night.'

'Thank you. That's very kind.'

A minute later, Don reappeared clad in his own jacket, and then he draped Pippa's coat over her shoulders. Together they let themselves out of the veranda and went down the steps to the long front garden. They stopped part way down the moonlit path and looked up at the start-studded dome of the inky sky above.

'Breathtaking, isn't it?'

They stood side by side, the older man and the young woman, breathing in the silence and the stillness of the night, for some while until the chill in the air made Pippa shiver.

'It's getting late,' she said to Don. 'Time for bed, I think.'
'Yes, I agree.'

Pippa smiled at him in the dark. What dear people he and Sylvie were. She turned back to the house, but as she did so, a blinding flash way in the distance caught her eye. She paused. A shooting star? She'd never seen one before. But then there was another. A frown wrinkled her forehead. It didn't seem right.

And then a hand rested on her shoulder. 'My dear girl, I'm so sorry.' Don's words quivered with sympathy. 'That's how it started last time. Those two dreadful nights last month. The nights when you . . . They're hitting Plymouth again.'

Pippa shuddered as a cold chill washed through her. It was what everyone feared. Had expected but had hoped against hope wouldn't happen. And now it was.

'Don't tell Mum. She won't sleep a wink, worrying about Dad,' she managed to murmur. And would she sleep either, knowing what she did? 'I think I'll stay here a bit longer.'

'If you're sure,' Don said questioningly. 'But our own sirens might go off. We've had hundreds of alerts, especially when Plymouth's being hit. You might want to come inside if we do get one. You're welcome to shelter down in the basement if you'd feel happier. We don't, though. We've had bombs exploding in the distance, but we feel pretty safe. Not that you can be entirely sure anywhere.'

'Yes, thank you for the warning,' Pippa muttered as Don mounted the steps to the veranda door. Tavistock did feel safe compared with Plymouth, but as Don said, you never knew.

She turned back to staring at the night sky in the direction of Plymouth, drawn by some horrified fascination and, she supposed, the reckless hope that she'd see nothing more. But she did. It started as a faint golden glow that gradually bloomed into the darkness in a shimmering orange arc. She could even see the daffodils dancing in the border by her feet, as if dawn was breaking. But it wasn't. Plymouth was on fire once again.

And somewhere among it was her father.

CHAPTER NINE

Pippa crept down the stairs soon after dawn. She'd hardly slept. How could she when she was so worried about her father? She was relieved that her mother was unaware of what had happened to Plymouth overnight, so at least one of them had slept well.

Now, though, Pippa was desperate for a cup of tea to soothe her nerves. She knew her way around the kitchen well enough by now to get the kettle on the go, and made for the stairs that led down to the semi-basement. Her foot was just on the top step when the telephone's ring pierced the early morning silence, and she sprang back to the table in the hall. Beatrice and her family were asleep in the front room and she hoped to stop the shrill noise from waking them.

'Hello,' she said, putting the receiver to her ear. 'Tavistock—'

'Is that you, Pippa, love?' her dad's voice crackled. 'So sorry to ring so early but I thought if you'd heard about the raid on Plymouth last night, you might be anxious, like.'

'Oh, Dad.' Pippa sagged with relief. 'I've been mortal worried. Mum didn't know about the raid, but I did.'

'Just as well I rang, then. But I'm fine. Tired and very dirty. At home now, so I'm going to get cleaned up and try and get a couple of hours' sleep afore I go to work. If the office is still standing. It was all pretty bad again. Are you and your mother coming back today?'

'Yes, of course. That's the plan.'

'I'll see you this evening, then. I'm not on duty tonight, so I'll go back to Tavistock with you.'

'Okay, Dad. See you then. And . . . I love you.'

'Love you, too, my flower.'

Pippa wasn't sure why she'd felt compelled to say that. Was it that horrible thought that you must say such things often? Just in case? Just in case what? The unthinkable?

'Oh.' Just as she replaced the receiver in its cradle, Beatrice appeared at the top of the stairs to the kitchen with baby Lucy in her arms. Pippa hadn't expected anyone else to be up yet, and it made her jump.

'Morning, my lover. I yeard the phone but I were feeding little madam down in the kitchen so I couldn't get up yere to answer it.'

'It was my dad to let us know he's safe after last night.'

Pippa could have kicked herself. Bea's husband and her son had also been in Plymouth that night, and she must be worried sick, too. But just then, the phone rang again. Pippa picked it up as she was nearest.

'It's Ernest here,' an unfamiliar voice said. 'Can I speak to Mum?'

Ernest. Ernie. Bea's son who worked on the railway. Pippa prayed he wasn't ringing with bad news, and she shook as she passed the phone over to Beatrice.

'Hello, love.' Bea shifted Lucy into one arm, then all went quiet as she listened to what her son had to say. Pippa held her breath. Please . . .

'See you later then,' Bea concluded, and put down the phone.

'Everything all right?' Pippa dared to ask. 'Did you hear about the raid on Plymouth last night?'

'Just yeard it on the local radio downstairs. But Len and Ernie, they'm all right and our home's still standing, so I can relax now. This one kept us up half the night, so I'm just a bit tired.'

'Still going home to fetch some things later on?'

'We certainly are. And it might be an idea if you and your mam do the same. Just in case.'

Pippa nodded in reply. It seemed a sensible idea, but how was she to suggest it to her mother? She chewed on her lip as she made her way down the stairs to the kitchen and put the kettle on the gas.

***

'I'm so pleased not to be on duty tonight.' Pippa's father released a weighty sigh as the adults relaxed around the fire that evening after the children had gone to bed. 'After the pasting Plymouth got last night, I couldn't face it again so soon. I'd been going out when there was a raid even if I wasn't on duty, but last night was something else.'

'I'm really glad of the break, too.' Pippa detected the tiredness in Bea's husband, Len's voice as he nodded in agreement. 'It's a wonder that the railways have escaped any serious damage all along. Last night there was a bomb that was obviously meant for the Pennycomequick Bridge, but it missed and blew a crater in the road below instead. And there was just a bit of damage to the track at Wingfield, but it was negligible really. Just think of the disruption to supplies if the railways had been hit. And my dear wife wouldn't have been able to bring everything but the kitchen sink back with her this afternoon. Lucky I was there to find some space in the goods van.'

Pippa saw Ernie trying to stifle a laugh, but couldn't help a chuckle herself. It had certainly been a sight, Bea pushing Lucy's pram piled high with heaven knew what when she'd finally returned late that afternoon, accompanied by the girls lugging heavy suitcases along. But then babies needed such a lot of paraphernalia, and the whole family needed clothing, footwear, books and toys and so forth if they were going to stay in Tavistock for the duration. There it was again, that expression. After last night's horror, it hung over them like a dark cloud, so it was good to have something to smile over. Pippa glanced about the room. It really was a full house with her father, Len and Ernie all come to stay for the night.

When Pippa and her mother had returned home that morning, they'd found that the gas was off as apparently the Keyham gasworks had been hit in the raid. So with no gas to cook on, her mum had rung Sylvie and arranged that they'd return early and eat with everyone else. Since they'd got back to Tavistock, Adeline had been busy helping out in the kitchen. Pippa had done what she could to help, but was limited as to what she could do with her wrist still in plaster. Wretched thing. But not long now before it would be removed and she'd be back at the hospital. What was her mother going to do then, she wondered. At least she'd persuaded her to bring back some spare clothes, underwear and so forth, in the two small suitcases they possessed. Pippa had reasoned with her that if the railway was hit or she couldn't get back home for some other reason, it would be a good idea to have a few things with her. But secretly she hoped it was a step towards persuading her mum to take up Don and Sylvie's kind offer to stay.

'Shall we go outside for a cigarette before it gets dark?' Len suggested. 'Our last chance as you know Mum doesn't allow smoking indoors.'

Pippa watched as the men, Mr Robbins and young Arthur Bell included, all traipsed out into the front garden. She drew in a deep, calming breath. Less than twenty-four hours ago she had stood outside with Don, watching as the raging inferno in Plymouth had lit up the sky for miles around. She knew that once darkness fell, the tiny light from a cigarette could be enough of a guide for a bomber, which was why the men had taken the opportunity for a smoke while it was still light. Thank goodness for Double Summer Time, at least. But it paled into insignificance when compared with the thousands of incendiaries that had set the city ablaze to light the way for the bombers on so many occasions.

The previous night's attack had been even worse, if that were possible, than those two raids a month ago when the hospital had been hit and the city centre decimated. Pippa had found a copy of that day's *Western Morning News* that someone had left on the train. Only six pages, so she'd been able to stuff it in her bag so that her mum wouldn't see, but she'd read it while shutting herself away in the bathroom.

She was hardly surprised to learn that tremendous fires had blazed all over the city. After all, from where they'd stood in Tavistock, it had seemed that the very sky over Plymouth had been burning. The inferno had apparently stretched from Cattedown in the east to Devonport in the west and even across the river into Saltash in Cornwall. But it was reported that the worst conflagration had once again been in the city centre where the few buildings that had escaped the March blitz had become raging furnaces. A short paragraph stated that ironically almost the only building left standing among the blast and heat all around it was Leicester Harmsworth House, the very building that published the *Western Morning News*, and that probably because it was newly constructed of fire-resistant materials. Tragically what hadn't withstood a direct hit was the Portland Square underground shelter. Over seventy people had been killed, and there were stories all over the city of entire families being wiped out.

Pippa had shuddered and lowered the paper on to her lap. She wasn't sure she could read any more. The horror of it was unimaginable. She had seen at the hospital some of the dreadful injuries people had suffered during earlier raids, and had come close to losing her own life. But she hadn't experienced at first hand the grime, the heat, the choking dust, the deafening explosions, crackle of fire and swooping of enemy aircraft, the fear as buildings gave way and collapsed. But her father had. And yet he'd said nothing. It must be too terrible to talk about.

She'd been about to hide the paper within her cardigan and take it downstairs to add to the pile ready for collection, when a final paragraph caught her eye. It was reported that

Devonport Dockyard and all its associated buildings had been badly hit with many personnel killed or injured, but exact information was withheld for security reasons. Pippa felt a cold wave stream through her. So what Lord Haw Haw had been saying was true. Hitler was going for Devonport and the Royal Navy. Of course he was. It was to be expected. But the dockyards weren't far from where they lived. So how safe would they and their home be?

'I'm going to bed now, love.' Her mother's voice brought her back from her reverie, and she realised that everyone else had gone up. 'Say goodnight to Dad for me when he comes in. Old stop-outs, men, when they get together. Nearly dark and they're still nattering away out there. And they say women are chatterboxes!'

Pippa gave a wry smile. Thank goodness her mother hadn't been reading her thoughts. 'Goodnight, Mum. I'll be up soon.'

But as her mother left the room, she almost collided with Beatrice coming in with a mewling baby Lucy.

'Don't mind if I feed her yere, do you? The men are all outside . . .'

'Hardly, with me having worked on the maternity ward. In fact, it's rather nice to see something good and wholesome with all these horrible things going on.'

A minute later, Lucy's protesting stopped and her noisy guzzling at her mother's breast took its place. A smile crept on to Pippa's face. It all seemed so peaceful, a world away from the terrors of war.

'I be turning in now,' Bea said a while later when Lucy lay contentedly asleep in her mother's arms. 'Hopefully I can slide this one into her cot without waking her. Go and tell Len to creep in quietly, would you, my flower?'

'Yes, of course. I think it's time my dad came in, too, if he's going to get to work on time in the morning.'

Pippa followed Bea out into the hall before observing all the blackout regulations to go outside without letting any light show. It was fully dark now, and the cool night air made her pull her cardigan more tightly around her. The men were standing together, all cigarettes extinguished now, looking out in the direction of Plymouth. Her dad turned as she came up to his side and he put his arm around her.

'Looks as if Plymouth's getting it again tonight,' he said grimly.

Pippa caught her breath as she turned her gaze southwards. Sure enough, way in the distance, a faint orange glow was bleeding up into the indigo sky.

'Come on, cheel. Time for bed.' Her father's voice was low as he turned her towards the house.

Fear gripped her stomach for a moment before she remembered why she'd come outside. 'Mr Chollacott, Len, Beatrice says to come in quietly so as not to wake Lucy. She's just got her off to sleep.'

'Thanks, Pippa. I think we'd all better try to get some shut-eye. Don't know what we'll all be up against tomorrow.'

There was a murmur of agreement as they all turned towards the front door. Pippa felt her heart as well as her feet drag as they climbed the steps. For indeed, who knew what horrors would await them in the morning?

* * *

She sensed something was wrong even before they turned into the street. They'd already seen terrible destruction from the railway carriage and Pippa's stomach was fluttering nervously as they made their way from the station towards home. Her father had gone on to the next stop to get to work, so she and her mother were on their own.

Pippa's steps faltered as they reached the corner. Instead of the normal peaceful quiet, she could hear raised, anxious voices and a sudden, loud crash followed by more shouts. Her insides screwed in protest but she felt compelled to walk on. But she and her mother came to an abrupt halt as the scene of devastation opened up before them.

The street was in chaos. Uniformed men, ARP wardens and other Civil Defence personnel, were milling about in the middle of the road. One side of the street should be in shadow at that early hour, but light was flooding across the tarmac. For a moment, Pippa stared in confusion. It wasn't right.

And then she realised.

Beside her, she was aware of her mother's horrified gasp, and dropping the small empty suitcase she held in each hand, Adeline grasped her arm in a fierce grip. Neither of them could move, numbed with shock, and then slowly, they inched their way forward, shoring each other up.

Their home, Ivy's house on one side and the one adjoining the other side were gone. Nothing. Not even a ruin. But gone. It didn't seem possible. Wasn't right. Couldn't possibly be true. They must be seeing things. Surely it was a mistake.

They tottered forward on shaky legs. Pippa felt strange and faint, trying to support her mother who seemed on the point of collapse. Heart pumping furiously, not wanting to believe. And then she saw Mrs Hodges' house on the end. Or what was left of it. And it was suddenly real. For they were standing near the edge of a giant crater that had swallowed up their home. Their life.

'Stand back, there!' an irate voice shouted at them. 'Don't want you falling in!'

Pippa shuffled back, dragging her mother, her bloodless lips trembling and a heavy, sick feeling in her belly. 'B-but it was our house. The one in the middle,' she protested.

'Sorry, miss.' The voice was more sympathetic this time. 'Sorry to ask, but was there anyone . . . ?'

It registered now that the man was an ARP warden like her dad. And that he couldn't bring himself to complete the question. Pippa shook her head.

'Not in ours or next door. I don't know about the other side. But . . . Mrs Hodges on the end . . .'

'Trying to get her out. So if you can keep back. I'll try and find someone to take you along to the nearest WVS centre and they'll sort you out.'

Pippa managed a brief nod, and remained staring at the nightmare in front of her. A sob broke from her mother's lungs and Pippa held her as best she could as she slithered down onto her knees. Pippa felt the blood draining from her own limbs as she sank down beside her, lost and fragile. She couldn't comprehend it. Their home. Gone, obliterated in an instant.

A soft mewing beside them crept into her senses and she turned her head. Willow. Her fur coated in dust, but alive and unhurt. Adeline scooped her up into her arms, holding her tightly as she wept. Pippa looked on, feeling a whimper flutter from deep inside. They'd lost their home, everything. But they were alive. And so was her mother's beloved pet.

Suddenly it was all too much, and Pippa felt the strength drain out of her. She, too, let the tears stream down her cheeks.

CHAPTER TEN

'Oh, my poor flowers!'

Pippa let slip from her left hand the handle of the small suitcase she was carrying and fell into Bea's ample embrace. She was aware of her mother putting down the box she'd been given by a lady at the WVS centre to transport Willow in, and of joining her in the comfort of Bea's arms. Pippa had to bite back her tears at the dear woman's kindness. She'd managed to hold it together throughout the traumas of the day, but now she was relaxing, her fragile emotions threatened to crack.

'You've a home here for as long as you need it,' Don said gravely from behind his daughter-in-law.

Pippa pulled back from Bea's embrace and thumbed away the moisture in her eyes. 'That's terribly kind of you when the house is already so crowded. But at least I'll be going back to the hospital soon.'

'And an official-looking envelope arrived for Arthur in the second post,' Sylvie sighed ruefully. 'Wouldn't surprise me if it isn't his call-up papers. If I'm right, it means the box room will be coming free soon, so we can expand out a bit when he leaves.'

Pippa drew in a shaky breath and nodded. Everything was just so awful. Such a pleasant young man, Arthur. It hurt to think he'd be joining all the other men going off to fight for their country.

'Come into the sitting room,' Don invited, picking up the box with Willow inside.

'I don't know what we'd have done without everybody's kindness today.' Pippa paused as a sniffle came from her mother's direction, and Bea led Adeline over to sit down on the sofa. 'I hope you don't mind about Willow. Mum's cat.'

'Of course not. Why don't you let the poor thing out of the box? I'll go and put the kettle on, and then you can tell us all about it. Always helps to talk about things, I find.'

'Thanks, Sylvie. You're an angel. I'll just take the case up to our room.'

Pippa went back into the hall and mounted the stairs, suddenly feeling so drained and weary. She put the case on the bed and snapped open the locks. Instead of their own clothes inside as they'd planned, there was a selection of second-hand, donated attire given them at the WVS centre. At least she had a few items of clothing at the hospital, whereas her parents only had what they stood up in, plus the few things they'd brought back the previous day. With her mother needing both hands to carry the box with Willow in, they'd only been able to bring one suitcase, so her dad had taken the other back to his office with him, once they'd finally sorted out everything else.

What a day it had been. Pippa rubbed her hand over her forehead. But her mum needed her, didn't she? So she went back downstairs to find Willow haughtily inspecting her new surroundings, much to the amusement of Bea's gaggle of offspring.

'Is your dad coming back tonight?' Don asked in a low voice as Pippa entered the room.

Pippa felt her throat close up. 'No. He's on duty tonight. Mum begged him not to after what had happened, but they'd lost a couple of wardens in our area to injury last night. So he felt he really couldn't get out of it, especially as they'd found him a new uniform with his being destroyed. And hopefully there won't be another attack. Not three nights in a row. But don't mention it to Mum, will you? She's in such a state she could do without being reminded.'

'Of course. Come and sit down, my dear. Ah, here's Sylvie with the tea. And you children, leave the poor cat to settle on her own, and go out and play in the garden.' Don shoo-ed them all out of the room and then sat back down in a chair. 'Back to school next week, thank goodness. I love having them around, but a few hours' respite each day won't come amiss.'

'I just hope they settle down all right in their new schools here,' Sylvie said, setting down the tea tray.

'Oh, I be certain Susie and Norman will,' Bea answered, her arm still about Adeline's shoulders as they sat side by side on the sofa. 'And Sharon will, once she comes to terms with the idea of making new friends, like. Arter all, I expect they'll be other chiller from Plymouth if they've friends or relations they can stay with yere.'

'That's right. And the town's already taken official evacuees from other cities so the classes will be big. And now that central government is finally listening to Plymouth's local authorities after these dreadful raids and planning to officially evacuate children from there, the classes could get even bigger.'

'It wouldn't be possible to bring all the Plymouth children to Tavistock, though,' Don considered. 'I believe some of the Plymouth schools who've already taken matters into their own hands have evacuated the entire school to Cornwall. So maybe many of these new evacuees will go there, too. But if some of them do come here to Tavistock, they might have to split the children into morning and afternoon school, to fit them all in. I've heard they've had to do that in lots of other places.'

'Oh, well, what will be, will be. Now here you are, Adeline, dear.'

Adeline had been sitting, seemingly oblivious to the conversation, and Pippa watched as Sylvie handed her mother a cup of tea. Bea had to nudge her to take it, and when she did, the cup rattled in the saucer. Bea at once took it back from her and quietly placing it on the table, removed the cup and helped Adeline to hold it as she sipped.

'There, get this down you, my lover. You'll feel better afterwards.'

Pippa's heart expanded with gratitude. Everyone, Bea especially, was so kind. Pippa herself was struggling with her own emotions and it would have been hard for her to cope with her mother on her own.

'Dinner won't be long,' Sylvie told them. 'When you telephoned with the awful news, Miss Polly and Miss Primrose came down to help in the kitchen to get the meal ready early as we didn't know if you'd have managed to get anything to eat during the day. And we thought you wouldn't want anything heavy so we managed to get hold of some fish.'

'Thank you,' Pippa said, gratefully. 'That was just so thoughtful.'

'Well, I'll leave you to it. And Don, love, would you lay up the table? And Arthur and Mr and Mrs Robbins will all be back from work soon, so perhaps you could tell them what's happened. And of course, the letter for Arthur?'

'Indeed, my dear.'

For a moment, the room went quiet but for the clatter of cutlery as Don set the table. Pippa wondered if she shouldn't help him with her one hand, but to be honest, she was so shattered, all she wanted to do was sit. But she also felt so tense as she watched her mother's fraught expression. Then Willow jumped up on to Adeline's lap and snuggled down, soon purring softly as her mistress stroked her fur. Pippa's shoulders dropped with relief. Her mum looked so much more relaxed with her beloved pet curled up in her lap. What had happened would take a lot of getting over, and this was just the beginning. Her poor mum. She wasn't the sort of person to accept something like this that easily, but thank God for Bea and her wonderful family.

The meal wasn't easy. Pippa could feel everyone was trying to make light conversation — apart from Norman who seemed to think the situation exciting and kept asking questions so that he was repeatedly having to be shushed. Pippa could see that her mum was almost on the verge of tears again and was eating very little of the carefully prepared meal. And then there was Arthur whose face had turned ashen when he'd opened the envelope as it indeed contained his call-up papers.

'Please excuse me, but I think I'll go to bed now,' Adeline murmured a little while after the meal was over and everything cleared away. 'It's been a long, hard day and I feel exhausted.'

'You try and get some sleep, my lover,' Bea answered, looking up from where she was now dandling baby Lucy on her knee. 'I know it be awful but things'll look brighter come the morning.'

'I'll come up with you, Mum,' Pippa said, 'and we can sort out those things we were given. I just left them on the bed earlier.'

She followed her mother's laboured steps up to their room. She could see her mum's face was stricken as she picked up the items of clothing from the case and dropped them mindlessly on to the bed. Pippa's heart was breaking but she had to do something to try and snap her mother out of her misery.

'Oh, look, this is nice,' she said with forced enthusiasm as she held up a pretty ice-blue jumper with a Peter Pan collar. 'It'll suit you, Mum. And look at this lovely skirt. Everything's in good condition and all freshly washed. People are all so generous.'

'You should have them, sweetheart. They'll look better on you.'

Pippa jolted. At least her mum was saying something at last. 'No, you have them. Don't forget I've got some clothes back at the hospital and anyway, I'm hardly out of uniform, they work us so hard. We even have to wear uniform to go to the lectures in our off-duty time. I only dress up when I'm going out with Steph, and that's not often. I can soon buy myself a couple of summer dresses when it warms up a bit. That's all I need.'

'Well, if you're sure. But look, take this,' Adeline said, holding up a floral blouse with pearl buttons. Well, at least she was beginning to show some interest, Pippa thought. 'I really want my lovely girl to have *something*, like.'

'All right. Thanks, Mum.' She pressed a kiss to Adeline's cheek. 'So what else is there?'

She watched as her mother had a final rummage. 'No nightdresses, so I've only got the one I already had here. Not that I'd fancy wearing someone else's nightclothes.'

'Yes, I know what you mean. But I'm sure Miss Polly will run you a couple up on her sewing machine. You know how she loves to sew things, the dear. We can go to the market tomorrow and get some material.'

She spied the hint of a smile on her mum's lips. 'That'll be nice. We can go shopping together, mother and daughter. But,' her face crumpled once again, 'I keep thinking of all our things that we've lost, not just our clothes. Pictures on the walls, knickknacks from here and there. Even the kitchen table. I remember when your dad and I bought it when we were first married. We were so thrilled. It made it feel as if we were really setting up our home together. And things like the best tea set. It were a wedding present from your gran, and now it's all been blown to smithereens.'

'Oh, Mum.' Pippa reached out and rubbed her mother's arm. 'Try not to think of such things. And when the war's over and we get a new house to live in, you can have fun buying all new stuff. It'll be like starting married life all over again.'

Adeline gave a loud sniff and managed a brief nod. 'Yes, you're right. And we'll have our lovely daughter to help us.'

'So let's put these things in the wardrobe and you get yourself off to bed. I still feel a bit jittery, so I think I'll go back downstairs for a while.'

'All right, my love. What would I do without you?'

Pippa chuckled softly. 'Now you try and get some sleep. I won't stay up long.'

Five minutes later, she was back downstairs in the sitting-cum-dining room. The children had all gone to bed, sisters Polly and Primrose and Mr and Mrs Robbins were playing cards up at the table, and Arthur had apparently gone to the pub to meet with some of his pals. Sylvie, Don and Bea were sitting in the chairs, amusing baby Lucy who always had some wakeful playtime in the couple of hours before her last feed of the day. At barely five weeks old, Pippa knew she'd be up at least once and probably twice in the night, so keeping her awake and amused for as long as possible in the evening and tiring her out perhaps gave Bea a chance of a longer sleep before she was up again to feed her.

The sight of the baby gurgling happily made Pippa feel more relaxed.

'Your mum settling down, the poor soul?'

'Yes, I think so,' Pippa sighed as she sat down. 'I just hope there's not too much going round in her head to stop her getting some sleep.'

'Must've been a dreadful day for you.'

'Yes, it was. There was just so much to sort out, like. We had to find a phone box that was working to ring Dad at his office and let him know what had happened. He came to meet us straight away. Which reminds me, we'll need to work out some rent for you. Dad's got a good job so there's no problem.'

'But he'll need to save up to buy a new home after the war,' Sylvie suggested.

Pippa shook her head. 'No, no. When we eventually found out where the housing department of the Civic Offices now is, Dad registered for compensation. There's this new Act that came out recently. Not that I expect he'll see any money until after the war's over. But he'll get the value of the property, less what he owed on the mortgage, of course. You don't get anything for your possessions, furniture and so on, but at least you're promised your own four walls again.'

'When you can find something. There's going to be terrible housing shortages,' Don said grimly. 'But at least you've got a home here for as long as you want.'

'You don't know how grateful I am for that. Which reminds me, we must give you our ration books, Sylvie. They were in the house, so we had to find where to register to get new ones, and then there was the WVS centre. Everywhere was in such chaos, as you can imagine. And we saw the city centre. It was bad enough after those raids a month ago when I was hurt, but now . . . It just doesn't look real. What's left of the buildings are burnt-out shells, just mountains of rubble. Any walls left standing are like ghosts, skeletons with their souls and their eyes ripped out. And Devonport, Fore Street and all around, residential streets, just like ours, blasted to bits.'

'Now, now, my dear, try not to upset yourself.' Sylvie patted her hand. 'You've just got to think that you're safe now. Possessions are just that. Inanimate objects. I know sometimes they have deep sentimental value, but it's all based on memories and you'll always have those.'

Pippa forced herself to nod and gave a watery smile. Sylvie was meaning to be kind, she knew, and attempting to give her some encouragement. But deep down she knew she'd miss her home and everything in it dreadfully. And how safe really were they? Unless Hitler did invade which was still a huge fear, her mum should be safe here in Tavistock, but Pippa knew she'd grieve over her lost home for some time. She herself would be returning to the hospital and she had to admit that she couldn't wait, but would it be hit again? And as for her dear dad, well, she wasn't going to wait until it was fully dark to see if Plymouth was going to burn and light up the sky again. Surely, it wouldn't be attacked for a third night in a row? But if it was, her dad would be in the thick of it again. She already knew of her two old school friends who'd lost their lives in the March raids, and then there were all those babies and the adults who'd been killed in the maternity unit. Hundreds more had been killed in the city, and many more wounded, but it was just so much worse when you had the personal connection. And now she was terrified her dad could be in danger yet again.

No, she would go to bed making herself believe that all would be well. How could she sleep if she didn't? But she knew in her heart that nothing was certain and that she'd only be able to relax once the night was over and that there was no bad news.

* * *

Goodness, was that the time? Pippa couldn't believe she'd slept so late, but then she'd lain awake for hours before finally drifting off into an exhausted, fitful slumber. Her mother must have slipped out of the room while she was still asleep. Pippa wondered what sort of night she'd had.

She hurried into the bathroom for a brief wash, dressed as swiftly as she could with her plastered arm, and then went downstairs. Bea was in the hallway, her shoulders slightly slumped as she replaced the telephone receiver in its cradle. But Pippa noticed her pin a wry smile on her face as she turned round.

'Good morning, my flower,' she said, but Pippa didn't detect the usual exuberance in her voice. 'Well, I might as well tell you as you'll find out soon enough. Plymouth were raided again last night. I've just been on to the telephone exchange, but a lot of the lines are down in Plymouth and I cas'n get through to the station yet. And there's been no call from your dad neither. But don't you fret none. It'll be a while afore they get more lines restored so we'll just have to be patient, like.'

Pippa felt her heart squeeze as she nodded back. On top of losing their home and everything in it the previous day, this agonising wait was going to be crippling. She wondered how her poor mum was coping. She found her down in the kitchen, frantically polishing cutlery for all she was worth as she helped Sylvie wash up the breakfast things. Her way of coping, Pippa realised as she wished her good morning with a peck on the cheek.

'Ah, Pippa,' Sylvie beamed encouragingly. 'Help yourself to some toast. Gone cold, I'm afraid, but I'm about to make a fresh pot of tea.'

Pippa nodded her thanks. Butterflies were trundling in her stomach and she wasn't really hungry, but she knew she should try to eat something. It all felt so strange, as if they were all treading on hot coals, everyone fearing for their loved ones, the Chollacotts for Len and Ernie, she and her mum for her dad, while pretending nothing out of the ordinary was happening. Stiff upper lip and all that, Pippa thought bitterly.

'I don't see no point in going home to fetch some more things,' Bea said quietly a while later. 'If it's still standing. The whole place'll be in chaos and we'd only add to it. That's if we managed to get there. I'm going to take the chiller across to play in the Meadows and feed the ducks in the canal if we can spare a crust of bread. Want to come?'

'Er, no.' Pippa tried to smile. 'Think I'd better stay with Mum. Until we hear from Dad.'

'Of course, cheel. See you later.'

Pippa turned back into the hall. Without the children, the house seemed so quiet. She was pleased that her mum was being kept occupied down in the kitchen with Sylvie, preparing vegetables for tonight's dinner, the gentle tones of *Music While you Work* drifting up the stairs. Don was digging in the garden, Mr and Mrs Robbins and Arthur were at work, and Miss Polly and Miss Primrose had gone to see what was available in the food shops. Pippa huffed out a breath. There was little she could do to help anyone. Fortunately, she'd brought her nursing text books with her some days previously so she sat down in the sitting-cum-dining room and tried to do some studying, but she couldn't concentrate and kept reading the same paragraph over and over again.

The telephone rang in the hall and made her jump. By the time she got to the door, Sylvie had already answered it, and Pippa could tell from the conversation that it was Len to say he and Ernie were safe. At least it meant more lines were working. If only her dad would ring! After Len had hung up, she tried calling his office again, but once more, all available lines were engaged. Oh, it was killing her. She would try again in ten minutes.

But before she did, the doorbell rang. It was quieter than the phone so Sylvie probably wouldn't hear it from downstairs. Pippa got to her feet and went to open the front door.

Her heart missed a beat and then started pounding. An ARP warden was standing there in the veranda, his uniform filthy and his face so covered in grime that his eyes stood out like golf balls. Pippa blinked at him, a knot tightening in her stomach.

'Yes?' she whispered.

'Erm, you Mrs Luscombe?'

'That's my mother. She's downstairs.'

'Better fetch her then, cheel.'

Ice froze around Pippa's heart. 'You'd better come in.' She stood back, her legs trembling as she showed the stranger into the front room.

'I won't sit down. Too dirty.'

The poor fellow looked as if he was in danger of falling down, but Pippa wasn't going to argue. Her limbs felt wobbly as she stumbled to the top of the stairs and called down. A few moments later, her mother joined her in the hall, her face paper white, closely followed by a concerned Sylvie.

'Mrs Luscombe?' the man said gently as they trooped into the room. 'You'd better sit down. I'm afraid I have some bad news.'

Pippa heard her mum gasp as she collapsed rather than sat down in one of the armchairs. A kernel of panic unfurled in Pippa's own breast and her hand went over her mouth. Oh, no.

She knew before he said the dreaded words.

'I'm so sorry, Mrs Luscombe. I were on duty with your husband last night. There were a bomb landed proper close. He were . . . caught in the blast. By the time I got to him, he were struggling for breath. He managed to say he loved you both. And then he were gone.'

Pippa stared at him, her mind somehow sealed to what he'd just said. Silence, heavy, fractured. No one moved.

'I, er, I wanted to tell you myself,' the stranger stammered. 'Rather than you hear it from a policeman or in a telegram. He were a good man, your Neil.'

Pippa felt the strength drain from her limbs and stumbled into a chair. Through a fog as dense as coal dust she heard her mother's unearthly scream.

CHAPTER ELEVEN

Pippa stood rigid. She felt sure that if she didn't move, she would be safe and the words she'd just heard and the scene before her would merely be part of a bad dream. Her dear, kind, thoughtful dad couldn't possibly be dead. It just couldn't be true.

But as the veil of shock slowly lifted, a cold, heavy emptiness settled in her stomach. Her mother's screams continued to echo in her ears, a dreadful, wailing sound, her mum bending over and drawing her clenched fists into her waist each time the blood-curdling noise shattered the quiet of the room. Pippa wanted to go to her but somehow she couldn't make her legs move. Instead, she watched as Sylvie went to comfort her mum, but Adeline angrily pushed her away. At a loss, Sylvie turned to the bewildered stranger.

'I'm so sorry. Would you like to come down to the kitchen for some tea?'

The poor man looked stricken. 'No, thank you, missis. I'd best be getting back. A lot to do, like. And I'm master sorry to have upset the lady so.'

Sylvie nodded and showed him to the door. While she was gone, Pippa managed to force her trembling limbs to work and stepped over to her mother, her own heart ripped apart. She tried to encompass Adeline in her arms but was met with a violent struggle and was hurled aside.

'Mum, please, stop!' she cried over the horrendous screeching, but there was no response as the hysterical keening went on and on.

She stood back, utterly flummoxed. *Please let it not be true.* It was like watching through a window, something she didn't want to be part of, but was. She felt she was being swallowed up into a great black hole, so helpless as her mother continued to vent her grief.

Sylvie slipped back into the room, followed by Don who'd been drawn in from the garden by the terrible noise. With that, there were shouts of laughter as the front door opened and Beatrice and her tribe came back in from their expedition to the Meadows.

'What on earth . . . ?' Bea was at the door, Lucy in her arms, her forehead corrugated with anxiety.

Pippa didn't hear Sylvie's brief explanation, but caught the words *go for the doctor*.

'I'll go,' Don said, turning from the room.

'And I'll take my lot downstairs,' Bea said. 'Get them out of the way.'

Pippa watched, and waited, as Sylvie tried again to pacify her mother but to no avail. She herself snatched at Adeline's hands but was fought off once more. What was worse, her own tearing shock and grief, or watching her mother's?

Oh, please, she thought, let the doctor come quickly! How long could she witness her mum's agony? But her prayers were answered as only a matter of minutes later Don came back into the room followed by a tall, elderly man carrying a medical bag. Pippa saw his eyes move swiftly about the room, assessing the situation in seconds. Then the lines on his face moved into a compassionate smile and his gentle, confident demeanour alone seemed to soothe the tense atmosphere.

'Ah, I'm so dreadfully sorry to hear of your sad news, Mrs Luscombe, isn't it?' he said, moving straight across to Adeline.

'I'm Doctor Franfield from two doors down. Doctor Franfield senior, that is. I'm afraid my son is seeing some of his patients at the hospital just now, so you've got to put with me. Now I can understand how terribly distressed you are, so please will you let me help you?'

His voice was soft and mellifluous yet had an air of authority about it. His compassion was evident but perhaps because he wasn't so emotionally connected to Adeline, she seemed to take notice of him and began to calm down. Her screams faded to heaving sobs as she turned her eyes to him.

'Now, shall we sit down, my dear? Would you like to talk to me about it?'

Pippa watched, amazed and relieved, as Doctor Franfield helped her mother to sink down on to the sofa and then sat down beside her. He took her hands, gently but firmly, and rubbed his thumb over her skin.

'It's a terrible thing to lose your spouse, and such a shock. What was his name?'

Adeline sniffed hard. 'N-Neil,' she barely whispered. 'And I'll never see him again!' she wailed, nearly breaking into tears again.

'And this is your daughter, I understand?' he said, glancing at Pippa with a scarcely discernible nod which she took to indicate she should sit on her mother's other side. 'And your name is . . . ?' he asked as Pippa dutifully obeyed.

'Philippa,' she managed to answer, 'but everyone calls me Pippa.'

'Right, then, Mrs Luscombe, I'm sure Pippa doesn't like seeing you in such distress, so will you allow me to give you a little injection? Just a low dose to help you relax and maybe have a little snooze? Of course, it won't change the situation but you might feel a little calmer afterwards. I'm not going to offer you any platitudes, but I am here to help in any way I can. So, what do you say?'

Adeline turned her tear-stained face to Pippa, her eyes wide and questioning.

'I think you should, Mum. You'll be able to face things better after a little rest.'

'Well, all right, then,' her mother faltered. 'If you think so.'

'Good. Well, shall we roll up your sleeve, then?'

Pippa helped her mother slip her arm out of her cardigan sleeve while the doctor took a box containing a syringe from his bag and then carefully drew up a small dose from a phial. Pippa watched. She'd observed injections being administered often enough in her training. One day, she'd be giving them herself. But for now, it was a weight off her shoulders to know that her mum was receiving some help.

'I suggest you go and have a lie down now,' Doctor Franfield told her. 'Could you go up with her, Mrs Chollacott? And maybe I can have a little talk with Pippa here.'

'Of course,' Sylvie replied. 'Come on, Adeline. Let's help you upstairs.'

Pippa waited, hands wringing in her lap, as Sylvie helped Adeline from the room. And then Don went down to the kitchen to make a cup of strong, sweet tea for herself and the good doctor.

'Well, my dear,' Doctor Franfield said, swivelling round to face her. 'I am so very sorry. Dreadful times we live in, but it hits you so hard when it directly affects you. Your poor mother gave vent to her grief, but what about you?'

Pippa blinked at him. What about her? She'd been so distraught watching her mum that only now was she able to look inside herself.

'I-I don't really know,' she answered truthfully. 'I suppose I feel . . . sort of empty. As if there's nothing inside me at all. I don't even feel as if I want to cry. Isn't that terrible of me?'

She felt her brow tighten with confusion and guilt as she gazed at the doctor, but his face creased with compassion.

'No, not at all. It's the shock. And in a way, it's your mind's own defence mechanism. I'm no stranger to grief in my line of work. You will cry once it all starts to sink in, and promise me you'll let it all out. It will help, I assure you. To have lost your father and, so Mr Chollacott told me on the way, your home is a huge amount for your emotions to process, and it will take time. And I see you've already been in the wars, too,' he concluded with a brief dip of his head towards her plastered arm.

'I'd almost forgotten that,' Pippa told him. 'I'm doing my nurse's training at the City Hospital and I was on duty in the maternity block when it was hit. I was lucky to survive when so many, mainly the little ones, didn't.'

She saw Doctor Franfield's eyes stretch wide. They were kind eyes, a striking green blue, one of them drooping slightly at the corner where she noticed a faint, tell-tale scar. So he'd suffered an injury himself at some point. No wonder he was so understanding.

Now he swung his head from side to side. 'Terrible, terrible business,' he muttered almost to himself. 'So I assume you'll be returning there soon.'

'Yes, in a couple of weeks when the plaster comes off. If Mum's able to cope without me, that is.'

'Of course. But it looks as if she'll have plenty of support around her here. And we're only two doors down if you need any help. Either my son, William, will be there, or myself. In fact, I'll call again this afternoon to see how you both are.'

'Thank you, Doctor Franfield.'

'Well, I think I'm going to be seeing quite a bit of you over the next few days. And we are neighbours, so let's drop all the official protocol that you'll be used to at the hospital, and call me Elliott.'

Pippa jolted in surprise. That was unexpected. But then she had the feeling Doctor Elliott Franfield could be full of surprises. What a pleasant old chap he was. She couldn't have wished for anyone better to keep an eye on her mother.

***

Pippa stood with her mother, Don and Sylvie, along with hundreds of other mourners, on one side of the long mass grave that had been hastily dug in Ford Park Cemetery. They'd been given a number to match up with the tiny wooden crosses spiked into the ground so that they'd know which of the shrouds laid out in the deep ditch contained her father's remains. How impersonal was that? But Pippa supposed it was the best anyone could hope for.

It had been the same at the morgue. So many bodies that there simply wasn't the capacity to put them into cold storage and they were set out on tables. It wasn't actually a morgue at all, but one of many halls that had been brought into use. Many of the deceased were only distinguishable by their identity cards, their injuries were so dreadful. Who'd had the macabre foresight to think of that, Pippa thought bitterly. At least they'd been permitted to pull back the sheet, hold her dad's hand, kiss his face. Not a mark on him. Blast lung they called it. He'd died almost instantly and not suffered the choking agonies of some. They should be thankful for that — but if only he'd been among those that pulled through.

Now Pippa gazed down on the shroud ten feet below her. Not even time for enough coffins to be made to give the poor souls dignity. All around, the echo of stifled sobs, crowds of families and friends united in grief. And yet, when it came to it, everyone had to face their sorrow alone. Her mum was barely being held upright by Don and Sylvie, and Pippa was so grateful for their support. It meant she could grieve herself, in her own little bubble. She wondered if she should try and find out where her two old school pals were buried, but there was already enough desolation in her heart.

On the opposite side of the trench, a line of vicars and priests were uttering funeral rites, *man that is born of woman, dust to dust, ashes to ashes*, but it all went over Pippa's head, a jumble of mutterings as they sprinkled Holy Water over the bodies. A string of choir boys began singing as the clergymen slowly filed away, floating, in silence, to gather in the covered arch in front of the stone chapel, ready to offer their condolences as the bereaved departed.

There was a murmuring among the crowds as people stepped forward to say their very last goodbyes. Pippa watched as her mum threw down the single red rose she'd managed to procure, then collapsed on to her knees in a flood of uncontrolled tears while Don and Sylvie knelt down on either side with their arms around her shoulders. Alone in her despair, a cruel pain raked Pippa's throat as she dug her fingers into the ground and tossed a handful of soil down into the grave. It landed, silently, on where she imagined her father's tortured lungs would be.

'Goodbye, Dad,' she whispered in her head. 'Rest in peace. I love you so much.'

Between them, Don and Sylvie raised her mum to her feet and half carried her away. Pippa followed, blinded by tears, and a tearing void gouged out of her heart.

CHAPTER TWELVE

Pippa knocked on the door and waited. Sister Tutor Honeywell had asked to see her as soon as she returned to the nurses' home. Having missed six weeks' training, she wasn't going to be put back with the latest intake, was she, despite what Sister Tutor had promised on the day she'd been discharged from hospital? It would just be about the last straw after all she'd been through, but she supposed she couldn't complain if that was to be the case.

'Come in,' she heard Sister Tutor's familiar voice, and quietly obeyed, shutting the door gently behind her.

'Ah, Probationer Nurse Luscombe.' Amanda Honeywell looked up with a welcoming smile. 'Do take a seat, my dear. And let me first say how dreadfully sorry we all were to hear of all your appalling news, you poor child.'

Pippa had to take a moment to compose herself. Sister Tutor's tone was so soft and compassionate that Pippa could easily have melted into tears again. But she had to make herself appear as strong and resolute as possible. She wasn't going to be told she needed more time off and have her training put back even further!

'Thank you, Sister Tutor,' she replied calmly, not wanting her anxiety to show.

'Well, it's good to see you back with us. Now, I've been looking through your file and as I said before, I believe that as one of our brightest students, I feel confident that you'll be able to catch up with your studies.'

'I have been trying to learn as much as I can from my text books while I've been away,' Pippa told her eagerly, mentally crossing her fingers.

Sister Tutor's smile broadened. 'Why does that not surprise me in someone as diligent as yourself? But are you sure you feel ready to return to the wards? After all, you've been through some terrible traumas.'

Pippa was ready with her answer. 'Yes, I do, Sister Tutor. I think concentrating on my work and my studies is just what I need.'

Amanda Honeywell steepled her fingers. 'And what of your poor mother? Will she be able to cope without you?'

'Yes. In fact, I think it'll be good for her. She leans on me greatly so that she's more sinking into her grief when I'm around, rather than trying to move on. She's living with a wonderful family in Tavistock, so away from all the bombing. I don't know if you ever met Mrs Beatrice Chollacott? She'd just given birth to her seventh child who was miraculously among the few who survived. Quite a character, like. I bumped into her on the street and we've become good friends. She's taken all her family to live with her in-laws who run a boarding house in Tavistock, and that's where my mother's living now. They're the most wonderful people and if anyone can help Mum get back on her feet, it's them. But,' Pippa hesitated only a moment, 'I would ask that when it comes to my time off, instead of having two half days, I could have a whole day so that there's time to go and visit her.'

Eyes downcast in order to concentrate, Sister Tutor had been slowly nodding her head as she listened. Now her incredibly blue eyes met Pippa's across the desk. 'What very wise words from one so young. And yes, I will do my best to facilitate that for you, though it might not be possible every time.

'Now I'm putting you on Men's Medical with Probationer Nurses Chappel and Saundercock. I believe you and Nurse Chappel are good friends, so I shall endeavour to keep you together. And being another excellent pupil, she can help you catch up on whatever you've missed. I think you've seen enough of the effects of war for the time being, so this should ease you back into things nice and gently rather than being on a surgical or emergency ward. I have also instructed the ward sister that you're to do no heavy work for the next couple of weeks with your arm only just out of plaster to give time for it to regain its strength.'

Pippa had to stop herself sighing with relief. Everything Sister Tutor proposed was perfect. 'Yes, Sister Tutor, thank you so much.'

'Now run along and get into uniform and on to the ward. Sister is expecting you.'

'Oh, yes, Sister Tutor, thank you again.'

'And, Nurse Luscombe, welcome back.'

Pippa stood up, bathed in Amanda Honeywell's beaming smile. She smiled back, her heart lifting as she left Sister Tutor's office and then made her way back towards the nurses' home and her room. Knowing she was returning, Steph, bless her, had laid Pippa's uniform out on her bed all ready for her, and as Pippa changed, she couldn't help but feel exhilarated. Donning the black shoes and stockings, pale blue check dress and spotless white apron really made her feel as if she was coming home, even if the starched collar did feel a bit stiff around her neck. But she'd soon get used to that again. And it did feel strange, using her right hand after six weeks of its being encased in the plaster cast. The skin was pale and a bit itchy in places, so it was a relief to be able to have a good old scratch until it settled down.

One thing Steph hadn't done for her, though, was to fold the stiff, white square of material into the nurses' butterfly cap. Different hospitals had different caps for the different nurses' ranks, and there were apparently various styles all going by the name of butterfly. Pippa folded and pinned, and smoothing her fair hair into a neat bun at the nape of her neck, she fixed the cap securely on to her head, before checking her appearance in the mirror. Detachable long sleeves with starched wrist cuffs to walk about the hospital and enter the ward, but elasticated elbow frills for when she was working stowed in her pocket. It was good to be back in uniform, feeling like a real nurse again. Just her dark blue cloak with the scarlet ribbons crossed over her chest, and she was ready to face her nursing world again.

She made her way to Men's Medical, almost dancing with excitement. It was one of the largest wards in the hospital so she knew she'd be kept busy. She went through the double swing doors and glanced down the rows of beds. She spotted Steph and Ruby and some more senior nurses further down, but no sign of a navy uniform with frilly cap, so the sister must be in her office. Reading the name plate slotted into the holder on the door, she knocked lightly and waited.

'Come,' she heard, and went inside, heart pattering nervously in her chest.

'Ah, you must be Probationer Nurse Luscombe.' The sister looked up, her eyes sharp and beady in a thin face framed by the lace cap tied beneath her chin.

'Yes, Sister Tyrrell.'

'Well, it's good to have you on board. We're rushed off our feet. Find whatever space you can in the cloakroom to put your things and then get out on the ward. Staff Nurse will tell you what to do. I've instructed her not to give you any heavy work for a few weeks as requested by Sister Tutor. I was so sorry to hear about your personal circumstances, but I do hope it won't affect your work. I shall expect the highest standards with no slacking.'

'Of course, Sister Tyrrell.'

'Good. Now off you go.'

'Thank you, Sister.'

Closing the door behind her, Pippa slipped back through the double doors to find the cloakroom. Hanging up her cloak, she removed the stiff wrist cuffs and detachable long sleeves from her uniform dress and slipped the elbow frills up over the remaining short sleeves. Then she went into the sluice room, gave her hands a good wash even though she'd done so on leaving the nurses' home, and walked on to the ward, a feeling of elation wafting over her.

She caught Steph's welcoming grin as she walked past her and approached a harassed looking staff nurse seated at the desk in the middle of the ward.

'Excuse me, Staff Nurse. Probationer Nurse Luscombe reporting for duty.'

The older woman looked up from contemplating the charts on her desk. 'Oh, and not a moment too soon for us! I'd like you to help Nurse Saundercock finish the bed baths so that Nurse Chappel can assist with the next round of obs before lunchtime at midday. Should have finished an hour ago but we're so short-staffed. But it'll help you to get to know some of the patients. Some of them are quite long stay. You'll be on second dinner after you've helped serve the patients.'

'Yes, Staff Nurse.'

Pippa turned away and went straight up to Steph and Ruby. But there was no time for pleasantries. Within minutes, she was wheeling in from the sluice room a trolley with all the necessary for her and Ruby to give the next bed bath while Steph went off to wash her hands before joining a second-year nurse on her observations round. Oh, yes, Pippa thought as she introduced herself to an elderly man with bronchitis. It would be good to be rushed off her feet again, to be thinking of others and not of that massive crater that had swallowed her home, and the rows of white shrouds in the deep ditch at Ford Park. Setting to, she felt the ache in her heart retreat below the surface. For a while at least.

***

After being busy with bed baths, bed pans, observation rounds and handing out drinks and meals, Pippa was exhausted when they went off duty at nine o'clock that evening.

'Phew, I feel proper worn out,' she groaned as she, Steph and Ruby made their way back towards the nurses' home.

'Forgotten what real hard work is like, have we?' Ruby said tartly, throwing her a sideways glance.

'Oi, Ruby, watch yourself,' Steph warned her. 'Pip had a bad concussion, remember, and badly bruised ribs as well as her broken arm. And then, well, everything else she's been through. You'd be just as tired out yourself on your first day back if it had been you.'

Pippa held her breath. She'd never taken to Ruby and it was good of Steph to defend her but she wished her friend hadn't risen to the bait. She didn't feel up to witnessing an argument. All she wanted was to have a quick wash and get herself into bed. But she was saved any further embarrassment by the sudden, haunting wail of the air-raid siren.

'Oh, no, not again,' Steph sighed as they crossed over to the old block that housed the nurses' accommodation. 'Is a week off from the raids the best Hitler can give us?'

'Hardly worth his while, is it?' Pippa scoffed bitterly. Anger and grief speared her heart. 'Nothing much left to bomb from what I've seen. And how many more innocent civilians does he want to kill?'

After the devastating raid that had killed her father and blasted mainly Devonport and the west end of the city into a further raging inferno, there'd been only a few nights' respite. It was during that brief time that they'd made the journey to Ford Park for the mass burial, and she'd seen the utter destruction, misery and ruin wreaked upon the population by the bombers. And then it had begun again.

The same area had been targeted, drenching the already stricken homes and businesses with incendiaries and high explosives, and lighting the night sky with a lurid glow that young Arthur Bell had let slip could once more be seen from the front garden in Tavistock. For two nights running, Plymouth had been subjected to vicious night attacks yet again and even the main street of Saltash over the river in

Cornwall had been heavily damaged by fire and blast. Pippa wondered if the rest of her street had been obliterated to join her own home in another massive crater or been reduced to mountains of rubble. She felt she ought to try and find out if Mrs Hodges survived her injuries, but really none of it bore thinking about, it was all so horrific.

But since then, there'd been a whole week without any raids. Surely Plymouth and Devonport had been so totally destroyed that there was no point attacking again? So, to hear the moan of the siren again swamped Pippa with despair.

'Well, we can either go to the dining hall and cower under a table, or brave it out in our rooms,' Steph reminded her glumly. 'At least our rooms are in the semi-basement so we'd be safe from flying shrapnel. And if you get a direct hit, well, doesn't matter where you are.'

Pippa knew that well enough! You could try and stay safe, but you never knew. Look at all those poor souls who'd been killed when sheltering in the underground Portland Square shelter. Just now she was so tired, she didn't really fancy going to the dining hall, and it would be great to have a good old natter with Steph and catch up on all the goings on at the hospital.

'Our room and bed, I think,' she replied.

'I'm with you there, cheel,' Steph grinned back. 'And you, Ruby?'

Pippa sincerely hoped that the other girl wouldn't want an invite to their room. Besides, there'd be plenty of other nurses coming off duty if she wanted some company. But oh, thank goodness, Ruby turned away from them.

'Well, I'm not risking myself,' she told them haughtily. 'I'm off to the dining room.'

'See you in the morning, then,' Steph called after her, and then bursting into laughter once Ruby was out of sight, she linked her arm through Pippa's. 'Come on. Didn't want her with us anyway, the sour old lemon. Acts like she knows everything when really she's not the brightest spark. What this fiancé of hers sees in her, I don't know.'

'Fiancé?' Pippa questioned in surprise. 'Well I never.'

'Oh, yes, of course, you missed that,' Steph answered with a hint of gleeful malice as they went through the doors into the old building. 'Remember she'd never say where she was going on her days off? Turns out she had a sweetheart back home somewhere near Ivybridge. A saddler or something. Makes harnesses for carthorses and that sort of thing as well. Anyway, she comes back one day shortly after . . . you know . . . giving herself all sorts of airs and graces and with a ring on her finger. Has to wear it on a chain round her neck while she's on duty, of course, but thinks it gives her the right to act all superior, like.'

'Well, I can't say I'll miss her if she leaves to get married.'

'No chance of that unfortunately,' Steph told her, opening the door to their room. 'She says they wanted to make their relationship official afore he gets called up, but not get spliced until the war's over, whenever that might be.'

As if to remind them, a loud explosion not that far away made them both instinctively duck, and their eyes snagged on each other's as they attempted to ignore it. It was what you did, wasn't it, carry on as normal. But Pippa felt anything but normal as she changed into her pyjamas and hung up her uniform ready for the morning.

'Fancy some Horlicks? If there's any left, that is.'

'Oh, that'd be proper grand.'

'You get yourself into bed, then, and I'll go to the kitchen. But don't you dare spill it on the sheets, or Matron'll have your guts for garters.'

Pippa knew the rules, but she was too tired to care about breaking them for once. Perhaps she had come back a bit too early, but really she did need something to take her mind off her grief. Her poor, poor dad. There was such a hollowness inside her whenever she thought of him, and she just wanted something to wash away the pain. More than anything, she prayed that what the kindly ARP warden had said was true, that the end had been quick and that her dad had suffered no more than a few moments of gasping breathlessness before he'd passed away.

She perched on the side of the bed, waiting for Steph to return with the hot drinks. Her saddened gaze was inevitably drawn to the two photos on the bedside cabinet next to her. Her parents on their wedding day looking so happy and in love, and a more recent one of the three of them taken on the now charred and twisted pier, laughing and joking and trying so hard to keep still enough for the photographer. Oh, she remembered that day so well. And now her dad was in a communal grave with not even a coffin to protect him.

Agony tore at her throat once again, and she was utterly grateful when just at that moment, Steph reappeared, pushing the door open with her rear end as her hands were occupied with two mugs of steaming liquid. Pippa gulped back her threatening tears. In one of her numerous moments of acute distress, her mum had wept that she didn't even have a photograph of her dad. Everything had been destroyed by the bomb that had obliterated their house. They'd lost everything except Willow, and that had been a miracle. But Pippa had not only the two framed pictures — all that each nurse was allowed to display in her room — but an envelope full of others in a drawer. So next time she went home — home? So strange to think that the boarding house in Tavistock was now home, although it wasn't really hers, was it? The hospital was her true home now — she'd take them with her. Although a relatively small market town, Tavistock had a thriving shopping centre. There was bound to be a chemist or a photographer's who could make copies. She hadn't said anything to her mum, though, as she wanted it to be a surprise.

Even though the thought was tainted with sadness, it went some way to cheering her up and quickly slipping into bed, she took the mug from Steph and settled back against the pillows to drink it. 'So, any other gossip I should know of?' she asked, trying to put a hint of cheekiness in her voice.

'No, not really.' Steph gave a disappointed shrug. 'Poor Geraldine had to leave. Remember how her poor hands reacted to being in Dettol all the time?'

'Yes, I do. Poor thing, they used to get red raw.'

'Well, it just got too much in the end. Her hands were in a mortal terrible state, knuckles bleeding and everything. So she was forced to give up. Broken-hearted over it, she was.'

'Oh, what a pity. I really liked her, and she seemed a good student to me. I'd be devastated if something like that happened to me. I've only ever wanted to be a nurse.'

'Me, too. Even if it means we hardly get any social life and I feel like a criminal when I sneak out to see Rusty. So I'm glad you're back to leave the window open for me when I overstay my late pass.' Steph laughed, but with a meaningful wink of one eye. 'I don't trust anyone else.'

'Things still good between you and Rusty, then?' Pippa asked, sipping her hot, sweet drink.

'Very much so,' Steph grinned, then paused momentarily as another nearby blast made her jump and nearly spill her Horlicks. 'I try to see him whenever I have proper time off,' she went on, trying to ignore what was going on outside. 'If I haven't got a lecture to go to and he's off duty, too, and not flying some sort of mission.'

Pippa closed her lips in a soft line. 'You must worry about him,' she said gently.

'Of course. I just try not to think about it. And I often wonder if it wouldn't have been better not to get involved with anyone until the war's over. But it happened. And the more I see of Rusty, the more I'm convinced he's the one for me.'

'What, really seriously, you mean? Serious enough that you'd give up nursing to marry him?'

'Well, he'd have to ask me first!' Steph giggled back, and Pippa distinctly saw a deep blush colour her friend's cheeks. 'But, yes, I think I would.'

'Well, I'd miss you terribly.' Steph had become such a good friend, Pippa couldn't imagine continuing her training without her. She couldn't bear to lose Steph on top of everything else. There was nobody else on the course who could take her place. 'So would you go to live in Australia when the war's over?' she asked, quite horrified but trying to hide it. It seemed a huge step and one she wouldn't fancy herself, if only because of what Jack had told them about poisonous snakes and spiders and other insects that lived there!

'I guess so.' Steph's eyes gleamed at the prospect while Pippa's heart sank. 'It'd be a proper master adventure, wouldn't it?'

Pippa shook her head with a wry smile at Steph's enthusiasm. 'But what about your folks? You might never see them again.'

'My folks?' Steph pulled a face. 'Well, I've never rightly got on with them. And I don't reckon as they'd miss me much, either. Oh, Pippa, I'm sorry!' She clapped her hand over her mouth in remorse. 'There's me putting my girt foot in it when you've just lost your dad. Me and my big mouth.'

Pippa felt anguish twisting her stomach again. She was going to have to grow a shield of resilience about herself. Steph's innocent remark was one of many she was going to have to weather.

'I wondered why you never mention them or go to see them,' she managed to reply, ignoring Steph's last words. 'I can't imagine not getting on with one's family.'

'Well, it'd be a strange world if we were all the same, I suppose. And I guess you wouldn't be interested in making up a foursome with Jack again some time?'

Pippa shook her head. 'Not at the moment. I've asked Sister Tutor if I can have my time off as a whole day instead of two half days so I've got time to get to Tavistock to see Mum, and she said she'd do her best. And for a while I'll need any other free time I have to catch up on my studies. Sister Tutor said I can borrow your lecture notes if that's okay with you.'

'Of course. But don't turn into an old blue stocking, will you? Jack'll be disappointed, but I'm sure he'll understand. I know he's a bit brash, but he's a good fellow at heart.'

'I'm sure he is, but to be perfectly honest, I've got other things on my mind at the moment.'

'Yes, of course.' Steph gave her a kind look. 'But you need a bit of enjoyment for yourself as well. Which reminds me, when Rusty and I had a couple of hours together the other day, we actually saw Winston Churchill and his wife! You know they came to visit Plymouth to see the destruction and boost the city's morale? Well, we just happened to hear all this cheering and followed our ears and there they were, waving to the crowds from the open back of their posh car. Rusty was proper chuffed, though more about seeing the car than Churchill. A Daimler Landaulette apparently. Lovely looking thing, but one posh car's the same as another to me.'

'Same here. And I have to say it'd take more than a visit from the Prime Minister to boost my morale at present,' Pippa said bitterly. 'And I'm sure there's plenty as would feel the same way.'

'I'm sure you're right. But it does show that they care.' Steph put down her mug and leaned over to squeeze Pippa's hand. 'This war's terrible and you've had more than your share of it. But we'll get through it together, you and me. We'll always be there for each other.'

Pippa smiled at the sincerity in Steph's voice, even though she could feel a lump in her throat. Beneath her happy-go-lucky attitude to life, Steph was as solid as a rock, a good reliable friend. Overcome with emotion, Pippa wanted to hug her. But just then, the eerie, single-note whine of the all-clear blared out over the city, and both girls breathed a huge sigh of relief.

'Ooph, thank goodness for that.' Steph rolled her eyes dramatically. 'Perhaps we can get some sleep now. Don't know about you, but I've never managed to sleep through a raid.'

'No, me neither. Let's hope no one was hurt. I only heard a few explosions. And hopefully they won't come back. I'm shattered and I really need some sleep ready for tomorrow.'

'So do I.' Steph stretched her arms with a wide yawn. 'Sister Tyrrell's okay, mind. She's strict, of course, but quite understanding underneath. Always happy for you to ask questions if you're not sure about something. Not like that dragon, Sister Pudifoot. Dreading being on her ward ever, I am.'

Pippa couldn't help but chuckle at the memory of Steph standing up to the harridan of a sister. Hopefully it would be some time before it was their turn to be on her ward, but Pippa could imagine some tense moments when the time came. But for now, she could look forward to the next day on Men's Medical. As she snuggled down in bed, she tried to focus on the day ahead, but the last image in her head as she finally drifted off to sleep was the photograph of her dear parents on their wedding day.

CHAPTER THIRTEEN

'Amen,' Pippa mouthed at the end of morning prayers on the ward the following day.

Somehow, she couldn't bring herself to say it out loud. Her faith had never been strong, but what faith she did have had been shattered by recent events. How could she believe in a God who'd taken away her beloved father? Who had only allowed those poor babies a few days, in some cases a few hours, of life? Had it been quick or had the poor mites suffered pain? Everything kept coming back to haunt her, and the best way to curb the memories was to throw herself into her work and give as much care and comfort as she could to the patients on her current ward.

She'd been so excited to be back that she hadn't been sure she'd be able to sleep the previous night. But so tired was she that she'd fallen almost instantly into a deep and restful slumber. The knock on the door at seven o'clock had been a rude awakening. Then a quick wash and donning of her uniform to be down in the dining room for breakfast by half past.

'You should cut you hair short, then you wouldn't have to bother to do all that,' Steph observed, watching Pippa twist her hair into a bun and fasten it with several pins while she herself merely ran a brush through her own cap of bouncing curls.

'Then I couldn't put it in a victory roll, could I?' Pippa grinned back. 'Anyway, I like it long. Dad likes . . . Dad used to like it long, too.'

Steph noticed the catch in her voice and briefly squeezed her arm. 'Well, don't be long. Mustn't be late on your first morning.'

'Nearly ready,' Pippa answered, fixing her butterfly cap securely on her head. 'At least we don't wear our aprons to the dining room.'

'No, that's right. D'you remember when we first arrived and one of the first things we had to learn was when to wear long sleeves and cuffs and when to wear short sleeves and elbow frills? Cuffs on, cuffs off. Still seems blooming daft to me sometimes.'

'What, long cuffs but no aprons for the dining room and lectures?' Pippa laughed, taking Steph's arm as they hurried along the corridor. 'And then on the ward, aprons on with long sleeves for serving meals, but elbow frills at all other times!'

'But long cuffs if you need to address a sister or a doctor.'

'Not that you're supposed to speak directly to a doctor anyway.'

'Except in a dire emergency or if he addresses you first!'

They looked at each other, giggling again as they made their way to the dining hall. They joined the others in their set at the probationers' table. Ruby gave them a smug glance at having arrived in plenty of time while they had only made it by the skin of their teeth — just before Sister Tutor entered the hall and everyone fell silent for grace. Pippa remembered to eat as quickly as possible, since the minute Sister Tutor had finished and rose to her feet, everyone else had to leave the table, too, whether or not they had finished. You wouldn't eat again until one o'clock if you were lucky enough to be on first dinner, or later if you were on second.

Hurry back to the nurses' home, then, to clean their teeth and tie on a clean apron, pinning the bib neatly on to the bodice of the uniform dress. Pippa faltered as she pinned on her nurse's fob watch. She remembered her father's face, so proud as he'd given it to her.

Five minutes later and they were on the ward, joining the night staff for eight o'clock prayers. The bottle round had already taken place and the patients been served breakfast, and now there was a change-over period when the night staff continued to care for the patients while the night sister and staff nurse briefed the day staff on each patient's overnight status. By nine o'clock, all care had been passed over and the day's routine was in full swing.

Pippa felt as if she'd never been away. Staff put her in charge of collecting the next round of sputum trays. Not a pleasant job, but it was quite an honour as each had to be accurately labelled in case the doctor wanted to examine them on his rounds.

'S-sorry . . . my flower,' one old man wheezed as she collected his. 'Not nice . . . mine.'

Pippa smiled and nodded. Poor fellow had acute double pneumonia and didn't stand much chance. She exchanged glances with the third-year nurse assigned to his constant care. You could always tell a heavy smoker as they coughed up yellowy-brown, gooey mucus.

'Don't worry, I'm used to it,' she said kindly, though to be honest, she knew that once it had been left to congeal, it would be extremely difficult to get the enamel dish clean and she'd have to use a horrible caustic solution that made the eyes water. The patients didn't need to know that, of course, and this old chap seemed a gentle soul and she wanted to ease his embarrassment.

It seemed next to no time before it was the appointed hour for the doctors' rounds. Pippa and Steph had been allocated the left-hand side of the ward and stood ready to follow the doctors down the line of beds. They stood at the back of the group, of course, but it was considered they could still learn by observation.

'Ah, it's my little nurse from Sister Pudifoot's ward, isn't it?'

Pippa blinked her eyes, taken aback that a doctor had addressed her, a mere first-year probationer. She'd recognised him at once, the registrar from Women's Medical, but of course, he would cover Men's Medical as well, together with the consultant who was leading the group now. Meeting his gaze, she realised he was quite attractive with a kindly smile, and couldn't be much more than thirty, though looks could be deceiving. But really, he shouldn't have put her in such an awkward position.

'Good to see you back on the wards,' he went on now. 'I trust you are fully recovered?'

Well, she had to say something, didn't she? Otherwise, she'd appear rude, even though she could feel Sister Tyrrell's eyes on her.

'Yes, thank you, Doctor,' she murmured.

She shuddered as the consultant cleared his throat.

'Let's get on, shall we, Doctor Curnock? Now, then . . .'

Pippa could have died on the spot and felt the heat in her cheeks as the party moved to the first bed on the left-hand side. Steph dug her in the ribs but she flashed her friend a warning glance. Please don't make it worse! She was sure she didn't hear a word of what was being discussed until they came to the fourth bed where the sweet old man with his individual nurse was propped up on pillows, gasping for breath.

The consultant studied the charts at the bottom of the bed and nodded thoughtfully. 'How are we doing today, Mr Cubitt?'

'Fair . . . to middling,' the patient rasped back. 'My nurse yere . . . be an angel.'

He winked up at the third-year nurse whose job it was to stay with him at all times, bathing him with tepid water every two hours to try and reduce his temperature. Pippa's heart flipped over. It would be a miracle if he survived.

'Well, keep up the good work, Nurse. And we'll continue with the M and B tablets every four hours. We'll see you tomorrow, Mr Cubitt.'

They moved onto the next bed and worked their way down the twenty beds on that side. When they reached the end, Pippa and Steph were released to return to their duties while Ruby and a second-year nurse took their places to cover the right-hand side of the ward. They weren't allowed to do much until the doctors had departed, and then it was back to work, changing sheets and making beds with envelope corners — all to be inspected by Sister Tyrrell — and putting screens around patients to give bed baths and bed pans, and accompanying Staff on her observation rounds.

'Well, with an extra pair of hands we seem to be ahead of ourselves today,' Staff smiled briefly, 'so time to see you take some temperatures. Nurse Luscombe?'

Pippa was thrilled. It was the first time she'd been entrusted to carry out any such procedure on a real patient. Not that it seemed a particularly difficult thing to do, but she felt very proud as she flicked the thermometer to make sure the mercury was down low, popped it under the patient's tongue and consulted her watch to time the reading, talking and smiling at the patient while she waited. Gently removing the thermometer and turning it in the light to see the mercury, she read the result out to Staff who then checked the reading and recorded it on the patient's chart.

'Well done, Nurse Luscombe. Nurse Chappel, you can do the next one.'

The morning went so quickly and before Pippa knew it, it was time to put on their long cuffs to serve dinner. Some patients needed help to eat, and her own stomach was rumbling. She'd forgotten just how hungry you could get on the ward, having had breakfast at such an early hour and using a lot of energy being on your feet all the time. All you had was a ten-minute break for a cup of tea. Thankfully, she and Steph were on first dinner at one o'clock, much to the annoyance of Ruby who glared daggers at them.

'I reckon that Doctor Curnock fancies you,' Steph teased as they made their way to the dining hall.

'Don't be daft,' Pippa scoffed. 'I could've crowned him, putting me in an awkward position like that. Nurses aren't supposed to fraternise with doctors, and anyway, I'm not interested. I've got too much catching up to do if I'm to pass my Prelims.'

'They're a few months away yet!'

'I know, but I don't want to risk being left behind.'

'Knowing you, you'll be top of the class, anyway. Come on, hurry up, I'm starving.'

With only forty-five minutes for dinner, they were soon back on the ward. The nurse who looked after Mr Cubitt went off for her break and Pippa felt proud and amazed that she was asked to cover for her, with strict instructions to report the slightest change. He wasn't due his next M and B tablets until the meds round at two o'clock, but Staff would be giving him those anyway.

'Pass me . . . the photos of . . . my grandchiller, would you . . . my flower?' Mr Cubitt wheezed. 'Top drawer . . . of my locker.'

With a smile, Pippa did as he asked. The poor chap's faded eyes were either watering or filling with tears as his shaky fingers held up each photograph in turn.

'They're beautiful,' Pippa said as she gazed at two identical little girls who were holding hands as they smiled into the camera. 'Twins, are they?'

'Certainly are.' Mr Cubitt paused for breath. 'Older now. Twelve. And these . . . are my grandsons. Fourteen and fifteen. Just hope . . . this war is over . . . afore they'm conscripted.'

Pippa's heart jolted. What a terrible thing to be watching your children — or in this case, grandchildren — growing up, knowing they could be sent away to fight as soon as they were old enough. She must divert Mr Cubitt's thoughts.

'D'you see them often?' she asked, forcing brightness into her voice.

'Oh, yes. They only . . . live around the corner. But . . . not so much . . . since I've been . . . in yere, like. With visiting . . . only once a week.'

'Yes, I know. If it were up to me, it'd be every day.'

'Now you . . . tell me about . . . yersel, maid, as I don't have . . . much breath.'

Yes, of course. Perhaps she shouldn't have let him talk. So she told him about her schooling, how she'd missed out on grammar school because she'd been ill on the day of the entrance exam but got in when she was fourteen instead, when her friends were leaving to go out into the big wide world. How she'd always wanted to be a nurse, and now her dreams were coming true. She didn't mention the fact that two of her school friends had been killed together in an air raid, or how she'd been injured when the hospital had been hit and that since then she'd lost both her home and her dear father. She just hoped Mr Cubitt didn't ask her any direct questions as it would be difficult to lie to this nice old man, but she was saved anything like that as the third-year nurse returned and resumed her duties.

'There's a lecture on bandaging for you three first years at three o'clock,' Sister Tyrrell informed her as she walked back down the ward. 'I want you back on the ward the minute it's over. You'll have to forego your afternoon break I'm afraid, but it can't be helped.'

Pippa almost smiled to herself. She was definitely back in the old routine now! The short lecture followed by a practice session was soon over, and they were back on the ward, serving tea while hunger pangs were beginning to gnaw at their own stomachs again. Various bottle, observation and drug rounds later, and they had to serve supper — long cuffs again — before nipping off for their own hasty meal.

Back on the ward, Pippa was dismayed to see Mr Cubitt on oxygen, poor fellow. Even so, he looked awful, and she noticed when his nurse removed the mask so that he could drink, that his lips were an alarming blue colour. At eight o'clock, the night staff arrived for the change-over, and by the time she and Steph finally returned to the nurses' home for the night, her legs were aching from the unaccustomed activity.

Thank goodness there was no lecture that evening! Pippa felt sure she'd have fallen asleep during it if there had been.

Again, she slept like a log, but felt refreshed and ready for the next day. She grinned at Steph as they hung up their cloaks and hurried onto the ward for prayers the next morning. She felt filled with happiness. Yes, this was what she'd been put on this earth for.

'Oh, Nurse Luscombe, can you hurry to Women's Medical and fetch Mr Jarvis as soon as possible, please,' Sister Tyrrell instructed the instant she set foot inside the door. 'It's Mr Cubitt. He's deteriorating rapidly.'

'Yes, of course, Sister.'

Pippa's heart lurched. Poor Mr Cubitt. And what a responsibility. She must hurry but not run. She ran through the checks in her head as she hurried through the corridors. She still had on her long cuffs for prayers so she didn't need to change those. You didn't address a doctor directly, not least a consultant, but had to find a staff nurse or sister to do so on your behalf.

Her pulse was pounding as she reached Woman's Medical. She knocked on Sister Pudifoot's office door, but there was no answer. The dragon must be on the ward, then. You were supposed to ask permission before going on a different ward, but if there was nobody there to ask . . . Girding her courage, she pushed open the doors.

Sister Pudifoot was standing with her back to her, about to start prayers. *Oh, heck.* But surely Mr Cubitt's life was more important than getting a ticking off.

'Excuse me, Sister Pudifoot,' Pippa said, bracing herself as she stepped forward. 'I'm so sorry to interrupt, but Sister Tyrrell has asked me to fetch Mr Jarvis urgently.'

Sister Pudifoot turned, her face like thunder, but Pippa was determined to stand her ground. However, despite her exasperated expression, the sister merely tutted.

'Staff, take over prayers, will you?' And then she bustled out into the corridor with Pippa in her wake. 'Wait here, Nurse,' she instructed brusquely.

Well, Pippa thought. She'd done her best. She was almost dancing on the spot in agitation. She felt she'd made some sort of connection with old Mr Cubitt and didn't want to let him down. It seemed an age but was probably only a few minutes before Sister Pudifoot reappeared, followed by, *oh help*, Doctor Curnock, looking a little dishevelled and with his white coat flapping as he wriggled into it.

'Mr Jarvis isn't here yet, so you've got to put up with me. Sorry, been on call all night,' he apologised with a stifled yawn.

Pippa thought he looked even more attractive in his tousled state, but what she'd said to Steph was true.

'It's Mr Cubitt,' she said swiftly, wanting to hide her embarrassment as they sailed down the corridor together. 'I think he must've taken a turn for the worse, though I don't know any details. I'd literally only just come on duty.'

'Well, let's hope we can do something for him,' Doctor Curnock smiled reassuringly at her, sending confusing sparks down her spine.

Back on Men's Medical, prayers were obviously over and the usual calm pervaded the ward — except that there were screens around Mr Cubitt's bed. Oh, no. As Pippa approached with Doctor Curnock, she could hear a terrible rasping coming from behind the screen. She'd heard of the death rattle, but this was the first time she'd heard it for real.

'Thank you, Nurse Luscombe,' Sister Tyrrell said, emerging from behind the screen. 'Back to your duties now.'

Pippa popped back to the cloakroom to remove her long cuffs and replace them with elbow frills. But as she helped Steph wheel along other screens — one between each three beds — as they gave bed baths and handed out bed pans, she had one ear cocked to try and listen to what was going on around Mr Cubitt's bed. Not that she could make out what was being said, although she could hear Doctor Curnock's gentle voice.

'Better call his family to come in,' she caught his words to Sister Tyrrell as he walked back down the ward, hanging his stethoscope around his neck.

Pippa saw the surprise on Sister Tyrrell's face. She wasn't sure that was usual procedure, but Doctor Curnock seemed both kind and one who would flaunt the rules if he saw fit. He threw Pippa a sad look as he passed. Presumably there was nothing more he could do.

Mrs Cubitt, her wrinkled face distressed, arrived a while later with the daughter Mr Cubitt had spoken of. As she went about her normal duties, Pippa couldn't help glance in the direction of the screens around the dying man's bed. Poor Mr Cubitt. Doctor Curnock was called again later. The dreadful noise had stopped.

'Give his family some time,' Pippa heard him say in a low voice to Sister Tyrrell.

So, the poor man had died. Pippa felt a constriction in her throat and had to dash outside to swallow down her tears. She mustn't let the other patients see, but it felt like her father all over again.

'Was it your first death?' a voice at her elbow asked.

She looked up into Doctor Curnock's concerned face. 'Yes,' she croaked. 'At least the first person I'd got to form a relationship with. I saw some terrible fatal injuries in Casualty but they were complete strangers.'

She didn't want to mention her dear dad. That was something too personal, too raw.

'You never truly get used to it,' Doctor Curnock sympathised. 'Even at his age. If only we had this new wonder drug, penicillin, it might have saved him. Only the army have limited supplies at present. But, maybe one day . . .'

He shrugged, gave a sad smile and walked off down the corridor. But not before turning to raise a hand to her before disappearing around the corner. Pippa stood for a moment before returning to the ward. Doctor Curnock had done something to her insides she couldn't understand.

CHAPTER FOURTEEN

'Lordy love, what time d'you call this?' Pippa groaned, stirring from her sleep as Steph climbed in through the window.

'I know,' Steph whispered as she landed on her feet. 'Two o'clock in the morning, and I'm mortal sorry to have woken you. Thanks for leaving the window open for me. Night Sister didn't come to check up on me, I take it?'

'No, but if she had, you'd never get a late pass again. And you'll regret it in the morning.'

'No worse than being on fire watch duty half the night. Or changing from day to night duty.'

'You don't know that. We haven't done nights yet. Anyway, I hope it was worth it, like.'

'It was. Being on the Hoe at midnight was proper lovely.'

'Well, I hope you didn't get up to anything you shouldn't have done.'

'As if I would,' Steph joked, but then her tone changed, making Pippa sit up in bed. 'It's just that . . . Oh, Pippa, Number Ten Squadron's being moved to Pembroke at the end of the month. God knows when I'll see Rusty again.'

Pippa drew in a breath, suddenly feeling wide awake. 'Oh, no! Oh, I'm sorry, Steph. But you can still write? And maybe he'll get a few days' leave sometimes and can come to visit?'

Steph let out a huge sigh as she plonked herself down on the bed and pulling up her skirt, fumbled in the dark to unhook her stockings from her suspender belt. 'Maybe. It wouldn't be so bad if we were able to talk on the telephone. But it's so difficult only being able to use a phone box. So, how was your evening? Get all your studying done?' she asked, changing the subject as she finished wriggling into her pyjamas and dived into bed.

'Some of us were on duty till nine o'clock, remember? I was going to start cutting out the material I bought in Tin Pan Alley. But I was so tired, I went straight to bed. Just as well as I've been woken up by some gadabout stop-out!'

'I really am sorry,' Steph whispered back. 'A pity our off-duty time doesn't always coincide. I'm sure you'd have made me come back on time if you'd been with me. That was a proper fun afternoon we had off together, mind, when we got that material.'

'Yes, it was,' Pippa agreed, her voice low. 'Those shopkeepers are amazing, not giving up when they were bombed out but moving to covered stalls in the open air instead.'

'Mmm,' Steph mumbled. 'Still, I don't know why you didn't buy something from Marks and Spencer. Would've saved you all the bother of making a dress yourself. Marks have only moved to Mutley Plain.'

'Lucky enough to be able to do that,' Steph answered wryly. 'Only the big businesses could afford it. No, I wanted my small contribution to support one of the smaller businesses. Besides, it would've cost more and I need every penny of my generous wages to help Mum,' she concluded, with a hint of sarcasm on the word *generous*.

It was absolutely true, she considered, saying goodnight to Steph and snuggling back beneath the bedclothes. Her mother would be eligible for some sort of widow's pension as her father had been killed while on duty, but it would be some time coming through, and the compensation for the house could take years. Her dad had a small life insurance, but it wasn't much, just enough to cover her mum's food and a small contribution towards coal and electricity and so forth. She'd moved into the box room now that young Arthur Bell had gone off to join his unit, and it wasn't the full rent he'd been paying for it. But as Adeline was helping Don and Sylvie run the boarding house, they kindly considered that she was earning the remainder of her keep. Nevertheless, Pippa wanted to stretch her meagre wages to give her mum a few shillings pocket money when she saw her next.

What would they have done without the Chollacotts, Pippa mused as she drifted off to sleep again. And poor Steph. She was going to miss Rusty terribly. Would they stay together? Was their relationship strong enough to continue when they were miles apart? This wretched war! It wasn't just bombs and people being killed and injured. That was the worst, of course, but it meant so much more. Families and loved ones separated, grinding fear, food shortages, rationing. Would life be the same for anyone ever again?

***

'I'm so sorry it's taken so long to get you a full day off-duty,' Sister Tutor Honeywell apologised several weeks later. 'And you'll need to confirm it with Matron this evening, of course, in the usual way.'

Pippa's spirits soared. It was the beginning of July and she'd been waiting for this for so long. She'd spoken to her mum on several occasions, calling from a public box as they weren't allowed to use the hospital phone except in an emergency. But the calls only lasted as long as her few pennies allowed as she fed them into the machine each time the pips went.

'Thank you, Sister Tutor,' she replied gratefully.

'But I'm afraid there's a sting in the tail.' Amanda Honeywell looked almost abashed. 'You'll have to go straight on night duty when you get back tomorrow night. Still on the same ward, so you'll know the patients and what have you. It isn't ideal for your first night duty, but we're generally so short-staffed and we couldn't see any way round it. We haven't even got a night sister, so you'll be with Staff Nurse Spinks. So, we needed a strong, reliable first year, and you came out top. If only we could attract more young women into nursing,' she sighed. 'And stop so many qualified nurses joining the army because of the better pay. You don't know anyone who could be persuaded to start training, do you? Any old school friends?'

'No, I'm sorry, Sister Tutor, I don't.' Pippa was pricked by a pang of sadness. She could only think of one person who might have been interested. They hadn't been close since they'd all left school at fourteen and Pippa had continued her education at the grammar. But this friend had been killed in the major air raid the night the City Hospital's maternity block had been hit and Pippa herself injured.

She was glad when Sister Tutor's voice interrupted her morose thoughts. 'Well, run along now. And don't forget to speak to Matron. In your supper break, I'd suggest. Matron will still be in her office.'

'Yes, thank you, Sister Tutor,' Pippa repeated as she left the room.

Returning to Men's Medical, she felt all topsy turvy and nerves began to trundle in her stomach. It would be wonderful to see her mum again, but at the same time, she wondered quite how her mum really was. She always sounded cheerful on the phone, but was she putting on a brave face for those few precious minutes? Deep down, she must be feeling just as raw and empty as Pippa did when she had time to think about her dad. How would her mother feel when they saw each other in the flesh again? Would it bring back the pain? But there was no question in Pippa's mind that being reunited if only for a few hours would help them both to work through their grief.

So, what should she wear? The new dress she'd made would be perfect. Lucky she'd got the material for it and a second one when she did, with clothes and material rationing having just come in. Dear Steph had helped her finish off the first one. Since Rusty had gone to Pembroke, Steph hadn't been going out much even when her off-duty time allowed. And Pippa thought she did seem a little distracted on the wards which was perhaps why she hadn't been chosen for night duty, as she was normally just as capable. Well, at least on nights, there was less actual work to be done and you had some time to yourself. With Prelims looming, it would give her a chance to do some studying. She really wanted to do well. A little voice inside her told her she was doing it for her dad. She knew he'd have been so proud.

With a little shake of her head to dismiss her thoughts, she hurried back to the ward.

***

Pippa walked up the steps to the veranda and rang the doorbell. She still had keys to both the inner and outer front doors, but it didn't feel right to let herself in completely unannounced. She knew she'd receive a warm welcome, but she still worried how her mum would react. Delighted to see her, of course, but would it cause her taut emotions to snap?

Bea, much slimmer now than when she'd given birth over three months ago, opened the inner door, her face illuminating with a beaming smile when she saw who it was.

'Pippa!' she exclaimed, pulling open the veranda door. 'How master grand to see you! Come in, my flower! Your mam's going to be that happy.'

'So good to see you, too!' Pippa rasped as Bea squeezed her in a hug that almost knocked the breath from her. 'How's everyone?'

'Proper grand, maid. With your mam in young Arthur's room now he's gone, I've moved into her old room with Lucy. So the other chiller have more room in the old dining room.'

'That's good. Is Mum here?'

'Oh, of course. There's me wittering on when you want to see your mam. She'm down in the kitchen, helping to wash up the breakfast things.'

Pippa nodded her thanks and then made her way down the familiar stairway. She could hear the clatter of plates and called out as she reached the bottom step. Both Adeline and Sylvie turned round in surprise, and then her mum dropped on to the table the tea towel she had in her hands and came towards her, arms open wide.

'Pippa, love! What a grand surprise!' They hugged tightly and when they pulled apart, Pippa noticed a tear in her mum's eye despite the grin that split her face. 'Why didn't you tell us you were coming? We'd have baked a special cake!'

Pippa laughed back. 'I didn't get the chance. I only knew myself last night, and this morning I didn't want to waste any time going to the phone box, so I decided to come straight here and surprise you.'

'Well, you've certainly done that. And what a lovely surprise it is! Expect you'd like a cuppa after the journey.'

'Yes, please. If you can spare one with tea being on ration.'

'I'll make it,' Sylvie offered. 'Why don't you go into the garden and I'll bring it out. Don's out there watering the veg with Bernard's dubious assistance.'

'Thanks, Sylvie. You're a brick.'

Pippa linked arms with her mother and they went out the kitchen door and up the steps to the garden. Don's face lit up in surprised greeting and Bernard at once ran over and grabbed Pippa's free hand, jumping up and down.

'You're back!' he cried excitedly.

'Just for today, I'm afraid,' Pippa answered.

'Oh-oh,' the little boy pouted.

'Leave Pippa and her mum alone for now,' Don gently admonished. 'Let them have a good old natter. You can talk to Pippa later.'

Pippa saw her mother throw Don a grateful glance. A thrill passed through her at the overwhelming welcome she'd had. It strengthened her conviction that the Chollacotts were the best people on earth to take care of her mum.

'Now tell me, sweetheart, what you've been up to at the hospital,' Adeline said, settling into one of the garden chairs while Pippa sat down opposite her.

'Well, I'm still on Men's Medical,' she replied. 'We've got a couple of peptic ulcer cases, but it's mainly older men with chest complaints. Careful nursing's the best we can do for them. We've got sulphonamides like M and B to give them, but this new wonder drug, penicillin, would be even better. But it's in such short supply that only the army has it. So we have to sponge the patients down and give them things like aspirin to reduce temperatures and frequent inhalations of Friar's Balsam or whatever. And then hope for the best.'

She was about to say that some, like dear old Mr Cubbit, didn't make it, but thought better of it. She'd been deeply upset by his death, coming so soon after her dad's demise, and didn't want her mum to feel the same way. So she went on in a more cheerful tone, 'We've got three patients getting over heart attacks, mind, all well on the way to recovery. The City's best known for its orthopaedics and only has a small cardiac ward, so the heart attack cases come to us to convalesce.'

'Goodness, my little cheel sounds so professional, like,' Adeline said proudly, nodding her thanks as Sylvie arrived with two cups of tea and then left them to chat.

'Not really.' Pippa felt herself blush. 'Officially we're not even allowed to do simple obs — that's observation rounds — until we're third years. And more complicated things like blood pressure and handing out meds until we're qualified as staff nurses. But if there's time, Sister Tyrrell lets us do temperatures and pulse rates under her supervision.'

'So what do you do all day, then?'

'Oh, still bed baths and bed pans.' Pippa laughed at her mother's aghast expression. 'Helping those who can get to the bathroom but need assistance. It's fine once you get used to it. Patients can feel embarrassed so one of the things is to make them feel at ease. And then there's sputum dishes. They're the worst.'

'Urgh,' Adeline grimaced. 'I don't know how you do it.'

'Well, it feels more like you're doing something to help, and better than all the cleaning we do. Essential, I know, to reduce infection, but hard work and boring. My favourite job's handing out food and drink, especially helping those who need it. We've a chap with such bad rheumatoid arthritis that he can't feed himself, poor fellow. But if I pass my Prelims next month, I'll be learning more interesting stuff.'

'Well, you can talk to Elliott about all that this afternoon,' Adeline told her. 'It's his birthday and his daughter-in-law, Deborah, is holding a tea party for him to which we're all invited. I'm sure they'll be happy for you to come, too. They've all become such good friends. Elliott's three granddaughters play with Bea's kiddies a lot. There's a grandson as well, the eldest, Edwin. He's twelve, same as Sharon, but he has a bosom pal, Daniel, who lives up on the moor with some great aunt, and no one else gets a look in.'

Pippa noted with pleasure the way her mum chatted about her new acquaintances with such enthusiasm. So the Franfields as well as the Chollacotts were helping her in her bereavement, and Pippa was indescribably grateful. But she wanted to know how her mum was faring deep inside, but didn't feel the moment was quite right yet.

'So the Chollacott children are settling in at school okay, then?' she asked instead.

'Oh, yes. Little Norman is delighted he only has morning school as the town's getting quite a few evacuees from Plymouth now, as well as the ones it already had from before. Even though most of the Plymouth kiddies went elsewhere, it were decided the schools here are getting so crowded they needed to be divided into morning and afternoon classes.'

'Well, at least the government's finally listened to the Plymouth authorities.'

'What, and organised official evacuation for those who haven't been able to do so for themselves, you mean? Somewhat shutting the stable door, like, if you ask me,' Adeline scoffed.

Pippa caught her mum's bitterness. Not that it would have made any difference to them personally, but it was all part and parcel of her mum's grief, she knew, since she felt the same. So maybe it was time to start broaching the subject.

'That's right. We've not had a serious raid in weeks now.'

'Huh, nothing much left to bomb since the night your dad were killed.'

There was a moment of silence so brittle Pippa thought the air might crack. She held her breath for a few seconds, then reached out a hand to squeeze her mum's arm.

'I know, Mum,' she choked. 'People are so kind and helpful, and it's good to keep busy. But at the end of the day, you have to deal with it in your own way.'

When Adeline glanced at her, Pippa could see moisture glistening in her eyes, and could feel a lump swelling in her own throat. Her mum was coping, just as she was, but it wasn't easy. Perhaps now was the moment, but she still wasn't sure if it would please her mum or upset her.

Summoning her courage, Pippa opened her handbag. To transport them more easily, she'd taken the two photographs out of their frames and put them in the envelope with the others.

'I have something for you, Mum,' she said tentatively, and handed over the envelope.

She watched her mother's expression, a tiny, inquisitive frown on her forehead and then her mouth falling open when she saw what was inside. Her face turned so pale that for a moment, Pippa was worried she was going to faint. But then her lips curved in a gentle line.

'Pip,' she barely whispered. 'I'd forgotten you had these. Thank you so much. I never thought I'd see your father again, and now I will.' She almost gagged on her last words, and Pippa could see tears rolling down her cheeks as she slowly shuffled through the pictures. Pippa was fighting back tears herself and considered the best thing for both of them was to start some light conversation.

'Remember that day?' she asked, pointing to the three of them on the Hoe when she was about eight. 'The only way you could get me to keep still for the photographer was to promise me some ice cream afterwards.'

'Oh, yes!' her mum laughed through her tears. 'You were never a naughty child, but we never found out what got into you that day. And your dad dropped the slip of paper from the photographer and it blew away and he had to chase after it.'

Pippa chuckled in response and felt the tension easing as the various photographs evoked tender memories. It was a bittersweet interlude, and Pippa felt gentle, healing waves lapping through her. Looking at her mum, she was sure it was the same for her.

'I'm hoping there's a photographer in the town who can make copies of some of them without the negatives,' Pippa said when they'd been through the photographs a couple of times, lingering nostalgically over each one in turn. 'I'd like to have copies of my own to take back to the hospital.'

'I expect there'll be somewhere.' Adeline gave a wry smile. 'Don and Sylvie will know. I'll try and have them ready for you next time you can visit. Now, then.' Pippa saw her mum give a little shake and square her shoulders resolutely. 'We can't sit here being all morose, like. I'm certain everyone else will want to chat to you, too,' she declared with conviction, rising to her feet.

Pippa nodded, smiling with relief. Her mum was managing her grief, and the photographs had helped. Pippa felt she could now enjoy the day and look forward to the party at the Franfields' house. How kind of them to invite the Chollacott tribe. But it was what the war made you do. People who barely knew each other sticking together.

CHAPTER FIFTEEN

The train jerked and slowly began to move forward. Pippa blew a final kiss out of the window and waved as her mother gradually became a small figure on the platform and was finally lost from view. Adeline had insisted on coming to the station to see her off, not knowing when she might be able to come again, but was then returning to the party.

Pippa sat back in the seat, ready to enjoy the wonderful views over Dartmoor. She felt relaxed and happy in the knowledge that her mum was being well cared for. During her waking hours, at least. Who knew how her mum really felt at night when the loneliness could steal in? Pippa knew that all too well herself.

She had really enjoyed the party. The Franfields were a lovely family. Elliott and his wife, Ling, were a wonderful elderly couple. Ling's son by her first marriage, Artie, had apparently run an antiques emporium in Plymouth, but had been bombed out and was now struggling to run a small business in Mannamead. Like so many, he wasn't crying over spilt milk, but was getting on with the situation. Ling and Elliott's daughter, Mary, had clearly been putting on a brave face as her husband, Michael, was in the Merchant Navy and both their sons were in the Royal Navy, so she must live in constant fear. Then there was William who Pippa guessed to be about forty. Medicine was a reserved occupation, of course, but with so many evacuees in the town, the workload for general practitioners had increased dramatically. So William had been glad when Elliott had offered to come out of retirement to assist. William's wife, Deborah, had been a fully qualified nursing sister, but now ran the administrative side of the practice as well as helping in a nursing capacity when needed. What a jolly, bubbly soul she was, Pippa reflected with a smile. How she coped with her work and four children, Pippa didn't know — and throwing parties at every opportunity, she'd gathered.

What with the Chollacott tribe and numerous other guests, it had been a noisy affair. But Elliott had found time to draw Pippa aside and have a little chat, asking about her training, which she thought was very kind. They talked about some new advances in medicine and Elliott lent her a copy of *The Lancet* that he thought she'd find interesting. He then went on to explain about Tavistock's Cottage Hospital. The local general practitioners looked after their own patients there, using the more extensive facilities, but seeking the assistance of specialist consultants when necessary. Being a small town, everybody knew everybody else, and it all sounded a very friendly atmosphere, very different from the City and other hospitals in Plymouth.

Pippa went over the afternoon in her thoughts as the train puffed around the edge of Dartmoor. As they approached Plymouth's North Road Station, they had to wait for a freight train to go through before they could complete the journey. No doubt carrying supplies for the navy, and so taking priority. But Pippa had deliberately left early in case there was any hold up. She mustn't be late for her first night duty.

At eight o'clock, she duly arrived on the ward, having eaten a good supper in the dining room as she didn't know when she'd get the chance to eat again. At least, the meal was the best the hospital had to offer. It was actually 'Hooray Pie' — not that she'd found a cube of meat among the vegetables and was able to proclaim so with a joyful *hooray* to her companions! In fact, to her knowledge, nobody had discovered any meat in their meal that night.

'Have a good day?' Steph dared to ask her in a hushed voice as they gathered for the change-over.

'Great, thanks,' Pippa whispered back. 'I'll tell you all about it when I can.'

She clammed up as she caught a warning glance from the night staff nurse she recognised from earlier changeovers. Sister Tyrrell was about to speak and bring the night staff up to date with all the patients' needs for the night.

'Well, good luck, Staff Nurse Spinks,' Sister Tyrrell concluded. 'Dr Curnock's on call if you need him, and you'll find that Probationer Nurse Luscombe is one of the best.'

She gave Pippa an encouraging smile as she led the day staff out of the ward. Pippa noticed Steph turn to give a little, surreptitious wiggle of her fingers in lieu of a wave as she passed through the doors. And suddenly it all seemed very quiet. Pippa turned to Staff Nurse Spinks, wondering how they'd get on together. It was going to be a long night if they didn't see eye to eye.

She needn't have worried.

'Sorry about that,' the staff nurse said. 'I wanted to make sure I heard every word, being in charge all night without a sister. I gather it's your first night duty.'

'Yes, it is,' Pippa answered, feeling encouraged.

'Well, it can be tough till you get used to it. And let's hope we have a quiet night with it being just the two of us. Well, first thing is to give all the patients a nightcap. If you wouldn't mind popping off to the kitchen and putting the kettle on. This is your day ward, so you know who likes what, and more importantly, who's allowed what. We had a new admission today and he's diabetic, but it's on the sheet.'

'Yes, Staff,' Pippa nodded.

'By the way, the name's Juliette,' Staff Nurse Spinks said, lowering her voice. 'But only when we're off duty and no one's listening. Off you go, then. And remember, as there's just the two of us, one of us needs to be on the ward at all times.'

'Of course. And I'm Philippa, but everyone calls me Pippa.'

Juliette smiled back, and Pippa went off to the kitchen to prepare the drinks. After distributing them and washing up, it was a bottle and hand wash and teeth clean round, followed by the meds round. Pippa could scarcely believe she was trusted to assist, double checking every item with Juliette and checking it off on the charts. She never expected that responsibility until she was a third year, at least. But needs must with the shortage of staff. She felt elated and nervous all at once, but felt exhausted when it was all over and the men were settling down to sleep for the night.

'Make us a cuppa now, would you?' Juliette asked, sitting down at the desk in the ward. 'Then you can have a break yourself. I'll call you if I need you. There are some bandages for winding in the off-duty room. If you could do some of those, that'd be great. But if you want to do a bit of studying, you're welcome. I'll come and get you when I need my break.'

Pippa gulped. Crikey. That meant she'd be left in charge of the ward on her own for a short while, didn't it? Well, it was what she wanted in the long run, but she hadn't expected it so soon. Goodness, she felt nervous, but there again, she also felt proud.

She made two mugs of tea and took one to Juliette who was reading through patients' notes by a dimmed table lamp. Then she took her own mug through to the off-duty room, which was really only a cupboard with an old armchair. She'd just have her drink, and then she'd wash her hands in Dettol solution and start winding some of the bandages ready for sterilising. It was nearly eleven o'clock and so far, she wasn't feeling tired, although she'd make use of the rest.

She'd only taken two sips of her tea when the dreaded sound pierced the quiet of the night. Why was it such a haunting wail? They hadn't had a serious raid for six or seven weeks and everyone hoped that with Hitler turning his attentions to

Russia, the attacks on Britain might have stopped. Evidently not.

She put down her mug and hurried into the ward.

'Oh, good,' Juliette said over her shoulder as she was helping a patient out of bed. 'If you can start ferrying down to the basement all those who can walk, I'll see what I can do to protect those who can't be moved.'

Pippa nodded and proceeded to wake all those who weren't already getting to their feet and pulling on their dressing gowns.

'All right, Nurse, I knows the way,' one old fellow grinned. 'Just put me teeth in an' I'll lead some of the others.'

Pippa glanced across at Juliette. Shouldn't she accompany each and every one? But the important thing was to get everyone to safety as quickly as possible.

'Those who are steady enough on their feet, yes,' Juliette assured her. 'The others you'll have to help.'

Lordy love. She'd have to think on her feet. She just prayed she didn't make a split-second decision that was wrong. Old Mr Stenhouse was leading some of his fellow patients out of the ward, and Pippa followed, with a slower patient on each arm. Out on the landing, patients from Men's Surgical on the other side were queuing for the lift. It was going to take ages, and should they be using the lift? What if there was an incendiary and the building caught fire? For a moment, Pippa was shot through with panic as the night the maternity unit was hit flashed across her brain.

'All right, Nurse, I'll take these down and you bring someone else.'

Doctor Curnock's voice was like a soothing balm as he appeared like a whirlwind, shrugging into his flapping white coat as he hurried towards her. Pippa was flooded with relief. At least she wasn't going to be the one in charge.

A quarter of an hour later, Pippa was ensconced with her charges in the crowded basement. Some were on chairs, others were lying on mattresses on the floor. Chaos reigned with patients from several wards gathered together. When the hum of engines roared overhead, people crossed their fingers and held their breath as distant booms quivered in the air. Someone was getting it. Pippa just prayed the hospital wasn't hit again as the nightmare rushed back at her. Mr Stenhouse tried to start a sing-song, but as a long-term bronchitis case, he was soon coughing and spluttering, although others soon took up his tune.

'I can't leave Staff on her own up there,' Pippa told Doctor Curnock as he passed by, checking to see if each patient was all right after the exertion.

'Don't worry, I'll go back up. You should be okay with these. Just try and keep them calm. And you've got Sister Walters over there if you're worried about anyone.'

'Yes, thank you, Doctor,' she murmured.

'Don't worry. You'll be fine.'

His encouraging smile as he turned for the stairs seemed to settle her nerves. For the next hour or so, she found herself chatting to the patients in a way she wasn't allowed to on the wards. It helped to pass the time, and once again, she thought how it would help them recover more quickly — or at least make them feel better — if they were allowed more communication with the nursing staff.

Thankfully the raid wasn't protracted and the all-clear wailed out across the city. Crossing her fingers the bombers wouldn't return as they often had in the past, the laborious task of getting the patients back up on the ward began in earnest, but at least there wasn't such a rush, and queuing for the lift didn't seem so frustrating.

Finally, with all the patients settled back in bed and drugs dispensed to those who were on four-hourly meds, Pippa left Juliette and Doctor Curnock talking in low voices by the ward desk while she went to make them all a much-needed mug of tea.

'You did really well there, Nurse,' Doctor Curnock told her as she handed him his drink.

Pippa found herself basking in his praise. Of course, she'd far rather not have had the experience, but it was good to feel she was appreciated. He was nice, was Doctor Curnock, not like some of the doctors who treated junior nurses as inferior. And he had kind eyes that seemed to light up when he smiled.

'Well, I'm off for some shut-eye while I can,' he said, stifling a yawn. 'I'm on duty all day tomorrow, so fingers crossed. I'll take this with me,' he concluded, carefully waving the mug in the air.

'You go and get your break at last,' Juliette instructed, turning to Pippa. 'I managed to get one during the raid while Doctor Curnock held the fort, so it's your turn now.'

Pippa nodded her thanks. Now all the hoo-hah was over, she felt drained. Half an hour relaxing would be most welcome, but she really didn't think she could concentrate on any studying, so once she'd finished her tea, she closed her eyes.

She must have drifted off as the next thing she knew, there was a knock on the door and Doctor Curnock poked his head around it.

'Sorry, Nurse, but I've been called down to Casualty. Most of the bombs fell on the west end of the city, but the Hoe was hit badly. Not that many casualties, and some have been taken to the other hospitals, but there's only one other doctor on duty downstairs and they've called me down. They need another nurse, too, and Staff has said you can come with me.'

Pippa at once felt the adrenaline pumping through her. She wished they'd taken *all* the casualties elsewhere. She'd had enough excitement for one night!

She followed Doctor Curnock downstairs and through the linking corridors to Casualty. It was nowhere near as crowded as the previous time she'd helped out, the night before she'd been injured herself at the height of the bombings. Then, there'd been what seemed like hundreds of victims strewn everywhere, but now there were a dozen at most. Last time, she'd awaited instructions as porters and rescue workers brought in the injured. She had merely given first aid to some of the less badly hurt, but tonight it seemed that though there were fewer casualties, many were serious cases.

'Stick with me, Nurse,' Doctor Curnock instructed. 'We'll assess these ones first.'

That was a bit of a relief, at least. She kept by Doctor Curnock's side as he worked his way along a line of waiting trolleys, while the other doctor dealt with those in cubicles. Pippa knew at once that the first patient, a young woman, was dead, but Doctor Curnock carried out the usual checks just to be sure before shaking his head sadly. Pippa lifted the sheet over her face. Poor woman, with so much of her life ahead, snuffed out like a candle. The next was an older man the remnants of whose scorched uniform declared him a railway worker. His blackened face was screwed in agony, but it was his arms and chest that were badly burnt.

'Morphine, Sister!' Doctor Curnock called, scribbling on the pad hung on the bottom of the trolley. 'And some strong scissors to cut his trousers! All right, old chap,' he then said to the patient. 'We'll soon have you out of pain, but I'll be injecting into your thigh. Okay?'

A minute later, the sister appeared with some scissors and a metal tray containing the loaded syringe. She was clearly harassed with so many patients to deal with and not enough staff.

'Nurse, you take the tray so Sister can get back. Give me the scissors. It's thick material and my hands'll be stronger and quicker.'

Pippa obeyed at once, smiling down reassuringly at the patient. 'You're in the best hands. Can you tell me what happened?' she asked, trying to hide her alarm. Railway worker. Bea's husband, and her son.

'Oil bomb . . . on a rail truck at Laira,' the man croaked. 'Like a fool, I tried to put out the fire, but—'

Not North Road, then. Pippa had to hide her relief. But at that moment, Doctor Curnock had taken the syringe and the patient flinched as the needle pierced his flesh. 'There.

The pain will ease pretty quickly and you'll feel drowsy. Might even get a bit of kip,' he winked. 'I'll be back soon.' And then he ushered Pippa onwards. 'Need to get back to him the minute we've finished assessing.'

A compound leg fracture next. More morphine.

'Where's Mr Stubbs?' Doctor Curnock demanded of the poor sister who was run ragged. 'This woman needs an operation *now* and it's not my field.'

'On his way, Doctor.'

'Good. Now what's next?'

Tragically, it was another body, crushed under rubble.

'Be he dead, like?'

'Sadly, yes, son,' Doctor Curnock answered the boy on the next trolley. 'Did you know him?'

'No,' the boy shrugged. 'I were just walking down the street, and he'm a stranger.'

'Right, so what's your name and where are you hurt?' Doctor Curnock asked.

'Peter. And a bit of shrapnel in me leg,' the boy answered, lifting the blanket that had been thrown over him. 'Nort much, really. Master hurts, mind.'

Pippa saw the doctor's raised eyebrows and followed his gaze to the piece of metal embedded in the boy's thigh. Blood had oozed around the site of the injury and it looked fairly innocuous to the untrained eye. Pippa knew better.

'Right, now listen to me, Peter.' Doctor Curnock's severe attitude confirmed her thoughts. 'I need to assess the other few patients here, but I'll be back shortly. In the meantime, do *not* move a muscle. Can I trust you to do that for me?'

'Yeah, course, doc.'

'Good lad. Let's move on, Nurse,' the doctor said to Pippa, lowering his voice as they went to the next patient. 'Can you keep an eye on him as I look at the others? You know why?'

'Yes, I do.'

Fortunately, the remaining patients only had minor wounds, except for the last, an elderly woman who'd been concussed. It was while Doctor Curnock was doing some checks on her that Pippa glanced down the line just in time to see the boy, Peter, fiddling with the shrapnel in his leg. She at once dashed to his side, just in time to see blood spurting out of his thigh.

'Femoral bleed!' she called out.

Catching the boy's horrified glance, she bundled the blanket into a ball and pressed down on the wound as hard as she could, but with her hands either side of the piece of metal as she didn't want to push it further in. Within seconds, Doctor Curnock was at her side, followed almost instantly by the sister with an instrument trolley.

'Well done, Nurse. Keep pressing as hard as you can.'

Pippa felt as if her brain was acting of its own accord. She was aware of the sister lying the boy flat and pushing a pillow under his legs to elevate them, while the doctor swiftly tied a tourniquet above the wound.

'Keep pressing, Nurse. The tourniquet won't be enough on its own. We need to get him straight into surgery.'

'Here's Mr Stubbs now,' the sister announced.

'Thank God for that,' Pippa heard Doctor Curnock murmur. 'This boy first, then the compound tib and fib.'

'What's happening to me?' the boy moaned. 'I feel all funny, like.'

'Don't worry, you'll be fine,' Pippa reassured him, praying that he would. 'We're going to get you into Theatre and when you wake up, you'll feel much better.'

She caught a swift glance from the doctor. 'I'll take over, Nurse. You'll be tiring.'

Yes, she was, and it would be easier for Doctor Curnock to take over the compression, being so much taller. Then it seemed that the whole ward burst into life with not only the consultant, Mr Stubbs' arrival, but other doctors and nurses, too. Porters were wheeling the boy in the direction of Theatre with Doctor Curnock running alongside as he continued with the pressure, Mr Stubbs hurrying ahead to scrub up while other staff began to swarm among the patients.

Pippa flexed her aching arms with relief.

'Get yourself cleaned up, Nurse, and then see what else you can do to help,' the sister instructed. 'And well done.'

She was gone before Pippa could acknowledge her praise. After that it was all a bit of a blur as Pippa did what she could before she was eventually told to go back to her own ward. With her apron splattered with blood, she removed it and hung it up with her cloak before creeping on to the ward and explaining to Juliette what had happened.

'Well, I think you deserve that break at last,' Juliette whispered. 'It's all been quiet here, so I'm fine for a while. It'll be all go at six o'clock, mind.'

Pippa didn't need telling twice. She was utterly exhausted, both physically and mentally, and grabbing herself a fresh mug of tea, returned to the off-duty room. Ten minutes later, a knock on the door startled her, and Doctor Curnock entered again. Oh, no! They weren't needed again, were they?

'Just wanted to say well done, Nurse,' he smiled.

Pippa drooped with relief. 'How's the boy?' she asked at once.

'Mr Stubbs removed the shrapnel and repaired the artery. The lad'll be sore for a while but should recover with a few weeks' bed rest. Provided there's no infection, of course. We put him on M and B just in case and gave him an anti-tetanus shot. Should be okay. He's young but a bit thin, mind. I just wonder what on earth he was doing out on the streets at that hour.'

'I expect his parents will be frantic.'

'Maybe, or maybe not. You never know.'

'And the railwayman with the burns?'

'Hmm, well, fingers crossed. First thing will be to soak off his clothes in a warm saline bath. They've had a lot of success with that on badly burnt pilots at Queen Victoria Hospital in East Grinstead in Kent.'

'Yes, I've read about that. And then applying tulle gras?'

'In between the baths, yes. And then growing skin for grafting but without detaching it so it has a full blood supply while it's taking. A lot of that's for facial burns. Remarkable pioneering work. But,' and here he paused to nod at her, 'I'm delighted to know you're taking an interest in matters beyond your current training. Anyway, well done, once again, Nurse. And good night.'

He left with a smile on his face, putting Pippa in a swirl of confusion. She'd had no interest in the opposite sex, just as she'd told Steph on more than one occasion. All she wanted was to be a nurse, but now she wasn't so sure. Doctor Curnock was so kind and had lovely warm eyes.

She shook her head. No. She was just so tired she couldn't think straight. Better to put all such ideas out of her head. She was there to work and to learn, and to make her dad proud of her if he was looking down. With that, she drained her mug and walked confidently back on the ward.

CHAPTER SIXTEEN

'Now, pay attention, ladies! I have some news I think you'd all like to hear.'

Pippa and Steph exchanged unsure, wary glances. They'd been on Women's Medical since September — thankfully for Pippa on day duty — and under Sister Pudifoot's rigid discipline. So to see her marching into the middle of the ward, clapping her hands loudly to gain everyone's attention, was both unexpected and disconcerting. Steph had managed to keep on the right side of her — just — but generally the dreaded sister ruled her ward, both staff and patients, with a rod of iron.

'You all know of the dreadful catastrophe a few days ago,' Sister Pudifoot began in a raised voice, 'when the American Pacific Fleet was almost destroyed by the Japanese at a place called Pearl Harbour, and some of our own overseas territories were also attacked, so that both we and the United States are now at war with Japan. Well, I have just been told that Germany and Italy have now declared war on America, so that our American friends are now completely allied with us in our fight against our enemies.'

'About blooming time! Left it long enough, just like in the first war,' a voice called out as murmurs erupted around the ward.

'That's enough, Mrs Fuggleden,' said Sister Pudifoot sternly.

'Nice Christmas present if you ask me. Means we'm not alone no more,' another voice declared. 'Not just little us against that monster, Hitler, now that he's taken most of flaming Europe.'

'Not getting far against Russia, mind, is he?' Mrs Fuggleden insisted.

'Ladies, please!' Sister Pudifoot virtually shouted now. 'I wouldn't have passed on the news if I'd known what a rumpus it would cause. Now settle down and let the nurses finish their work to prepare you all for doctors' rounds.'

Disgruntled mutterings hummed around the ward. Steph cocked one mocking eyebrow towards the huffily retreating sister so that Pippa had to give her a warning frown. The news was serious indeed. They'd both wondered why the hospital almoner had come unexpectedly to speak briefly with Sister Pudifoot. She must be spreading the news throughout the hospital, as it was considered so important. Which it was, of course. But what exactly would it mean for the future? For all of them? Since the summer, there had been hardly any raids on Plymouth and very few casualties, with several enemy planes being successfully shot down either by ack-ack fire or pursuing fighters. So, together with the news of the United States joining in the war, Pippa wondered if the tide might be turning.

She was evidently not the only one thinking the same thing as despite Sister Pudifoot's instructions, muted conversation was breaking out throughout the ward again.

'Now, Mrs Fuggleden, please can we have you out of bed so we can make it all neat and tidy for doctors' rounds?'

'Course you can, flower,' Mrs Fuggleden beamed back, swinging her podgy legs over the side of the bed and dropping into the chair. 'What d'you make of the news, then?' she asked as Pippa and Steph began smoothing out the bedclothes. 'D'you think old Hitler might be giving up on the idea of invasion, us have had so few raids of late? And now with the Yanks on our side . . .'

'Would be nice to think so,' Pippa smiled back, giving the top sheet a final stroke. 'The Blitz attacks over the whole country seem to have calmed down. Now, can we have you back in bed and please try not to untidy it until the doctors have been,' she said cajolingly.

'Course, cheel. Especially if it's that handsome young Doctor Curnock,' Mrs Fuggleden winked, shifting herself back into bed.

Pippa shook her head with an amused smile as she and Steph moved on to the next bed. She hoped the irrepressible Mrs Fuggleden wouldn't wriggle about too much, and that her speculations on the war would prove correct. But as for the conflict being over soon, Pippa had serious doubts, what with Japan joining in now, and then there was everything going on in North Africa as well as over the whole of Europe. But there was no use pondering on it now. There was work to do.

By the time Doctor Curnock appeared, Sister Pudifoot having cast a critical eye over the ward just as he came in through the doors, everything looked ship-shape to Pippa's own eye. Pride swelled in her chest as her gaze travelled over the line of beds on either side of the ward. Not that Doctor Curnock ever seemed worried about such details, unlike the consultant, Mr Jarvis. Doctor Curnock's presence in the ward made Pippa feel more relaxed as Mr Jarvis could be sharp at times. But on the other hand, something inside always tingled when the handsome young doctor — as Mrs Fuggleden had put it — was in close proximity.

'Right, Sister, let's begin,' he said, walking towards the first patient, an elderly lady with pancreatitis. 'Now, Miss Hansen, how are we today? Feeling a little better, I trust?'

Sister Pudifoot and the staff nurse trotted behind him, the latter pushing a small trolley with a few items on it the doctor might require for his examinations. Pippa and Steph followed on with the portable screens, wheeling them into position around the bed. Then they stood at the back while the doctor talked to Miss Hansen, examined her stomach and consulted her charts.

'Well, I think we can come off the drip now, but continue with the very light, little-and-often diet,' he announced pleasantly. 'We'll see how that goes and we should have you home soon but you will need to be careful with your diet. So, I'll see you again tomorrow.'

Pippa noticed him give that kind, reassuring smile as they moved on to the next patient, a newly diagnosed diabetic. After that, they moved on to Mrs Fuggleden, whose face lit up like a glowing sun, much to Pippa's amusement.

'Nurse, I think I'm going to be sick!' she heard a voice call from the other side of the ward.

'I'll go,' Steph offered. Anything to get away from Sister Pudifoot, Pippa mused.

'I'd better come with you,' the staff nurse sighed. 'It's Mrs Day and you know what she's like.'

'Right, Mrs Fuggleden, let's have a listen to your chest, shall we?' Doctor Curnock began. 'Sister?'

Pippa stepped forward to help Sister Pudifoot sit the patient forward and then pull up her nightdress so that the doctor could listen to the back of her lungs, first warming the chest-piece of the stethoscope in his hands, Pippa noticed. Mr Jarvis wouldn't have done that, she considered.

'That's sounding much better,' Doctor Curnock pronounced. 'Should have you home in a day or two. Tell you what, before you sit back, would you mind if Nurse Luscombe here has a listen? Nothing like practical learning.'

'What, this lovely cheel? Be only too happy to!'

Pippa was astounded — and noticed with dismay the affronted look on Sister Pudifoot's face. But a doctor's word was sacrosanct, and the sister couldn't be seen to be arguing with a higher authority. Doctor Curnock took a Dettol swab from the trolley and wiped the ear-pieces of the stethoscope before handing it to Pippa. Their fingers touched as she took it, and a frisson of delight tingled up her arm.

'Now, Mrs Fuggleden, if you could take a deep breath in and slowly out again, please,' he asked. 'And Nurse, you should hear a soft, whooshing sound.'

Pippa listened carefully, and then a smile blossomed on her face as she nodded. 'Yes, I can, Doctor,' she said, wiping the ear-pieces again before handing back the stethoscope. 'Thank you, and thank you, too, Mrs Fuggleden.'

'Not at all, my maid,' the woman said, giving her saucy wink again as Pippa settled her back in bed before following on to the next patient with the screens. Poor Mrs Wonnacott had been admitted the evening before with double pneumonia and was struggling to breathe, despite the oxygen mask she was using and being propped up on pillows. Once again, Doctor Curnock invited Pippa to listen, having first asked the patient's permission.

'So, what do you hear, Nurse?' he asked.

'A sort of loud crackling,' Pippa answered thoughtfully.

'Good, that's right. But not so good for you, Mrs Wonnacott,' he smiled kindly. 'But we'll have you feeling better in no time. M and B, inhalations, and aspirin to bring the temperature down. You're in excellent hands, Mrs Wonnacott,' he reassured her, writing on her chart before moving on to the next bed where the staff nurse and Steph joined them again, having attended to Mrs Day.

An hour later, the round was over and Pippa was taking the trolley back to the facility room, feeling exhilarated from the opportunity Doctor Curnock had given her. But she also recognised there was something stirring within her she'd never felt before... He was a lot older than her, of course, and she'd always told herself she wasn't interested in the opposite sex. But really Doctor Curnock's presence made her pulse rate quicken.

He was coming along the corridor behind her now, and she caught her breath. But before he caught up with her, Sister Pudifoot appeared from her office and asked to speak with him. Not knowing if she was relieved or disappointed, Pippa popped the trolley into the facility room and went to make her way back to the ward. However, as she passed the sister's office, she noticed the door wasn't quite shut, and paused in her step as she heard her name.

'Really, Doctor Curnock, you shouldn't pay Nurse Luscombe such attention,' Sister Pudifoot was saying. 'It simply isn't appropriate.'

'What?' Doctor Curnock sounded genuinely taken aback. 'I'm only encouraging her in her studies. Surely you can see that she has the makings of an exceptional nurse? She was top of the class in her Prelims if you remember. And did you know when she goes to visit her mother in Tavistock, she's friendly with some of the doctors there, one of them extremely senior? She discusses medical advances with them and even reads their copies of *The Lancet*. And after all she's been through—'

'You seem to know an awful lot about her, Doctor Curnock.'

'Only because I chatted to her a couple of times when she was on night duty on Men's Medical and I was on call. In her break, of course. And I'm not singling her out, as you might imply. If Nurse Chappel hadn't been called away, I'd have given her the same opportunity. Now, if you don't mind, I have other patients to see.'

Pippa felt her heart flutter and she hurried back into the ward before anyone realised she'd been eavesdropping. She squeezed her eyes shut for a moment, not knowing what to make of it all. Doctor Curnock thought she could be an exceptional nurse. How proud that made her feel! And yes, she had got the top marks in her exams at the end of the summer. Thank goodness, as she could have ill-afforded the two guineas to retake them! How elated she'd been when she'd put on her new uniform to denote that she was now a second-year nurse, progressing from the pale blue check dress to pale blue and white stripes. It was still the butterfly cap, and would be until she was qualified and became a staff nurse, but the small change in uniform meant the world to her.

But now another emotion was creeping into her heart and she felt caught up in some sense of strange euphoria. Had there been some element of truth in what Sister Pudifoot had said to Doctor Curnock? Did he have some feelings towards her? Certainly, a warm gladness seeped into the very core of her whenever he came on to the ward. Was that how Steph felt about her Rusty, who she missed terribly?

Pippa shook her head as she marched down the ward. It really didn't matter how she felt. She wouldn't let anything get in the way of her vocation, her love of nursing. And yet, when she thought of Doctor Curnock, she wondered if perhaps, one day, she might, just might, end up falling in love.

* * *

'Now, remember, it's "Away in a Manger" followed by "Oh, Little Town of Bethlehem" on the children's wards,' Matron reminded everyone as they lined up in the corridor at six o'clock on Christmas Eve. 'Those of you carrying the lamps, hold them high and don't forget, you have actual candles in them. Only tea-lights, I know, but still be very careful, please. Right.' Pippa saw her take in a deep breath and give a satisfied, gentle smile. 'I must say, you all look quite angelic, and the little ones will find it all quite magical. Now, off you go.'

Surely this was the happiest she'd felt since that horrific time in the spring when she'd lost both her home and her dear father, Pippa thought as the procession moved forward. She couldn't wind back the clock — would that she could — and the only way to find peace was to look forward. Just now, there was something mystical with all the lights turned off and only the glow from the hand-held lanterns illuminating the way. The nurses all wore their blue cloaks, those nearer the front with their white butterfly caps, while the staff nurses and sisters bringing up the rear had on their frilled or veil caps. Pippa couldn't help feeling that the continuity added a sense of both solemnity and beauty to the proceedings. They advanced slowly, their footfall as quiet as possible as their voices echoed softly around the ward.

Judging by the wonderment on their little faces, the children were spellbound by the spectacle, their eyes wide and transfixed. It was such a shame they weren't well enough to go home for Christmas, Pippa thought, but every effort would be made to make the time special. Even if she wasn't able to go home herself, she wouldn't have missed all this for the world. The children looked on in awe as the nurses glided up one side of the ward and back down the other, the melody of the carols sweet and silvery.

It took the best part of two hours for the carol singers to visit each ward in the hospital. Some of them Pippa hardly knew, but she would spend time on most of them as her training continued. Oh, there was still so much she had to learn and she'd relish every minute. In the new year, she'd be moving on to Women's Surgical. She was really excited about that. She already felt that surgery would be fascinating, and she wouldn't be sorry to leave Sister Pudifoot's harridan discipline, even if she had learnt so much from her. But she would be sorry no longer to be seeing Doctor Curnock on a regular basis. He'd been so kind to her, and her heart still gladdened whenever he was near. She wondered if she'd have the opportunity to speak to him again. Whether he'd seek her out.

Then, oh, joy of joys, as she was preparing to return to her own ward for the evening handover, there was Doctor Curnock coming towards her now, his handsome face in a broad smile. Wouldn't it be amazing if he asked her out, if only for a quick drink to celebrate Christmas? It would make up for not being able to get home over the holiday. She hardly dared to breathe.

'May I wish you a very Merry Christmas, Nurse Luscombe,' he said, and Pippa noticed his eyes sparkling. 'The carol procession was lovely, I must say. I always enjoy it. Something quite ... sublime about it.'

Pippa felt a light bursting into flame inside her. 'Yes, there really is, isn't there? Especially in the children's wards.

Seeing their faces. And there'll be a special tea for them tomorrow, I believe. For those who are allowed, of course.'

'Few who are not, I believe. And I'm going to be Father Christmas for them in the morning. If I can't be with my own children, it'll be the next best thing. But I've got a week's leave from the day after Boxing Day, so I'll be going home. Well, not home exactly. My wife took the girls to stay with her parents in deepest Wales nearly two years ago, before the bombings ever started. I hardly ever see them, so you can imagine I just can't wait!'

His face was glowing like burnished gold — burning a hole in Pippa's heart. *Married? Children?* Oh, what a fool she'd been to have read so much more into his attentions! It was just as he'd said to Sister Pudifoot. He was encouraging her because she had the makings of a good nurse. Nothing more.

She must put on a brave face, though she felt as if she was crumbling inside. Not just devastated, but so very, very naive and stupid. What could he, a senior registrar, see in a mere student nurse? And he was probably at least ten years older than her. Of course he'd be married with children, he was so kind and good-looking. She felt all screwed up, empty and angry at herself at the same time, but she must remain calm and dignified, and not let it show.

'Well, have a wonderful time with your family, Doctor,' she managed to smile.

'I will, thank you,' he beamed. 'And good luck on your new ward. And if there's anything you ever need any help with, you can always come to me. I know some other doctors aren't always so approachable.'

Oh, she knew that well enough. But his words only served to push the knife deeper into her side. 'Thank you, Doctor, I will.'

'The name's Chris, by the way. In private at least.'

'And I'm Philippa.' Not Pippa, she thought. She needed to keep some distance between them at least.

'Well, Happy Christmas, Philippa. And I'll see you next year some time.'

She nodded, planting a smile on her face as she watched him saunter away down the corridor with a spring in his step. What an idiot! Why had she let herself become distracted when she was determined to be the best nurse the hospital had ever produced? Really, that was all that mattered, though regret still persisted in her breast.

'Think he's got a soft spot for you,' Steph joked as she joined her, digging her in the ribs.

'What?' Pippa shook herself from her thoughts. 'Oh, no. Whatever made you think that? He's just happy because he's off to see his wife and children in a day or two.'

'Oh?' Steph's face fell. 'Oh, well, never mind. Plenty more fish in the sea.'

Her expression made Pippa chuckle. *Oh, Steph, what would I do without you?* 'I don't know why you're always trying to partner me off!' she found herself laughing. 'I've told you afore like, all I'm interested in is nursing. Now come on, or Sister Pudifoot'll have us strung up!'

She linked arms with Steph and together they hurried off back to their ward. From now on, she would stick to her guns, and the likes of Doctor Chris Curnock could take a running jump!

CHAPTER SEVENTEEN

Pippa almost danced her way back from taking the early breakfast in the dining room. A whole three days off duty! She couldn't wait to change back into her civvies — ridiculous that she could only go to the dining room in uniform — and hurry to the station to catch the next train to Tavistock.

As she hurried along the corridor, she spied Steph coming towards her, doubtless on her way to late breakfast. Steph had been put on night duty, so they were literally like ships passing in the night, even though they shared a room. If their paths had crossed, Steph had been full of yawns, but now Pippa could see stars glinting in her eyes as she hopped towards her.

'Why are you looking so mortal pleased with yourself?' Pippa asked teasingly.

'I've just collected a letter from Rusty,' Steph answered, taking an envelope from her pocket and waving it joyfully in the air. 'Number Ten Squadron are coming back to Mountbatten! Isn't that great news!'

'Oh, I'm proper happy for you!' Pippa grinned back. 'You must be thrilled!'

'That's an understatement! I'm only on nights for a couple of weeks, and then we'll be able to see each other again.

And maybe you'll join us to make up a foursome with Jack. Seeing as Doctor Curnock is no longer on the cards,' she finished cheekily.

'I told you, that was all just professional,' Pippa insisted, annoyed at the colour she could feel rising in her cheeks. 'Anyway, I've told you afore, I'm not interested in men, though I'd be happy to act as chaperone for you and Rusty to make sure you don't get up to anything you shouldn't.'

'Spoilsport.' Steph pulled a face, then burst out laughing. 'Well, I'd best cut along. Quick breakfast then back on the ward for change-over, and then I shall fall into bed.'

'Sleep well.'

'Thanks, I shall. And you have a fabulous few days off.'

'I will. See you afterwards.'

Pippa skipped along the corridor as she made her way back to her room to change. It was likely to be bitterly cold if she was kept waiting on the station for any length of time. January had ushered in arctic temperatures, and she'd need to put on as many layers as she could. She wondered quite how people were going to manage to keep their houses warm with the coal shortages.

She set out with a brisk step, carrying her little suitcase with just the few bits she'd need for her short stay, plus a few belated Christmas gifts for her mum and the Chollacotts, seeing as she hadn't been able to get away over the holiday period. Even with her hat rammed down over her forehead and a thick scarf wrapped about her face, she could still feel the icy chill, and it felt like frost was forming on her eyelashes. She was grateful that the trains were running on time, and soon she was huddled in a carriage that was at least warmer than outside.

The train was relatively full, with the usual good number of servicemen, mainly seamen in their distinctive uniforms. Coming away from Plymouth, she guessed they must be going on leave. She wondered where they'd been serving, patrolling the coast or further afield, perhaps. She shivered. Thank goodness she had nobody to worry over. Even if her feelings over Doctor Curnock hadn't been crushed, she wouldn't have had that anguish to contend with, medicine being a reserved occupation. She felt a little foolish over the whole matter now. It had been her own mistake for taking his friendship for something more, and now she must put it behind her.

As the train skirted the western fringe of Dartmoor, her eyes were drawn to the wild uplands. The landscape was covered in a magical hoar frost, but she knew that to be out there in these sub-zero temperatures would be brutal. Come the summer, it would be wonderful to escape to the savage beauty and sense of timelessness to be found on the moor, but then again, it could bring back sad memories of expeditions there with her old schoolfriends. Maybe, though, their souls were hovering over the tors and valleys and would be looking down on her.

She shook herself from her morose thoughts. She was going to see her mum and the lively Chollacott family and must focus on that. Before she knew it, they were passing through the long tunnel at Yelverton to arrive at Horrabridge Station, and soon after that, flying over the Magpie Viaduct. Another short tunnel before a short stop at Whitchurch, then chugging into Tavistock. The biting cold nipped at Pippa's nose as she stepped down on to the platform and she pulled her scarf up tightly as she hurried down into the town and along the broad street to the Chollacott household in Plymouth Road.

She went to spring up the stone steps to the veranda door, and then checked herself. They could be icy in this biting cold and a bad fall was the last thing she needed. So she stepped up carefully and rang the doorbell. Although this time they knew she was coming, she still didn't feel right letting herself in.

The inner front door opened and Bea came out into the veranda, her face adorned with its usual welcoming smile. But as she opened the outer glass door, Pippa noticed that while her eyes were dancing, she held a finger up to her lips. Pippa was confused. It wouldn't be a surprise for her mother as she was expected, so she wondered what Bea was up to.

'Hello, my lovely!' the kindly woman greeted her in a whisper. 'Sorry to ask, but can you come in quietly? Lucy's having her morning nap, not that ort'd wake her. But our Duncan's home on leave and he'm exhausted, poor lad, and fast asleep.'

'Oh!' Pippa mouthed. Bea didn't talk about her eldest much. When she did, it was with deep pride, but also Pippa could sense with a feeling of dread. Best not to think about the dangers he was facing on a merchant ship on the high seas. But now he was home, Pippa could see the fathomless love in his mother's eyes. 'You must be so thrilled!' she whispered as she followed Bea into the house, softly closing the doors behind her.

'I am that. Take off your coat and come into the sitting room. Nice and warm in there. Your mam's waiting for you. Just finishing off a difficult row in the jumper she'm knitting for Lucy. Really complicated pattern and she didn't want to lose her place.'

Pippa hung up her coat and gas-mask box, and followed Bea into the living room. That was typical of her mum. Liked to give herself a challenge. But concentrating on something like that probably helped to keep her mind off her grief. Nine months nearly since her dear dad had been killed and every day as raw as the previous one. Pippa knew only too well how it helped to keep occupied with other matters.

Her mother must have finished the row as she thrust the knitting needles into the ball of wool and stood up with a huge smile on her face. Pippa hugged her tightly. She felt thinner, but it was so good to hold her close.

'Great to see you, love,' her mum whispered in her ear before they drew apart.

'Hello, Pippa, good to see you again,' Miss Polly and Miss Primrose chorused. 'How are you?'

'Good, thank you,' Pippa beamed at them over her mum's shoulder. 'And yourselves?'

'Fair to middling for our age, cheel.'

Just then, as Bea went to close the door, she opened it again as Sylvie appeared with a teapot, followed by Don carrying a tray of teacups. Little Bernard, who'd just celebrated his fourth birthday, sidled past his grandparents to greet Pippa with a hug, and the room seemed to burst into life. Pippa couldn't help thinking it was lucky the school term had started again so that Norman wasn't there with his endearing but boisterous personality to throw everything into chaos.

'Welcome back, Pippa,' Sylvie said as she and Don put everything on the table. 'Tea's only weak, I'm afraid. Having to use the leaves a couple of times over to make them last. So many things on ration now.'

'I'm so lucky that I don't have to deal with any of that,' Pippa told them. 'Everything's done for us. We just have to hand over our ration books. But tell me, how is everyone?'

'Bearing up, I'd say,' Bea answered cheerfully. 'Not so many alerts nowadays, but that must be the same for you in Plymouth.'

'That's right. And how's Susie getting on?' Pippa asked, taking the cup of tea she was offered. 'Still enjoying her work at the British Restaurant?'

'Loves it, even if it's open twenty-four hours a day to help feed the refugees, so sometimes she'm working through the night. Run by the WVS, of course. But sometimes she goes out in their mobile canteen, all over the place. People be camping out in the fields and up on the moor. And your mum has some news, as well,' Bea concluded with satisfaction.

Pippa glanced across at her mother, whose expression was one of pride mixed with gloom. 'Well, I had to do something for the war effort, like,' Adeline explained. 'I know your dad would've wanted us to. So I've joined the WVS. I help out at the other British Restaurant, the one on the wharf. I work mainly in the hut that prepares the meals, but sometimes in the dining hut. Children from the rural areas who go to the Dolvin Road School have their lunch with us, poor little mites. The school can't cope with feeding all the extra kiddies they have, so they come to us instead. Just fourpence for the meal, to cover the costs. But adults can come to us as well. Sixpence for a main course, tuppence for a pud and a penny for a cuppa. Have to say, I rather enjoy it.' She looked so proud of herself. 'I'm on dinner duty today, so I'll have to leave you for a few hours.'

'Oh, Mum, that's great news!' Pippa beamed. 'I mean, not that I won't see you for a few hours, but that you've found something you enjoy.'

'I'd join as well if I weren't so master busy with all the tackers,' Bea put in. 'But I do help out, like, with all the Town Hall dances, exhibitions, concerts and so forth they put on to raise money for the war effort. So I feel I'm doing my bit. But I be so pleased I'm not doing ort these few days when Duncan's yere.'

'Yes, you must be delighted he's back. How long's he here for?'

'Huh,' Bea scoffed. 'Tavistock's what they call a closed town now. Visitors be only allowed to stay three days without official approval. So you'm all right, my flower, as you'm only staying three days any road. But our Duncan didn't have no time to go through all that palaver, so he'm yere for three days, and then he'm going back to our house with Len and Ernie. Still standing, thank the Lord. Windows got blown in and the ceilings have come down in the front rooms, but it's still liveable. Not much of a break for a lad risking his life on the high seas, mind.'

Just as she finished speaking, everyone's attention was drawn by the door opening.

'Did I hear my name?' a softly spoken voice asked.

Pippa sensed the gentle humour in the words and turned her gaze towards the door. A tall figure clad in a thick, cable-knit navy tunic walked in, his presence seeming to fill the room. Pippa's eyes stretched wide with pleasant surprise and her heart performed a little patter. Duncan Chollacott had every inch of his father's height, but though slender of waist, his shoulders were strong and so much broader. He was also possessed of his mother's large, expressive hazel eyes, yet had a shock of dark blond hair that flopped casually over his forehead. That didn't come from either of his parents, Pippa mused. Neither was it shaved militarily short at the back and sides, she noticed, but sat rather appealingly on his collar. Perhaps the Merchant Navy wasn't quite as strict about such matters, she pondered.

Goodness, what was she thinking of? She was still feeling bruised over her mistake with Doctor Christopher Curnock, her own stupid fault entirely for reading something that really wasn't there. She'd vowed herself right off men, and yet here she was, almost mesmerised by this handsome stranger who crossed the room to drop a kiss on his mother's head.

'Have a good sleep, my lover?' Bea enquired, her face split in a grin as she looked up at her beloved eldest son.

'I did, but it'll take a few days for me to catch up entirely,' he answered, and Pippa was once again struck by the softness of his voice which was at the same time confident and commanding. 'And this must be Philippa,' he went on, turning to her with a broad smile just like his mother's. 'I've heard so much about you.' He held out his hand and Pippa took it. 'But I believe you prefer to be called Pippa.'

His grip was firm, but Pippa suspected there was a great deal more strength in those long, artistic fingers that felt only slightly rough. His warm smile showed off perfect teeth in a generous mouth set in a chiselled jaw.

'Pleased to meet you,' she replied, praying the heat in her cheeks didn't show. She couldn't help feeling an instant liking for him. But she must shake herself out of this. He probably had a girl in every port, he was so good-looking and with such an endearing manner to boot!

Feeling flushed — and not just from the warmth from the fire in the grate — Pippa glanced about the room. The only seat free was on the sofa next to her, and sure enough,

Duncan sat down by her side. But she was saved any embarrassment as no sooner had he done so than Willow jumped up on to her lap.

'Hello, puss,' Duncan said in surprise. 'Where did you spring from?'

'She was our cat in Plymouth,' Pippa explained, grateful for a topic of conversation. 'Don and Sylvie kindly let us bring her with us when our house was destroyed.'

'Oh, yes, I heard about that.' Duncan's voice was grave as he leaned over to stroke Willow's head. 'So dreadfully sorry. And your dad. I can't possibly imagine . . .'

He didn't finish the sentence. There was no need to. The sincerity with which he spoke was enough. It made Pippa feel less awkward. As if he really did understand.

'Thank you,' she replied, almost under her breath, and then realised that other conversations had started up in the room and nobody was listening to them in particular. 'She likes you,' she smiled wryly as Willow began to purr and tipped her head to push against Duncan's caressing hand.

'Yes,' Duncan chuckled softly. 'So, you're just staying for the statutory three days, too, then?' he asked, looking her straight in the eye.

'Yes,' she answered, feeling at ease with him now. 'It's all the off-duty time I've got, anyway, and lucky to have that. Once you're into nursing, it completely takes over your life. Even if you're off duty from the wards, you're either at lectures or studying. You're hardly away from the hospital at all. Hardly ever get out, and even then, it's usually only for a few hours.'

'Don't I know the feeling,' Duncan sympathised. 'When you're stuck on a ship in the middle of the ocean, there's no escape. Of course, I knew that when I first went to sea. But then I wasn't expecting a war and having to face the idea of being blown out of the water at any minute.'

Pippa heard the hint of bitterness in his words. Having the personal connection now, she felt it really brought home to her what it must be like for anyone in either the Royal or the Merchant Navy. It must be unimaginable wondering if you were about to go to a watery grave at any moment.

'How long have you been at sea?' she asked, wanting to change the subject.

'Seven years now.'

Pippa raised an eyebrow. 'A long time, then.'

Duncan puffed out his cheeks. 'Maybe. But the sea's always got more to teach you. I'm Second Officer now. The war's slowed down the progression process, but I'm hoping to make First Officer in time. I'll never be captain. You need to attend one of the posh training schools in your youth to make that, and Mum and Dad couldn't afford it. I was lucky to pass through grammar school, though. But I'll be quite content with First Officer eventually.'

'I know what you mean. I want to make it to sister with my own ward to look after, but I wouldn't want to become matron or even something like Sister Tutor. Too much admin rather than dealing direct with the patients.'

Duncan nodded in agreement. And there Pippa feared the conversation would stumble, but just then young Bernard appeared in front of them, thumb plugged in his mouth as he stared into Duncan's face.

'Hello again, little man,' Duncan said affably, and it somehow pleased Pippa to see how easy he was with the child.

'Me mam says you'm my big brother,' Bernard stated solemnly without taking his thumb from his mouth.

'That's right. I saw you briefly last night. You were just going to bed when I arrived. We met twice before when you were just a baby, but I don't suppose you remember.'

'No, I don't,' Bernard frowned. 'Mam says you'm a sailor.'

'That's right, I am. That's why I don't come home very often because I'm away at sea for long periods.'

'Hmm.' Bernard thrust out his chin. 'Can we go and feed the ducks?'

'I should think so. Just let me have a cup of tea and some toast or something, and then we can go if Mum says we can.'

'And can Pippa come, too?'

'Oh, poor cheel's only just got yere,' Bea put in, catching their conversation. 'She don't want to go out in this snipey weather again.'

'No, it's fine. I'm happy to go,' Pippa smiled. In truth, she was curious about Duncan. He clearly took after his father's side of the family in many ways. Although there was a slight Devonshire burr to his voice, she'd yet to hear him use any of the local expressions that peppered Bea's speech and that some of the other children used. On the other hand, he appeared possessed of his mother's easy-going, big-hearted nature.

Ten minutes later, they were crossing the road to the Meadows, Bernard holding tightly on to Duncan's hand, a stale crust of bread held jealously in the other. They all breathed out clouds of mist into the freezing air as they headed for the canal where Bernard expertly broke the crust into tiny pieces before throwing it to the ducks that flapped around him, eager for a morsel. Ice sparkled on the edges of the shallow water, glinting in the pale sunshine.

'Poor things look frozen,' Pippa sighed.

'Oh, I don't know,' Duncan replied. 'They probably feel the cold less than we do. Nature has provided them with good insulation. I've seen many a sea bird happily diving into icy water to catch fish when we've a foot of ice clinging to everything on deck and the sea's almost freezing around us.'

'All the bread's gone,' Bernard wailed. 'But can we go to the swings?'

'Yes, of course, if that's all right with Pippa. Not too cold?' he enquired, turning to her.

'No, not at all,' she replied, falling into step beside him while Bernard bounced around them like an excited puppy. 'I like it here in the Meadows. People were camping out here to get away from the bombings in Plymouth, not that we're getting many raids nowadays, thank goodness. Most of them have found somewhere proper to stay now. You couldn't camp out in this weather.'

'Poor sods,' Duncan muttered under his breath. 'But you can understand it. I mean, Mum told me everything that happened to you. I can't say how sorry I am.'

Pippa gave a wistful smile. 'I don't know what we'd have done without Bea and your grandparents' kindness. It's the one good thing that's come out of the war, meeting them all.'

'That's Mum for you. Heart as big as the ocean, even when she's so busy with all my brothers and sisters. Talking of which, is Bernard all right there?' he asked as the child ran on ahead.

'Oh, yes. He's the sensible one. If it was Norman, now, we couldn't take our eyes off him,' Pippa chuckled. 'He's only got morning school so he'll be home to jump all over you at lunchtime.'

Duncan rolled his eyes and groaned before giving a soft laugh. 'I really don't mind. But we should make the most of the peace and quiet here while we can. It's so good to be able to relax properly for once,' he concluded, his voice fading as his gaze seemed to move off into the distance for a moment.

'I can understand that,' Pippa said gently. 'It can't be much fun for you.'

'No, not with the war on,' Duncan murmured back. 'Fighting the elements is one thing, but knowing you're likely to be attacked at any moment either from above or below the water is another. I've seen ships torpedo-ed and sunk in minutes, tried to rescue survivors while being under fire ourselves.' He breathed in deeply through his nostrils and then glanced sideways at her. 'You're a nurse. You must keep secrets all the time. Patient confidentiality and all that. Can you . . . keep a secret for me? I don't want anyone else knowing, especially not Mum. She'll be worried enough as it is. I just feel . . . I need to tell someone else. Silly, I know, but . . .'

'Yes, of course,' Pippa answered. She couldn't explain it but she felt that in the short time they'd known each other, some strange sort of trust had developed between them.

'Well, it's no secret that it exists,' he said in a low voice. 'The Germans know what we're doing. I can't give you any details, of course, but . . . we're on the North Atlantic Run.'

'The North Atlantic Run?' A tremor shivered through her. 'We don't often hear a lot about what's going on, but I've heard of that. Transporting arms to Russia to help them fighting back against the German invasion.'

'That's right. The Russian winter's probably their greatest ally, but the supplies, weapons, tanks and so forth from Britain and America are vital. Thousands of tonnes twice a month. We go in large convoys with a heavy naval escort, destroyers, minesweepers. They protect us as best they can from enemy attack, but losses are heavy. And the conditions at sea are the worst I've ever known.' He shook his head. 'Fog, almost constant dark now it's winter, ice floating in the seas and so thick on deck we have to break it off with pickaxes. Cold like I've never experienced before. We're right up in the Arctic Circle, sailing round the northern tip of Scandinavia to get to Murmansk. So conditions like that are only to be expected, but it's not exactly what I went to sea for. Oh, I'm sorry,' he said with a rueful sigh. 'Sounds like I'm complaining and yet . . . It's war. Others are facing just as dreadful conditions elsewhere, on land, in the desert. We've all got to do things we wouldn't normally. Face grief and fear and horror. You've had enough of it yourself. But . . . I just wanted to tell someone so that if I don't come back, you can tell Mum and Dad what I was doing. They just know I'm at sea somewhere. We decided it was best that way once the war started. Of course, I don't suppose we'll be on that route indefinitely. But I'd like Mum and Dad to know how I was doing my duty.' His voice had quivered on his last few words and he appeared to hesitate before concluding, 'I hope you don't mind. But you seem so sensible and just detached enough to be able to explain.'

Pippa had been listening intently as they strolled along the frozen path. It seemed that Duncan Chollacott had needed to talk to someone and that someone had turned out to be her. She'd let him speak uninterrupted, letting him get it off his chest. She knew how talking helped. How Steph had listened to her, how Bea had listened to her mum.

'No, I don't mind,' she answered as they came to a halt by the playground where Bernard had climbed on to a swing and was waiting to be pushed. 'I do understand. And ... I do hope you come back.'

Their eyes met and she gave him a compassionate smile. It was strange how they'd taken to each other in the hour or so since they'd met. But she wouldn't let herself become attached. She had to shield herself from hurt. The war had hurt her enough already, and after her error over Doctor Curnock, she wasn't going to let herself be hurt again. She was Nurse Luscombe, halfway through her training nearly. One day she would be Sister Luscombe, and beyond her mother, that was all that mattered to her.

'I think we'd better give Bernard a push for a few minutes, and then head back, don't you, it's so mortal snipey.'

She watched as Duncan's face broke into a grin at her use of the sort of expression Bea would have used. He strode up behind the swing and gave Bernard a hard push that sent the boy swinging upwards with a joyful laugh.

CHAPTER EIGHTEEN

'Ssh! Keep your voice down!' Pippa warned in an anxious whisper as they came into the nurses' home.

'Why? It's not as if we're coming in late or anything,' Steph queried. 'Hardly likely to, with it being cold enough to freeze your nose off out there.'

'No, but others might be trying to sleep. It's not everyone who sneaks out to the flicks with their Australian sweetheart the minute there's no lecture during their off-duty time.'

'It were good of you to come with me and make up a foursome. Especially when you're not so keen on Jack.'

'Oh, Jack's okay. But I wouldn't see him as anything more than a friend.'

'Makes a change, anyway, to go the cinema, doesn't it? One of the few left standing, anyways.' Steph opened the door to their room and hanging her gas-mask box on the hook on the wall, flopped down on her bed to take off her shoes. 'And I did enjoy the film. I wasn't sure from the title. *The Black Sheep of Whitehall*. Didn't make it sound like a comedy, but it was very funny.'

'But with Will Hay, what would you expect? I loved the bit where he's posing as the professor and has to give a BBC radio broadcast.'

'I thought when he's posing as a nurse was the funniest bit. Imagine if we had a man trying to infiltrate our hospital here,' Steph chuckled. 'And the car chase where they're towing the real professor along in the bath chair.'

'Yes, it was funny,' Pippa giggled, yawning as she undressed. 'The *Pathé News* was pretty sobering, though, wasn't it? Can you imagine living through the siege of Malta? And now Singapore has fallen to the Japs. Must've been terrifying, and God knows what'll happen to everyone they took prisoner.'

'Yes.' Steph's tone was serious now. 'It's put the wind up Australia, Rusty says. But I'm going to try not to think about it. I want a good night's sleep afore facing the ward tomorrow.'

'I'm enjoying Women's Surgical, though, aren't you?' Pippa replied. 'Better than the medical wards. More interesting. I'm just going to pop along to the kitchen to make myself a hot-water bottle, it's so mortal cold.'

'Make us one while you're at it, would you?' Steph asked, launching her own rubber bottle at her friend.

'Oh, you!' Pippa laughed, at the same time rolling her eyes.

Five minutes later, both girls were tucked down in bed. Pippa closed her eyes, cuddling her hot-water bottle as she waited for its heat to penetrate her body. My, it was cold. Heavy snow had fallen on the day she'd returned from her stay in Tavistock late in January, and it had been freezing ever since. She recalled that day, traipsing through the deep white sea to the station with Duncan by her side as he was on his way to the family home in Plymouth at the same time. As the train had chugged along, they'd marvelled at the sparkling wilderness of the moor they could see out of the carriage window, shivering as they imagined being out in its frozen wastes.

'Rather be out there than doing what I am, mind,' Duncan had muttered bitterly.

Pippa had given a sympathetic nod. He couldn't have said more than that, she knew, as there were others in the compartment. He'd been in uniform as most men were when out and about, and few would know the difference between Royal and Merchant Navy attire. He'd looked smart and less weary than that first day they'd met. They'd enjoyed each other's company, but Pippa was determined not to let herself become involved. So she'd been glad when they came out of the station and he'd merely held out his hand.

No, she wouldn't let herself think of Duncan Chollacott in any other way than as a friend. It wasn't even as if he'd asked if he could write to her as she knew some men did when they were returning to duty and had found themselves attracted to a girl. He had seen her as someone he could trust, a kindred spirit who'd experienced at first hand what war could do and so understood. Someone he could rely upon to carry out his wishes should the worst happen.

Would things have been different if it weren't for the war, Pippa asked herself. Probably not. A merchant seaman spent his life sailing the oceans of the world, didn't he, war or no war, and she was pursuing her career in nursing. There was no room for romance in either of their lives. She must put him out of her mind, though the thought that once he was back at sea, he could be lost to a watery grave made her shudder.

Now she must get some sleep. They needed to be up bright and early for their day's work on Women's Surgical. The operating list wasn't until the afternoon. Among others, there were two gall bladder removals, a gastric ulcer that hadn't responded to medication and needed surgical intervention, a woman with such bad haemorrhoids they needed operating, and another who was to have a suspicious lump removed from her breast. For the last few days, they'd been preparing the operation sites with antiseptics and today, of course, they had to make sure the patients were nil-by-mouth from the appointed hour. An important part of the nurse's job was to reassure patients that all would be well, and Pippa liked to be the one to assist when they were given their relaxing pre-med. One day, it would be her administering the injection.

The thought brought a gentle smile to her face as she drifted off to sleep.

* * *

'Good morning, nurses. And welcome to Men's Surgical, second-year Nurses Luscombe and Saundercock. Nurse Luscombe, you've come from Women's Surgical so you'll know a lot of the ropes already. Perhaps you will help Nurse Saundercock as she hasn't been on a surgical ward before. But neither of you must feel afraid to ask anything you're unsure about. I expect all my nurses to work hard, but you will find me very fair and I consider you are here to learn. You've all been listening to the changeover and we've said morning prayers, so let us begin. Everyone about their duties. Nurses Luscombe and Saundercock, go with Staff Nurse, and she will show you which patients she would like you to assist with their bathing.'

Sister Kitt's brown eyes twinkled as they swept around the circle of nurses. Pippa felt herself wrapped in the sister's warm smile. It was just what she needed, wasn't it? It was exactly a year since her father had been killed. In gardens that hadn't been flattened by the bombings, daffodils were waving their heads in the breeze, welcoming the spring, but for Pippa, spring would always revive the horrible memory. *Oh, Dad. I wish with all my heart you were still here. But I'll work and study and make you so proud if you're looking down on me.*

'Huh, trust you to be the instant favourite.' Ruby's snide whisper swept away the comfort Pippa had taken from Sister Kitt's kind welcome. 'I could hardly get surgical experience closeted on Geriatrics, could I?'

Pippa had to bite back an angry riposte. Why was Ruby always so flipping nasty? It wasn't Pippa's fault she'd just come from Women's Surgical. She didn't choose the training rotations. Sister Tutor liked to mix them up so that nurses worked with different colleagues and if possible each nurse had the chance to see life on each type of ward before she qualified.

Pippa had the feeling Ruby resented the friendship between her and Steph. But then if Ruby were less cutting towards her fellow student nurses, she'd be more popular. She was also so smug about her engagement, as if it put her above the others. Pippa wasn't the only one who wondered if her fiancé actually existed! Maybe it was her way of making up for the fact that she was often bottom of the class in the tests they regularly took.

Stifling a sigh of exasperation, Pippa followed Ruby as she stepped over to the staff nurse who allocated them the five men who were virtually recovered and able to wash themselves if provided with the necessary items. With there not being enough movable screens for each bed, they had to initiate a rota whereby one patient gave himself a full wash behind the screens and the others shaved and washed their faces while awaiting their turn of privacy.

'Think we can't handle a bed bath, do they?' Ruby grumbled as she carried a bowl of used water towards the sluice.

'Well, we are the most junior nurses on the ward and it is our first day,' Pippa retorted. For what did it matter? Each patient wanted to feel fresh and clean, and she was sure she and Ruby would get their chance another time. You had to be really careful giving a bed bath to someone who'd just had major surgery. You could cause them severe pain or even rupture something inside if you didn't know what you were doing. It seemed logical to her even if she hadn't spent nearly four months on Women's Surgical. Being a nurse wasn't some ego trip. It was about doing the very best for the patient.

As it was, after doctors' rounds and distributing mid-morning tea and biscuits — for those not nil-by-mouth, of course — Sister Kitt took her and Ruby around the ward, introducing them properly to the patients, though there was only time before dinner to work their way down one side.

'Nice to see such a mortal pretty face!' an older chap recovering from a hernia repair declared, winking at Pippa. 'If I weren't in so much pain when I move, I'd like to waltz you up and down the ward, my pretty maid.'

'Mr Horrell, do behave yourself!' Sister Kitt reprimanded. 'Nurse Luscombe doesn't want to dance with you, I'm sure!'

'Oh, come on! When I's well enough to do so, I be certain she would!'

Pippa grinned back at the cheeky fellow as they moved on to the next bed. Seemed a bit of a character did Mr Horrell, and a bit of humour would liven the place up a bit. She caught a suppressed smile on the sister's face. She was maybe thinking the same thing, and it made Pippa feel warm inside. But then she saw Ruby glaring daggers at her. Was the girl jealous that Mr Horrell had directed his remark at Pippa and not her? For heaven's sake! It really was just a bit of fun!

Dinner time came round before she knew it, and Pippa helped prepare light meals in the kitchen for those who were recovering from stomach surgery of some sort, boiled fish and creamed potatoes in the main. Afterwards, Ruby and the staff nurse were sent on their two-hour break, and Sister Kitt took Pippa to one side.

'Now I understand you've been practising removing stitches in your practicals,' she said.

'Yes, Sister, we have. On a pig's trotter.'

'Well.' Pauline Kitt gave a knowing smile. 'I hear you're one of the best. I have a little spare time, so how would you like to try the real thing?'

Pippa's skin tingled with pride and excitement, if not a little nervousness. 'Really? D'you think I could? I mean . . .'

'Well, you're not far off your final year and I've heard such excellent reports about you from Sister Tutor. And sometimes we're so short-staffed that it can be useful to have nurses capable of a little extra. Mr Horrell's stitches are due out. It's an inguinal hernia so it might take the wind out of his sails a little to have a pretty young thing like you seeing to his down-belows,' she winked. 'If you'd like to tell him the good news and put the screens around his bed, then meet me in the facility room and we'll get the trolley ready.'

Pippa grinned back and then trotted off to tell Mr Horrell what was about to happen. Despite Sister Kitt's prophesy, he seemed not the least bit daunted though his cheeks did colour a little. Back in the facility room, she scrubbed up under Pauline Kitt's watchful eye, masked up and prepared the sterile trolley. The sister, scrubbed up herself, pushed the trolley itself, opened the doors and moved the screens so that Pippa touched nothing else. She turned down Mr Horrell's sheets and helped pull down his pyjama bottoms so that his groin was exposed. Pippa gave him a matter-of-fact, reassuring smile — but as much for her own benefit. If she felt nervous, she really mustn't show it.

'You are happy to let Nurse Luscombe do her first stitch removal on you, Mr Horrell?' Sister Kitt repeated.

'Well, she has to do it on someone,' he answered. 'In fact, I can claim I were the first to let this pretty maid get her hands on the real thing!' he declared proudly.

'Well, thank you, Mr Horrell. Now, Nurse Luscombe, what is the first thing you must always do when removing stitches?'

There was a slight sternness to her voice that made Pippa smile to herself. She wasn't going to be tricked.

'Check the doctor's orders,' she said calmly, and Pauline Kitt smiled back.

'Well done, Nurse. I've already done that, so let's get on. Do everything slowly so that I can make any comments as we go along.'

Pippa nodded and carefully opened up the sterile pack. Gently removing the dressing from the wound, she first inspected it to make sure she, too, was satisfied it was sufficiently healed. The type of stitches were simple interrupted sutures and Pippa proceeded to swab them with disinfectant.

'Should I remove every other one, just in case?' she asked the sister.

'Good. I was waiting for you to ask that. Top marks,' Sister Kitt replied, removing the lid from the metal tray containing the sterilised instruments.

Pippa took up the tweezers in her left hand and the special scissors in her right, making sure she touched only the handles. She chose the second stitch along, it being under less strain than the first, lifted the knot to snip the thread beneath, then used the tweezers to ease the stitch out from the opposite end so that the thread that had been on the outside of the wound wasn't pulled through underneath, thus increasing the risk of infection. Instinctively she curved her hand as she did so, reducing the pull on the flesh and therefore making it less sensitive for the patient. Having completed the process on the other chosen sutures, she swabbed the tiny holes where the stitches had been.

'What do you think, Sister?' she asked with an inward sigh of relief.

'I think you did that perfectly.'

'Certainly did!' Mr Horrell enthused. 'Didn't feel a mortal thing!'

'But shall we leave it at that? There's just a tiny ooze of plasma.'

'Yes, I would agree. We'll let the doctor decide on the remaining stitches tomorrow. If you'd like to apply a fresh dressing?'

That was something else Pippa wouldn't have expected to do until her third year. When she'd finished, she almost felt weak, but also so proud and excited. Her first attempt at advanced nursing had gone brilliantly. When everything had been cleared away, she returned to Mr Horrell to remove the screens.

'Hey, everyone,' he called out, 'when you has your stitches out, ask for this yere maid! I honestly didn't feel a thing!'

'Now, Mr Horrell, don't embarrass the poor girl,' Sister Kitt chided as she walked down the ward. 'Nurse Luscombe isn't qualified for such procedures yet and was only able to do so because I was able to supervise. All my more senior nurses are perfectly able to do the job. Though I have to admit Nurse Luscombe is a natural. Ah, here comes Nurse Saundercock returning from her break, so Nurse Luscombe, perhaps you'd like to take your break now.'

'Thank you, Sister.'

Pippa turned towards the doors, sparkling with elation. As she did so, she passed Ruby who shot her a snide glare.

'Hear you've been showing off again,' she spat in a low voice as they passed each other.

Pippa drew in a gasp. Little minx. It wasn't her fault Sister Kitt had invited her to carry out the procedure. But if she'd pointed that out to Ruby, Sister Kitt might have overheard and she didn't want to upset her after her kindness. So she carried on towards the doors, head held high, and trying to hide a proud smile.

***

'So, how was your day?' Steph asked that evening, rubbing her feet as she sat on the edge of her bed.

'Proper grand!' Pippa declared as she stripped off her uniform. 'Sister Kitt supervised me taking some stitches out of an inguinal hernia.'

'Never!' Steph was speechless for all of ten seconds. 'You lucky thing! Wouldn't expect that until we're third years at least.'

'I know! I was nervous but it felt so good. Old Ruby was as jealous as hell afterwards, mind.'

Steph gave a wry chuckle. 'I bet she was, the old cow.'

'But enough of my day. How about yours?'

'Well, Geriatrics is no fun. It's so sad.' Steph's brow knitted ruefully. 'A lot of incontinence to deal with. Particularly hard for those who are still with it and are obviously embarrassed about it. But then a lot of them don't know what time of day it is. I found one chap wandering along the corridor. I asked him where he was going, and he said he was looking for his dog. He said he was so worried because dogs weren't allowed down the public shelter and Fido was left outside on his own. I told him I'd go and look for the dog once I'd got him back in bed. Such a sweet old fellow. And so horrible to think they were all strong, fit young men once upon a time.'

'And that the war's so imprinted in their minds that it's something that stays with them even when they've lost so much of their mental capacity. It really is heartbreaking.'

'At least we've not had any raids for months,' Steph reminded her. 'So maybe the threat of invasion's over.'

Pippa blew out through her lips. 'I wouldn't bank on it. I don't think Hitler's likely to give up that easily.'

As if on cue, the haunting siren that they hadn't heard so far that year suddenly blared out across the city, its echoing wail making their blood run cold. Their eyes met, full of exasperation and fear. Just when it appeared life might be safer again.

'So, what's it to be?' Steph spoke on a sigh. 'The dining room or here?'

'Well, I'm so tired, I think I'll just go to bed. When your number's up, your number's up, and cowering under a table in the dining room isn't going to offer much protection.'

Steph nodded in agreement and ten minutes later, when they were both curled up in bed, she groaned, 'I hope Rusty'll be all right and Mount Batten doesn't cop it.'

'Oh, he'll be fine,' Pippa assured her, though she knew it was just a platitude.

She closed her eyes, listening out for the booms of explosions and dreading what the night would bring. But silence rang in her ears and she began to relax. Her last thought as she drifted off to sleep was of a merchant ship, encased in ice, rising and falling in a raging sea.

There were no thunderous crashes to disturb her slumber. The planes that had appeared on the radar were headed not for Plymouth but for nearby Exeter, where the city was badly bombed and eighty people lost their lives. Slightly further north east, Bath was attacked on the same night, killing four hundred civilians. In the next few weeks, cities across the country were raided with severe destruction and loss of life.

The war was far from over.

CHAPTER NINETEEN

'Nurses Luscombe and Saundercock.' Sister Pauline Kitt's expression was a blend of kindness and efficiency. 'We have an emergency appendectomy coming up from Theatre. He's in recovery at the moment but will be coming up to us as soon as he's recovered from the anaesthetic. Poor chap, the appendix had actually burst. But he's young and fit, so with careful nursing and sulphonamides, he should make a good recovery. Now, I want you two to make up the empty bed for him. So, Nurse Saundercock, what position bed are we looking at?'

Pippa glanced across at Ruby and saw the anxiety on her face. She opened her mouth as if in thought, but no words came out. *Oh, dear.* It wasn't the first time Ruby couldn't answer a question. Pippa almost pitied her and cringed slightly when the sister said briskly, 'Nurse Luscombe, perhaps you can enlighten us?'

'Oh, well, we're looking at Fowler's Position,' Pippa answered, feeling embarrassed and yet proud at the same time. 'So there's less pressure on the diaphragm and any fluid and other matter that might collect will do so in the pelvis and not in the upper abdomen which would be more dangerous.'

'Well done, Nurse. And can you tell me what extra items will be required, Nurse Saundercock?'

Pippa could see the relief on Ruby's face now that her memory had been jogged. 'Two firm pillows and three or four soft ones, one of these for the small of the back and another behind the head and neck.'

'Anything else?'

'Erm . . .'

'Nurse Luscombe?'

'An air ring to support the buttocks and a knee bolster to be removed at intervals to reduce the risk of thrombosis.'

'Excellent. Now get on with the task and don't forget . . . ?' she finished in an enquiring tone.

'Disinfect the bed first,' Pippa allowed Ruby to say as she could see the other girl was ready to speak.

Sister Kitt nodded sharply then marched off down the ward. Pippa looked across at Ruby and jabbed her head towards the facility room.

'Come on,' she encouraged as they walked down between the rows of beds.

'Huh, why do you always know all the answers?' Ruby scoffed under her breath.

Pippa was taken aback as they went out through the doors. 'Maybe because I study more than you do,' she replied reasonably.

'Well, it's not natural the way you've always got your head in a book. Hardly ever go out. You're obsessed.'

Pippa jerked her eyes wide. She'd had enough of Ruby in the three months they'd been on Men's Surgical together. Always directing snide remarks at her. She'd jolly well retaliate this time.

'Well, if you spent more time studying and less time bunking off to see your fiancé, maybe you'd remember more,' she said firmly, trying to keep her voice calm.

She saw Ruby's face colour. 'I'll have you know Archie's just on home leave for a couple of weeks afore he's shipped out abroad somewhere. Rumour has it they'll be going to North Africa. Huh! You don't know what it's like, not having a sweetheart of your own.'

'Oh.' Pippa pulled herself up short as she poured disinfectant into a bowl of warm water. Ruby had a point. 'I'm sorry, Ruby. I didn't realise. Of course, you'll want to spend as much time as you can with him afore he goes.'

'And then I'll study as hard as you,' Ruby said in a huff.

Pippa's heart softened. 'Well, if you've missed anything, you can borrow my notes.'

'Yes, very kind,' Ruby sneered sarcastically as she pushed the trolley out through the door.

Pippa followed, exasperated, as they approached the bed and wiped it down with the disinfectant. Without a word exchanged, they went to the linen room, collected what they needed and then proceeded to make up the bed. Pippa worked in silence, smoothing and tucking, applying perfect hospital corners, but all the while, Ruby's words were echoing in her head.

Was Ruby right? Was she obsessed with her studies? Nursing was all she'd ever wanted to do. Besides, burying herself in her work was a way of coping with her gnawing grief over her dad and the sense that she needed to feel he'd have been proud of her. Should she go out more, instead of poring over her books? She did more, though, now it was the summer, didn't she?

The thing was that, true to her word, Sister Tutor Honeywell allowed her to save up her half days off so that she could have a whole day to visit her mum in Tavistock. As a result, she often only had her couple of hours break to get away from the hospital, and it wasn't long enough to get down to the Hoe, one of her favourite places, and back again in time. Recently, though, she had used a half day off to go with Steph when she was meeting Rusty and Jack. A smile twitched at her lips now as she remembered how close Steph and Rusty had seemed. And now she was looking forward to her evening off the following week when she and Steph were planning on going to see the much-acclaimed film, *Mrs Miniver*. It had such a good cast and was supposed to encompass the spirit and determination of what they were all going through.

She glanced across at Ruby as they finished preparing the bed and together turned the bedding down ready for the patient to be slid across when he was brought up from the recovery room. She wasn't keen on Ruby. She didn't know anyone who was. But if the girl was worried about her fiancé being shipped out to fight in North Africa, then she had every sympathy for her. Tobruk had recently fallen to Rommel, and now there was fierce fighting in what was being called the Battle of El Alamein. Together with the atrocious desert conditions, it would be unimaginable to think of one's other half on his way to join the forces there.

Just for a fleeting moment did Pippa's thoughts go to Duncan, not that he was anything but an acquaintance of a few days. Leonard and Beatrice had received a communication from him recently, and Pippa felt relieved for them that at least they knew he'd been alive when he'd written it. As she began to wheel the now empty linen trolley back down the ward, Pippa thanked her lucky stars she had no one that close to her heart to worry about. She knew her mum was safe but she'd lost her dear dad, and that was enough for anyone.

Pushing her thoughts aside, she got on with her duties, emptying bed pans and later, distributing the afternoon tea and biscuits. It was quite late before the appendectomy patient came up from recovery. Must have had quite a time of it, poor fellow. The portable screens were already around the prepared bed, and when he was brought up on the trolley, Pippa and Ruby and all the available nurses were called to assist. He clearly needed to be transferred to the bed with as little movement as possible.

'Has everyone got a bit?' Sister Kitt asked as they each took a hold on the sheet beneath him. On the sister's count, the young man was carefully slid across to the bed and settled in the half propped up position. He still had an oxygen mask over his face, the cylinder fixed to its own special trolley. Standing by his feet, Pippa and Ruby lifted the folded bedding up over his legs, but then turned away as the more senior nurses were left to complete the task.

'How are we feeling now, Mr Yelland?' Pippa heard Sister Kitt ask softly as they went to walk down the ward.

Pippa glanced across at Ruby. She was sure she'd heard her take a sharp intake of breath. The other girl's face was suddenly as white as a sheet and she swayed slightly.

'You all right, Ruby?' Pippa asked under her breath, forgetting that they were only supposed to refer to each other by their surnames when on the wards.

Ruby's eyes were wide in her pale face and she seemed unable to speak. Puzzled, Pippa's eyes swept about them. Sister Kitt was coming away from the patient now as other nurses were wheeling the screens from around his bed. The need for privacy was over, and it was better to be able to see the patient so as to keep an eye on him.

'Sister, shall Nurse Saundercock and I start preparing supper in the kitchen now?' she dared to ask. It wasn't her place, and hopefully kind Sister Kitt wouldn't reprimand her. 'The canteen have sent up two large saucepans of soup and it'll take a while to heat them through.'

'Good idea, Nurse Luscombe,' the sister said, a little surprised. 'You can prepare the bread and butter and lay the trays while you're watching the soup.'

'Yes, thank you, Sister,' Pippa replied, praying she hadn't noticed Ruby's distress.

Pippa hurried Ruby out of the ward, keeping an eye on her as they went. The girl almost looked as if she might faint. As the doors swung closed behind them, Pippa caught her arm just in case. She could feel her shaking, and quickly ushered her into the kitchen.

'Whatever's the matter, Ruby?' she quizzed her once the door was shut.

Ruby looked at her through eyes swimming with moisture. 'That was . . . it's my Archie,' she whimpered. 'I didn't look at his face. I mean, you don't, do you? Especially when they've still got the oxygen mask on. It were when Sister said his name. And then I realised. I had no idea. He were proper clever when I saw him the other day. And now . . . I pray to God he'll be all right!'

The words had come out in a squeal and she put her hands over her face as she burst into tears. Pippa felt herself moved, and wrapped her arms around her.

'You heard what Sister said,' she soothed. 'He's otherwise fit and strong, and with careful nursing, he'll be fine. And look at it this way. He'll be here two to three weeks, then another few weeks convalescing. And then he could only be on light duties for a while, so it could mean he's never sent to North Africa at all. The fighting there could be over by then.'

'Fat chance of that.' Ruby gulped, and thumbed the tears from her eyes. And then an expression of horror came over her face. 'You won't tell Sister Kitt, will you? Oh, please, Pippa! She'd have me transferred to another ward and I so want to be with him. You know we're not allowed to treat a family member or anyone we know personally. You won't tell on me, will you?'

Her voice had risen on a note of hysteria, and Pippa couldn't help but blink at the irony of the situation. She knew darned well that Ruby would be the first to tell if the boot had been on the other foot! But she herself wasn't like that.

'No, of course not,' she assured her. 'But you'll have to warn him not to let on. I'm sure Sister Kitt wouldn't be cross that you'd kept it a secret, but she'd have to follow protocol and have you transferred.'

'Thanks, Pippa. You're a true friend.'

Friend? Well, Pippa would hardly call it that. She just felt it was the right thing to do.

'Well, if it were to come out, I know nothing about it, and we haven't had this conversation. Now let's get this soup on the go and start buttering the bread or there'll be trouble to pay,' she said, lifting the first saucepan onto the hob and turning on the gas beneath.

What a turn up for the books!

* * *

'Proper grand, wasn't it?' Pippa enthused, linking her arm through Steph's as they stepped outside from the cinema. It was the start of August and although well past the longest day, with double British Summer Time, they could still get back to the hospital by dusk.

'Yes, it was,' Steph replied. 'It's somehow quite rallying to see what we're all going through portrayed on screen.'

'And at least with Rusty not being there, you saw it all rather than snogging through it all in the back row!' Pippa teased.

'What, you think I'd have missed watching Walter Pidgeon, and in such a brilliant role?' Steph retorted with mock offence. 'And Greer Garson wasn't bad either, was she?'

'No,' Pippa agreed. 'I reckon *Mrs Miniver* will go down as one of the best wartime films ever. It really made you think about all those little boats that braved the Channel to get to Dunkirk.'

'And what about the bit with the German airman? I thought that was a bit scary. Didn't you say you and your mum thought there was a German in your house once?'

'Yes, we did. It was just the blackout blind got ripped, but we were terrified.' Pippa shuddered at the memory. 'A bit too close for comfort, but hopefully the risk of invasion's over now. And Plymouth's not had a raid this year, either.'

'No.' Pippa saw Steph raise a rueful eyebrow. 'I reckon Hitler's too busy pushing into Russia and with the fighting in North Africa to bother bombing Plymouth again. What's left of it. But talking of North Africa, how's Ruby's young man doing? Managed to keep it a secret, still? That he's Ruby's fiancé, I mean.'

'Oh, yes. Can't be easy for them, mind.'

'So, what's he like, then?' Steph asked as they joined the queue at the bus stop.

Pippa paused to consider. She'd expected Archie Yelland to be as objectionable as Ruby, but in fact he appeared just the opposite. He'd been utterly polite, expressing his gratitude for everything that was done for him, eyes sparkling a little mischievously as his condition improved. If anything, Pippa found him rather attractive — not that she'd want Steph to gain an inkling of that. She'd pull her leg wholesale, and besides, it wouldn't be fair on Ruby. Much as she disliked the girl, she had no intention of upsetting her if she could help it.

'Quite nice, actually,' she answered Steph with what she hoped was a casual shrug. But she didn't want to appear over-dismissive, so she went on, 'And good-looking, surprisingly. Quite a catch for Ruby, I'd say. Can't quite see how they're suited, to be honest. He seems too easy-going and, I don't know, chatty and friendly. And with quite a sense of humour, especially now he's feeling better. Be with us another couple of weeks, I should imagine, and won't be passed fit to go back to the army for a few more weeks after that, I shouldn't wonder.'

'And then what, eh?' Steph released a wistful sigh. 'We've patched him up and then he'll be sent to fight who knows where?'

'Much as I don't like Ruby much, I don't envy her having someone to worry about. Oh, I'm sorry, Steph.' Pippa flushed with remorse. 'I know you have Rusty to worry over all the time.'

Steph gave a wry smile. 'Not your fault, my flower,' she said in an exaggerated tone. 'I know he's flying out over the Channel under Coastal Command, escorting naval and merchant ships and picking up survivors from other downed aircraft. What you'd expect from a sea-plane. But . . .'

'You just wish . . .'

She didn't need to finish the sentence. They both knew what the other was thinking. What everybody else in the bus queue, everybody else in the cinema and over the whole country was thinking. They just wished that this blessed war was over. Or that it had never started in the first place.

CHAPTER TWENTY

Pippa straightened up from smoothing the bedclothes over Archie Yelland's slim figure.

'Is there anything else I can get you, Mr Yelland?' she asked pleasantly.

Archie wrinkled his forehead in a half doleful, half cheeky expression. 'No thank you, Nurse. Not unless you have an anti-boredom pill.'

Pippa couldn't help but chuckle. 'I'll ask the doctor on his next round,' she bantered back. 'But in the meantime, I can fetch you a book of some sort. We've a bookshelf in the kitchen. Not much choice, I'm afraid. A few Agatha Christies and some wartime Penguin Classics. You know, the ones printed on tissue-thin paper.'

'Because there's a war on and we can't waste paper on such trivialities as books,' Archie sighed. 'Nothing with horses in, I don't suppose?'

'I don't believe so, but I'll check,' Pippa smiled. 'Like horses, do you?' she asked, not letting on that she already knew he was a saddler by trade. Nobody, not even Archie himself, must realise she knew he was Ruby's fiancé.

'Well, they come with the job. I'm a saddler and harness maker. Or repairer, more often than not.' Then his face fell. 'Before I was conscripted, of course. But to be honest, there's been less business since the war started, just enough to keep my dad in work. People who've managed to keep their horses for pleasure have to make do with what tack they've got, and most farmers use tractors in their fields nowadays. When they can get the petrol, of course.'

'I've only been up close to ponies on the moor,' Pippa told him, pouring some water into a glass for him from the jug on his bedside cabinet. It wouldn't do to be caught chatting to a patient if she wasn't doing some sort of nursing at the same time! 'It must be daunting to be up close to some of those mortal big carthorses.'

'Gentle giants, mostly. Would've loved to own one myself, but never had the chance. D'you have pets, Nurse Luscombe?'

Pippa jolted with surprise. He must have heard Sister call her by name, but even so, not that many patients remembered their nurses' names. 'My mother has a cat called Willow,' she answered as the surprise subsided. 'Now, shall I fetch you a book or not? One of the Agatha Christies has a dog on the cover. I think it's called *Dumb Witness* or something. Probably as near to a horse as I can offer you for now.'

'That'd be proper grand, thank you.'

He presented her with a grateful smile that strangely gave him an almost aristocratic air. He was a working-class man and yet there was what Pippa could only describe as something classy about him. How intriguing, she thought as she made her way towards the kitchen. No wonder Ruby had fallen for him. If he wasn't already spoken for, she'd have found him attractive herself.

'There we are,' she said, returning to his bedside with the well-thumbed book. 'I hope you enjoy it.'

'Well, it'll give me something to do other than watch you nurses flitting about. I've asked my mum to bring me a pencil and some paper when she comes next. But with visiting only once a week, I've got to wait for that,' he said with a roll of his eyes. 'I can't wait to be allowed out of bed. You don't think you could take me to the bathroom, do you? I'm sure I'm up to it.'

'Sorry.' Pippa shook her head with a wry chuckle. 'More than my job's worth. It's only a week since your operation, and I don't think you realise how ill you've been.' Knocking on death's door, if the truth be known, though she wasn't going to say so. 'Ask the surgeon on his rounds tomorrow and see what he says.'

'Oh, well, it was worth a try,' he sighed despondently.

'Surgeon. Tomorrow,' she encouraged, waving a finger at him. And as she went about her duties, the conversation left a smile on her face.

* * *

'Nurse Luscombe, I've had the golden seal of approval,' he called to her as she passed his bed later the following day. 'So would you do me the honour of accompanying me to the bathroom?'

Pippa paused, a little taken aback but also somewhat amused at his chivalrous request. *Please, Nurse, I need the lav*, was the usual sort of slightly embarrassed question, or *Take us to the bog*, she'd heard on occasion. But Archie Yelland made it sound as if he was inviting her to a grand ball! But shouldn't he be asking Ruby, she queried in her head. Although maybe that was a little too intimate for their relationship whereas she was just that step away.

'I'll just check with Sister,' she answered. 'She might want you to go in a wheelchair the first couple of times.'

Indeed, she discovered that was exactly what Sister Kitt wanted, so having disinfected it first, she wheeled the chair up to Archie's bedside and put on the brakes. She instructed him to sit on the edge of the bed for a few moments to let any dizziness pass as it was the first time he'd been upright in over a week, before helping him into the wheelchair.

'How was that?' she asked once he was settled. 'Any discomfort?'

'A tiny bit,' he admitted, 'but I don't think I'm going to burst open. So, wagons roll!'

Pippa shook her head in amusement as they progressed down the ward and out to the bathroom. She parked Archie next to the lavatory which had assistance bars around it.

'I'll leave you to it,' she told him. 'But I'll stand outside the door. Just shout if you feel faint or anything, and call me when you're ready.'

'I will, Nurse, thank you. And,' he lowered his voice, 'no one can hear us in here, but you know Ruby and I are engaged? It's been hard keeping it secret, so it's a sort of relief that someone else knows.'

'Ssh,' Pippa warned. 'Yes, I did know, but unless you want Ruby transferred to a different ward, you need to keep quiet about it.'

'Yes, I know. And thank you. You've done such a marvellous job at keeping our secret, I wasn't sure myself if you knew or not. But I guess you have to keep a lot of things to yourself in this place.'

Pippa replied with a faint smile. Quite astute was Archie. And yes, patient confidentiality was paramount. She saw things she'd rather not, and at other times, moments of great pride and happiness as patients were well enough to go home and walked out of the ward with a grateful goodbye. That was the best part of nursing and why she was determined to make it to the top.

***

'You really are looking a lot better, Mr Yelland,' Pippa pronounced a few days later as she was cleaning out and disinfecting his bedside cabinet.

'Being allowed to go to the bathroom on my own has done me a world of good,' Archie grinned back. 'Makes me feel human at last, even if that's the extent of it. And it's helped to relieve the boredom. I've never read so much in my life. I'm half way through my second Agatha Christie and my mum brought me the paper and pencil I asked for.'

'So what are you writing?' Pippa asked as she began to put everything back.

Archie pouted his lips. 'Mainly my observations on the ward. So that I don't forget my time here.'

'Oh, dear, nothing bad about us, I hope?' she teased.

'On the contrary, it's quite interesting watching the way Sister Kitt runs the place like clockwork, and all you nurses are the well-oiled cogs of the machine. I watch you, doing such hard work without a murmur, flitting around like a butterfly. The edges of your cap fluttering like wings.'

Pippa felt her thoughts perform a little hiccup. *A* butterfly. Not *butterflies* in the plural. Was it a slip of the tongue, or was he intimating that he was watching her in particular? She sincerely hoped not!

'Well, our caps *are* called butterfly caps,' she told him efficiently, as much as by way of diversion, for this really would not do! 'In fact, there are various styles all called butterfly. It varies from hospital to hospital. We'll have different caps when we're qualified, like the staff nurse, you see? But I'll let you into a secret. You get told off if you have too much hair showing. But I expect a little bird has told you that,' she concluded, lowering her voice.

Archie's face lit up with a chuckle. 'Yes. But it's a pity not to see more of your golden tresses, Nurse Luscombe. It'd add more to the picture in my mind I'll take with me when I leave. Of you alighting on each patient, bringing tenderness and comfort, like.'

Pippa felt hot under the collar. This was too much, and she felt herself recoil.

'That's what nurses are for,' she replied in a matter-of-fact tone. 'As well as the actual nursing, of course. All nurses care deeply about their patients, including Ruby,' she added under her breath, hoping to shut him up.

Archie shrugged his eyebrows then dropped his voice conspiratorially. 'She only went into nursing because she thought it'd be glamorous,' he said in a whisper. 'You know she very nearly gave up, and only stayed on when they brought in conscription for women last year because it was better than working in a munitions factory or joining the ATS or whatever?'

Pippa pulled back, startled. No, she didn't know that. No wonder Ruby was so slack in her studies. And of course, once she and Archie were married, she'd have to leave. Not that there was any sign of an actual wedding as yet.

'Well, that's as maybe,' Pippa said, replacing the last of Archie's personal items back in the cabinet. 'But I have work to do and I'm not allowed to stand around chatting. Fraternising with patients is forbidden, so I shall have to leave you to your books and your scribbling.'

There was a slight edge to her voice as she moved away. It was all very well being polite and friendly, but Archie Yelland had actually unsettled her. Yes, she found him quite charming, but at the end of the day, he was someone else's fiancé and was forbidden territory in more ways than one.

She walked away down the ward, carrying the bowl of used water towards the sluice room to replenish with fresh water and disinfectant for the next bed along. But as she passed Ruby who was carrying out the same laborious task on the opposite side of the ward, she saw the girl glaring at her with venom in her eyes.

Oh, blow you, Archie Yelland! Why couldn't you just behave like most patients and keep yourself to yourself!

***

For the next few days, she kept away from him as much as she could. She didn't want to upset Ruby and despite being drawn to Archie, any involvement was the last thing she wanted. Steph wasn't much help. When she'd confided in her, her friend had hooted with wry laughter.

'Bet you've put Ruby's nose right out of joint!' she chortled.

'Well, it wasn't my fault!' Pippa protested. 'He's a nice chap, too nice for Ruby if you ask me. But I'm really not interested and I'll be master glad when he's discharged. Shouldn't be long, thank goodness, and we can get back to normal.'

'Interesting what he said about Ruby, mind. About her not really wanting to be a nurse. Suppose it shouldn't come as a surprise, though. Not that she likes it when she's shown up on the ward when she can't answer Sister's questions.'

'Well, I did offer to lend her my notes to help her catch up when Archie's gone off to wherever they send him to. Not sure I've a mind to now, though, after the looks she's sent me.'

'You're too soft-hearted by half. Just carry on as your usual lovely self, if I were you.'

Well, that was what she was trying to do, wasn't it? So when she brought a fresh jug of water to place on Archie's bedside cabinet, she gave him her normal cheery smile.

'Won't be long afore you're discharged,' she said breezily.

'Mmm. Still slightly tender, but other than that, I feel fine,' he answered, though he looked a little wistful, Pippa thought.

'I expect the doctors will prescribe a month or so's convalescence afore you can go back to your army training centre.'

'Yes, I reckon so,' Archie sighed. 'But I'll miss this place.'

'Really? I am surprised. Most patients can't wait to get home.'

'But I'll especially miss you, Nurse Luscombe. Watching you and the way you treat all your patients with such kindness.'

Pippa drew in a sharp, wary breath. 'All we nurses do. And what about Ru . . . Nurse Saundercock?' she corrected herself just in time.

Archie gave a soft snort. 'She just does her job. But with you, when I observe you, you treat everyone as if they're someone special.'

Pippa knew she blushed, but rather from irritation. 'That's because they are.'

'There you are, then. But as a thank you for your care, I have something for you.'

'Oh, no, Mr Yelland. That's terribly kind, but we aren't allowed to accept gifts from patients.'

'It's not that sort of gift. Here. I've written it out in my best handwriting for you. Keeping the original rough to remember you by.'

He held out a sheet of paper. Well, that was a surprise. She supposed that didn't constitute a gift, so she took it from him with a smile and folding it in half, slipped it into her pocket.

'Thank you,' she said cagily. 'I'll read it later when I have time.'

'I'm afraid I'm not really much good at poetry, but I like to try.'

She smiled again, not knowing what to say, and then went on with her duties. A poem... She supposed she was flattered. Nobody had ever written a poem about her afore. But as long as that was all it was and Archie Yelland wasn't after anything else.

She didn't have time to read it all that day, she was so busy, and by the end of her shift, she'd pretty well forgotten about it. It wasn't until she was getting ready for bed and changing out of her uniform, that she felt the paper in her pocket.

'Oh,' she said, remembering. 'Ruby's fiancé gave me this today,' she told Steph who was yawning away as she climbed into bed. 'It's a poem, apparently.'

'Really? Give it here!' Steph cried, jumping out of bed and attempting to snatch it from Pippa's hand.

'No, I haven't read it myself yet,' Pippa protested.

Steph's face fell. 'Oh, all right, then. Let's read it together,' she suggested, brightening at the prospect. 'Fancy that. A poem. I don't suppose Rusty would ever write a poem about me. So come on,' she encouraged, slipping back into bed. 'Squeeze in beside me and let's take a butcher's.'

In her pyjamas now, Pippa wriggled next to Steph as she unfolded the paper. It was certainly set out as a poem, and the handwriting was surprisingly neat. The girls exchanged glances and then bent their heads together as they began to read.

The Butterfly Girl
She flits from bed to bed, alighting softly on her gauzy wings,
To soothe a fevered brow with a touch as light as gossamer threads.
Her golden hair shimmers in the sunlight beneath her fluttering butterfly cap,
Her words as gentle and caring as angel's breath,
Her eyes as blue as the ocean, deep pools of compassion and concern.
She lifts your heart with a smile as radiant as the sun.
Is she real, this ephemeral fairy who hovers in the air,
Yet brings you comfort and sees to your every need?
She moves through a dream world, bringing hope and calm.
To watch her is to bring peace to my soul.
When the haze lifted, she was there at the foot of my bed.
She seemed always there through my darkest hours.
Yes, she is just like a butterfly, hovering, ready to land so delicately.
To help and succour and make me smile.
And yet now it is time for me to go, for she has restored me.
But I will never forget her, her gentleness like summer rain,
My Butterfly Girl

Pippa held her breath as her gaze met Steph's. For some moments, they were both speechless. And then Steph stretched her eyes wide.

'Wow,' she breathed. 'I reckon he's got it bad for you, kiddo,' she went on in an American accent. 'I dread to think what Ruby'd say if she ever saw that.'

'God, yes.' Pippa found her voice at last. 'But she must never know. No one else must ever see this. I'll burn it the moment I have the chance.'

'Oh, but that seems a shame,' Steph frowned. 'It's rather lovely. Hide it somewhere safe. Besides, there's nothing on there to say who wrote it.'

'I know. But I feel quite bad about it.'

'Take my advice, and just look at it as something from a grateful patient. Something to show your children and grandchildren.'

Pippa chewed thoughtfully on her lip. 'Maybe. For now, I think I'll hide it under my smalls. Nobody's going to rifle through those.'

But as she slid the folded paper into her drawer and climbed into bed, she felt truly unsettled. What was she to do about it? And then the answer came to her. The next time she went to visit her mum in Tavistock, she'd take the poem with her and leave it with the few possessions she kept there.

* * *

'Right, I'm to see you off the premises.'

Pippa gave a false smile. If only Sister Kitt hadn't asked her to do the honours! Archie was dressed in the clothes his mother had brought in the previous day in a small case, and all his other bits and pieces had been packed into it instead. Now she picked it up and made for the doors, with Archie following on behind.

'Thank you, Sister, for everything,' he said politely as they passed the sister's desk.

'You're welcome, Mr Yelland,' Sister Kitt smiled back and then got on with her work.

Pippa's heart was doing a jig in her chest. Out of the corner of her eye, she saw Ruby throw a glance across at them from where she was making up a bed. Lips drawn into a knot, they only spread into a smile when Archie gave her his best, charming grin.

'Now you look after yourself,' Pippa said automatically as they went down in the lift. Goodness, she'd be glad when

Archie Yelland had left. And that should be in a few minutes when they met his parents in the front hall. The moment couldn't come quickly enough for her.

'What did you think of the poem?' Archie asked, his face raised in expectation.

'Very good,' she answered stiffly. 'But it doesn't rhyme.'

'Oh, it doesn't have to,' he laughed. 'As long as you liked it. But . . . I really will miss you, you know. I mean, you wouldn't consider coming out with me for a drink or to go the flicks, I suppose, before I go back to the army?'

Pippa's jaw dropped a mile. First the poem, and now this? The affrontery of the man was unbelievable!

'No, I'm sorry, but I would not!' she declared in no uncertain terms. 'It'd be more than my job's worth to break the rules and go out with a patient. And you're engaged to Ruby, for heaven's sake!'

Archie's face twisted for just a moment before he put on his most cajoling expression. 'But no one would ever know if we were careful. And Ruby, well . . .'

He broke off as the lift arrived on the ground floor. Pippa was never more grateful than when the doors opened into the front hall of the hospital, and she saw the woman she recognised as his mother with a man who must be his father waiting for them on one of the benches. She strode across to them and handed the case to Archie's father.

'Well, good luck, Mr Yelland,' she said efficiently, and turning her back, made towards the lift before the doors closed again. Maybe Archie Yelland had charmed her just a little, and she'd felt flattered, but now she couldn't be more relieved than knowing he was walking out of her life for ever.

Really, whatever next!

CHAPTER TWENTY-ONE

'I do so wish I hadn't been put with Ruby again on our new ward,' Pippa sighed as she pinned on the bib of her apron. 'Four months with her on Men's Surgical was as much as I could bear, and now I've been put with her again.'

'Didn't Sister Tutor say it was to help Ruby along?' Steph answered, looking in the mirror as she secured her butterfly cap on her head. 'D'you think this is okay, or am I showing too much hair?'

'Don't ask me! I've not been on Women's Orthopaedics, so I don't know how strict the sister is there. I wish so much I was going to be with you, like. It'll be so interesting.'

'But you'll love being on the children's ward, won't you? Whenever you go to visit your mum, you're always full of stories about Beatrice's kiddies.'

Pippa hesitated. And then lowered her eyes. Steph was perhaps the only person in the world she could admit her true feelings to. 'Maybe,' she said quietly. 'But some of the children on the ward are so young, they remind me of . . . Well, you know. The maternity ward.'

Steph turned to her, all thoughts of how she looked fled. 'I know. And don't forget, I was there, too. I probably saw more than you did since you were knocked unconscious. But . . .' She took Pippa's hands and stared earnestly into her face. 'We really must put that behind us. We've got our second-year exams in two weeks and we must concentrate on those. And don't let that Ruby bother you. Or memories of that two-faced fiancé of hers.'

Pippa gave a wry snort. 'At first, I thought he was quite nice, but my opinion of him changed when he wanted to two-time Ruby. I almost feel sorry for her.'

'Well, that's as maybe, but right now, we need to get going. The first rule of nursing is punctuality!' she mimicked in Matron's strict voice.

'Second only to cleanliness, perhaps?' Pippa teased as they went out through the door and made their way to the main building where they parted company to go to their different wards. Pippa gathered her courage. Another day spent with the obnoxious Ruby. She was hardly looking forward to it.

She wondered vaguely if the girl had any news of her fiancé, though Pippa wouldn't risk asking. Archie probably hadn't gone back to his training unit yet. And when he did, would he eventually be shipped out to North Africa? It looked as if it would be the most likely destination. Churchill had now appointed a General Montgomery as Commander in Chief or whatever it was, and the Eighth Army was holding its own against Rommel. It was the one bit of good news on the war front. Would they begin to see the tide turning? After three years of war, everyone had had enough, but it seemed to Pippa it would be a long time before it was over — whatever the outcome was.

But at least there hadn't been any more serious raids on Plymouth, and they should be grateful for that.

Pippa hung up her cloak and gas-mask box in the cloak-room. No sign of Ruby yet, she noted. Late again. It wouldn't be a good start to the day. But, Ruby aside, Pippa was looking forward to seeing the children on her ward again. With official evacuation now in place — at long last, though somewhat a case of bolting the stable door, she scoffed — the ward wasn't as full as it might have been. Pippa didn't like to see any child suffering, but it was good to be able help them as much as possible. The rules about connecting with patients were thrown to the wind here, and provided all other duties were covered, comforting or playing with the children was even encouraged.

A happy smile bloomed on Pippa's face as she pushed open the doors to the ward.

***

'Well, congratulations, my flower! Top of the class again!'

Bea enveloped Pippa in her warm embrace. The exams were over a couple of weeks ago, the results published, and Pippa had three days' leave to visit her mum in Tavistock. Adeline had already proudly told everyone of her daughter's success. Now Pippa felt embarrassment flooding her cheeks as Bea finally released her, and everyone else in the room wanted to congratulate her, too. Thank goodness the older children were back at school, and she could suffer their boisterous — but most welcome — greetings later in the day.

'My goodness, Lucy, look at you!' she cried, grateful to change the subject as she spied the little girl toddling across the room to her, arms outstretched and her face lifted expectantly. Pippa duly obliged, scooping the child in her arms. 'You remember me, then?' she asked delightedly.

'Pi-ppa!' Lucy beamed, and everyone in the room laughed.

'Let Pippa sit down and have a cuppa after her journey, like,' Adeline protested, fussing over her daughter.

'I'll get it,' Sylvie offered. 'Anyone else while I'm down in the kitchen?'

'I'll help you,' Don said, following her out of the room.

'And I need to change Lucy's nappy,' Bea announced.

Pippa handed Lucy over to her mother and then sat down next to Adeline on the settee. Miss Polly and Miss Primrose offered their congratulations, too, and went on with their knitting so that Pippa and Adeline could have a chat, undisturbed.

'This time next year I'll be buying you your nurse's buckle,' Adeline grinned, pride almost coming out of her ears, Pippa mused, if such a thing were possible. 'I just hope, with the war on, I can get you a decent one. Your dad . . . would've been so proud of you.'

'Yes, I know,' Pippa faltered, and was glad that Willow chose that moment to jump up on to her mistress's lap and her mum comforted herself by stroking the cat's furry ears. It made Pippa feel able to go on more brightly, 'And I'll have my staff nurse's uniform. I've got my third-year one now, of course. Dark blue and white stripes instead of pale blue and white. Still the same butterfly cap, but we get a veil cap once we qualify. More flattering, I think. But enough of me. How's your work with the WVS going? Still enjoying it?'

'Oh, yes, but I'm not on duty today. Susie's out somewhere on the moor again, with the van. Proper loves it, like. I reckon Sharon's quite jealous of her big sister. Just started her last year at school, of course.'

'And have you seen anything of Elliott and the Franfields recently?'

'Yes, we see a lot of them. You remember their son-in-law, Michael, is in the Merchant Navy? Well, he were home on leave for a week recently, so his wife, that's Mary, she were proper relieved to see him. Their home's in Plymouth, in the Barbican area, which weren't so badly bombed. Not like us.'

Pippa caught the sadness in her mother's voice and squeezed her hand. 'I'll pop round and see them all later. They're all always so kind and always want to know how I'm doing in my studies, being quite the medical family.'

'That's right. Young Edwin's thirteen now, of course, and desperate to become a doctor. I think Sharon quite fancies him, but he only ever has his nose in one of his dad's or grandad's medical journals!' Adeline chuckled. 'Even little Celia, she's the youngest, if you remember. Six years old and all she ever plays is nurses with her dolls as patients. Just like you used to do.'

Pippa smiled wistfully at the memory. 'Yes, I remember. And you and Dad made excellent patients, too.'

'Right, here we are,' Don announced, entering the room with a tray of mugs while Sylvie followed with a plate of Nice biscuits. 'Managed to scrounge a little extra tea from somewhere, so it's got a bit more flavour than usual.'

'That's proper grand, thank you,' Pippa said, taking a mug. 'Mum's just been catching me up on all the family news.'

'Did she tell you our Ernie's got hissel' a sweetheart?' Bea put in, coming back into the room with Lucy in her arms before setting the child on her feet. 'Works at Lyons Corner House. And we had another letter from our Duncan. Says he's safe and well. And he asked arter you. Wanted to know if he could write to you,' she finished with a meaningful jab of her head.

For a moment, Pippa didn't know what to say. She'd got over her stupidity with Doctor Curnock, and recently her experience with the flirtatious Archie Yelland had put her right off the idea of men altogether. But now her mind was flooded with the image of a tall, imposing young man with warm, hazel eyes, a shock of dark blond hair and an earnest, honest expression on his serious face. And yes, she had to admit that her thoughts had wandered to Duncan Chollacott on more than one occasion, wondering where in the world he was, praying he was safe. They might have only known each other for a short space of time, but they'd seemed to find some sort of common spirit, and if truth be told, she'd been a bit disappointed when they'd parted and he hadn't asked for permission to write to her. So now, the idea of corresponding with him was more than welcome. They both had their careers to follow but being pen friends could do no harm.

'Well, yes, I'd be delighted to hear from him,' she answered with a smile she hoped didn't appear over enthusiastic. 'Do tell him when next you write.'

'Better still, why don't you write to him first, while you'm yere?' Bea suggested with a hopeful gleam in her eye. 'I'll give you the address. You has to write care of his shipping line's offices and they pass it on to wherever he be. Takes a while cuz there's a war on, you knows,' she joked, using the quip on everyone's lips, 'so you has to be patient. But it'll be proper grand for him to hear from you, I be sure.'

Pippa nodded back, smiling a little. Yes, the more she thought about it, the more content she was with the idea. She liked Duncan very much. Doubtless Steph would want to know who she was writing to. You couldn't keep anything a secret from Steph! And my, she could just imagine how her friend would pull her leg about it!

'Any more tea in the pot?' she asked in an attempt to hide the pleasure on her face.

* * *

'That's right, sweetheart.' Pippa smiled encouragingly at young Rick Dashper as she withdrew the thermometer from beneath his tongue. 'Are we feeling better today? Less sore, I hope.'

The boy nodded, and his eyes flicked in discomfort as he swallowed. Pippa really felt for him. The previous day, the poor lad had undergone a tonsillectomy, quite a painful procedure but one that should put an end to his recurrent bouts of severe tonsilitis.

'You'll feel better as the day goes on. And at least there'll be plenty of ice cream on the menu,' she winked as she twiddled the thermometer in the light so that she could see to read the level the mercury had reached. 'There, perfectly normal,' she assured the boy, and flicking the instrument so that the mercury went back to its starting point, popped it into its little box on the wall. 'You've been a very brave boy, Rick,' she said as she entered the reading on his chart. 'And very grown up to have your temperature taken sublingually. That means under the tongue,' she explained, as in the couple of days he'd been under her care, she'd learnt that he was interested in everything medical going on around him. 'Now, can I get you something to read? A *Beano* or *Dandy* perhaps?' For what would a twelve-year-old boy like to help pass the time?

'Please,' Rick whispered, and Pippa winced for him. He obviously didn't want to use his vocal chords yet. 'I brought in some of my schoolbooks. In my locker. We're reading *Huckleberry Finn*. Can you pass it to me?'

'Of course. At grammar school are we?'

'I was till it was bombed.'

'Oh, dear. Well, let me get you this book, then.'

She bent down to open the bedside cabinet and select the novel from a small pile of books there. She straightened up, passing the requested item to her young patient. As she did so, she heard a quiet tap and the ominous tinkling of glass. To her horror, the thermometer lay smashed on the floor, a tiny puddle of liquid silver spilling from the shattered inner tube.

Pippa stared at it, disbelieving. She was sure she'd replaced the thermometer safely in its container on the wall. But there it was, in splinters on the linoleum. Had she been distracted by talking to young Rick? It looked as if it had fallen off the cabinet, yet how could it have done?

For an instant she glanced down the ward, utterly shocked. The first thing she saw was Ruby, standing at the foot of the next bed with a smirk on her face. Good Lord. Surely . . . surely Ruby wouldn't have had the nerve to move the thermometer behind her back while she was elsewise occupied? And then place it on the cabinet where it was sure to get knocked off? But how could she accuse Ruby without any proof?

She was struggling to work out how to handle this, but before she could do so, Sister Drakewell was striding past Ruby and came to a stop, glaring down at the crime scene, her face like thunder.

'Really, Nurse Luscombe! How careless of you! You came with the highest recommendation, top of your year, and yet your cock-sure belief in yourself has led to this. You will go to Matron at the end of your shift and she'll deduct the cost of the thermometer from your wages. Now, have you broken one before?'

Pippa wanted to die on the spot as humiliation burned inside.

'No, Sister,' she mumbled.

'But you do know how to clear it up?'

'Yes, Sister.'

'Then go and get the necessary. I'll stand guard until it's done. Broken glass and toxic mercury! I don't know, I really don't.'

Pippa walked down the ward, feeling utterly ashamed and disgraced. She couldn't help feeling Ruby's eyes on her and anger churned in her stomach. She was sure it had been Ruby's doing. How could she? Mercury was so dangerous, and with children around, what was the girl thinking of?

Gathering all she needed, she quickly returned and knelt down on the floor at Sister Drakewell's feet. Sliding two pieces of stiff paper along the floor towards each other, she carefully scooped up the broken glass and as much of the liquid metal as possible and funnelled it into the glass jar she'd brought with her. Inevitably, some tiny fragments of mercury escaped the paper and rolled themselves into minute balls. It would have been quite fascinating if it wasn't so poisonous, and Pippa used a pipette to suck up the remaining silvery specks. She then patted sticky tape over the whole area to pick up any glass splinters or blobs of mercury too tiny to be seen, followed by a piece of damp lint, before placing everything she'd used into the glass jar and sealing the lid.

'Well, at least you cleared it up perfectly,' Sister Drakewell said from above her. 'Put the jar in the dangerous waste bin and give your hands a thorough wash.'

'Yes, Sister. Thank you, Sister. I just want to give a final check with my torch,' Pippa answered, taking the said item from her apron pocket.

'Very well.' Sister exhaled heavily. 'We'll say no more about it, but I will have to report it to Matron.'

Yes, Pippa thought as she swept the light over the floor at a low angle. Satisfied, she got to her feet, carrying the contaminated jar out of the ward with the utmost care. She dared not look at Ruby. But she dared not accuse her either, even though she was convinced the other girl had deliberately contrived the situation. Not only would she have one and sixpence deducted from her meagre wages, but she'd have a black mark against her name. What she couldn't understand was why Ruby should be so spiteful. The only thing she could think of was that Ruby had found the rough of the poem Archie had written. After all, Archie had said he was going to keep the original copy as a memento and perhaps he hadn't hidden it properly. Ruby would know it wasn't about her because it mentioned golden hair, while hers was dark brown. And Pippa had been the only fair-headed nurse on Men's Surgical at the time.

Oh, damn you, Archie Yelland! Why hadn't you just kept your feelings to yourself?

* * *

'The cow!' Steph whistled as they got ready for bed later that evening. 'Are you sure?'

'As far as I can be,' Pippa sighed in a shaky, upset tone. 'I'm ninety-nine point nine per cent certain I put the thermometer back. And d'you know what? Later on, Ruby set out the afternoon drinks on the trolley. Usually we make Ovaltine for the children, but if anyone doesn't have it for any reason, we just do warm milk instead, and put those drinks to one side with a list of the patients. Just as you would in an adult ward if someone's on a special diet. Anyway, she was pushing the trolley and handing me the mugs to give to each kiddie. And d'you know what? She passed me an Ovaltine for the one diabetic child we have on the ward. I mean, I know I'm supposed to check each one, too. But I'm sure she was hoping

I wouldn't notice and then I'd get the blame for it, like. I mean, can you imagine? It could've been so dangerous for the poor child if I hadn't been on my toes! And doubtless Ruby would've argued that it was my fault. Would've been her word against mine, and after the fiasco with the thermometer, I'd have been sure to be blamed for something that could've had serious consequences.'

She saw Steph shake her head in disbelief. 'Takes the biscuit, that one. But . . . don't you think you should say something? I mean, what else might she get up to?'

Pippa plonked herself down on the bed. 'I don't know, really I don't. I mean, would anyone believe me? It just seems too fantastical. Plus I have no proof.'

'Hmm, I see your point. But look on the bright side. You'll be on night duty from next week, so dear Ruby'll out of your hair.'

Steph shot her a teasing glance. They both knew that night duty was neither of their favourites, even if it meant Pippa would be free of the conniving Ruby. It wasn't exactly a jovial matter, but Pippa grabbed her pillow and playfully swung it about Steph's head.

'Right, it's a pillow fight you want, is it?' Steph laughed, grasping her own pillow.

A few pillow swings later, they both stopped and stared at each other, bursting with mirth, before collapsing in a heap of giggling. Pippa grinned at her friend, the tensions of the day melting away. Thank goodness she had Steph. What on earth would she do without her?

CHAPTER TWENTY-TWO

'Oh, Steph, keep still, will you, or I won't be able to get it straight,' Pippa complained as she attempted to draw a seamline down the back of Steph's legs so that it looked as if she was wearing a pair of virtually unobtainable stockings.

'I'm sorry,' Steph answered, her voice alive with joyous anticipation as she tried not to wriggle. 'It's just that I'm that excited to be going to an actual proper dance with Rusty. It's amazing that we're both off duty at the same time, and that it coincides with such an event!'

'And that you were able to get a late pass,' Pippa said, leaning back to check on her handiwork.

'Oh, but you will leave the window open so I can climb in, won't you? Blowed if I'm coming home that early even if it is a late pass. Lucky to get tickets we were, and I'm not cutting the evening short. And you sure you won't come?'

'Absolutely,' Pippa sighed as she straightened up. 'Jack can't go and I'm not playing gooseberry to you two lovebirds. And even if Jack could go, you know I'm not overkeen on him. Anyway, there probably wouldn't be any tickets left on the door. Besides, if I came, who'd leave the window open for you?' she laughed.

'True. Thanks, Pip, you're a brick! And thanks for doing my legs.'

'Get away with you! Just hope you won't be cold with bare legs.'

'Well, I shall have my love to keep me warm!' Steph chanted cheekily, breaking into song. 'Now you get a good night's sleep, my lover,' she winked as she slipped into her coat. 'I know how hard it is getting back into the old sleep pattern when you've been on nights.'

'At least on nights I didn't have to put up with Ruby, so that were one compensation. I wonder how long I'll be on the same ward as her. Hopefully the next time we get moved on, I won't be with her again. I've just about had enough of her shenanigans.'

'Yup. It'd be good if we're put back together at long last and can have a bit of fun on the wards. But look, I must be off!' she grinned, glancing at her watch. 'Mustn't miss the bus into town.'

'Well, have a great time!' Pippa hugged her friend. 'Don't do anything I wouldn't.'

'Oh, spoil sport!'

'And try and come in quietly,' Pippa said hopefully.

'Quiet as a mouse I'll be. Next time you see me will be in the morning.'

Pippa shook her head with a chuckle as Steph danced out of the room. She was incorrigible!

Now, Pippa sighed, should she study for an hour or so before turning in? She was shattered after her first day back on day duty. She adored being on the children's ward where some of the rules were a bit more relaxed. Of course it wasn't pleasant seeing young ones unwell, but a joy to watch them recovering and finally going home.

Right. She'd make herself some Horlicks in the little nurses' kitchen and then get into bed with her books, and if she couldn't keep her eyes open, then she'd settle down. By the time she'd finished her hot drink sitting up in bed, the letters were dancing around on the page. Time to snuggle down.

Oh, the window. Good job she'd remembered! She jumped out of bed, undid the latch and dived back under the blankets. What a miserable November evening it was, wet and blustery, and she could hear the wind rattling the open window. It was breezy in the room, too, but fortunately mild for the time of year and with a hot-water bottle, she was as warm as toast.

She hoped Steph was having a good time. She really was head over heels in love with Rusty. It hadn't been an easy relationship with their off-duty shifts sometimes not corresponding for weeks on end, but they were both still as keen as mustard on each other. And good luck to them! The only thing was, Pippa worried so very, very much that one day, there'd be bad news. The Sunderland sea planes were perfect for rescuing survivors from other downed aircraft or sunk ships. But they were in danger of being shot down themselves especially when they were on escort duty for both naval and merchant shipping. What would Steph do if one day Rusty and Jack's aircraft was among one of those that didn't return? Though she didn't feel the least romantically drawn to Jack, Pippa would of course be sorry if he was lost, too. And what of their families back in Australia who hadn't seen them for so long now?

It was all so horrible. Pippa tried to drag her mind away from such thoughts but even though she was so exhausted, sleep was eluding her. Things were said to be looking up in North Africa, though. She wondered briefly if Archie was out there now, but she hardly wanted to broach the subject with Ruby! But that was just one theatre of the war. Hitler had occupied pretty well the whole of Europe, was continuing his assault on Russia, and heaven knew what was going on with Japan, Singapore, the Philippines, Malaysia and now Burma. It didn't bear thinking about.

And where was Duncan among all of this? He could literally be anywhere in the world. She'd heard that back in the summer, the North Atlantic Run had been suspended for a while after one convoy had been attacked so disastrously that hardly any of the ships had survived. As Bea and Don had received a letter from him after that date, Pippa knew that Duncan either hadn't been among that particular convoy, or had been among the lucky few who came back from it. He could have been anywhere in the meantime, but now she understood that the runs to Murmansk and other northern Russia destinations had resumed, perhaps he was engaged on that route yet again.

Pippa had written to him. Twice, in fact, but hadn't heard back. But that wasn't to say he hadn't replied. Or indeed, he might not even have received her letters. The more she thought about him, the more worried she became, and the more involved she felt. It was because of her love for the Chollacott family, wasn't it? At least that was what she kept telling herself. In truth, she was beginning to think she felt more for Duncan than she wanted to admit. When she finally drifted off to sleep, a vision of his handsome face with its soft, hazel eyes and dark blond hair kept creeping into her dreams.

Wait, what was that? She came to with a start, a dart of unease stinging through her. She glanced up at the window to see that it had been opened wide from the outside and in the darkness she could just make out a leg appearing through it . . . Nothing to worry about. Just Steph returning from her night on the tiles, so she could just turn over and go back to sleep.

But then she realised there was something else. She heard the lock to their bedroom door click, and the next moment, the door opened and the night sister waltzed in. The light from the corridor dazzled Pippa's vision for a moment, but she distinctly saw Ruby standing outside in her pyjamas, a satisfied smirk on her face.

Oh, no! Pippa flicked her head towards the window but there was no time to warn Steph as she climbed in backwards. Aghast, Pippa sat up in bed, rubbing her eyes, only to see the look of horror on Steph's face as she turned round to find the night sister glaring at her.

'Well, well, well, what have we here?' The woman's voice was like ice. 'You two are supposed to be our star probationers, and this is what I find! And don't try telling me, Nurse Chappel, that it was quite by chance that you found the window open. And draw that blackout curtain at once! Now, it's quite obvious that Nurse Luscombe left it open for you, and on such a blustery night! It was a good job you woke Nurse Saundercock with your antics and she brought it to my attention. Honestly, you should be ashamed of yourselves! As third years, you're supposed to be setting an example to those below you, not breaking one of the most fundamental rules! I'll be leaving a report on Matron's desk for her to be dealing with you both in the morning. Now goodnight, and I don't expect to see either of you late on duty tomorrow, or yawning on the wards.'

With that, she swept out of the room, closing the door behind her. Turning on the bedside lamp, Pippa stared after her, open-mouthed, and heard her remove her skeleton key from the lock. Her eyes met Steph's horrified gaze and for a few moments neither of them moved as what had just happened sunk in.

Steph was the first to speak as she plonked herself down on her bed. 'Oh, Pippa, I'm so sorry!' she wailed. 'I've got you into trouble and it's all my fault!'

As the shock subsided, anger took its place in Pippa's heart. 'No, it isn't. Half the nurses do the same thing, though there's bound to be a crackdown on it for a while after this. No! It was that flaming Ruby's fault. She's got it in for me, and you're the one who's going to come off worse. No, Steph. I'm the one who should be apologising to you.'

'Stuff that,' Steph retorted. 'We're best mates and we'll stand shoulder to shoulder against that creep, Ruby. We'll get back at her somehow.' Pippa saw Steph lift her chin stubbornly and push her lips forward before a cheeky grin illuminated her face. 'Still, it was worth it. We had a fantastic time. And you'll never guess what?'

Her pulse still pounding, Pippa glanced quizzically at her friend. 'No. What?'

Eyes dancing mischievously, Steph held out her left hand. On her ring finger, a single diamond in a gold setting twinkled in the glow from the lamp.

Pippa blinked her eyes wide as realisation dawned. 'Steph! He asked you to marry him?'

A wave of happiness for Steph wafted through her as the other girl jumped up and came over to give her a huge hug.

'So you see, it was worth it!' Steph crowed. 'I can face Matron and even that bitch Ruby for this!'

'I'm so pleased for you!' Pippa beamed, lowering her voice so as not to wake anyone who hadn't already been disturbed by the rumpus. 'So when's the big day going to be? I'll miss you so much, mind!'

'Oh, don't worry, it won't be for some while,' Steph assured her, stripping off her glad rags. 'I want to finish my training. We might even wait till the war's over.'

'That could be years,' Pippa said doubtfully. 'Could you really wait that long? You know . . . for . . . ?'

'Don't have to wait for that,' Steph answered with a cheeky wink. 'And if I fell, well, then we'd have to get married straight away.'

'Oh, Steph, you're terrible,' Pippa chuckled. 'But, right now, I really would like to get back to sleep.'

'Ready to face the dragon in the morning?'

Pippa nodded with a rueful twist of her lips before snuggling down in the bed again. Oh, she was so pleased for Steph and blow the inevitable consequences that would come in the morning! But then doubt started slithering into her mind. When Steph got married, at whatever point that was, she'd have to leave nursing. It was the unwritten rule. Pippa really couldn't imagine life without her dear friend and companion around her all the time. And when the war was over, whenever that might be, would Steph go back to Australia with Rusty?

She didn't get on with her own family so there was nothing to keep her in Blighty.

Except Pippa.

Her thoughts were tumbling around in a tangled web until she thought her head would burst. It all came down to this wretched war. It had so much to answer for!

***

Pippa made her way back to the children's ward, on the verge of tears and smarting under the degradation and shame Matron had heaped upon her. But it wasn't so much the reprimand as the unjust punishment that was being meted out that was so devastating. Apparently she was about to begin a stint on Gynaecology. As cases tended to be planned rather than emergencies, the ward would be fairly empty over Christmas and Sister Tutor had put in for her to take three days' leave over the actual Christmas period. Oh, what joy it would've been to spend the big day itself with her mum and the Chollacotts! The last time she'd spent the festive holiday with her family, she'd still been at school. The war had started but so far there'd been no bombs falling on Plymouth, and she'd been at home with her mum and her dearest dad. And now another Yuletide was going to pass without her being able to comfort her poor mum.

Sorrow overwhelmed her as she hung up her cloak and her gas-mask box. She smoothed down her apron, consciously pulling herself together as she removed her detachable sleeves and slipped her elasticated frills over her upper arms. Exhaling heavily, she marched towards the swing doors, but as she did so, she noticed that the kitchen door was open and Ruby was in there alone, preparing elevenses for their young patients.

The empty hole inside her instantly filled up with burning rage. Nurses stayed out late and climbed in windows all the time. So why had Ruby turned a blind eye on so many occasions — had been known to do the very same herself — and yet chose just now to betray her fellow probationers? It was spite, wasn't it? But what for, Pippa really had no idea.

She strode into the kitchen and shut the door.

'You evil little snake!' she hissed at Ruby.

The other girl turned on her with an angry sneer. 'Well, that's a case of the pot calling the kettle black,' she spat.

Pippa jolted back. That were unexpected. 'What the hell d'you mean?' she demanded. Was Ruby mad? 'What have I ever done to you?'

'Huh! Can't you guess? Stolen my Archie from me, that's what!'

'What?' Pippa scoffed incredulously. 'Well, if you're referring to the advances he made towards me, I can assure you I turned him down flat. I'm simply not interested. You can ask him yourself.'

'No, I can't. He's broken off our engagement.'

Pippa heard a catch in Ruby's voice and for a moment, experienced a pang of compassion. 'Well, I'm sorry to hear that but it has nothing to do with me.'

'Oh, yes, it does.' Ruby's eyes were like burning coals. 'He said it were all cuz of you. He said what he felt for you were summat special. He said you were his butterfly girl, and that even if you didn't feel the same, it made him realise that he'd never felt like that about me. He said he only got engaged cuz his best friend had, and he wanted someone to write to when he were sent overseas. And now cuz of you, I'll never hear from him again.'

Pippa stood for a moment, watching as Ruby's face suffused with scarlet. The poor girl really was upset. She reached out a hand to comfort her. 'I really am sorry, Ruby.'

The girl scornfully threw off her hand. 'Oh, you will be. Mark my words, you will be!'

And with that, she stormed out of the kitchen, leaving Pippa at a loss for words. My goodness. She'd have to watch her back from now on. Ruby was a devious, nasty piece of work. What would she be capable of next?

***

'At least we had the Christmas Carol procession to look forward to,' she told her mum and all her friends at Don and Sylvie's when she was at last able to get a couple of days' leave in January. 'It's always lovely, walking round the wards by candlelight. The children loved it especially. Their little faces! Of course, I'm on the gynae ward now, but it was super to see the kiddies again. Sadly some of them are long-term cases and they were as happy to see me again as I was to see them. And then one of the doctors dressed up as Father Christmas and gave them little presents.'

'Oh, yes, Elliott still does that at the cottage hospital here,' Adeline commented with a fond smile.

'So how are all the Franfield family?'

Pippa had only just arrived and there were so many strands of conversation buzzing around the room, her head was in a whirl.

'Proper clever,' her mum replied. 'We still see quite a lot of them, when they're not too busy, of course. Artie, Ling's son by her first marriage if you remember, were here for Christmas. And Elliott and Ling's daughter, Mary. Poor soul's all on her own, with her husband, Michael, a captain in the Merchant Navy and both their sons in the Royal Navy.'

'Talking of which, it were such a shame you missed our Duncan!' Bea said pointedly, her face breaking into that huge, proud smile of hers. 'Fancy him actually being yere for Christmas. Arrived at the last minute, totally unexpected, like. I were cock-a-hoop, I can tell you. He were so disappointed you wasn't yere. But he left a letter for you. I put it up yere on the mantelpiece.'

Bea bustled across the room to take an envelope from behind the clock. She handed it to Pippa with a look of expectancy on her face. Pippa had to chuckle to herself. Did Bea have a notion she'd like to see her eldest son and her together? It wouldn't work with their careers, but Pippa had to admit that her thoughts were drifting towards Duncan more and more, though mainly because she worried about him. Didn't she?

'Thank you, Bea,' she smiled, taking the letter and stuffing it in her pocket. 'I'll read it later.' She saw disappointment on Bea's face at her casual reply, but really, she wanted to keep her feelings to herself. Instead, she went on, 'When the children are all home from school, I'll tell them about the little panto we put on. It was really quite funny. We had George — that's the skeleton we have in the lecture room — with his gas mask on, and another nurse stood behind him all in black so as you couldn't see her, and wiggled his arms and sang. And then we did a pretend operation. I was the surgeon with a great wood saw to pretend to cut open the patient's stomach — another nurse, of course — and I pulled a string of sausages from her. We did it in various wards and you should've seen the kiddies laugh. I'm sure it was quite a tonic for them.'

'Norman'll love to hear about that!' Bea laughed. 'The more gruesome the better for him!'

Everyone was chuckling and Pippa glanced about the familiar room. It really did feel like home now, and everyone her family.

It wasn't until she retired that night and slid into the Z-bed squeezed into her mother's room that she opened Duncan's letter. The day had passed in a whirlwind with the children coming home from school and Mr and Mrs Robbins returning from work, and everyone eager to chat to her. Now as she unfolded the letter, she found her heart bouncing in her chest. What would Duncan have to say? Would he be thinking of her in the same way she did of him? She shook her head. That was quite ridiculous. And yet . . .

She unfolded the letter and began to read.

Dear Pippa,

I hope this finds you well. I was delighted that you took the time to write to me. Thank you so much for your letter. I did reply straight away, but I don't know if you received it. Post can take so long or not arrive at all.

It was such a pity you couldn't be at home for Christmas. It would have been wonderful to see you again. I know we only had those few days together a year ago now, but those walks in the Meadows, bitterly cold as it was, refreshed me. I hope you enjoyed them as much as I did.

I was really interested to read about your nursing life, although it was distressing to learn about the kiddies with long-term illnesses. I didn't realise there is such a lot of diphtheria around, in adults as well as the young, and that so many refuse to take up the vaccinations that could help prevent this terrible and painful disease. Putting cases in side wards to be barrier-nursed sounds hard work but rewarding when they recover, I'm sure.

For myself, I'm sure you remember what we discussed. I'm no longer on that run, but am somewhere less cold if just as dangerous. All I can say is that we're taking civilian supplies to the Med. You will understand that I can't say more than that. I truly value the trust that developed between us and know that I can rely on you to do as I asked should the need arise.

I'll leave you now to enjoy the company of my crazy family. Do look after yourself and write again as soon as you can and tell me more about your daily life. I think of you often and hope that we can remain friends.

With love and best wishes,
Duncan

Pippa stared at the letter for some moments before folding it and replacing it in the envelope. So Duncan thought of her often. As she did him. He had replied to her first letter, but nothing had arrived from him. Neither had he received her second letter, but she had this precious one from him now. Carefully she tucked it under her pillow and then snuggled down, a whirlwind of emotions in her breast so that she wasn't entirely sure what she truly felt.

Life could be so complicated!

CHAPTER TWENTY-THREE

'Well, that was some jolly good tucker!' Jack declared, licking his fingers. 'I can see why you Poms love your fish and chips.'

'And you'll never get fresher!' Pippa countered proudly. 'Straight off one of our trawlers.'

'Yeah, I know. Risking their lives at sea to feed us.'

Pippa shot him a sideways glance. She knew what he was implying. They were all risking their lives. But that was the way of war, wasn't it?

The four of them, Pippa, Jack, Steph and Rusty were sitting on a bench on the Hoe in the spring sunshine, munching their lunch from one small piece of greaseproof paper and just one sheet of old newspaper each, paper being so scarce because of the shortages. Pippa was glad to be away from the hospital for a few hours, though she wished it were just her and Steph. That was a bit mean and selfish, she knew, but it was how she felt.

'If it weren't for the poor old pier, from here you'd hardly know there was a war on,' she commented lazily, her eyes scanning the Sound spread out in front of them. 'You can't see the barbed wire along the shore or the damage to the Belvedere or the yacht club.'

'What about our Sunderlands?' Jack sounded affronted. 'You didn't have those before the war, or all the extra naval ships coming and going.'

'That's true,' she conceded.

'Well, I'm glad the war brought you here to me!' Steph put in, linking her arm through Rusty's and leaning her head on his shoulder.

Pippa looked at her friend and smiled contentedly. Steph looked so happy when she was with Rusty. They did seem made for each other.

'At least the bombing raids on Plymouth seem to have stopped,' Rusty said, dropping a kiss on his fiancée's head. 'So I can feel my sheila's safe.'

'There were that raid back in February, though,' Steph reminded him. 'Thank goodness we weren't at that dance at the Continental. It's the sort of place we might've been. At least nobody was killed, just a few injured.'

Unlike the bomb in Stoke that same night not far from where my house used to be, Pippa considered. One of the biggest craters seen in the city that yet again had swallowed up homes. In all six people had died that night, a reminder that Hitler hadn't forgotten Plymouth. But looking at the relaxed joy on Steph's face, Pippa didn't want to spoil things by voicing her thoughts, so she popped another chip in her mouth instead.

'At least it looks as if the tide could be turning, in Europe anyway,' Rusty observed, swallowing a mouthful of fish. 'Especially with the Yanks involved now. Things are going well for the Allies in North Africa and Russia's fighting back against her Nazi invaders.'

'Talking of the Americans, when I was in Tavistock last, I heard they're building a massive field hospital up on the edge of the moor at a place called Plaster Down.'

'So you think they might be planning on moving a whole load of GIs into the area?'

'I guess so. Something must be afoot anyway, like. But I don't see the war being over for ages yet,' Pippa concluded despondently.

'Little ray of sunshine,' she heard Jack murmur.

She sighed. Yes, she hated to admit it, but Jack was right. Of course, he didn't know that she was becoming more and more anxious over a certain merchant seaman she hadn't heard from again yet, and neither had his family. The worry burrowed like a little worm at the back of her mind, even if she kept telling herself that she hardly knew Duncan. Yet she couldn't help herself. But just now she should turn the conversation towards happier thoughts.

'So, have you two love birds decided on a date yet?' she asked merrily.

'I still want to get my nursing qualifications first,' Steph assured her. 'Then maybe once I'm married, if I have to leave nursing proper, I can get some private nursing or work in a nursing home. Don't you fret none. I'll tell you as soon as we've set a date. You will be my chief bridesmaid, after all.'

Pippa felt her spirits soar. 'Oh, yes, I'd be honoured!' she cried delightedly.

'And Jack's going to be my best man,' Rusty grinned.

'Oh, our special day's going to be such fun!'

Pippa felt her face shining with happiness for her friend, but for her, it was tinged with sadness. 'I will miss you on the wards, though. It's been such fun being back together on gynae these last few months.'

'Yes, but you're moving on to Theatre next week. You've always said you think surgery's what's going to interest you the most. So this is your chance to find out for sure.'

'True enough. But I do wish you were going to be with me. And unfortunately Ruby took great pleasure in telling me yesterday that she'll be with me,' Pippa groaned. 'I thought I might've shaken her off, at last. But Sister Tutor had other plans.'

'Don't blame our lovely Sister Honeywell. She doesn't know about Ruby's vendetta against you.'

'No, I don't. I just hope Ruby's grown up a bit and lets bygones be bygones. But talking of the hospital, we'd better get moving as soon as we've finished eating. We're due back on duty at four o'clock.'

'Pity, with Jack and me having the rest of the afternoon off,' Rusty said. 'But we'll walk you to your bus stop.'

There were nods of agreement and smiles all round. Five minutes later, they were all making their way back towards the devastated centre of the city and the bus stop. Steph and Rusty walked in front along the narrow pavement, and Pippa couldn't help noticing how lovingly they held hands. And somehow a vision swam into her mind of her holding hands with a tall man in Merchant Navy uniform with a shock of dark blond hair and shining hazel eyes.

***

What the blazes was that? Pippa was dragged from her sleep. She hadn't heard the moaning shriek for so long that she thought she must just be dreaming and turned over, ready to return to her deep slumber. But the all too familiar droning wail penetrated her brain and she came to, realising she wasn't dreaming after all.

'Oh, Lord,' she heard Steph groan from the other bed. 'I thought we were done with all that.'

'Apparently not,' Pippa sighed. 'But let's just wait and see what happens. It could well be a false alarm and the all-clear'll go in a few minutes and we can get back to our beauty sleep.'

'Well, we could all do with that. I'm shattered.'

Pippa smiled to herself as she snuggled down beneath the blankets again. It would have been a different story if Steph had just returned from being out on the razzle with Rusty. She'd have been full of beans, then! Let it please just be a false alarm and she could just go back to sleep.

Five minutes later her hopes crumbled when they heard the whine of an engine tearing across the city. A pathfinder flying low and fast, dropping flares for the bombers that would soon follow. A sinking feeling in her stomach made Pippa sit up in bed.

'Here we go again,' she mumbled.

Scarcely had the sound of the lighter aircraft receded than the thrumming roar of the heavy bombers resounded through the June night air. This was for real. And from the terrific sound of it there must have been about twenty or so of the deadly machines streaking through the sky. And they were dropping their bombs close.

Steph jumped out of her bed and came to huddle with Pippa in hers. They clung to each other, wincing at each tremendous explosion. Despite the blackout curtain, the room flickered with flashes of light from the full power of the new rocket defences the city now possessed, the night sky alive with tracers and exploding shells, and the screaming of falling bombs and other debris. From the way the building shook and the deafening bangs and crashes, the area all around was the target. Oh, dear God.

It seemed the longest half hour of their lives, but at last the droning lessened as the attackers receded and the all-clear sounded, only to be replaced by the clanking of fire engines and ambulance bells. In the gloom, the two girls looked at each other, knowing what the other was thinking. How could they go back to sleep? Without a word, they clambered out of bed and reached for their uniforms.

In Casualty, the staff were preparing for the arrival of the dead and injured. The explosions had sounded really close, so the casualties would come to them and the neighbouring Prince of Wales, being the two nearest hospitals. It would take some time for the victims to arrive, some having to be dug out from beneath collapsed buildings. Doubtless there would be burns cases as well.

Remarkably, Ruby had turned up, bleary-eyed and her cap awry.

'Nurse Saundercock, go and straighten yourself up, and then you and Nurse Luscombe should get yourselves along to the theatres as that's where you're currently on duty,' the night sister instructed. 'At the moment, you'll be more use preparing for operations. We have plenty of volunteers here. Nurse Chappel, come with me.'

Pippa needed no more telling. Gone was her tiredness at having been woken when she'd only had a few hours' sleep, and instead, eager adrenaline was rushing around her body. She was loving her time in Theatre. She'd told Steph on more than one occasion that was where she felt her vocation lay. So, she and Ruby were only what were known as the *dirty nurses*, but Pippa had known from her very first day that she wanted to be a theatre sister.

Their job as probationers was to wash down with disinfectant the walls, floor, operating table, trolleys, cabinets, lights, gas cylinders, in fact every inch of surface and artefact. They assisted the sister in making sure everything that would be needed was to hand, and in sterilising all the equipment including surgeons' gloves which then had to be dusted inside with sterilising powder. Scrubbed-up, masked and gowned themselves, they had to assist the surgeons and anaesthetists into their gowns, masks and even their gloves, holding them open at the cuff so that the consultants could put them on without touching the outsides. During the operations, without getting in the way, they had to mop the surgeon's sweating brow, and be ready with sterilised bowls to take the used instruments, bloodied swabs and anything that was removed from the patient's body to be inspected later. Finally, when each operation was over, they had to clear everything away and disinfect all over again, ready for the next one.

Pippa had attended all sorts of surgery, everything from plating together badly broken bones, tonsillectomies and hysterectomies, to the removal of tumours, appendectomies and even surgery for a cranial tamponade. Although as dirty nurse, she couldn't see directly what the surgeons were performing, she always listened and observed as much as she possibly could. It was fascinating, the cutting edge of modern medicine, and sometimes a life and death situation where the surgeon's skill saved the patient's life.

'There's a staff nurse on her way, but in the meantime, Nurse Saundercock, you will prepare Theatre One, and Nurse

Luscombe, Theatre Two,' the sister instructed. Then, lowering her voice, she whispered to Pippa, 'I can trust you to do it all properly, but I'll just keep an eye on Nurse Saundercock next door if you can get on here.'

'Yes, Sister,' Pippa answered as she went to get on with her tasks, her heart swelling with pride that she was trusted to carry out such important work unsupervised. An aseptic theatre was just as important as the surgery itself. Even the fact that she saw Ruby, who must have heard the sister's words after all, glaring at her daggers didn't diminish her sense of pride.

At last, all was ready and they just had to wait. Sure enough, it wasn't long before surgeons and patients began to arrive. Pippa waited to be instructed with a heightened feeling of anticipation. Of course, she wished the poor souls hadn't been injured in the first place, but she was there to do her small bit to put them back together.

'Compound arm fracture in Theatre One, Nurse Sandercock,' the sister directed as two trolleys bearing semi-anaesthetised patients arrived together. 'Punctured lung in Theatre Two, Nurse Luscombe.'

'Why d'you always get the best cases?' Ruby murmured under her breath as she went off.

Oh, for heaven's sake! What was *wrong* with the girl? But as Pippa attended the procedure in her theatre, all thoughts about Ruby dissipated as she heard the rush of breath as the patient's lung was drained of fluid and the woman began to breathe normally again. Both she and the patient with the broken arm had just been taken away back to a ward when the doors to the theatre prep room crashed open and Pippa's pulse jumped a beat as Doctor Curnock rushed in alongside a trolley with a male patient whose face was as white as a sheet, his brow cold and clammy.

'Severe abdominal crush injury,' he announced, before disappearing again.

Mr Hathaway, the surgeon who dealt with internal cases, picked up the clipboard at the bottom of the trolley, a deep frown on his face as he glanced at it.

'Right, it's going to be all hands on deck for this one. Mr Stubbs, may I have your assistance? Mr Hobman on anaesthetics. Sister, you and staff, and both your nurses.'

All was calm pandemonium, Pippa thought as she got to work, even if that was a contradiction in terms, everybody doing what was needed as orderly yet swiftly as possible. There was no time to waste if they were going to save the man's life, yet no mistake must be made. When all was prepared, Pippa stood back with her empty bowl, Ruby behind her with a second dish, while the sister and staff handed the surgeons whatever instruments and swabs they needed.

'Well, this chap's going to have to manage without a spleen and part of his liver, though that'll regenerate,' Mr Hathaway announced slowly as he inspected the opened abdomen. 'There's a tear in his stomach and I'm going to have to remove part of his small intestine that's damaged beyond repair, then I think we're okay. Going to be touch and go, mind. Now, is everyone all right? You nurses?' he asked, glancing briefly at Pippa and Ruby.

'Yes, sir,' Pippa answered, hearing a muttering from Ruby. When she looked over her shoulder, Ruby was looking a little green, but standing behind her, she wouldn't need to see anything and would only need to hold out the empty dish without looking into the open operation site.

With several procedures in one, progress was slow and laborious, but Pippa was all eyes and ears. She it was who took away the spleen and kept an eye on the surgeon's brow in case it needed wiping. Ruby did her bit, too. Glancing at the clock, the operation was taking a long time and twice had to be interrupted when the anaesthetist was concerned about the patient's blood pressure, but at long last, Mr Hathaway was satisfied and announced he was about to close up the patient's stomach.

'Swab check,' Sister announced.

Standing back at one of *dirty* trolleys, Pippa began to count. Oh, no! A thrill of horror ricocheted through her and her blood turned to ice.

'Wait, we're one short!' she squealed. 'Let me recount!'

'Useless nurse!' Mr Hathaway fumed. 'Now hurry up!'

Pippa's heart was beating like a sledge hammer. No! How could she have miscounted? She counted again, moving each bloodied swab to one side as she counted. Still one missing!

'Oh, no, I'm so sorry, but we're one short,' she had to admit, shame flaring hot in her cheeks.

'Oh, for God's sake, I'm going to have open everything up again! He could die because of you!'

Hot tears scorched at the back of Pippa's eyes. No! How could she have made such a terrible mistake? And then . . . thank God!

'Oh, it's all right, I've found it! It's on the floor!'

'Well, pick it up quickly, girl, and then get out of my theatre!'

Pippa swiftly bent to retrieve the swab with some used forceps and placing it back on the counting tray, used the clean swab the sister passed her to wipe the floor before fleeing the theatre. As she did so, she noticed the nasty smirk on Ruby's face. All became clear. She knew she hadn't dropped the swab. She would have known. It was Ruby, wasn't it, while her back was turned as she was concentrating on the operation? Ruby would have known she'd be in severe trouble.

Good Lord, her career could be in ruins! She would never be trusted again! Hurrying out through the theatre doors, she stripped off her gloves, mask and gown, and burst into tears of anguish and frustration.

* * *

'You're just going to have to tell them about Ruby,' Steph insisted firmly as Pippa tidied her uniform ready to answer her summons to Matron's office.

'Oh, but how can I?' Pippa groaned, rolling her head back as if to distance herself from the present. 'It'd be her word against mine. It'd just sound so preposterous and I have no proof.'

'Of course you do.' Steph took Pippa utterly by surprise as she yanked open Pippa's undies drawer and pulled out the piece of paper hidden there. 'The poem. Look, it's actually signed by that Archie fellow. You said yourself you were the only blond on the ward, so it was clear he meant you.'

'Oh.' It was a long, drawn-out moan. 'It'd be like telling tales, and there's no way they'd believe me.'

'Well, *make* them believe you, kiddo, because you and I know the truth. Now, promise me!'

Pippa's face screwed up with anxiety. She really didn't know what to do. What was the right thing to do.

'Well, all right,' she relented. 'If it really comes to it,' she said, taking the paper and slipping it into her pocket.

'Promise?' Steph repeated, and when Pippa reluctantly nodded, she hugged her and wished her good luck.

A few minutes later, Pippa was standing outside Matron's office, heart thundering so hard she felt it might break out of her chest. With trembling hand, she knocked on the door, and when Matron's voice replied, she went inside, feeling weak at the knees. Sister Tutor Honeywell was sat at the side of Matron's desk, while Matron herself eyed Pippa as if she was something the cat had dragged in.

'I'm sure you know why I called you,' she began sternly.

'Yes, Matron,' Pippa just about managed to reply, her mouth was so dry.

'The incident in Theatre yesterday was not your only misdemeanour but it was the most serious,' Matron continued. 'If a swab had been left inside or if Mr Hathaway had needed to go in again to retrieve it, the patient could well have died. It's still touch and go with him as it is. Now, you have always been top of your set both in exams and in your assessment on the wards with the ability to be one of our top nurses. Sister Tutor here had high hopes of you. Yet recently your conduct has been not only lax but disobedient. I know you had some personal tragedies to contend with near the beginning of your training, but you should have put those behind you by now. You're not far away from your finals, of course,' she said, glancing down at the file open on her desk.

Pippa could have wept. She was going to be made to repeat a year, wasn't she? And all because of that vixen, Ruby.

'Well, I'm sorry,' Matron went on fiercely. 'But I cannot have a nurse like you in my hospital. You will leave your probationer course with immediate effect, and I will see to it that no other hospital will admit you ever again. You are a liability and a danger to your patients.'

Pippa stared at her. Her senses reeled, and she rocked on her feet, almost swaying backwards. No. She couldn't believe her ears. Everything she'd worked so hard for, the only job she'd ever wanted to do, to be whipped away from her. Humiliation, disbelief erupted inside her, choking her, and she turned begging eyes on Sister Honeywell. But the good Sister Tutor could only reply with a look of sympathetic agreement.

'B-but . . .' Pippa stammered, but she was so shocked she could barely speak.

'You will go with Sister Tutor to collect your ration book and all other necessities and then you will pack your bags and leave.'

Pippa's mouth fell open but she couldn't speak. No chance to say goodbye to her colleagues. To Steph? And then Steph's words sprang into her brain. The promise she'd made to her dear friend.

'I have something to say,' she announced, her voice gaining strength as she spoke. 'On each occasion, Ruby — Nurse Saundercock — was involved. When I broke the thermometer on the children's ward, I actually didn't. I'd replaced it on the wall. I believe that while I was on my knees getting a book for young Rick Dashper out of his locker, Nurse Saundercock took it out and put it on the edge of the locker so that it would get knocked off and I'd get the blame.'

Pippa's gaze swept from Matron to Sister Tutor's face. Amanda Honeywell leaned forward enquiringly, her expression eager. Encouraged, Pippa went on, 'That same day, she tried to trick me into giving a little diabetic girl Ovaltine, only I realised in time. And then, I mean I know leaving the window open for Steph — Nurse Chappel — was breaking the rules and I deserved to be punished for it, but it was Ruby who told on us, and I know for a fact that she'd done the same thing often enough so that she could stay out later with her fiancé.'

'Fiancé?' Sister Tutor questioned. 'I wasn't aware that Nurse Saundercock was engaged.'

'Well, she was. But she isn't any longer. And that's the whole point. His name's Archie Yelland and he was a patient when we were on Men's Surgical, an emergency appendectomy. I know I should have reported it, but they both begged me not to. Anyway, he developed a thing for me. Asked me out. I refused, of course. And I thought that was that. But apparently afterwards he said his feelings for me made him realise he didn't really love Ruby — Nurse Saundercock — and he broke off the engagement. And ever since, she's had it in for me, like. And that business in Theatre yesterday, it was Ruby who deliberately dropped the swab on the floor, not me. I would never have been so careless.'

Both Matron and Sister Honeywell looked amazed and exchanged glances. 'And how do we know you're not just making this up?' Matron asked.

'You can contact Mr Yelland and he'll confirm it. And here.' She thrust her hand in her pocket and held out the sheet of paper. 'He wrote this and gave it to me. If you look up the duty rotas, you'll find I was the only fair-haired nurse on the ward at the time. I was going to throw it away but Nurse Chappel thought it rather sweet and said I should keep it.'

'Well,' Matron hesitated. 'We shall certainly look into this. And in the meantime, Nurse Luscombe, I suggest you hurry along to Theatre. You'll be late on duty, but I would ask you to send Nurse Saundercock to me immediately.'

'Yes, Matron. Thank you, Matron, thank you, Sister Tutor.'

'Well I never,' she heard Amanda Honeywell comment as she closed the door.

***

'Ruby's gone!' Steph chortled that evening, dancing Pippa round in circles. 'Gone for good. We'll never need to see her sly little face again!'

Pippa nodded, so relieved after her interview in Matron's office that she was ready to cry. She gave a wry, watery smile. She prayed Steph was right. Yet all the incidents with Ruby had left her so upset, she felt really unsettled. There was only one thing for it. An hour or so of study before she turned in. Finals were only a couple of months away.

CHAPTER TWENTY-FOUR

'Congratulations again, my darling,' Adeline crooned as Pippa gazed down at her shiny nurse's belt buckle.

'Oh, thank you so much, Mum,' Pippa breathed.

'You deserve it after all your hard work. Deborah, you know, Elliott's daughter-in-law, helped me choose it.'

'It's beautiful, Mum. When I go back, I'll take it to the uniform room and they'll attach it to my new staff nurse belt. And look, let me show you my City Hospital nurses' badge. I'll be wearing it on my collar. And when I go back, I'll have a brand-new uniform, as well. Plain mid-blue and a veil cap.'

'You'll look proper grand, cheel!' Bea put in, adding her congratulations. 'We'm all so proud of you!'

Pippa glanced around the living room. All her dear friends were there to welcome her back. A warm aura of contentment engulfed her, soothing away every memory of the feud with Ruby and all the tensions of her final exams. She was a qualified state registered nurse now and nothing could take that away from her.

'I just wish you weren't in Plymouth with the raids still going on,' Adeline sighed.

'I know, Mum,' Pippa answered gently. 'But we have only had two real raids the whole year.'

'But both times the hospital had a lucky escape,' her mum insisted. 'That raid in June were centred on Mannamead and Mutley, just down the road from you.'

'You know half the bombs the Germans are dropping aren't exploding?' Don put in. 'Keeping the bomb disposal units busy, so I've heard.'

'That's as maybe, but they can still cause a lot of damage and kill people,' Adeline protested. 'And what if they had exploded? One fell right outside the City Hospital in that second heavy raid in August. Heaven knows what would've happened if it had gone off! And one ward were completely burnt out from an incendiary, weren't it?'

Reluctantly, Pippa nodded her confirmation. That night had certainly been a terrifying one, the worst raid they'd had for over two years. By then, Pippa had been on a geriatric ward but had gone across to help in Casualty. Over the entire city, it was estimated over a hundred and fifty people had been injured, some seriously, and forty odd killed. Once again, the civilian population had taken the brunt of the attack, and Pippa and Steph had seen some appalling injuries inflicted on innocent people.

'Tell you what, though,' she neatly changed the subject. 'Tavistock's heaving with American troops, isn't it? I didn't realise how many. I saw jeeps and transport lorries and even a tank on my way here. D'you think that—?'

'It's the start of something, yes,' Don nodded gravely. 'They started arriving in the summer but I'm sure there's many more to come. The camp up on Plaster Down is massive by all accounts. A huge, fully equipped hospital, stores, a barber's shop, even a full-sized cinema. And there's smaller camps elsewhere around here. One up on Whitchurch Down, for instance. And it's rumoured, all over the South West. No one knows what's being planned, of course, but it's going to be big when it comes.'

'Yes, well,' Miss Primrose put in, 'look how the Allies took Sicily and are fighting their way up through Italy from the south now Mussolini's gone and Italy's surrendered.'

'Churchill's idea to hit the Axis powers in the so-called soft underbelly, wasn't it?'

'Theoretically. The Germans are resisting like hell, mind, and the fighting's been atrocious. I expect you've seen it in the *Pathé News* at the cinema. But if the Allies are gradually succeeding, then perhaps all these GIs are amassing for an attack from a different direction. But,' Don tapped the side of his nose. 'We shouldn't speculate.'

'Well, it can't come soon enough for me,' Bea declared. 'I just want to go back to not being scared for my Duncan.'

The sudden anguished outburst from the good lady who normally seemed to take everything in her stride shook them all. For a second or two, there was a shocked, sympathetic silence, then Pippa thought of a way to ease her distress. But that was often part of her job, wasn't it, to think of some comforting words to utter?

'I've had several letters from him recently,' she said brightly. 'After that one he left here for me at Christmas, I didn't hear for months, and then suddenly they all arrived at once. And I had another one only last week.'

'Oh, yes!' Bea perked up. 'What did he say? The last one we got were about six weeks ago.'

Pippa gave her a broad, reassuring smile as she popped the belt buckle back in its little box and, accepting the cup of tea Sylvie offered her, sat down on the settee. 'He's well,' she said, taking a quick sip of her drink. 'And it still being summer when he wrote it, he says the weather's been good. Too hot, sometimes. He talks a lot about all of you. And about growing up in Plymouth. How he was always escaping down to Sutton Harbour, talking to all the old fishermen as they mended their nets and trying to persuade them to take him out on a fishing trip. They always refused without your permission, of course. But he says once he managed to stow away and there was a brave old uproar when he was discovered.'

'There were that!' Bea's face moved into a half fond, half reprimanding smile. 'The mate wanted to return to port, but the skipper insisted they went on with the trip. Thought he'd teach the little nipper a lesson and put him to work. All it did were make him more keen to go to sea. Three days they were gone. I were beside mesel' with worry.'

'I'm sure you were!' Pippa sympathised.

'Us can look back on it now and maybe smile at his determination, but it weren't funny at the time. He's a good un is our Duncan, but I could've throttled him just then.'

Pippa chuckled ruefully as the conversation took a different direction and she went back to her tea. Some of the stories Duncan had related to her in his letters were amusing and sometimes quite revealing. She almost wondered if they were getting to know each other better by letter than if their relationship had been solely in person. In her letters to him, she related all sorts of little incidents of her childhood but also of her nurses' training. She might have only spent a few days with him physically, but through their letters, she really felt as if she was getting to know him like an old friend.

While general chatter went on around her, her eyes were drawn to the photographs on the mantelpiece. There was one of Duncan in naval uniform but with his hat held under his arm. She guessed it must've been taken a few years back as he looked much younger, but that kindness still radiated from his eyes. How she prayed he'd survive the war, for her own sake as well as Bea's and the family. There couldn't be any future for them with their differing careers, but she hoped they could always be friends.

'Deborah's throwing a little tea party for you on Sunday,' she realised her mum was telling her. 'Being a qualified nurse herself, she said you deserved one. And we didn't have the chance to celebrate your twenty-first, of course. But it won't be quite as jolly an affair as some of Deborah's do's. I told you their nephew, Dick, were killed back in the summer, didn't I? Ship blown up and all hands lost. Terrible business.'

Pippa felt her heart sink. Yes, her mum had told her. She'd never met him, of course, but it still affected you if you knew someone's family.

'Must be awful for them,' she murmured sadly, for didn't she and her mum know what it was to lose someone so close to you through the horrors of war?

'Well, anyway,' Adeline went on more sombrely, 'we've all pooled our rations and we're going to contribute towards it as well, so it's going to be a joint affair.'

'Really?' Pippa was overwhelmed. 'Oh, that's so kind of everyone. Thank you all so much. I must pop in and see Deborah a bit later on.'

Her gaze swept about the room at all the familiar faces beaming at her. If it hadn't been for the war and the kindness of strangers, she'd never have met them or the Franfield family next-door but one. Of course, if only she had the power to turn back the clock and make it that her beloved dad hadn't been killed and their home destroyed, she'd do so like a shot. But she couldn't, and so she thanked God that these lovely, generous people had come into her life.

* * *

'So, have you decided yet if you want to specialise in any particular field?' Elliott enquired during a quieter moment on the Sunday afternoon.

As luck would have it, the late September weather had decided to be kind and the tea party was taking place out in the large back garden. Just as well, Pippa chuckled to herself, with the entire Chollacott brood rushing about, together with the four Franfield children. It would have been chaos if they'd had to hold it indoors, although the two eldest, Edwin and Susie, were each keeping a stern eye on their younger siblings, Pippa noticed with an amused smile.

'Yes, I have,' she replied, turning her attention back to Elliott. 'I want to be a theatre sister when I have enough experience and the opportunity arises. I'm on Orthopaedics at the moment which is the next best thing, but I'm waiting for a staff nurse post to come up in Theatre.'

'Could you not look elsewhere?'

'I'm supposed to stay on at the City for a year after qualifying,' she explained, taking a sip of the sherry the Franfields had supplied. 'And it's all nicely familiar. Besides, I wouldn't want to leave my friend, Steph, behind. She qualified at the same time, you see.'

'But I thought you said she's getting married? To an Australian airman I think you said? So she'd have to leave nursing.'

'Well done for remembering,' Pippa smiled. 'Yes, she is, but they haven't set a date yet. Rusty wants them to get married straight away, but Steph wants to get a bit more experience so that she can hopefully get some private nursing work or something once she's married. So they're thinking of a spring wedding.'

'Ah,' the elderly doctor nodded. 'And by then you might have got a post in Theatre.'

'Well, if not by the time my year's up, then I'll look elsewhere.'

'I think your mother would like you to be nearer her,' he said kindly. 'She puts a brave face on it, but she misses you. Perhaps you'd consider coming to work here at the cottage hospital?'

Pippa nodded thoughtfully. 'Yes, it's a possibility. It certainly sounds like a nice set-up. But talking of brave faces, I haven't seen you all since, but I'm terribly sorry about your grandson.'

The old man's expression changed and he suddenly looked haggard. 'Thank you for saying so,' he mumbled. 'It's what you dread, losing a young family member. You wish it was yourself instead. I'm eighty now. I should've gone in his place. Mary's taken it really hard as you might expect. Though she knows what war is all about. She was a fully qualified Red Cross nurse out in France in the last war, you know. Ah, here comes Ling. Let's pretend we were talking about something a bit brighter.'

'Congratulations again!' Elliott's wife beamed as she came over. 'We're all very proud of you, you know.'

'Thank you,' Pippa blushed as Ling threaded her arm through Pippa's. 'It was so kind of Deborah to put this on for me.'

'You deserve it,' the elderly lady smiled. 'Now come along over to the table. I think Elliott wanted to say a few words before we cut the cake. Just a simple thing made with dried egg, I'm afraid, so it won't be very good, and no icing, of course, but it was the best we could do.'

'Oh, I'm sure it'll be great,' Pippa grinned. 'And so kind of everyone.'

'Well, we have to make the best of things, don't we?'

Make the best of things. That was what they all said, with a resilient smile. For what else could you do?

***

'It's been proper grand having you here these last few days,' Adeline declared as they enjoyed a leisurely breakfast around the table after Sharon had left for her new job at Woolworths, dropping Norman and Bernard off to school on her way. Mr and Mrs Robbins had both also left for work and Susie was on a late shift that day, so was catching up on some sleep. Miss Primrose and Miss Polly had volunteered to do the shopping, queuing for whatever was available, so that left Bea, Sylvie and Don around the table, and Lucy sucking on a biscuit in her high chair.

'It's been a lovely rest for me, too,' Pippa agreed, 'but I am looking forward to getting back. As a staff nurse,' she grinned proudly. 'No more studying every spare moment, or going to lectures in my off-duty time. Still have to keep up with everything, mind. Any new drugs or what have you. And I might be assisting probationers in their practicals. But my spare time'll be much more my own, so with luck, I should be able to come and visit more often.'

'That'd be master grand!' Her mum beamed. 'I miss you so much in between your visits, like.'

'I know, Mum. And I miss you, too.'

Pippa glanced around the table. Yes, she missed her mum and all her new family here, as well. She hadn't mentioned Elliott's idea that one day, she might be able to work at Tavistock's Cottage Hospital. She didn't want to get her mum's hopes up. It was just an idea for the future, and while Steph was still around, she'd be torn between her mum and leaving her dear friend.

Her thoughts were interrupted by the front door bell ringing. 'I'll go,' she offered, and jumped up before anyone else could. She wondered who it might be as it was unusual to get a caller. Maybe it was Elliott popped round, as he did on occasion.

She opened the door. A young lad in uniform. Holding a telegram.

Her heart was seized with panic. Telegrams could only mean bad news. She felt her pulse quicken as she took the flimsy envelope from the boy's hand.

'Any reply, miss?'

'O-oh,' she mumbled. 'It's not for me. I'll take it inside.'

'Then I'll wait till you comes back.'

'Y-yes. Thank you.'

She went back inside, wrapped in her own tortured thoughts. There'd been no raid over Plymouth, so it couldn't be Leonard or Ernie. And if one of them had had an accident on the railway, the other would have rung. No. It had to be Duncan. Time fractured, everything around her dropping away. She knew then how much he meant to her.

'It's a telegram. Addressed to Len,' she faltered, stepping back into the living room.

Don at once stood up, suddenly ashen. 'Perhaps I'd better open it,' he said grimly.

Pippa saw the expectant smile slide from Bea's face as she nodded her agreement, too choked to speak. Oh, Lord.

Don tore open the envelope, read it, and dropped down in his seat. He pushed the telegram in front of Bea without saying a word. Pippa watched Bea's eyes move along the words, dread trundling through her own body as she leaned over Bea's shoulder.

SHIP UNDER ATTACK STOP REGRET 2ND OFF CHOLLACOTT SEVERELY WOUNDED EXPECT WORST

Black sorrow cut into Pippa's heart. Poor, generous-hearted Bea and all her family. A leaden weight dropped down inside Pippa. Please, no. Not Duncan.

For a few moments, an impenetrable silence smothered everyone in the room. Bea broke it with a cry of anguish.

'What the hell do that mean?' she wailed.

'I . . . I don't know,' Don finally gulped. 'I'll try ringing the shipping line offices. They might know more.'

'And will you speak to the telegram boy?' Pippa put in, suddenly remembering the young lad on the doorstep. 'He's waiting to see if there's a reply.'

She caught Don's sharp nod as he exited the room in a flash, leaving the four women locked in a fog of shock. None of them spoke a word, but gathered in a cluster around Bea, holding her hand, squeezing her arm, as they heard Don's voice on the telephone out in the hall. Pippa found herself too numb to think of anything useful to say, any words of comfort, for her own heart was breaking.

It must have been a good ten minutes before Don returned, shaking his head. 'That really is all they know at this point,' he announced grimly. 'We've just got to sit and wait. All they know is that the ship didn't go down, so there's still hope.'

'I suppose that's summat,' Bea barely whispered.

'I'm so sorry,' Pippa barely breathed at last. 'Let's pray he'll be all right. I wish I could stay longer, but I'm back on duty tomorrow and I've got to sort out my uniform. But you will let me know the minute you have any news, won't you?'

'Bless you, cheel,' Bea muttered with a gut-wrenching sigh. 'Of course we will.'

Pippa nodded, biting hard on her bottom lip as she left the room, and mounted the stairs to the little room she shared with her mum. She only had a few things to pack, but in truth, she needed a few moments alone. It was like when her father had died. She felt strangely empty, but for the crushing fear inside her. Please, *please*, let Duncan live. For his own sake, his family's sake. And for her sake.

Not long after, she was walking into the town centre in the direction of Tavistock South Station. In the last few days, she'd become accustomed to all the GIs milling around the streets, on foot or in jeeps, and sometimes catching a glimpse of someone obviously of higher rank. Don was right. They must be building up to something big. But what? And when? It could take months to plan something as huge as everyone felt it might be. And with autumn on its way, was it a sensible time to begin action? But whatever it was, whenever it was planned for, it could already be too late for Duncan.

She climbed the hill to the station, acknowledging with a faint smile the American soldiers who politely doffed their caps at her. How could they know the anguish that was churning in her stomach — or the future that lay ahead for any of them?

CHAPTER TWENTY-FIVE

Pippa sat at the sister's desk in Women's Orthopaedic by the dim light of the night lamp. There was no night sister available, so she had been left in charge. She had notes to copy up, order forms to fill out, but little nursing to carry out as most of the patients slept through the night. There hadn't been any operations for a few days, so other than one or two who woke needing pain medication or who were due an M and B tablet against infection, there was little for her to do. Anyone needing to be taken to the bathroom or requesting a bedpan was dealt with by the lower ranking nurse.

But there were other demons afoot, and Pippa almost wished she had more to do than oversee the ward and be there just in case. It was seven weeks since her visit home to Tavistock, and she felt she'd been living under a cloud. There was still no news of Duncan. She supposed the ship's captain had greater worries than just one injured officer, but the uncertainty was killing her. She kept reminding herself how dreadful communications were, and just clung to the thought that she was sure they'd have been informed if . . . if he hadn't made it. What poor Bea and her family were going through, she dared not imagine.

Five o'clock in the morning. Another hour and it would be time to wake the patients gently with a cup of tea. The younger nurse couldn't do it all on her own, and Pippa would be grateful for something to occupy her. Greeting her charges, enquiring how they felt this morning and doing the first obs round of the day was something to look forward to, especially taking everyone's blood pressure that she was now fully qualified to do.

Her spirits dropped like lead as the dreaded wail echoed out across the city. It was mid-November, three months since the last attack in August. Everyone thought the raids must be over now especially with the Germans fully occupied in Italy and Russia as well as continuing to rule all the occupied countries, but apparently not.

Pippa sighed heavily. The ward was her responsibility and she needed to do her best for everyone. She had some patients in traction and unable to be moved, but some of the walking wounded could be taken down to the basement. Some of the women were already groaning as they were wakened from their sleep by the siren, while others had to be roused and got into dressing gowns and slippers. Pippa was grateful when a couple of the day nurses arrived to help with the chaos.

The ward seemed eerily quiet once everyone who could be had been evacuated. Pippa stayed with the remainder, issuing cups of tea and reassurance, despite the numerous explosions, a huge one that sounded quite close while most were further away. By the sounds of it, there were many fewer unexploded bombs than on previous raids that year. Pippa could imagine her ward could be overflowing with wounded by the time she came back on duty that evening.

By seven o'clock, the all-clear had sounded and all patients were back in their rightful place. Pippa tried to catch up with the morning routine, but the day sister was quite understanding that not every task had been completed due to the *unforeseen circumstances*. Pippa stayed on late to catch up, managed to grab a late breakfast in the dining room, and then made her way, exhausted, to her room. Now they were staff nurses, they'd been moved to a separate accommodation block where they had individual rooms. It seemed strange not sharing with Steph anymore after three years of being bosom pals, but Steph occupied the room directly opposite, so they were near enough to share as much time as possible with each other. Amazingly, Steph had taken up a post on Women's Medical with the harridan Sister Pudifoot. To her delight and surprise, Sister Pudifoot had turned out to be far less of a tartar to her qualified staff nurses and even seemed to appreciate what a good nurse Steph was. Or was it that in her happy state, Steph was more tolerant of Sister Pudifoot's strict discipline?

Pippa hung up her uniform and changing into her pyjamas, dived into bed. She closed her eyes, trying to block out all her thoughts. She always found it hard sleeping during the day when she was on night duty, but she was so tired after the extra-long shift as she helped to settle the ward down after the alert, that she soon felt herself drifting off.

Then— what the hell was that? A stray bomb? No, it was more like a fusillade of gunfire. She dragged herself from sleep, dread racing round her body. As she came to, she realised it was none of those things, but someone knocking on her door.

She glanced at her clock. Ten past twelve. Oh, goodness, whoever it was had better have a jolly good reason for waking her. Grabbing her dressing gown, Pippa opened the door a crack and peering out, saw it was the almoner standing there.

'So sorry to wake you, Staff Nurse Luscombe,' the older woman apologised, 'but there's a telegram for you. We thought we'd better . . . The boy's waiting to see if there's a reply.'

'Oh,' Pippa mumbled, taking the telegram from the woman's hand.

'I'll wait out here.'

Pippa nodded as she shut the door. A telegram. Oh, God. She felt as if her body had collapsed in on itself and dropped down on to the end of the bed. She could feel her heart vibrating in her chest as she stared down at the telegram in her shaking hands. She didn't want to open it. But she had to. The woman was waiting. The telegram boy was waiting.

Here goes. She ripped it open.

DUNCAN ALIVE HOSPITAL MALTA STOP DON

The tension pulsed down through her core, then ratcheted up again. What did that mean . . . But he was alive, wasn't he!

She peeled herself from the bed and opened the door.

'Thank you,' she said to the almoner. 'Please tell the boy there's no reply.'

'Oh, dear.' The woman's brow creased into a concerned frown. 'I hope it's not . . .'

'No, no,' Pippa assured her. 'If anything, it's good news.'

'Oh, good. Well, I'll leave you to it. And apologies again for waking you.'

'Not at all. You did the right thing.'

'Well, I'll let you get back to sleep now.'

Back to sleep? She must be joking! Pippa turned back into the room, reaching immediately for her civilian clothes. If only they were allowed to use a hospital phone, but she'd need to be a sister before she could do that. It was still the telephone box on the street outside the main gates. She grabbed her purse and opened it. At least she had the right change.

A quarter of an hour later she was back in her room, her mind all upside down. If only she'd been able to find out more. Apparently, Don had once again rung the shipping company on Bea's behalf, but they had little more knowledge to reveal. Duncan had been so seriously wounded that it was thought unlikely he'd survive. But he had, and was now recuperating in hospital in Malta.

Poor Bea, she'd been in tears as she'd spoken to Pippa on the phone. Tears of what, it was hard to say. Relief, sadness, but maybe the fear of not knowing. Pippa felt exactly the same.

Would Duncan make a full recovery, or would his injuries be life-changing? He could be horribly burnt. God knows, Pippa had seen enough horrific results of both explosives and fires. The ship had survived the attack, limped into Valetta, was all the shipping company were prepared to say. Better than the alternative, Pippa supposed. At least they'd have been able to give Duncan some sort of medical care. Hopefully they had, anyway.

Strong, kind Duncan with his gentle sense of humour and those soft, caring eyes. She could see his handsome face smiling at her now, remembered the thrill that had fizzed through her as he'd looked at her. There was no room in her life for love. But there was room enough in her heart.

She felt she was tottering on the brink of confusion. She'd never wanted to fall in love. But had she? How could she when she hardly knew him? But she couldn't deny there was something inside her that was breaking. It felt so ridiculous, she couldn't tell anyone. Not even Steph.

She sank down onto the edge of her bed again, steepled fingers against her lips in contemplation. She couldn't imagine she'd go back to sleep now. All she could do was hope. And offer up a silent prayer.

***

'Good night, Mrs Baines.'

Pippa nodded at the elderly lady who'd become a particular favourite of hers. The poor thing had been thrown across the room by the blast from a nearby bomb in the early morning of the sixteenth of November, and had broken her femur in her fall. She'd been in traction ever since, her old bones expected to take longer to heal than the usual six weeks. It was so hard on the dear old girl, but she never complained and bore it all with a grateful smile. Pippa was back on days now, and though she was run off her feet, she always had a kind word for Mrs Baines. Poor soul was likely to remain in hospital over Christmas.

'Good night, dear,' the old lady smiled back. 'You have a nice evening.'

That would be good, Pippa silently sighed as she turned away. Sister Tutor had asked if she'd mind helping out with a practical session for the current first-year probationers. Pippa liked Amanda Honeywell. She'd been really good to her, and didn't like to say no. She'd have liked to wallow in a nice hot bath — if you could call it wallowing in the statutory five inches that you were allowed — but by the time she'd grabbed some supper in the dining room and helped out with the practical, she'd be ready to fall into bed. She and Steph had arranged to meet up with Geraldine, the nurse in their set who'd had to give up because her poor hands had been allergic to the constant use of Dettol. Now Steph would have to go on her own.

But never mind. Pippa had been told that morning that unless there was another raid resulting in serious orthopaedic injuries, the ward wouldn't be accepting any patients in the run-up to Christmas, and she'd be allowed to go home for the festive period. She couldn't wait! It was three weeks away, but the time couldn't go quickly enough for her.

As she entered the accommodation block to find Steph, she noticed there was an envelope in her pigeon hole. A letter from her mum. That'd cheer her up even more. But when she picked it up, it wasn't her mum's handwriting. It was Duncan's. And her heart leapt into her mouth.

Like much overseas post, it was dog-eared and crumpled. How long ago had it been written? Before or after he was wounded? Would it be his usual informative missive with a little gentle banter, not knowing what was in store? Or would it be *afterwards*, when he'd maybe lost an arm or a leg, or been hideously burnt? Pippa felt sick and her legs wobbled as she stumbled to her room. Should she knock on Steph's door first, seeking her moral support? That would be unfair on her friend who was doubtless titivating herself for her evening out, even if she wasn't meeting up with Rusty. No. It was better if Pippa read the letter alone, and let her emotions run their course before she faced the outside world again.

With trembling hand, she let herself into her room and lowered herself on to the edge of the bed. Deep breaths. Try to calm herself before tearing open the envelope with shaking fingers.

Dear Pippa,

By now I'm sure you'll know that I was injured when our convoy came under attack in the Med. I was one of the lucky ones that the ship's doctor kept alive until we reached our destination of Malta. Then I and a couple of others were rushed to part of the Royal Naval Hospital where a skilled surgeon operated on my wounds. I'd caught shrapnel down my left side. The worst was a piece embedded in my leg above the knee and another in my gut which I guess was the most dangerous. But they managed to patch me up and then the real danger was infection. But I was lucky enough to be given this new wonder drug penicillin which I'm sure you know all about, and I eventually pulled through. When I was considered fit enough, I was moved to a civilian hospital way outside Valetta. I can't tell you exactly where. The places on the island have the strangest names with lots of Qs and Xs and aren't pronounced anything like they're written.

So here I am recovering in hospital and longing to come home. My injuries have put paid to my career at sea. I'm likely to be left with a limp and a weak intestine or something. That you'll understand better than I do myself. I can't say I'm sorry, about my career, I mean. I've seen enough of the sea, especially having been under attack on more than one occasion. I know the tide is turning in the war and we will win in the end, but I'm sick of it and can't wait until they tell me I'm well enough to travel home.

I've written to Mum and Dad and also Gran and Gramps in the hope that one of my letters will get through. So I'd be grateful if and when you receive this, you could let them know in case my letters home don't arrive. As always, very many thanks, and I'll tell you all more details when I see you which I hope won't be long.

Take care my dear Nurse Luscombe or Staff Nurse Luscombe I'm guessing it will be now. I trust congratulations are in order!

With love and best wishes,
Duncan

Pippa sat and stared at the letter, joy sparking through her. Duncan had survived thanks to the skill of a naval surgeon and modern science. Thank God for penicillin! Without it, she knew there would have been little chance he'd have made it. And he'd be coming home for good. Her heart performed a little dance, but then she pulled herself up short. She imagined he'd be brought back on one of the merchant ships of his shipping line, and that, too, could come under attack. It was all a case of chance, a sort of Russian roulette. She just prayed that Duncan got home safely.

And what then? Would they find they liked each other as much as she thought they did from their letters? Duncan's career might be over, but hers was just beginning. Mind you, that was jumping the gun a bit. She shook her head, feeling as if she were on the edge of a precipice. For now, she must put it out of her mind. She needed to get off to the lecture theatre to help with the practical session. She hoped it wouldn't take too long as she then needed to get to the public telephone and let the Chollacotts know the good news if they hadn't already heard it from Duncan themselves.

With a huge sigh, she crossed the corridor to Steph's room to tell her that she'd have to meet Geraldine on her own tonight. And she wouldn't be able to resist telling her about Duncan, too. Mind you, she'd have to brace herself against the teasing words she was sure Steph would have to say about that. Good old Steph! For the umpteenth time, Pippa wondered what she'd do without her!

* * *

'Rusty and I have settled on a date!' Steph crowed gleefully.

'Oh, that's proper grand!'

Pippa gave her friend a big hug. About time, too! Not that she welcomed the news from her own point of view. She was going to miss Steph dreadfully when she had to leave. But a lot of things were going to change once the war was over, weren't they?

'So, when is the big day to be?' she asked enthusiastically, pushing aside the thoughts that spiralled in her head.

'The fifteenth of April,' Steph told her excitedly.

'Is that Easter?'

'No, the Saturday after. We're hoping for St Andrew's — or what's left of it. They're still holding regular services there, even though there's no roof and no windows and the floor's now grassed over. We thought it'd be appropriate as it's the war that brought us together.'

'That's quite a romantic notion,' Pippa agreed, 'but what if it's raining? Or cold? And have you thought what you're going to wear?'

'Well, unless Rusty can pinch some parachute silk which he can't, a new dress is out of the question,' Steph answered, pulling a wry face. 'But my mum's still got hers, so I thought I could maybe bring it up to date a bit, like. I haven't asked her yet, mind. But I'm taking Rusty to meet Mum and Dad on Boxing Day, so I'll ask her then.'

'Bit nervous, are you, about them meeting?'

Steph answered her with a shrug. 'No, not especially. They'll love Rusty, and even if they don't, it doesn't matter. I'm twenty-one, so I don't need their permission. And you know I'm not that close to them anyhow, but I would like their blessing.'

'Yes, of course, I understand that. But, I've just thought, my mum loves knitting and she's master good at it. If she can get hold of enough wool, I'm sure she'd be delighted to knit you a warm cloak or bolero or something to keep out the chill, like. It's all right saying *you've got your love to keep you warm*, but—'

She smiled as Steph giggled at her. 'You know me too well,' her friend chuckled. 'But that sounds a wonderful idea if your mum wouldn't mind. And what about you? I can't expect you to use your clothing coupons to get a bridesmaid's dress even if such a thing could be found. But you look mortal pretty in that blue summer dress you made after you lost everything when your house was bombed.'

'Perfect,' Pippa agreed. 'And I expect Rusty will be in uniform so it'll all look proper grand.'

'He will, yes, and Jack, too, as best man. Rusty's got to get some sort of permission from his commanding officer or someone, I think, but after that, it'll be all systems go! And I'll have to apply for the extra rations for the guests, not that you get much.'

'Allowed up to forty guests, aren't you?'

'Yes, but it'll be much smaller than that.' Steph suddenly grasped hold of Pippa's hands and jumped up and down. 'Oh, Pip, I'm getting so excited! I just can't wait! I just wish I didn't have to leave here. And you.' Pippa noticed her face drop then, and felt her hands being squeezed. 'I'm sorry. There's me behaving like a schoolchild and you worrying over your Duncan.'

Pippa stretched her eyes open wide. 'He's not *my* Duncan. I like him very much, and yes, I am worried about him. And I worry for his family worrying about him, if you see what I mean. They've been so good to Mum and me, they're really like family. But I hardly know Duncan, except through his letters.'

'But you've grown fond of him.'

'Yes, I suppose I have,' Pippa agreed pensively. 'But there's really nothing romantic about it. You know all I want is to be a theatre sister. We've trained so hard over the years, and nothing's going to get in my way.'

'Tell you the thing I'm going to miss most of all this Christmas,' Steph told her ruefully. 'And that's the daft sketches we used to put on for the patients to cheer them up. Supposedly beneath our dignity now we're qualified.'

'Yes, we had some fun doing those, didn't we? But life moves on, doesn't it?'

Yes, it certainly did. Come April, Steph would be a married woman and no longer at the hospital. Soon after that, Pippa herself would have completed her year as a staff nurse at the City and could move on to be a sister anywhere she chose. And what of the war? Would it be over by then? She doubted it. But doubtless Tavistock wasn't the only place in the country where something seemed to be afoot.

Only time would tell.

CHAPTER TWENTY-SIX

Pippa paused for a moment as she stepped down from the train at Tavistock South Station, remembering the day nearly two years previously when she had travelled back to Plymouth with Duncan. Then it had been bitterly cold, heavy snow having fallen overnight. It had made for treacherous conditions underfoot, but the moor had looked magical, coated in white, as the train had chugged its way around the edge. Today was so different. The weather had been exceptionally dry recently, the skies draped in fog that had caused havoc for the RAF, resulting in some tragic losses. The fog wasn't heavy today, but there was a light mist in the air, and as the train's engine inched forward, slowly gathering speed, the steam it belched out billowed in a great cloud that completely enveloped the platform.

Pippa waited patiently for it to clear. She didn't mind a bit. It was good to pause and drink in the delicious sensation of feeling she was home. So, the hospital was where she lived and worked, and she wouldn't have had it any other way. But she'd come to look upon Tavistock as her home. Was that because her mum was living there, and the Chollacotts who she looked upon as family? Maybe. But right now she was so master happy to be back there for Christmas.

She set off down the hill towards the town centre, knowing there was a big smile on her face. A group of American GIs were coming towards her, smart in their pristine uniforms but larking about as only young men let loose for a few hours can.

'You look happy, miss,' one of them said, giving her a mock salute.

How was she supposed to respond to that? So she just nodded and smiled back. Her eyes moved about them, noticing one breaking a square of chocolate from a bar he was carrying. Oo, chocolate. She couldn't remember the last time she'd tasted chocolate. It was almost impossible to get hold of it.

Her gaze must have lingered too long.

'Want some chocolate, miss?' another soldier asked. 'A pretty girl like you should have a treat now and then. Here.' He produced a bar from his pocket and held it out.

Pippa felt herself flush. 'Oh, I couldn't possibly—'

'Course you can. Sure, we're given loads of it,' he drawled. 'Go on. Take it.'

Well, it was too hard to resist, wasn't it? She just hoped he wasn't expecting any favours in return. Cautiously, she held out her hand and took it.

'Thank you,' she murmured. 'I'll share it with the children.' Well, she would, but that should stop him getting any ideas.

'Children? Must be brothers and sisters?'

Oh, Lord. 'Well, sort of . . .'

'How many?'

'Er, five.'

'Come on, guys.' He turned to his comrades. 'Cough up all you've got for this little lady.'

Within seconds, she was festooned with enough chocolate bars to fill a shop, shaking her head in bemusement. 'Oh, I can't carry—'

'Course you can't with your little case. We'll stuff them in your pockets for you. Staying long, are we?'

'Just a few days.'

'There's a dance on at the base on Boxing Day if you're interested. Maybe see ya there? Have a great Christmas!'

With that the group moved on. Pippa stared after them. She needn't have worried.

'Thank you!' she called out, and a couple of them turned round and saluted again before carrying on into the mist.

Pippa found a smile on her lips as she crossed over Abbey Bridge towards the Town Hall. How very kind. She'd heard tales of the Americans' generosity and now she'd experienced it for herself. The place was teaming with even more of them than ever. It was Christmas Eve so she presumed they'd been allowed to come into the town en masse to enjoy themselves, even if they had so many facilities such as a full-sized cinema at the base. They might have been larking about and having fun, but there was no rowdiness among them, and in a way, it made her feel safe. A couple of officers coming towards her as she passed St Eustachius' Church raised their hands to her in salute as their paths crossed, and she replied with a smile.

She sensed a real festive atmosphere as she walked along Plymouth Road towards the Chollacotts' house, probably the most optimistic Yuletide since the war began. Dusk was falling early because of the mist and soon the town would be enveloped in the darkness of the blackout. Any GI who didn't leave soon would be either walking back to base by the dim light of a tissue-paper covered torch or equally dimmed headlights from one of the many jeeps that scuttled around the town like ants — or maybe they were reserved for the officers. Whatever, she hoped they had a good time this Christmas, all these brave young men. If the *Big Push* was coming, for many, it could be their last.

Thrusting the thought aside, she hurried up the front garden path and up the steps to the door and rang the bell. They were expecting her, so she wasn't surprised when her mum came out into the veranda to let her in.

'So good to see you, love!' Adeline declared, giving her daughter a hug. 'Come on in.'

Pippa followed her inside, closing the blackout curtain across the door behind her. She was immediately surrounded by the three youngest children, all wanting her attention.

'Is they'm chocolate bars in your pockets?' Norman immediately demanded, his eyes opening like saucers.

'Yes, they are,' she laughed. 'A group of GIs gave them to me just now. Gave them to *me*, mind. Not you. Though personally, I'd have preferred a pair of silk stockings.'

'I don't suppose they carry those around with them,' Bea joked, coming into the hall to greet her. 'Now, you lot, buzz off and let poor Pippa get settled arter her journey.'

Pippa noted the disappointment on the children's faces. Should she give them the chocolate now and put them out of their misery? Or give them to Bea to put in their stockings?

'Hello, Bea, how are you?' she managed to splutter as the good woman crushed her in a bear hug. 'I thought you might like to put the chocolate bars in their stockings? Unless you think that having seen them, they might put two and two together and realise that Santa doesn't really visit them at night?'

'No chance of that!' Bea assured her. 'They'm still crazied about Father Christmas. Now you come into the sitting room, my flower, and I'll pop down to the kitchen to let Sylvie know you'm yere and fetch you a cuppa.'

Pippa smiled her gratitude. Parking her little case on the hall floor and hanging up her gas-mask box and coat, chocolate-filled pockets and all, Pippa followed her mum into the main room. Miss Primrose and Miss Polly were in the process of putting up the blackout blinds and called their greetings over their shoulders. A few moments later, they were joined by Bea carrying a mug of tea, and Don and Sylvie, while the children hovered by the door, obviously in hopes of Pippa's relenting on the chocolate front. As she sat down in one of the armchairs, her eyes travelled about the room. Coloured paper streamers were strung across from the corners of the ceiling, sprigs of holly with bright berries adorned both the fireplaces, and in the corner stood a tall Christmas tree hung with glass baubles and tiny electric lights.

'I'll just turn those on,' said Don, bending to the plug. 'Artificial tree we've had for donkeys years and all the decorations are ancient, too. Can't get any new ones for love nor money. I'm amazed the lights still work.'

'Well, I think it all looks lovely!' Pippa declared as the tree suddenly lit up. 'It really feels like Christmas this year.'

'Especially with you here, my love,' her mum grinned.

'So tell me all the news,' Pippa said excitedly, sipping her tea. 'Where is everyone?'

'Well, Mr and Mrs Robbins have gone to her sister in Okehampton,' Sylvie told her. 'Haven't seen them since the war started. And to tell the truth, things will be jollier without them.'

'Susie's helping prepare the charity Christmas dinner tomorrow at the British Restaurant on the Wharf,' Bea said proudly, 'and Sharon's at work. Don't finish till closing time, even if it is Christmas Eve. She's trying to get transferred to the Woolworths in Plymouth in the new year, if you can call it that. Just great long stalls in the market since they was bombed out. Wants to be back with her old school pals, and live back home with Ernie and her dad. We'm not proper keen. Who knows if there'll be another raid, but there's no telling her. But,' Bea slapped her hands on her thighs, 'we'm all going to be together for Christmas. Len and Ernie'll both be yere later. Just be missing our Duncan, but at least we know he'm on the way to recovery.'

Pippa didn't voice her immediate thought that if Duncan was on a ship somewhere sailing home, he could still be in danger, but instead she said in an enthusiastic tone, 'Goodness, we're going to be a houseful.'

'And we've one other coming to Christmas dinner,' her mum said shyly. 'I've made a new friend. Mr Yates, the grocer. Walter. He's all on his own so Don and Sylvie kindly agreed that he could join us.'

Was her mum blushing? Crikey. Or was she reading something into it that wasn't there? Pippa hid her surprise by saying, 'What a lovely idea! The true spirit of Christmas. Just like all these Americans being so kind and generous. Seem very friendly and polite.'

'They are, for the most part. Except there's so many of them, they drink the pubs dry,' Don grumbled. 'Not that I'm a great one for going to the pub myself, am I, dear?' he added with a sly wink at Sylvie.

'And I'll tell you this for nort,' Bea added confidentially. 'Elliott's eldest granddaughter, that's Joanna, she's taken up with a young GI. She'm just fourteen and he'm eighteen. Nice lad, mind, and she's a sensible head on her shoulders. But they'm worried her little heart'll be broken when . . . well, who knows? But let's not spoil this evening with such thoughts. Why doesn't you go up to your mum's room and get yersel sorted, Pippa?'

'Yes, of course.' To be honest, there'd been a lot to take in and she'd appreciate a few quiet moments to herself.

'I'll come and help you, love,' her mum offered, getting to her feet.

'Yes, all right,' Pippa smiled and followed her outside to retrieve her case and take it up to her mother's room where the folding bed was made up for her. She undid the latches on the case, but Adeline put a hand on her arm.

'Come and sit by me a while,' she said, patting the bed beside her. 'I need to talk to you about something. Well, about Walter actually.'

Pippa had been a little taken aback and hadn't known quite what to think. So to hear more about this stranger would be good.

'Walter's a very kind man,' her mum said gently. 'Does whatever he can for all his customers. So difficult in these times. And he helps supply the British Restaurant. That's how we met. We sort of . . . got friendly. But once he shuts the shop, he's lonely. Just like me, really. Despite having Bea and everybody all around me. So we've... walked in the Meadows and along the canal path. Been to the cinema a few times. You'll like him. He's very quiet. And very attentive to me.' She paused. 'I just don't want you to think I'm being disloyal to your father,' she concluded in a whisper.

'Oh, Mum,' Pippa breathed. 'Of course I understand. I'd bring Dad back in a flash if I could. But I can't. It'll be three years in April. You can't expect for life not to move on, and to live as a hermit. Or *hermitess*,' she joked in an attempt to lighten the atmosphere. 'It's a surprise, but if you like this Walter and he likes you, then I'm really pleased for you. And I'll look forward to meeting him tomorrow.'

Pippa could see tears glistening in her mum's eyes. 'Thank you, darling.'

They both missed her dad so much. But if he was looking down, she was sure he'd be giving her mum his blessing.

* * *

Walter seemed a very pleasant fellow, Pippa considered, glancing surreptitiously at him as she and her mum laid the table for Christmas dinner the following day. And a gentle soul, too. He'd offered to help but Bea, who was running up and down the stairs to and from the kitchen with various items, told him he was doing a grand job entertaining the younger children and keeping them out of her hair while she helped prepare the meal.

And he certainly was doing a *grand job*, Pippa mused. He'd been crawling around on the floor, pushing along the little tin trains Norman and Bernard had been given, making up stories about where they were going and making train whistle noises that had the boys hooting with laughter. He didn't forget little Lucy either, and was rocking the tiny pram with its baby peg-doll with his other hand and crooning a lullaby in between being a train. For a bachelor approaching fifty who had no offspring of his own or young relatives, he seemed a natural.

'You look as though you've found your vocation,' she teased, setting out home-made crackers of painted newspaper tied with string and containing a walnut each and last year's silly jokes.

Walter looked up with a grin, but before he could reply, the front doorbell rang. Pippa met her mum's surprised look. They weren't expecting anyone, but perhaps it was Elliott popped round to wish them a happy Christmas. It certainly would be lovely to see the old chap.

'I'll go,' Pippa offered and skipped off to greet him.

But as she went out through the veranda, she could make out two figures, and both appeared to be in uniform. She frowned suspiciously. Who one earth could they be? She suddenly felt worried. No bad news, she hoped, especially on Christmas Day.

She opened the door and gasped as she recognised the tall figure and the handsome face with its kind hazel eyes and generous, smiling mouth. She immediately noticed he carried a walking stick in his left hand and there was a small scar on his left cheek that thankfully did nothing to spoil his good looks. Joy bubbled up inside her.

'Duncan!' she cried, and before she could stop herself, she stepped forward and wrapped him in her arms — which she noticed he returned as eagerly with his free hand — and kissed him on the cheek.

'Well, I couldn't have wished for a better welcome!' he answered in his soft voice, and the thrill that passed through her took Pippa by surprise.

She stood back, suddenly confused and embarrassed. 'Well, come on in!' she urged. 'And I'm sorry! Who is this?' she asked, turning to the older man standing behind him with a case and a kitbag.

'Alec Sanderson, captain retired, at your service, miss,' he replied.

'I wasn't considered fit enough to carry my own luggage,' Duncan explained, 'so Captain Sanderson has driven me all the way from Liverpool. We only got as far as Bristol last night, so here we are. And don't ask where the company got the petrol from,' he added in a low voice.

'Welcome, Captain,' Pippa put in. 'Do come in.'

'Thank you but I won't, if it's all the same to you. I want to visit a very old aunt on my return journey while I have the opportunity. But thank you, miss. Good luck, Second Officer Chollacott.'

Pippa watched as the two men saluted each other, not quite the salute of the Royal Navy, she noticed, but a recognition of respect that spoke of a common knowledge of things unspoken. She watched as he trotted back down the path, and then turned to Duncan, almost breathless with excitement.

'You go in,' she urged. 'I'll bring your luggage. Everyone's here,' she went on. 'Your dad and Ernie arrived last night. Bea's going to go mad with excitement!'

That was the understatement of the year, Pippa chuckled, as the existing chaos in the house turned into an utter riot of joyful cries and shouts of delight from adults and children alike. Susie was out at the British Restaurant and Sharon had volunteered to help. Their pleasure at seeing their eldest brother returned would have to wait.

'What I want to know is where we'm going to put you to sleep,' Bea declared later over a plate full of vegetables, mainly from Don's patch in the garden, and a slither of chicken. Elliott's wife, Ling, who'd been brought up on the moor and was used to rearing hens, had been keeping a small flock in their garden and had killed a couple of birds that had ceased laying, kindly giving one of them to her neighbours.

'With your dad and Ernie here, every bed is taken,' Bea went on, waving her fork in the air. 'And we can't use Mr and Mrs Robbins' room, can we?'

'How long are you here for?' Pippa asked.

'The company did all the paperwork and got me a permit for two weeks,' Duncan explained. 'After that, my permanent address has always been registered as the family home in Plymouth. So I guess I'll be going back there afterwards.'

'Well, I've got a spare room in my flat over the shop,' Walter chipped in. 'I did have a young mother with her two little ones evacuated there. Gone back to London, not that I think that were a wise decision. You're welcome to stay with me, lad, if you've a mind.'

'Really?' Duncan's expressive eyes opened wide. 'Why, thank you, Walter, that's most generous.'

Adeline exchanged a glance with Pippa that said *I told you what a kind man Walter is*. Pippa answered her with a nod and knowing smile. So had Walter's little evacuees been the source of his natural ability with young children? Whatever, her mum had found herself such a worthy gentleman friend, and Pippa couldn't have been more pleased.

The afternoon passed in a flurry of fun and laughter. It wasn't until the evening when the younger children were persuaded to go — reluctantly — to bed, that the older siblings and adults were able to sit round quietly and Duncan was given the opportunity to relate what had happened to him.

'Well, I can tell you now that for a long time, I was on the North Atlantic Run, taking supplies to the Russians at Murmansk, along with mainly Canadian and American ships.' He evidently heard the various stifled intakes of breath around the room, and flicked his eyes towards Pippa. It was clear she'd kept her promise to him not to reveal anything to his family unless the worst happened, and it seemed to strengthen the bond between them.

'That was suspended for a while after one convoy was decimated,' Duncan continued, 'but by the time it was resumed, our ship was already engaged in taking supplies to Malta. We were operating there during the siege, but our vessel seemed to be sailing under a lucky star and always got through, even if she were attacked en route. When the main siege ended and the Axis powers were being driven out of North Africa, it made things a bit less dangerous for us. Then the Allies eventually invaded Sicily, driving out the Germans. Eventually Italy surrendered and the Allies landed in south-west Italy.

But Hitler had occupied Rome, and was determined to fight back with all his might.'

Pippa saw him glance around the room at the nodding heads as he went on, 'Of course, I'm sure you know all this, but it helps to see the whole picture. Naturally, as well as the brutally fierce fighting on the Italian mainland, one of the ways the Germans are still able to show their force is by attacking any Allied shipping in the entire area, and our dear old girl's luck finally ran out. We were just a small convoy still sailing to Malta with civilian supplies, with just one escort ship, when we came under attack from both the air and a corvette-sized enemy ship, at a guess. I remember . . . I just saw this one shell coming towards me.'

Pippa shuddered as she saw the shuttered look come over Duncan's face as he paused and then lowered his eyes to his hands. The memories of it must be awful for him, but she knew from speaking to patients, that sometimes talking about such things often helped. She'd noticed at dinner that the tip of the little finger on his left hand was missing. It was Norman who'd commented on it, and Duncan had shrugged it off saying that it wasn't much use, anyway. But now he was gently rubbing the stump as if it was concentrating his mind.

'I dived for shelter,' he murmured, and it was as if everyone in the room was holding their breath. 'So I didn't get caught in the actual blast, but it was the shrapnel that got me, several small bits, and the one that caught my cheek missed my eye, thank God. But it was the bigger pieces that went into my side and my leg that did the real damage. But,' and here he looked up with a wry smile, 'I've lived to tell the tale. Literally. Oh, Mum. Don't cry. I'm here and I won't be going back to sea ever.'

Pippa glanced across at poor Bea who was openly weeping, Len's arm firmly around her shoulder. Ernie, Susie and Sharon were all gazing at their elder brother with a mixture of awe and sympathy, while Don and Sylvie exchanged concerned glances. Pippa noted that Walter was holding her mum's hand, while Miss Polly and Miss Primrose were squeezing each other's hands as tightly as their arthritic fingers allowed. It all looked rather incongruous with the Christmas decorations draped about the room and the tree with its twinkling lights.

Then Pippa's nurse's training kicked in. She was used to handling delicate situations especially now she was a senior nurse, and all at once, found herself taking charge.

'Well, I think we should all be celebrating Duncan's return,' she announced, fixing a broad smile on her face. 'It's Christmas Day after all. Come on, everyone, charge your glasses. A toast to Duncan and all our brave chaps, and women, of course!'

'Pity we don't have any champagne!' Don grumbled.

'Oh, yes, I'd love to try that!' Sharon declared.

'Well, you'd be far too young even we had any, my maid!' Bea immediately scolded, and everyone laughed as they got to their feet.

Within minutes, normal conversation had resumed. Duncan caught Pippa's eye across the room and she saw him mouth a thank you at her. A warm shiver of pleasure tingled down to her toes.

CHAPTER TWENTY-SEVEN

'So, what was it like being in the naval hospital?'

It was the day after Boxing Day. Mr and Mrs Robbins were due back that evening, and Len, Ernie, Susie and Sharon were all back at work. Some of the other members of the Chollacott household had gone for a walk in the Meadows, the three children eagerly running on ahead to the swings. With his limp and walking with a stick, Duncan had lagged behind even Miss Polly and Miss Primrose who ambled along at their own pace, and Pippa had dropped back to fall into step beside him.

Now he cocked a sceptical eyebrow at her. 'Morbid curiosity?' he asked enigmatically.

'Curiosity as a nurse, yes,' she answered easily. 'But morbid, no. I'm used to that in my line of work. I just wondered what it would be like to work in a forces hospital. The pay's so much better and you can join up once you're qualified.'

'You're not thinking of doing that, are you? Joining the QAs or whatever?'

Pippa heard the alarm in his voice. It was a warm feeling that he was concerned about her. 'Oh, no. My life is firmly here. I really was just curious.'

'That's a relief,' he mumbled, before going on, 'Well, I'm not sure how much I can tell you. It's all a bit of a blur. I was high on morphine and all I can remember is this strange feeling of being wheeled around with lights and strange faces looming over me. It was quite weird when I came to after the operation. That section of the hospital being in the tunnels underneath Valetta. All white stone and glaring lights and ... so claustrophobic. Incredible, though. Some of the tunnels date back hundreds of years. Jolly useful when the Jerries are bombing the hell out of what's above.'

'Yes. They say Malta's the worst bombed country in the world.'

'Wouldn't surprise me. And the people refused to surrender. That's why they were awarded the George Cross, of course. It's an amazing place, Valetta Harbour. The ancient fortresses that guard it are just so massive, they're beyond belief. Tell you what.' He stopped and turned to her with an expression she couldn't quite fathom. 'One day, when the war's over, I'll have to take you there.'

She looked up into his face, her eyes narrowed in questioning for a moment. And then her mouth curved in a smile. 'Yes, I think I'd like that.'

They stood for a moment, Pippa lost, just fleetingly, in his steady gaze. Did he feel the same way towards her as she did him? But she mustn't ... Nursing was what she was meant for. Nevertheless, it just felt so natural when she found herself slipping her arm in his as they continued along the path.

'So, how much more leave have you got?' he asked as they caught up with the others. Don and Bea were overseeing the children on the swings, while Miss Polly and Miss Primrose had sat down on a bench. There wasn't room for Pippa and Duncan but they found another one that was unoccupied.

'Well, officially, my third day here ends tomorrow,' Pippa replied. 'But I've got a few more days of leave and I don't suppose anyone's going to tell on me for staying on.'

She saw Duncan wince slightly and stretch out his leg as he sat down. 'Aching?'

'A bit,' he nodded. 'But it's good for me to walk. And they've given me exercises to strengthen it. But you'll know all about that.'

'Yes. I'm on Orthopaedics for now. But it's Theatre I want to work in.'

'Hence the morbid interest.'

She saw the teasing light in his eyes and chuckled back. 'Perhaps. But the human body is so amazing, it's incredible to see inside it. And to feel you're helping mend somebody's life.'

'You really do love your nursing, don't you?'

'Yes, I do. But what about you? What are you going to do now?'

'I'm not sure, to be honest,' he sighed. 'The company have offered me a desk job back in the offices in Liverpool. But I'm not sure it's really me. I suppose it'd be doing something for the war effort, and I know about cargoes and convoys and so forth. But I can't see myself sitting at a desk for the rest of my life. When my permit here runs out and I move back to the family home in Plymouth, I'll try and find some useful employment of some sort. And perhaps I can see you sometimes when you're off duty.'

For the second time in the last ten minutes, Pippa found herself looking into his searching eyes. Yes, there was something there. Something she mustn't return. But she couldn't prevent the words that came from her lips.

'Yes, that would be lovely. Though you'll have to fight over me with my friend Steph. She leaves to get married in the spring, so I'll be wanting to see her in my off-duty time.'

'Well, I'll have to make sure my duelling pistols are in working order.'

And there the conversation ended as Norman came running up to them wanting Duncan to take him down to the canal. Duncan shot Pippa a wistful glance as he heaved himself to his feet and began to limp after his little brother.

'No peace for the wicked,' he grimaced, but Pippa saw the smile on his face as he turned away. She had the feeling he was enjoying getting to know his siblings, and it gladdened her heart as she followed them towards the canal.

***

'Lovely lunch, Gran,' Duncan said as he stacked some of the dirty plates. 'Let me help you.'

'I'm not having you going up and down the stairs, young man,' Sylvie admonished. 'You've been on that leg enough this morning, hasn't he, Pippa?'

'I'd have thought so, yes,' Pippa replied. 'You're supposed to be convalescing. Bea and I can bring everything down. Duncan, you sit with your leg up for a bit and read to the kiddies if you want something to do. Mum'll be back from her WVS shift soon and she was planning on doing some drawing with them. They just use pencil so they rub it all out and re-use the paper. Such a shame. I know Mum kept . . . She kept lots of my early attempts, but of course they all went when we lost the house.'

She paused, throwing out the awful memory. She must put such thoughts behind her, but every so often something would slip, unguarded, into her head. Almost angry at herself, she picked up the plates Duncan had stacked and carried them down to the kitchen where Don had already started the washing up. She'd taken up the tea towel and dried the dishes that had been washed so far when Bea and Sylvie arrived at the bottom of the stairs with more dirty crockery. Pippa stood aside to let them pass before starting up the stairs again herself, and heard the telephone ring as she went up. By the time she got to the top, Miss Primrose had answered it, and she saw the expression of concern on the old lady's face as she held the receiver out to her.

'It's for you, cheel. But . . . the young maid sounds mortal upset.'

Utterly bemused, Pippa took the telephone from Miss Primrose's hand. 'Hello?' she said cautiously.

There was a great sob at the other end of the line. 'Oh, Pip,' Steph's voice wailed. 'It's Rusty. He's . . . Oh, Pip, he's dead!' she squealed down the phone.

What? Every muscle in Pippa's body stilled. No. Oh, no. This wasn't right. She was dreaming. It couldn't be true.

'Say that again,' she croaked down the phone, praying desperately she'd heard wrong. 'You're a bit muffled.'

'He's dead, Pip. Knocked down by a car, well, a taxi, in the blackout last night on his way home.'

It was a moment before Pippa could pull her thoughts together. 'Oh, my God, Steph. I can't believe it.'

'Well, it's true,' Steph wept. 'Can you come?'

'Well, yes, of course. I'll pack my things and get the next train.'

'Thank you,' a thin voice answered, and then the line went dead.

Pippa staggered into the sitting room, seeing the concern on Duncan's face as he looked up from the book he was reading to the little ones.

'It's . . . my friend, Steph,' she muttered. 'She says . . . her fiancé's dead. But she was only taking him to meet her parents yesterday afternoon.'

Duncan at once sat up straight. 'God, that's awful.'

'Did I hear right?' Miss Primrose's mouth had dropped open in horror.

'Y-yes, you did,' Pippa stammered. 'I'd better go and pack my things.'

'And I'll explain to everyone what's happened,' Duncan offered.

Pippa took the stairs two at a time. In the bedroom she shared with her mother, she quickly packed her little case, popping in the Christmas presents she'd received. No one could get hold of much. Her mother had knitted her some new gloves, multicoloured as she used up odds and ends of wool she had left over, Sharon had got her a lipstick from Woolworths, and she'd been given other small items that all fitted in the case. Within minutes, she was downstairs and slipping on her coat while Don, Sylvie and Bea had all appeared anxiously from the kitchen.

'Say goodbye to Mum for me, won't you?'

'Yes, of course. And we're really sorry about your friend.'

Pippa nodded and hurried out to the street, walking as briskly as she could to the station. She wasn't sure when the next train was due, and often they were unable to keep to the timetable anyway, especially with more and more American troops arriving all the time, though perhaps not today. As luck would have it, it wasn't long before a train was chugging alongside the platform, and she climbed aboard.

Looking out of the window, she watched the heights of Dartmoor rising up solidly to her left, not enshrouded in mist today. Oh, God. Poor Steph. Memories of when she lost her father slithered evilly into Pippa's mind. She knew what it was to stand on the edge of a great abyss of darkness. Poor Steph would be tottering there, too, shocked, numbed, disorientated. How could fate be so cruel, just when Steph had been so bursting with joy? Then doubt and guilt entered Pippa's heart. Was it her fault, for not looking forward to the time when Steph would leave the hospital? To losing her constant companion? Don't be so silly, she thought. It had nothing to do with that. It was just that . . . such strange things entered your head when grief took hold. And she did feel real grief for her friend.

She got to the hospital as quickly as she could, wondering where Steph would be. But when she hurried along the corridor to drop her things in her room, Steph's door was slightly ajar, and she could hear soft, soothing voices. She gently pushed the door open. Steph was sitting on the bed, weeping, and dear Sister Tutor Honeywell had her arm around her, trying to comfort her.

Steph must have sensed someone was there and lifted her tear-ravaged face. 'Oh, Pip!' she cried as soon as she saw her.

Knowing how close they were, Sister Tutor moved out of the way to let Pippa sit next to her friend. Steph at once let out a brutal howl, and clung to Pippa, sobbing against her shoulder. Pippa held her close, stroking her tousled hair, and glanced up at the sister.

'I'll leave you,' the good woman whispered. 'You know where I am if you need me. We're arranging some compassionate leave for her.'

Pippa nodded, and watched as Sister Tutor gently closed the door behind her.

'Oh, Steph, I'm so very sorry,' she crooned, holding her friend tight. What else could she say? Steph was lost in her ocean of grief and Pippa could only wait until her tears began to lessen into hiccups and she pulled away slightly, drawing the back of her hands over her wet cheeks.

'Th-thank you for coming,' she gasped. 'I know it was your leave—'

'Shush, now. That doesn't matter.' At a loss as what to say next, she finally uttered in a low voice, 'It was good of Sister Tutor to look after you when we're no longer her responsibility.'

'Yes,' Steph croaked. 'Matron was terribly kind, too, but too busy to stay with me. She has the hospital to run.'

'Yes, of course.' Pippa's voice was soft. 'D'you . . . d'you want to tell me what happened? Or . . . ?'

She watched Steph nod. 'It was last night,' she sniffed. 'We'd had a great afternoon at Mum and Dad's. They got on well. And then, when it was dark, R-rusty,' she stuttered, her chin quivering, 'he saw me on to the bus to come back here, and then was walking to the harbour to catch the ferry back across to the base at the appointed hour. One or two airmen had come across for the afternoon, you see, including Jack, to see a new lady friend. He . . . he saw it all. Rusty waved and called across to him. It was pitch dark, and he didn't notice the taxi creeping along with its dimmed lights. Jack yelled at him, but it was . . . it was too late. They . . . they took him to the Prince of Wales Hospital in Lockyer Street, being so near.

Jack came for me and took me there. I . . . I stayed with him all night, but he . . . died this morning.'

'Oh, Steph, I'm so sorry,' Pippa murmured, trying to soothe her, but Steph let out a wail and her tears began afresh.

'It was my fault, don't you see? All those missions he flew, but he took care and survived them all. But . . . I made him so happy, he didn't take care just crossing the road. It wasn't the taxi driver's fault, Jack said. And now he's dead. Oh, Pip,' she gulped, 'what am I going to do without him?' she squealed.

Pippa tried to comfort her, but what was the point? Grief would take its own path. So she sat quietly, stroking Steph's back and waiting.

***

Steph walked slowly up the aisle of the roofless, windowless, charred skeleton of the ruined church. Beside her, holding her hand, Pippa noticed the resolute look on her face, despite her faltering step. Her feet were treading the path that, in a few months' time, would have taken her to the remains of the altar to pledge her life to that of her fiancé. Now she was following his coffin, carried on the shoulders of six of his RAAF comrades, to receive the church's blessing into the next world.

Glancing across at Jack on Steph's other side, Pippa saw he was staring directly ahead, his expression set. He'd witnessed his best friend, elated and happy — so happy that he hadn't paid due attention to the road in the blackout — being knocked down and fatally injured. Much as she'd never been sure about Jack, Pippa's heart went out to him now.

But, perhaps worst of all, possibly even more so than to Steph, Pippa's thoughts went to Rusty's family, his parents and two sisters, on the other side of the world. He had done his duty, travelled thousands of miles, to serve his king and the Commonwealth, risking himself on an almost daily basis, only for his life to be cut short in such a futile manner. His family couldn't come to his funeral, say their final farewell to their beloved son. He'd be buried in a foreign land as far away from home as it was possible to get, in a grave they would likely never be able to visit.

Pippa bit the inside of her bottom lip to quell the rising sorrow in her throat and the desire for tears. She must be strong. A rock for Steph. Her friend's parents were following immediately behind. Much as they had accepted Rusty and had given Steph their full support and sympathy, Pippa wondered if they weren't secretly relieved. They might not be the closest family, but they probably didn't relish the prospect of their only daughter emigrating to Australia to be with her husband once the war was over.

Pippa's gaze wandered over the standing congregation as they moved forward. On one side, a contingent of solemn-faced Australian airmen, smart in their uniforms. On the other, some strangers she believed were former neighbours, together with those of Steph's nursing colleagues able to snatch a few hours' off-duty time, Sister Tutor and former probationer nurse, Geraldine. Pippa felt her heart strengthen as she spied her mother, and Bea and Duncan.

She met his concerned, hazel eyes for a fleeting moment, and the hint of a supportive smile flickered across his face. She acknowledged it with a brief smile and nod. Duncan. How kind and thoughtful of him. Just like his mother but in a quieter, more reserved way.

Those who were following the coffin took their seats on the few folding chairs that had been provided for them. The service was short, just the necessary ritual. Rusty's squadron leader said a few respectful words. With the organ destroyed in the bombing, choir boys, shivering in their thin robes, led the congregation in 'Abide with Me'. Pippa put her arm around Steph's shoulders as the poor girl shook with silent sobs.

When it was over, they got to their feet and followed the coffin back out of the church ruins. Then, as the closest to the deceased, Steph, Jack and Pippa stood outside where the church's doors would have been, to receive the condolences of the congregation. Not just from people who knew Rusty, but strangers from this war-ravaged city. A collective grief. For hadn't everyone had a loved one, a family member or friend taken from them? At least Rusty would have his own grave with its own stone, Pippa thought. Not like her father and so many who'd been buried together in a mass grave.

When her mother filed past, Pippa knew that she, too, was thinking of her dad. They squeezed each other's hands. They needed no words. Behind Adeline and Bea, Duncan dipped his head gravely when it was his turn. He passed a slip of paper into Pippa's hand and whispered, 'Keep in touch,' before moving respectfully onwards.

Later, Pippa remembered the paper she'd slid into her pocket. The address and telephone number of the Chollacott's family home in Plymouth. Of course. It struck her that she'd never had any reason to know it before. But now she did. She knew that Duncan would be moving back there in a week's time. Bomb-damaged but still standing. And yes, she did want to keep in touch. At that moment, she thought it was perhaps the only thing that made any sense in her life.

CHAPTER TWENTY-EIGHT

'So, how's your friend Steph doing?'

It was a blustery day at the end of February, and Pippa was walking along the Promenade on the Hoe with Duncan. They'd managed to meet up two or three times since Rusty's funeral and Pippa felt more and more at ease with him, enjoying his company immensely. It was good to get away from the hospital and breathe in some fresh air that didn't smell of disinfectant. Nothing romantic had passed between them. Pippa wasn't sure if she was disappointed or relieved, though at the moment, with poor Steph's recent bereavement, it felt better to keep her relationship with Duncan on a platonic standing.

She released a long sigh. 'Hard to say,' she reflected. 'She said she was glad to get back to the hospital after her two weeks' compassionate leave staying with her parents. And she's saying that throwing herself into her work helps keep her mind off it. I can understand that. It really helped me when my dad was killed. But . . . I don't know. She's hardly her old, carefree self. We have an hour or so together when we come off duty each evening and I try and cheer her up, but it's difficult to broach the subject and we've not had a real, in-depth chat. So I don't know how she's really feeling, you know, deep down.'

She shook her head. 'I guess that's a pretty stupid thing to say. She must be broken inside. I wish I could help her more. But at least she's moved to Paediatrics which she's finding brighter and more uplifting, I suppose, than Women's Medical.'

'Especially with the dreaded Sister Pudifoot, I imagine.'

Pippa looked up, startled, and gave a short laugh. 'Yes, you remembered. Steph wasn't finding her so bad, but the sister on the paediatric ward is so much nicer.'

'I guess you couldn't have a dragon in charge of children, flying around the ward and breathing fire.'

Pippa pushed his arm gently and chuckled, then tipped her head as she pondered her thoughts. 'You seem to have a natural way with children yourself,' she remarked. 'Considering you've never had any contact with them, you're really good with your younger brothers and sisters.'

'Ah, well, I've enjoyed getting to know them properly. Ernie and I were always quite close, but there was a bit of an age gap between us and the girls. Susie and Sharon were still little girls when I joined the navy, and the other three not even born. I've hardly ever seen them, but I often wondered about them, though. The good thing about being invalided out is that I can see my family again now. I always missed Mum and Dad, and Gran and Gramps, of course.'

'A pity you're having to live here in Plymouth, then. Though it means I can see you sometimes.'

She wasn't quite sure why she'd said that. Was it a good idea to let Duncan know how much she relished his company? Oh, heck. She wished she hadn't let it slip out. But fortunately he didn't seem to pick up on it.

'And living with Dad and Ernie is great,' he continued. 'And Sharon, now she's got her transfer. And when the war's over, Mum and Dad and the others will be coming back home, of course. Not sure about Susie, though. She's really put down roots in Tavistock.'

'Just as well. I imagine your parents' house will be pretty crowded.'

'Well, it's quite a big house,' Duncan told her. 'And Ernie's really keen on the young lady he's walking out with, and it wouldn't surprise me if we hear wedding bells soon. He's a good job on the railway and they could afford to move into their own place. If they could find anywhere, that is. And with any luck, I might be moving out soon, too.'

'Really?' Pippa couldn't help the surprise in her voice.

'Yes. It was Mum who spotted the advert in the paper. As you know, up until now, I've not had any luck finding a new job. What they need in Plymouth is manual workers to continue clearing all the bombsites, and with this stupid leg, I'd be no use at that. I can drive a car but wouldn't have a clue about a bulldozer. And I couldn't stand for hours in an armaments factory, either.'

He gave a wistful sigh. 'Anyway, I've plenty of navy pay saved over the years, so it's not been a problem financially. And in the meantime, I've become quite the handyman.' He threw her a sideways glance and she saw a proud look come over his face. 'You know the house had some bomb damage, but it's been inspected and it's perfectly safe. But all the windows at the front were blown out and Dad hadn't been able to get them replaced. So I trawled the city and eventually found somewhere that could provide the glass, so I've re-glazed and painted them all. Then a big piece of shrapnel had fallen through the roof and down into one of the bedrooms. Dad had just put a bucket underneath to catch the rain. I scrounged some tiles from a demolition site and managed to replace them from the inside, and we had some roofing felt left over in the garden shed, so I patched up underneath with that. I replaced the boarding in the loft and made some laths, again from some wood we had in the shed, nailed them over the hole in the bedroom ceiling and plastered them over. It'll need skimming by a professional plasterer at some point, but I reckon I made a pretty good job of it. Oh, and the wooden frame of the bunk beds in that room had been damaged, too, so I mended that as well.'

'I'm impressed,' Pippa said truthfully. 'But what's that got to do with this job you've found?'

'Ah, well, the job Mum spotted was for a caretaker at Mount House School in Tavistock. D'you know it? On the road that goes up steeply on to the moor? The job comes with its own accommodation, so it'd be perfect. I know about electrics and plumbing from the navy, as well, and I could give classes in navigation and seamanship. Not as an official part of the curriculum, of course. I'm not a trained teacher. But for any of the lads who were interested in their spare time. So, I'm really hoping I'll get it.'

'I hope so, too.' Pippa tried to inject some enthusiasm into her voice. But she'd hardly ever be able to see Duncan if he moved to Tavistock, would she? In that moment, she realised just how much he meant to her. She felt consumed with guilt. She didn't want him to get the job, did she? Just as she'd never wanted Steph to leave nursing.

Duncan's enthusiasm brought her back from her thoughts. 'The interview's next week, but I'm going to Gran and Gramps the day before. Now this is the really interesting part. It turns out Dr Franfield senior — you know, Elliott — his wife, Ling—'

'Yes, they're a lovely old couple.'

'Well, apparently, going back years, she was great friends with the wealthy widow who owned Mount Tavy House. Back then, it was a huge estate, covering extensive grounds and several farms. Anyway, when the old lady died, she had no family to leave it to, so she left it to Mrs Franfield in trust to do something for the good of the local community. It was shortly before the last war, and they opened it as a hospital for soldiers, mainly suffering from shellshock, but other trauma as well. Apparently, Dr Elliott became quite an expert in the field.'

Pippa raised her eyebrows in surprise. 'I didn't know that. But I can well believe it. He's such a kind man.'

'Yes, he is. And so eventually, their last patient left, a year or so after the war ended. They weren't quite sure what to do with the property. It's a beautiful big old house, apparently, with lots of outbuildings that were used for basket-making and what have you for the patients. In the end, they sold it into private hands, and put a lot of the money into the cottage hospital, and the rest they invested into a fund that supports the hospital to this day. In the meantime, the estate changed hands a couple of times, a lot of the farms and so forth being sold off separately. Then in 1940, a boys' private school from Plymouth called Mount House School could see all the bombings coming and wanted to move out of harm's way, so they bought it, and have been there ever since. So the day before the interview, I'm going to have a chat with Dr and Mrs Franfield, and they're going to tell me all about the place, which might put me at an advantage. I hope so, anyway, as I'd really love the job. Whether or not the school will stay there when the war's over, I don't know. But it'd suit me nicely for now.'

Yes, Pippa could see that it would. But what about her? She'd miss seeing him so much. He'd be bound to find someone else. But why should she feel like this, pulled in so many different directions? Her career. She must concentrate on that. It was her true desire, but it was also tearing her apart.

'That's what we all keep saying, isn't it?' she said instead, forcing the crucifying dilemma to the back of her mind. '*When the war's over*. It's been going on so long now, I wonder if it'll ever be over. I don't feel as if the Allies will ever beat the Japs, and in Italy, they've been halted at this monastery fortress place.'

Duncan nodded grimly. 'Monte Cassino, you mean? Looks impregnable, doesn't it? The Allies have been pouring bombs into it to no effect so far. But we will get there, I'm sure. We have to.'

He stopped walking and turned to her, his eyes deep and intense. 'We've made such progress against Hitler, we have to believe. We can't give up now. And all those American troops amassing around Tavistock and other parts of Devon and elsewhere. All the military exercises they've been carrying out. We're going to be ready. And we're going to win. I just wish I could still be part of it.'

Pippa stared up at him, and her heart bucked. She was glad he couldn't be. Even if nothing ever happened between them, he would still be alive. Unlike Rusty.

'It's time I was heading back,' she murmured, swiftly turning away. 'I might just catch Steph when she comes off duty.'

'Of course. I'm afraid I've kept you too long. I'll walk back to the bus stop with you.'

'Yes, thank you. And good luck with the interview.'

She saw him nod appreciatively, and felt rotten to the core. Yes, she really ought to want him to get the job. And she would be happy for him. But in her heart of hearts, she wanted things to stay as they were. She knew she was being selfish, but . . . he'd come to mean too much to her.

***

Pippa took the hand that was politely held out to her as she stepped down from the train at Tavistock South Station. She could manage perfectly well, but the American soldiers she'd shared a carriage with had been so chatty and friendly that she felt she couldn't refuse. Excited to be in *quaint old England* as one of them had put it, and eager to be doing their bit. Pippa tried not to think about it. If the fighting in Italy was anything to go by, so many of them wouldn't make it when the time came.

Surrounded by GIs, she hurried along the platform and handed in her ticket at the barrier. It was the first time since Christmas she'd managed to have a whole day's leave, giving her time to make the journey to the market town to see her mum and the Chollacotts. She hoped so much that she'd see Duncan, that he'd make the effort to be with her if only for a short time. He'd walked the interview and had been moving into the caretaker's accommodation that week. She'd found that she really was pleased for him, but prayed it wouldn't herald the end of their relationship, such as it was.

Crossing the long bridge over the Tavy, she strode purposefully past the church and down the road towards the Chollacotts' house. Daffodils were nodding their heads in the long front gardens, brightly coloured primroses nestled in between their tall stalks. Spring. Would it be the last one of the war? Could it truly be over soon? There'd recently been another massive Allied assault on Monte Cassino lasting over a week — all to no avail. It was the last day of March. Would the coming months bring more success? And as for the fighting out in the Far East, well, the Japanese seemed even more fanatical than the Nazis.

But Pippa needed to be back at the hospital that evening, and didn't want to spoil her brief time here with such morose thoughts. She opened the gate and hurried along the path and up the steps to the veranda. Her mum had been waiting for her and the door opened as if by magic.

It was proper grand to be back after three whole months, and her mum waltzed her into the living room. The adults were all there to greet her, except for Susie and Mr and Mrs Robbins who were all at work. It was the last day of school for Norman and Bernard, but Lucy climbed on to Pippa's lap the instant she sat down. Pippa felt a relaxed calm flow through her as she chatted with her mum and all her dear friends, catching up on everyone's news.

'Don't be forgetting about Elliott, now,' Bea appeared to remind Adeline, jabbing her head at her friend.

'Oh, he's all right, is he?' Pippa asked in alarm. She was so fond of the old fellow, but he was getting on.

'Yes, he'm proper clever,' Bea assured her. 'But he . . . Adeline, come on, you tell her.'

Pippa blinked at her mum. What was this all about?

'Well, he popped in the other day, wanting to know when you were coming next,' Adeline said mysteriously. 'Said he had some news which might interest you. He didn't say what. But when I told him you were coming today, he said he'd call in about eleven o'clock.'

'I wonder what it's all about,' Pippa pondered. 'And in the meantime, how's Duncan getting on?'

'You'll see him later on, as well,' Bea beamed. 'Coming for arternoon tea,' she added, preening herself, then gave her jolly laugh. 'That's if you can call arternoon tea sandwiches made from that awful National Loaf and mashed-up, tinned sardines!'

'Not forgetting a cake made with powdered egg and grated carrot instead of sugar!' Sylvie put in.

Everyone chuckled. You had to. The only way to cope with such things was to laugh at them. Still, Pippa wondered what Elliott had to tell her and a little frown puckered her forehead as she chatted with her mum and all her friends.

She didn't have long to wait. Elliott arrived dead on the dot of eleven and asked if they could go somewhere private. There wasn't much room for privacy in the crowded Chollacott household but Sylvie suggested they went down to the kitchen as lunch — a vegetable, mainly potato, soup — was already prepared and she wouldn't need to go down to heat it through until later.

'You have the chair,' Pippa said when they reached the bottom of the stairs. 'This is all very mysterious.'

'Well, I wanted you to know first so that you can have a think about it,' the elderly doctor told her, gratefully perching on the only chair in the room. 'But you'll have to think quickly. Now, I know you've always said you wanted to be a theatre sister.'

'Yes, that's right,' Pippa answered, intrigued.

Elliott nodded pensively. 'Well, Sister Eastercott, the theatre sister at the cottage hospital here, is retiring at the end of June, and we currently have no one suitable to take her place. Heaven knows there's a huge shortage of nursing staff everywhere, and we're no different. So I wondered, well, that is to say, I discussed it with William, and we wondered if you'd be interested.'

Oh. Oh, goodness. Excitement burst through Pippa's heart. It was exactly what she wanted! When she'd heard Elliott and William talking about the hospital, it sounded such a marvellous set-up, she couldn't wish for anything better!

'Well, yes!' she stuttered. 'But, d'you think I'd be capable?'

Elliott tipped his head in consideration. 'Well, you've done your basic Theatre training, haven't you? And if you could start at the beginning of May, Sister Eastercott would have two months to train you up, and for you to get to know everyone. The theatre isn't in full-time use as I assume it is at the City, so you'd be helping out on other wards and in other capacities as well. So . . . what d'you say?'

Pippa blew out through puffed cheeks. 'I'm quite overwhelmed that you have such faith in me. But . . . I'm not sure I'd be released from the City. We're supposed to do a whole year as a staff nurse after qualifying, and that wouldn't be up until the end of August.'

'Maybe we could pull some strings,' Elliott suggested.

Pippa released a deep sigh. She'd be over the moon! But then a heavy weight pulled down on her shoulders, like darkness descending on a winter's night. She shook her head.

'No, I'm afraid I can't,' she whispered, disappointment rampaging through her so that she felt on the brink of tears. 'I can't possibly leave my friend. The one whose fiancé was killed at Christmas. I've got to stay with her.'

She lifted her head up with determination. No matter what, despite the stab in her heart, her place was at Steph's side. Steph's needs had to come first.

Elliot paused. 'Oh. That's a pity. But . . . she's a qualified nurse, too, isn't she? Doubtless we can find her a position, too. God knows we're so short-staffed, we could do with her.'

Hope burst out afresh in Pippa's chest. It all sounded perfect. And it also meant she could be near Duncan as well as her mum.

'Certainly sounds tempting,' she answered cautiously. 'I'd have to talk to Steph, of course. But maybe a change of scene would help her.'

'I understand you'd need to think about it. But in the meantime, would you like to visit the hospital with me this afternoon? Say, two o'clock?'

'Oh, yes, please!' But then she thought of Duncan. 'I'd need to be back by four, though. The Chollacotts are laying on afternoon tea in my honour.'

'Perfect. Come round to us at a quarter to two, then. William has his gynae clinic there this afternoon, so he'll drive us. It's only a stone's throw, but the hill's a bit steep and my old legs don't cope with it as well as they used to.'

'I'll certainly look forward to it,' Pippa replied with enthusiasm. 'So let me see you out. And thank you so much for thinking of me.'

'You'd be the answer to the hospital's prayers,' Elliott answered as a warm smile crinkled his old face.

* * *

'It's such a fantastic set-up,' Pippa told Duncan excitedly later that afternoon. 'Of course, there are all the strict rules you need to run a clean and efficient hospital, but it's so much friendlier than the City. All the staff know each other well, and so do half the patients, it seems,' she added with a chuckle. 'The local GPs have their own specialist clinics on different days, and perform most of their own ops there. Anything that requires really specialist surgery, they call in a consultant from one of the Plymouth hospitals. One of the orthopaedic consultants I work with is someone they call on occasionally, though I didn't realise.'

'You sound really keen,' Duncan observed, biting into one of the sardine sandwiches.

'Yes, I am. It'd depend on being released from the City, of course, and whether Steph could come, too. Or want to.'

'You're a true friend to her. She's a lucky young woman in that respect. But wouldn't you need to go for an interview?'

'I think I more or less had one this afternoon,' Pippa answered with a smile. 'I met so many people and chatted to them about my experience so far. And Elliott is very influential. He's been involved with the cottage hospital all his working life, from way back when it was just a house at the top of West Street. He's only just retired from being Chairman of the Board apparently, which I didn't realise.'

'So, it's almost certain the job's yours if you want it.'

'Well, we'll see. I don't want to get overexcited, but I'd love it. And it means I'd be near to Mum. And all your lovely family.'

Duncan lowered his head and then looked at her from under raised eyebrows. 'And it'd mean I could see more of you, too.'

A dart of confused hope pierced Pippa's heart. Yes, it seemed that Duncan did have feelings for her. But, oh, crikey. If she became the theatre sister at the cottage hospital, it was even more of a reason for her not to have a romantic relationship. She felt as if she were being pulled in so many different directions at once.

'Yes, it would,' she answered evasively. Really, she didn't know what to think, what to say or feel, so she neatly changed the subject by saying, 'But how about you? How are you getting on?'

'Well, my job's barely started, but so far I'm loving it,' he grinned. 'I only moved in this week. Officially, the Easter holidays began yesterday. Being a private school, they break up a bit earlier. But most of the boys are staying on in case the Luftwaffe haven't finished with Plymouth.'

'There's not been a raid since that one in November, and even before that, they'd been few and far between.'

'I know, but if it were your son . . . ? One of them has parents stuck out in South Africa, and another one's home is in Guernsey, heaven help them. The housemasters and matron all live in, so they're there during the holidays anyway. Their accommodation is in the main house next to the dormitories. Beautiful house, it is. I thought mine was just going to be a flat, but it's a converted outbuilding, single storey but with two bedrooms and a little private area at the back. So all together, I'm really made up. And I hope you will be, too.'

Pippa met his gaze, his eyes questioning pools. A torrent of fractured emotions welled up in her breast. Oh, yes, she wanted that post more than anything in the world. It was what she'd dreamed of for so long, and heaven knew how long it would be before another such opportunity presented itself. It would also mean she could see her mum regularly, support her, even if she had Bea and her family — and now Mr Walter Yates as well — all around her. And she could see Duncan.

But no matter what, she would only accept the post if Steph could come, too. Her dear, happy-go-lucky friend who'd helped her through so much. She would never, *ever* abandon her in her own hour of need.

A knot of uncertainty tightened in her stomach. All she could now was to wait and see what happened.

CHAPTER TWENTY-NINE

'Well, this is highly irregular.' Matron looked up with a deep frown from perusing the open files on her desk. 'You know that when you signed up as probationers, you agreed to stay on here as staff nurses for a year after you qualified, and that will take you to the end of August. However...'

She bowed her head slightly and standing before her, Pippa crossed her fingers behind her back. She knew this wasn't going to be easy and she could feel her pulse banging against her temples. She'd have to be so careful what she said in answer to any questions.

'Staff Nurse Luscombe,' Matron continued, 'I can understand why you want to be nearer your mother after what you've both been through, losing your father and then your home. And the not inconsiderable matter of being injured in the tragic event when the maternity block was bombed. But what else have you got to say for yourself?'

She directed her steely gaze at Pippa who straightened her shoulders to give herself confidence. Matron was a strange mixture of compassion and strict authority. Pippa only hoped she could tap into her compassionate side.

'Well, I've loved every moment of my training here,' she began cautiously, 'and I believe I've given my studies and my work here absolutely everything I could. And it's because of that, I've learnt that what I really want is to be a theatre sister. Now, this is a unique opportunity for me to feel that I'd be serving a more close-knit community. But in the long run, I don't see a post as theatre sister coming up here for some while, so I'd be looking elsewhere for such a position soon, anyway.'

She waited with bated breath while Matron pursed her lips and nodded. 'Well, I can't disagree that you've given your all to this hospital in the time you've been here. You've been exceptional from the start. Now, Staff Nurse Chappel, I sympathise with your recent loss. But are you sure you wish to move away completely? Your parents live here in Plymouth, after all.'

Beside her, Pippa was aware of Steph gulping hard. 'Yes, I am sure,' Pippa was relieved to hear her say confidently. 'I have to admit that I'm not particularly close to my parents, and Tavistock isn't so far, anyway. I just . . . Whenever I have time off and go down to the Hoe or anywhere else in the city, I just keep seeing Rusty. All the places where we used to meet up. And . . . No.' She lifted her head defiantly and Pippa caught a spark of the old Steph. 'I really need to get right away. It really would be the best thing for me.'

'Hmm.' Matron steepled her fingers. 'Sister Tutor, what do you think? You know these girls better than I do.'

Sister Tutor Honeywell gave her kind smile. 'If it weren't for that tragic event, we would've lost Staff Nurse Chappel to marriage by now, anyway. I should be very sorry to lose two such exceptional nurses, but in their time here, they've both been utterly dedicated. I think we should be grateful for that, and under the exceptional and tragic circumstances they've both had to face, I believe we should let them go. Let them make a complete fresh start. And who knows, in the future, they might come back to us.'

Matron took some moments to consider, and Pippa felt the air sizzle between them. But then, Matron nodded. 'I'll be sorry to see them go, too. But I wouldn't want to stand in the way of what for Staff Nurse Luscombe will be, as she rightly says, a unique opportunity. So, reluctantly I have to say, I will agree to your leaving. But you will work here until the end of the month, the thirtieth of April and not a day sooner.'

Pippa inhaled deeply. 'Thank you, Matron. Sister Tutor. Your decision is much appreciated.'

Beside her, Steph muttered similar gratitude, and Pippa caught the hint of a smile twitch at Matron's lips while Sister Tutor beamed at them. What a relief.

The two friends walked back down the corridor together, Pippa realising she had hardly breathed throughout the interview. 'Phew, that was close,' she murmured. 'But . . . do you feel happier now?'

'Happy?' Steph's voice was unsteady. 'I'm not sure I know what happy means anymore. I just feel as if there's this big empty hole inside me that can never be filled. But I am really, *really* grateful for this, Pip. Thanks so much.'

'Don't thank me. Thank Elliott. He's such a lovely old fellow. You'll love him when you meet him, and his son, Dr William. And, Steph.' She caught Steph's arm and turned her towards her. 'Things will get better. I know how you feel. When Dad died, I never thought life would be the same again. Well, it won't. But the pain will get less. And I'll always be there by your side.'

'Yes, I know you will. I could never have wished for a truer friend.' And then Pippa saw her take a huge breath. 'Come on. To our future.' And linking her arm through Pippa's, Steph walked determinedly down the corridor.

***

Pippa turned over in bed and pulled the pillow over her head. Something was trying to drag her awake, but it was the middle of the night. She needed more sleep. Today was to be her and Steph's last day at the City. They'd said their goodbyes the previous evening and were packed and ready to leave. When they finished their shifts that evening, they were to hand in their uniforms, as they'd have brand new ones at the cottage hospital, and get to the station as quickly as they could to catch whatever train was available at that late hour to take them to their new lives in Tavistock. They were due on their new wards at eight o'clock sharp the next morning.

Perhaps if Pippa squeezed her eyes tight, she'd drop back to sleep. But something familiar wormed its way into her brain and triggered a response . . . Oh, no! The dreaded rising and falling wail was rolling out across the city. Surely not. It was nearly six months since the last attack. Hitler had other things to occupy him now, she thought, so it was probably just a false alarm.

The air-raid siren stopped, and Pippa could hear movement in the corridor. Well, at any moment the all-clear would reassure everyone and she could go back to sleep. Minutes passed, and there was nothing. Oh, come *on*. And then, in the distance, she could make out the droning of aircraft gradually increasing in volume as it drew nearer. It really was a raid!

A knock on the door, then, and Steph came in, ready dressed in her uniform. 'Wakey, wakey. Thought I'd go along to Casualty and see if I can help. You coming?'

Pippa threw back the bed covers. 'Might as well. Couldn't sleep through—'

The clacking of ack-ack guns cut her short as the familiar thrumming of heavy bombers roared overhead, followed by the whine of the night fighters endeavouring to chase them off. The first thunderous boom shook the building as the bombs began to fall, suddenly coming thick and fast as the aircraft swooped over the sleeping city.

'Sounds like there's a lot of them,' Steph groaned.

'And they're close,' Pippa just had time to say, pulling on her uniform just as several nearby explosions rent the air. 'Might as well finish our careers here on a bang!'

Within minutes, they were hurrying across to the main building of the hospital, running with others with the same idea, while some were heading for the relative safety of the dining room in the semi-basement. But when your number was up, your number was up. They both knew that only too well.

In Casualty, there was an air of nervous anticipation. Who knew what terrible cases they'd have to deal with? It would be a while before the victims could be dug out of the ruins of their destroyed homes or workplaces. Depending on where the bombs hit, the injured could be taken to the different hospitals in the city, but from the sounds of things, the raid was concentrated quite near and so the majority would be brought either there or to the branch of the Prince of Wales just down the road.

All instrument trolleys were prepared, cubicles waiting with staff in attendance. At last, the doors banged open and the first victim was hurriedly wheeled in. A junior doctor rushed in, panting as he slung his stethoscope around his neck and joined a waiting Casualty consultant as the trolley was whisked into the first cubicle and the curtains drawn. Pippa and Steph exchanged glances. They weren't needed yet.

The lull didn't last long. Three patients were wheeled in together, quickly assessed as ambulance crews delivered summaries of their wounds. Pippa noticed the orthopaedic consultant from her ward, Mr Longman, peering anxiously over one of the victims, then on his command, the trolley was being dashed down the corridor at speed.

'Ah, Staff Nurse Luscombe.' Pippa jerked with surprise as she heard him call her name, and hurried over. 'I understand we're losing you today to be the theatre sister at Tavvy,' he said rapidly. 'I'll be working with you there on occasion. I'd like you to assist me as staff nurse now. Let me see if you're as good as Dr Franfield says you are. Theatre Number One. Come on, now. Let's see if we can save this poor young woman's legs.'

A hundred thoughts swirled in Pippa's head. Dr Franfield, whether Elliott or William she didn't know, had been singing her praises. She shot Steph a swift glance, and Steph jabbed her head at her encouragingly. There was no time to lose.

Pippa hastened down the corridor in the direction of the theatres, her heart racing. This was her big chance.

* * *

'Ooph!' Pippa heaved her case up into the luggage rack and sat down with a huge sigh. Opposite her, Steph did the same, and they took a moment to gaze at each other as they caught their breath. 'That was lucky,' she went on. 'With trains all over the place, especially with those bombs falling at Laira station, we're lucky to get this one, like. At least we had the choice of the two different lines. Heaven knows when the next train will be. Or even if there'll be another one tonight. Then we'd have been stuck.'

'We'd have had to go back to the nurses' home.'

'And then be late on our first morning, if we couldn't get a really early train. Wouldn't have been our fault, mind. Hitler's, for deciding to bomb Plymouth again. I thought that was all over with.'

'At least we're alive,' Steph muttered. 'Did you hear, there was an Anderson shelter got a direct hit and everyone was killed, and a public shelter, too?'

'Yes, I did. And the victims that came to us were from Oreston. A dozen or more killed, one of the rescuers reckoned.'

'Did Mr Longman manage to save that poor woman's legs?'

'One of them, yes. But . . . the other had to amputated below the knee. It was horrible. I like to feel operations are mending people, not leaving them maimed.'

'But you saved her life. And you shouldn't have anything like that to deal with where we're going.' Steph bit on her bottom lip before she looked intently into Pippa's eyes. 'You know, I'm really grateful for this new start. For the first time since . . . I actually feel I'm looking forward to something.'

Pippa lifted her eyebrows. 'I'm really pleased to hear you say that. And . . . you're certain you don't mind starting as a staff nurse when I'm going to be a sister? At least I will be in two months' time.'

'Not at all. In fact, I'll be proper proud of my best friend,' Steph smiled. 'And I'm going to be on the kiddies' ward permanently, and that's my favourite. And I'm looking forward to getting to know Tavistock, too. I've only ever been there a couple of times, and it looks lovely.'

'It is, but a bit different now with all the Americans there,' Pippa told her as the train pulled out from its stop at tiny Bere Ferrers Station. 'I'll be really glad to get there. Having been up half the night and then on a long shift, I'm whacked.'

'Me, too. Is it far to walk when we get there?'

'Ten minutes, maybe? Actually, having got this train and arriving at Tavistock North rather than South, I'd say it's nearer. And it's downhill!' she grinned. 'And our rooms in the nurses' home will be ready and waiting for us, with our new uniforms, and all.'

For a while, she sat back, watching the countryside fading into dusk as the train continued northwards. But as they neared their destination, she leaned across and took Steph's hands. 'So, how does it feel, Staff Nurse Chappel, starting out on a new life?'

'It feels . . . really good. Thank you so much, Pip.'

Pippa could see tears welling in Steph's eyes, tears of sorrow, but also tears of hope. 'It was all quite by chance. But about time we had some good luck, don't you think?'

Steph didn't have time to reply. The train was slowing as they crossed Tavistock's magnificent viaduct and approached the station. They lifted down their luggage as the train lurched to a halt, and then climbed down from the carriage as a dozen or so other civilians and several GIs joined them on the platform. Leaving the station, Pippa led the way towards the cottage hospital as a late dusk settled on the town. Passing the opulent, Victorian villas in Watts Road, they turned down into Spring Hill towards the nurses' home and their new life.

***

'How are you doing, Phillipa, dear?'

Pippa looked up as Sister Eastercott entered the theatre anti-room, her round face in a beaming smile.

'Well, we scrubbed the theatre to within an inch of its life after yesterday's operations,' she replied, 'and Nurse Wilkins is going over everything — walls, floor, trolleys, lights, operating table — with disinfectant ready for this afternoon's surgery, as per your instructions.'

'As per *your* instructions, my dear,' Sister Eastercott smiled.

'Oh, well, I suppose so.' Pippa's voice was a mixture of surprise and pride. 'I was really only passing on what you told me, Sister.'

'Fiddlesticks. You'd have given her the exact same instructions. And Nurse Wilkins is extremely reliable. But do call me Shelley when it's just the two of us. I do hate formality.'

Pippa's mouth curved in a smile. 'I'll try and remember. And I've disinfected in here and sterilised all the equipment for this afternoon's list. Dr Franfield's doing a hysterectomy and two D and Cs. I've checked all the gas cylinders ready for the anaesthetist and all is in order, but I think we should put in an order for some more oxygen.'

'Well done. If you fill in the form, I'll sign it,' Shelley Eastercott agreed.

'And how was your meeting?' Pippa asked.

'Most informative.' Shelley bobbed her head up and down. 'I was able to report that you're doing brilliantly and that I have every confidence in you to take over as sister when I retire. And I have the most wonderful news.'

Her eyes shone and Pippa held her breath in anticipation. She watched as Shelley Eastercott took a deep breath as if to add emphasis to what she was about to reveal.

'We're getting penicillin!' she announced with glee.

Pippa caught her breath, her mouth dropping open. 'Really? Oh, glory be! At last!'

'Indeed!' Shelley nodded. 'Think how many civilian lives we'll save now. But it's been decided that staff nurses upwards are going to be taught how to prepare the injections. Apparently it comes solid, but it floats sufficiently to draw it up into a syringe already loaded with saline. Once it's all mixed, it's given intramuscularly into the buttock every three hours day and night.'

'Yes, I'd heard that. A friend of mine was treated with penicillin in the Royal Navy Hospital in Malta. He said how the repeated injections became terribly painful. And preparing them sounds extremely time consuming,' Pippa considered.

'Yes. Which is why it could be one of the duties you're called upon to perform when the theatre's not in use.'

'That makes sense. Oh, Sis . . . Shelley, I really think I'm going to love working here.'

'And how's your friend getting on? Is the change of scene helping her?'

'Yes, I believe it is. We've only been here a couple of weeks and she already seems happier.'

'Good. Oh, and the other bit of news is . . . Well, there was a lot of animated chatter going on in the outpatient waiting room so I popped my head round the door. Apparently, well, you might not know it, but there's a big old house up the road from here on the outskirts of the town that the Americans have been using as their HQ. Abbotsfield it's called. Field Marshall Montgomery has been seen there a lot. But today it's rumoured that Eisenhower's joining him there. Can you imagine that? People are out on the streets hoping to catch a glimpse of him. And everyone's guessing what it could all mean.'

Her voice had become more earnest as she'd spoken, and Pippa nodded gravely. What with all the American troops stationed around the town, especially the massive hospital camp up on Plaster Down, it had long been thought all was in preparation for the big push. An invasion of France by the Allied forces? No one knew exactly, or where and when. All was swathed in secrecy, of course. But did this mean it was coming closer? Would it be successful, or doomed to failure? She dared not think the latter.

Pippa drew in a deep breath. There'd be hundreds, thousands of lives lost. So many of these polite young GIs in the town, both black and white soldiers, would be making the ultimate sacrifice or returning with life-changing injuries. No wonder the extensive hospital at the Plaster Down Camp had already dealt with thousands of injured, mainly from the campaign in Italy or so it was thought. But . . . could it mean the end of the war was in sight? Would it be possible to drive the Nazis back? To liberate France and eventually all the other countries they had occupied? Were the Allied Forces ready at last? Strong enough?

She sincerely hoped so. But more than anything, she was relieved that Duncan couldn't be part of it.

CHAPTER THIRTY

Pippa could almost have skipped down the hill into the town, were it not for the brisk, blustery wind that whipped around her. It hardly felt like the beginning of June and she was glad she'd decided to wear her light summer coat. But she wasn't going to let the weather spoil her lightness of heart.

It was Sunday, and her regular day off. That was another advantage of her new role. No operations took place on a Sunday, so she was always off duty. And no night shifts during the week, unless she was covering for someone on one of the wards. In case an emergency operation cropped up, she was obliged to leave contact details if it were feasible, but she was assured that was a very rare occurrence. She had expected Steph to be envious of her regular shifts, but Steph seemed to be immersing herself with gusto in her work on the children's wards. They spent time together when they could, but today Steph was on duty, and Pippa was secretly pleased. She was going to spend the day at the Chollacott household. Steph would have been welcome, too, but Pippa was hoping for some private time with Duncan who also had Sundays off, unless there was something that needed urgent attention.

As she came down into the town centre, it seemed unusually quiet. Yes, there were families walking along the road, children playing on the swings in the Meadows, but no American jeeps moving along the streets or GIs fooling about, enjoying themselves on their free day. Black soldiers were only allowed out on Wednesdays which the locals considered racist and unfair, but there wasn't an American of any creed or colour in sight, the buzz they created in the town utterly silenced.

With a tiny frown creasing her forehead, Pippa hurried up the Chollacotts' long front garden. Having turned most of the back garden into a vast vegetable plot, Don had been busy in the beds at the front, too, and the feathery leaves of young carrots were poking up in the flowerbeds between the died-back leaves of the spring bulbs. Hmm, fresh carrots would be lovely in a few weeks' time, and Pippa wondered what home-grown vegetables would be on the Sunday dinner menu today, alongside, well, probably rabbit as it wasn't on ration and was easier to come by than other meat.

The house was bursting at the seams and utterly chaotic. Ernie was on shift and Sharon was with her friends back in Plymouth, but the rest of the Chollacott family including Leonard were all present. Walter was a regular visitor on Sundays, always bringing with him something from his grocer's shop. Then as paying guests, Miss Primrose and Miss Polly were there for lunch, as well as Mr and Mrs Robbins. Sylvie, Bea and Adeline were busy in the kitchen with so many mouths to feed, and when Don let Pippa in the front door, he went back to laying up the table, trying to squeeze in all the settings.

'I'll just pop down to say hello to Mum, and then I'll help you,' Pippa offered at once.

'Actually, if you can help Susie entertaining the children, that would be much appreciated. They're out in the back garden.'

'Yes, of course,' Pippa chuckled, knowing how demanding Norman in particular was.

She hurried down the stairs to the kitchen where the three women were buzzing around, with several pots steaming on the cooker. 'Hi, everyone. Hello, Mum.' She hugged Adeline, placing a kiss on her cheek. 'Don said I'd be most use keeping an eye on the little ones.'

'Yes, you do that,' her mum answered, her face hot and flustered.

'Probably find Norman up a tree,' Bea told her, tipping potatoes into a roasting pan. 'Least if he falls out, he'll have first-hand medical help,' she added with a grimace.

An hour later, Duncan and Walter had both arrived and there followed the not inconsiderable task of carrying all the food upstairs and dishing it out. It wasn't until everybody's meal was served and the children were tucking into theirs that peace descended and decent conversation could begin.

'I noticed how quiet the town is as I came along,' Pippa observed. 'Not an American to be seen.'

'Yes, looks like they've gone. Disappeared almost overnight,' Duncan said gravely. 'You know what that means.'

Glances were exchanged all around the table. Yes, they all knew. If the Americans had gone, it meant the Allied invasion of France was imminent.

'So, d'you think this might be, dare I say it, the beginning of the end of the war?' Pippa asked quietly. At the hospital, she had little chance to discuss the world outside.

Beside her, she heard Duncan draw in a huge breath. 'Let's hope so. But it's hardly going to be instant. Look at what a fight the Germans were putting up in Italy. Some say Monte Cassino only fell because they'd decided to pull back anyway.'

'There'll be many, many Allied losses,' Walter put in, shaking his head sadly. 'The town might be devoid of Americans now, but I don't suppose it'll be long afore many of them are back, badly wounded, and going to that there huge hospital on Plaster Down. And many of them won't be coming back at all.'

Pippa shuddered. She knew it was true. 'Let's just pray their sacrifice will be worth it.'

'I wonder when we'll get any news,' Don pondered. 'I know everyone's guessed what the build-up of troops in the area was for, but exactly how or when or where has been top secret.'

'That's right,' Len agreed. 'The build-up's been going on so long, it's hard to believe it's actually happening.'

'Well, I think we should forget about the war for now, and enjoy this lovely meal the ladies have cooked for us,' Miss Primrose declared.

'Yes, of course. This rabbit pie is delicious,' her sister confirmed, though everyone knew the pastry was made entirely from lard and some grey substance that was supposed to be flour. Oh, for the end of the war and better food on their plates!

Later on, the sun had peeped out and Pippa sat on a bench with Duncan in the back garden on the small area of lawn that was left. He stretched out his bad leg, gently rubbing around his knee.

'Still giving you jip?' she asked gently.

'Sometimes,' he muttered in reply. 'I'd say it's over a mile walk from the school down to here. And then I've got to get back and most of it's steeply uphill. I can't use the van with the small ration of petrol it's allowed. Just enough for transporting any large items I need for repairs and maintenance around the school. But,' he paused, turning to her with fire burning in his eyes, 'I'm hoping that before long, I can manage a walk in the Meadows with you on top of that on a Sunday. That is . . .'

He broke off, gazing at her intently. Yes, there was definitely a strong, unbreakable thread linking them together and an eruption of pure joy burst into Pippa's heart. When she was at the hospital, she was completely immersed in her work, but more and more, Duncan was in her thoughts when she was off duty. Yes, she knew she was falling in love with him, but she mustn't let it happen. In a few weeks' time, she would be *the* theatre sister at the hospital. It was what she'd always dreamed of, and a magnitude of jumbled confusion choked her throat.

Despite the cool day, a slick of sweat broke out down her back. She was rescued by the realisation that Norman was standing in front of them. 'I want you to play football with me,' he demanded.

Pippa heard Duncan's sigh of exasperation and came to his rescue. 'Now you know Duncan mustn't use his leg too much,' she told a pouting Norman. 'Not that there's much room and your granddad would be cross if we damaged his vegetables. But would I do?'

She got to her feet, acknowledging the grateful smile Duncan threw her — and which sent a warm feeling spreading down to her toes.

* * *

'It's happening. At last.'

Pippa glanced up with surprise. It was Tuesday morning and already two tonsillectomies had been carried out, and now she was selecting the instruments that would be required for the afternoon's operation list, ready to place in the sterilisers. Sister Shelley Eastercott had been to the office to collect the operating list for the following day, and now her face was alight with a mixture of excitement and consternation.

'Sorry, I'm not with you,' Pippa said, her concentration broken. 'What's happening?'

'The invasion.' The sister bobbed her head emphatically. 'There was an announcement at half past nine this morning on the BBC Home and European Services. That chap with the nice clear voice, John Snagge.'

'Oh.' It seemed to Pippa herself a fairly mild reaction to such a momentous event, but they'd waited for this moment for so long that it seemed strange and almost incomprehensible now it had come. 'What did it say?' she asked eagerly now.

'Not a great deal, apparently. He just read out what he called *Communiqué Number One*. That under the command of General Eisenhower, Allied naval forces, supported by strong air forces, began landing Allied armies this morning on the northern coast of France. That was it. But if you ask me, there'll be other announcements throughout the day and the king's supposed to be giving a speech this evening.'

Pippa took a moment to take it all in, and blew out a breath through pursed lips. 'This is it, then,' she murmured. 'Goodness, I pray it works. There'll be so many casualties. All those young men. So many of them having been here in Tavistock. Well, I sincerely wish them God speed.'

'Yes, God speed,' Shelley nodded gravely.

* * *

'Well, I don't know, really I don't.'

Bea shook her head despairingly as a group from the Chollacott family took a walk in the Meadows. It was another Sunday early in July, and after now what had become the ritual of a gathering of the clan for lunch, it had taken a while to clear everything away and complete the task of washing up. Pippa was delighted that Duncan felt able to join the constitutional after-meal stroll. He no longer used a stick, although he still walked with a pronounced limp. Pippa stayed by his side, not wanting to miss a moment of his company, even if they were surrounded by other family members.

'What's that, Bea?' she asked, sensing the dear woman's concern.

'I were just saying, there's all our brave lads, not forgetting all the Americans and Canadians and all the others, fighting their hearts out and giving their lives, and making progress against they bugger Jerries in France, and us thinking that in time, us *will* beat them. And then they start launching they dreadful flying bomb doodlebug things at us.'

'I know, it's awful, isn't it?' Pippa replied. 'They sound absolutely terrifying. And they're so high calibre, too.'

'The sooner the Allies get as far as the launching sites and destroy them, the better,' Walter, who was walking arm in arm with Adeline, put in. 'Trouble is, they've apparently built portable launch sites now.'

'Well, there was me thinking earlier on that maybe us'll move back home to Plymouth at the end of the summer term, and leave poor Don and Sylvie in peace,' Bea ranted. 'Especially now you've done those repairs to the house, bless you, Duncan. I know he works odd hours, but I do miss seeing my Len all the time. But then first there were that big raid at the end of April, your very last day in Plymouth, Pippa, maid,' she said, bobbing her head at Pippa, 'and now they devils are sending over they horrendous bombs that don't even need planes and pilots. They'm saying up to a hundred a day be reaching London.'

'Yes, over London, Mum,' Duncan said gently. 'Flying over the narrowest part of the Channel. I don't think they'd have the capability to reach as far as Plymouth. And I'd have thought Jerry had enough on his plate attempting, unsuccessfully we hope, to repel the Allied invasion without sparing planes to raid the West Country again.'

'Well, I wouldn't put it past them, so I think us'll stay put a while longer. But when us do go, I don't see that Don and Sylvie will have any difficulty renting out my room in the house. And I'm sure they'll be glad to have their dining room back, and all.'

'Knowing Gran and Gramps, they'll likely rent that out for a while, too,' Duncan considered. 'With so many homeless, I expect they'll want to be as helpful as they can.'

'Yes, you'm probably right,' Bea agreed. 'We'm so lucky our house is still standing. Oh, sorry, Adeline, dear. I didn't mean to upset you.'

'No, you haven't,' Adeline assured her. 'That's in the past now. I've come to accept it. Just as I've come to accept that my darling Neil's never coming back. I miss him dreadfully, of course, but . . . You've all helped me so much. And now I know I must build a new life for myself.'

Pippa saw her mother turn her head and look up at Walter, an enraptured light in her eyes, a look he returned with a loving smile. Oh, she wanted so much for her mum to be happy again. Her dad could never be replaced, but Walter was such a kind soul and he could be just the one to make her mum's life complete again.

'Sharon, would you keep an eye on Lucy for us?' Bea called out. 'And, Norman!' she shouted as the nine-year-old shinned high up in a tree. 'Get down from there at once!'

Beside her, Pippa heard Duncan chuckle. 'That would've been me as a tacker and Mum wouldn't have turned a hair. I think she's getting more protective in her old age.'

Pippa smiled secretly. Duncan barely had a Devonshire accent, so to hear him use one of his mother's local dialect words was both amusing and endearing. 'Not surprising, when you think what—' she began.

'Oi, I heard that! Not so much of the old, if you don't mind!' Bea laughed aloud. 'And soon us'd better be getting back for our tea. I believe Sylvie's got hold of some ham, and Don were going to pick lettuce and tomatoes from the garden.'

'Funny how obsessive we've all got about food,' Duncan commented. 'But I must say, I wouldn't mind getting back soon. Give my leg a chance to recover before the long haul up the hill back to the school.'

'I'll walk part way with you again,' Pippa said softly.

Duncan glanced down at her, the look in his eyes almost tentative. 'Yes, I'd like that. But you don't have to, you know. It's in the wrong direction for you.'

'No, I want to,' she answered, her voice low. 'It's the only chance we have to be alone together. I think . . . I think our mums would like us to be maybe more than friends.'

'And . . . would that be a bad thing?' he asked, his face suddenly tight and intense. 'Or is there some dashing young doctor at the hospital?'

'Good heavens, no,' Pippa laughed uneasily.

'So I'm safe from any rivalry there, then?'

'Yes, I should say so.'

Oh, dear. Was she leading him on? She mustn't! Her career must come first. But could she possibly bring herself to tell him to look elsewhere? It was breaking her, but she must put him right.

All through the rest of the afternoon, she felt all jumbled up inside. When it was finally time to go and she said all her usual goodbyes, it was as if someone else had taken over her voice. She walked down the long front garden path with Duncan, nerves stretched and taut. She barely noticed what they were talking about as they crossed over Abbey Bridge and along past the cottages and the little school in Dolvin Road.

'I wonder what the news will be this evening?' Duncan mused as they crossed the end of Vigo Bridge and almost immediately began the ascent up Mount Tavy Road. 'At least, even with my peg-leg, I'll be back in time for *War Report*. But there's no need for you to come any further, you know.'

'Well, yes, there is.' Pippa's heart was rattling in her chest. The moment she was dreading, that was tearing her apart, had come. 'In fact, well . . . I need to tell you something.'

Duncan stopped dead and turned to her, gazing deep into her eyes. 'And I've got something to tell you,' he grated, his voice suddenly like gravel. 'I felt it the moment I set eyes on you, and it's done nothing but grow ever since. All the time I was away from you, every letter we exchanged, was like a dagger in my heart. Because all I wanted was to be with you. And this damned leg has been a blessing in disguise.'

'No, don't say—'

'Ssh.' He pressed his finger against her lips. 'Let me finish. These months I've been back and I've been able to be with you more often, has only made my feelings run deeper. Pippa, Sister Luscombe,' he said with a teasing smile, 'I love you.'

Pippa stared up at him as a quiet and steady euphoria spread through her bones even as confused bewilderment stuck in her gullet. This couldn't be. This mustn't be. But she didn't move a muscle as he leaned forward and his lips touched hers, soft and gentle and sending ripples along her skin. Her senses dropped away, her entire being wreathed in enthralled rapture.

'So, what was it you wanted to tell me?' he barely whispered as they drew apart.

Pippa gulped, her head spinning. How could she tell him? She didn't *want* to tell him.

'Let me guess,' he said, his smile so gentle and understanding. 'You wanted to tell me that you've worked so hard to get where you are in your career, and that there's no room in your life for romance. Well, I understand that. But surely you can still have your career, but find a little bit of your heart for me as well? I'd like us to be more than good friends, and then see what the future brings. I just want to know if . . . if you think you could love me, too.'

Pippa stared up at him, a maelstrom of emotions swirling inside her. But, yes. Duncan had lit something inside her that couldn't be denied. And the fact that he understood how she felt made that flickering flame flare even brighter.

'Yes,' she managed to croak. 'I think I do love you already, Duncan.'

She saw the light blaze in his eyes, and she was in his arms. This time, his kiss was more confident, and she felt herself responding. When they finally pulled apart, each was as breathless and embarrassed as the other. Then they both went to speak at the same time. And laughed. And the ice was broken.

'Well, at least you've given me something to get me through until next Sunday,' Duncan smiled. 'If it weren't for this leg, I think I'd skip all the way back.'

'Well, be careful you don't trip over,' Pippa chuckled. 'I don't want to find you among my patients.'

'You won't find me on the broken heart ward now, anyway,' he teased. 'But we'd both better be getting back. Until next Sunday, then.'

'Yes. But . . . what do we tell the family?'

'Nothing.' Duncan looked surprised. 'They have eyes. Mum'll guess in seconds, if she hasn't already.'

'Yes, bless her, she will. Well, see you next week, then.'

It was an awkward moment, neither wanting to leave but knowing they had to. Pippa turned away, but a few seconds later, looked back over her shoulder to see Duncan limping up the hill. He, too, turned back and blew her a kiss, and then they both went on their way, Pippa with a joyous sensation calmly simmering inside her.

CHAPTER THIRTY-ONE

'A bit like old times, this,' Steph commented. 'Can't remember the last time we were on a ward together.'

'But we could be anyone behind these masks,' Pippa answered, tying hers behind her head as they prepared to enter the children's side ward reserved for diphtheria cases.

'What, you wouldn't recognise me by my scintillating personality?' Steph quipped back, and Pippa was pleased to catch a hint of the old, buoyant young woman she knew.

'But, of course. I'm not sure that masking up puts the children at ease, mind.'

'That's where being bright and cheerful comes in. Some hospitals don't gown up for diphtheria, but Dr Whitelock insists on it. He says it protects us, even though we've been vaccinated. But it also protects the patients from us giving them something else on top.'

'Well, that makes sense.'

'And the kiddies soon get used to it, poor lambs. They'll be in here for weeks, flat on their backs with no pillows, and kept utterly still and quiet. Poor things look so pale and ill, and are so bored.'

'Poor mites. Can you imagine? I can't understand why some authorities won't cover vaccination programmes.'

'They would if they were to come in here and see for themselves how awful it can be. Come on. You ready?'

Pippa nodded and then followed Steph on to the ward. A nursing orderly looked across at them from washing a little boy as he lay in his cot, and another nurse was emerging with a bed pan from the screens placed around another bed. Pippa at once was aware of the distinctive sickly sweet smell of the horrible disease that for a few moments until she got used to it, almost made her feel nauseous.

'Good afternoon, children!' Steph called brightly. 'I've brought a friend of mine to help look after you today. This is Sister Luscombe, and she's been dying to meet you all.'

Her jolly words were hardly met with a response, and Pippa's heart bled. These poor children were too ill to make a sound, and their dreadfully painful throats weren't going to help. In the gap between Steph's cap and her mask, she saw the compassionate expression on her friend's face.

'What would you like me to do?' she asked, wanting desperately to help.

'Help me with the drugs round would be good. The number of units of serum for each child is on their charts. If you can measure them out, I can help them swallow it down. That'll save time, and then we can read to them or entertain them in some way afore tea time. All really soft food, so you can help with the preparation. We've got a couple just on bottles, they're so young, so we have to be careful they don't choke. An extra pair of hands always comes in useful.'

Pippa nodded as she glanced around the ward. With the children having to be washed, toileted and fed lying on their backs, they could do with one-to-one nursing. The whole set-up made her feel woefully inadequate, but she knew that the patient-to-nurse ratio here at the cottage hospital was much more favourable than at some of the large city hospitals.

She counted eight children in the ward. 'So many for a small town like Tavistock,' she said to Steph in a low voice as they made their way around.

'It's the overcrowding from all the evacuees. Now they're bombing London again with those wretched doodlebugs, some who might've gone home have stayed, and others who had gone home have come back, bringing disease with them and spreading it through the schools. Though being the holidays now, hopefully we won't get any new admissions for a while.'

Pippa nodded as Steph took the next dose from her. She could see from the notes that the little girl was only five years old, though she was by no means the youngest on the ward. Watching as Steph tried to get the child to swallow the serum, she saw her frown and put the little cup to one side.

'Let me look at you, Annie, sweetheart,' she heard Steph say. 'Can you open your mouth for me?'

A moment later, Steph had abandoned the attempt to administer the drug. 'The membrane on her throat and larynx is getting worse and she can hardly swallow,' she told Pippa in a whisper. 'I'm going to find Sister on the main children's ward and ask her to call Dr Whitelock and ask if Annie can have the serum intravenously. Can you stay with her while I'm gone? I think she's getting distressed.'

'Of course. Hello, Annie,' she said, stepping up to the little bed. 'I'm Sister Luscombe, but you can call me Pippa.'

'That's a funny name,' the little girl croaked.

Pippa smiled. 'It's short for Philippa. Now I don't want you to talk, but shall I tell you a story?'

The child nodded, her eyes sunken in her pale face, and Pippa started making up a story about a naughty pixie on Dartmoor. By the time she got to the end, Steph was back, wheeling in a trolley and a mobile stand.

'Now, Annie,' she said, 'we're going to put a needle in your arm so we can put your medicine straight into you and you won't need to swallow anymore. And it'll make you get better more quickly. It'll sting for just a minute but then it won't hurt. Just need you to keep very still. Sister Luscombe will hold your arm for me. Okay?'

Five minutes later, Annie was linked up to her drip and encased in a steam tent. Pippa helped Steph for the rest of the afternoon, the time flying by until they went for their own break.

'You're not obliged to stay to the end of my shift,' Steph told her as they finished their tea.

'No, I want to. I've nothing else to do this evening, like. I can see why Matron redirected me here when there weren't any ops planned for this afternoon.'

'Well, I'm grateful for your help,' Steph said warmly. 'I need someone to keep a strict eye on little Annie.'

Pippa duly sat by the child's side. Annie had settled down to sleep but as the time ticked by, she was becoming more restless and her breathing noisier. Pippa took her pulse. It was becoming more and more rapid, and Pippa motioned Steph over.

'Before we go off duty, I think we should get Dr Whitelock to take a look,' she told her.

A quick glance at the child, and Steph nodded. 'Yes, thanks, Pippa. I agree. I'll go and try to get hold of him now.'

Twenty minutes later, Dr Whitelock scurried into the ward, tying on his mask. Pippa had assisted him for several operations and thought what a kind man he was and nice-looking in a self-effacing sort of way. She was impressed by the tender way he examined little Annie, and then, oh goodness, she caught something in his eyes when he looked at Steph. Something that reminded her of the way Duncan looked at her . . .

'She needs a tracheotomy,' he said gravely. 'Staff Nurse Chappel, can you arrange for her to be taken straight down to Theatre? And that's Sister Luscombe behind the mask, if I'm not mistaken? You okay to assist? I know it's out of hours for you.'

'Of course. It's an emergency. I never come away from Theatre without it being sterilised and ready.'

'Good. Come on, then.' He rushed towards the doors, but not before, Pippa noticed, throwing Steph another glance.

***

'We must do this more often,' Steph said jauntily as they followed Dr Whitelock down the school corridor, each carrying a box of equipment.

'Well, I've no ops until this afternoon and everything's prepared, so it was something different to be assigned to,' Pippa replied. 'And after that time with you on the children's diphtheria ward, I was keen to be involved. It was awful seeing what that poor little girl, Annie, went through. She was lucky to survive.'

Steph nodded. 'Yes, I can't understand why some people are against vaccination. Hopefully we won't have any objectors this morning. But I think if anyone's refused consent for their child, Dr Whitelock will go and knock on their front door and persuade them otherwise.'

'And who would refuse the lovely Dr Whitelock?' Pippa commented, lowering her voice.

'Ssh, he'll hear you,' Steph warned.

'No, he won't. Look, he's talking to the headmistress now. Anyway, he *is* rather lovely. And he's just so gentle with the children. Not all the doctors here are so human. I see them all, don't forget, in Theatre.'

'Pippa?' Steph quizzed her. 'What about Duncan? I thought you and he . . . ?'

'Oh, we are. I didn't mean . . . I just mean Dr Whitelock's very nice, that's all, isn't he? You're lucky to work quite a lot with him.'

She shot Steph a sideways glance. Her dear friend probably hadn't noticed the way Dr Whitelock looked at her sometimes, but she wasn't going to say anything more. It was September now, and only nine months since Rusty had died so tragically. But Steph couldn't bury herself in grief for ever. She already seemed brighter, a little more her old self. And Pippa was sure her work on the children's wards was helping her. And she'd see the kind Dr Whitelock every day. He was a lot older than they were by a good dozen years, but did that matter? He was highly regarded by the other doctors in the town, and she knew for a fact that he was single.

Could there ever be something between him and Steph? Pippa would like to think there might be, but the last thing she wanted was to see Steph hurt again. She'd said just enough maybe to set Steph thinking that way, but she'd not say anything more. She was just so enthralled with her relationship with Duncan, rejoicing when he swept her into his arms each Sunday, that she wanted Steph to be as happy as she was. Losing Rusty had broken Steph, but Pippa wanted desperately to put her back together. She'd sown the seed, and now it was up to time to see if it grew.

***

'What did you think of the film?' Pippa asked as she walked arm in arm with Steph up West Street from the old corn exchange cinema back towards the nurses' home. It was October and so dark that they had to make their way with the aid of a torch with a piece of cardboard with just a slit in it over its light. It was scarcely any help but it was what you had to do. 'Bit of an old Victorian melodrama, if you ask me,' she went on.

'Yes, it was rather,' Steph agreed. '*Fanny by Gaslight*, indeed. Supposed to be so good, I was pleased they were showing it again, but I think we wasted our money.'

'But at least we've had a good night out together. And fantastic to see in the *Pathé News* how the Allies are gradually liberating France. Really does look as if the war is coming to an end. In Europe at least.'

'Wouldn't be too sure about that,' Steph scoffed. 'They thought they'd destroyed all the doodlebug launch sites, and now the Nazis are sending over even bigger ones from the Hague.'

'Yes, the V2s,' Pippa agreed with a shudder. 'And there are so many injured GIs coming back here to the hospital up on Plaster Down, and heaven knows where all our own wounded are going to. I just wish it could all be over.'

'Don't we all!' Steph replied vehemently. 'Then maybe we wouldn't have to be creeping back home in the dark. I really wouldn't feel that safe walking home from the flicks on my own now the evenings have drawn in and we can only use a dimmed torch like this. Worse than useless. And of course . . .'

She broke off. Pippa knew exactly what Steph was thinking. It was because of the blackout that Rusty had died. It wasn't something she ever expected her friend to get over, no matter what other happiness the future might hold for her.

'Yes, I've always hated it when autumn kicks in,' Pippa said, neatly changing the subject. 'I never mind the colder weather so much as the dark. And even with daylight saving, it's dark when you come out of the cinema.'

'I know what you mean. But it was good of you to give up an evening when you could've been seeing your Duncan,' Steph was saying now. 'I do appreciate it.'

'Well, we don't normally see each other during the week,' Pippa informed her. 'After a full day's work, his leg still aches a bit and it's quite a walk for him. And we both feel it'd be a bit awkward for me to go up to the school. Besides, with the dark evenings now, I wouldn't want to be walking back from there on my own. But come on, we'd better hurry back. Need our beauty sleep.'

'You might,' Steph scorned as they turned up steep Spring Hill towards the hospital and the nurses' home. 'Who have I got to look my best for?'

'Not a certain young doctor who frequents the children's wards?' Pippa suggested softly, not wanting to push Steph too far.

'Oh, well.' Pippa could almost hear her blushing and her heart rejoiced. 'He is very nice. And always very pleasant to me. But he is to everyone.'

'And . . . would you object if he were especially nice to *you*?'

There was a brief silence before Steph gave a short laugh. 'No, I suppose I wouldn't. But he isn't.'

'You know, I'm not so sure about that. Just so you know, I've seen the way he looks at you sometimes.'

There was a short pause before Steph replied in an unsure voice, 'Oh, d'you think so?'

'Yes. And . . . I'm saying this as your dearest friend, but you are allowed to look to the future, you know. Coming here was meant to be a fresh start for both of us. For me it's meant that Duncan and I have got to know each other better, and all the time we're growing closer. And for you, well, I know how hard things have been for you, but if there's a chance of happiness for you, you must take it.'

They'd reached the nurses' home now, and let themselves in the front door. Their rooms were on different floors, and they paused by the stairs.

'Yes, you're right, Pip,' Steph said thoughtfully. 'It's hard, but I must let go of the past. Let go of Rusty. It . . . it needed you to tell me. To say it out loud. So, thank you.'

She enclosed Pippa in a hug, and then they parted. Pippa made her way up to her room, filled with relief that she hadn't upset Steph, the film forgotten. Before long, she was snuggling down in bed and summoned Duncan into her thoughts. With any luck, she'd dream of him all night long.

***

Pippa took off her veil cap and slipped on her outdoor coat over her uniform. Unlike at the City Hospital, there were no strict rules here about wearing one's uniform beyond the hospital grounds. She had two hours off duty and was popping down to see her mum. The November day had turned cold and windy, and her winter coat would be far warmer than her nurse's cloak.

She'd scarcely turned down into Spring Hill when the figure of a man emerged in front of her, making her jump. Her heart settled and she went to side-step the stranger, tossing a laugh into the air and expecting him to do the same. But he stepped across in front of her, blocking her path, and she looked up warily. His smiling face seemed vaguely familiar but she couldn't quite place it.

'You must remember me,' he said in a friendly, casual manner. 'It is my butterfly girl, isn't it?'

Pippa jerked back with a gasp of surprise before uttering another subdued laugh. 'Heavens, I do remember you,' she answered, keeping her voice steady and polite. He was the last person she was expecting to see. 'Archie Yelland, isn't it? What a coincidence! What are you doing here in Tavistock?'

'Looking for you, actually. So this is no coincidence.'

His tone was utterly polite and affable, his expression quite genuine, but Pippa at once felt on the defensive. 'Really?' she asked cautiously. 'But why? And how did you find me?'

'Easy,' he smiled. 'I went to the City Hospital and asked some of the nurses going in and out. Eventually spoke to someone who knew you'd come to work here. I said I was an old friend, which I'd like to think I am. I guessed if I hung outside this place long enough, I'd find you.'

'So you've been hanging around, hoping I'd appear. Well, look, I'm sorry,' she said briskly, 'but I haven't got long and I'm on my way to visit my mother.'

'Oh, well, I can walk with you if you don't mind?'

Yes, she did mind! But she didn't like to appear rude and Archie wasn't being in the least obnoxious. Just the opposite, in fact.

'All right, then. But I really am on a tight schedule,' she told him, setting off down the hill at a pace. 'But I don't understand why you've gone to such lengths to find me.'

'Oh, that's easy. I really wanted to see you to see if you'd change your mind and would like to come out with me. It's just that . . .' Pippa noticed his face fall slightly before he gave a wistful smile. 'I've been invalided out of the army. My shoulder was smashed up by a bullet. In Italy. So I'm no good for active service anymore. I'm back home now, helping in the family business again. Not making any new saddles as yet, though hopefully that trade will pick up once the war's over. No, we're mainly mending tack for farmers and others who still use horses. And mending shoes as well nowadays,' he added with a small laugh.

'So...' He stopped, and turned to her, biting his bottom lip. 'I've thought about you so much. You were never far from my thoughts, and when I was wounded... well, thinking about you helped me get through it. So, yes, I literally just wanted to see you again.'

His tone was utterly sincere, his brow knitted in earnest. Pippa drew her lips together. She supposed it wasn't his fault he'd taken to her and broken off his engagement to Ruby. Neither was all the trouble she'd had from Ruby his fault either.

'Look, I'm sorry, Mr Yelland—'

'Archie, please.'

'All right. Archie it is. I'm sorry you were wounded. And I'm sorry you've gone to all this trouble to find me. But after all the trouble Ruby caused me when you broke off with her, nearly getting me thrown out of nursing—'

'Oh, don't talk to me about Ruby!' Archie surprised her with an exasperated sigh. 'She's been hounding me ever since I got back. News travels fast in a small town, and word got to her, even though she's stationed in Exeter. In the ATS,' he scoffed. 'That was something she always hated the idea of. Fully trained as a driver and mechanic, and doing very well for herself if she's to be believed. But she won't leave me alone. Pestering me all the time to get back together. I keep telling her, but she won't take no for an answer. What a fool I was to propose to her in the first place! I regret it from the bottom of my heart.'

Well, knowing Ruby as she did, Pippa could well sympathise with him. 'I can understand that. But I'm afraid you're out of luck with me. I can see you're a nice chap, and maybe under other circumstances... But I'm already spoken for. I have a sweetheart and it's serious.'

She watched as Archie's handsome face fell. 'Oh,' he said flatly. 'Then I wish you well. I expect you can't wait for the war to be over and for him to come back to you.'

'As a matter of fact, he's here in Tavistock. He was invalided out, too. Of the Merchant Navy.'

'I'm sorry to hear that, too. So there's no chance for me.'

Pippa shook her head with a wry smile. 'No, I'm sorry. But you'll find someone, I'm sure. There'll be plenty a young woman thrilled to go out with you.'

'But none of them will be my butterfly girl.'

Pippa couldn't help but chuckle as she came to a stop outside the house in Plymouth Road. 'The poem was very good. And I was flattered. But look. This is where my mum lives.'

'Time to say goodbye, then. And good luck with your man.'

She saw the sadness in his face as he turned away. He looked so forlorn, walking down the road, and she felt sorry for him. Her opinion of him had been coloured by circumstances, she considered now, and she really did hope he escaped Ruby's clutches and found happiness. But now she put him right out of her mind and she turned in at the gate and hurried up the path.

CHAPTER THIRTY-TWO

'Brrh, proper snipey, isn't it?' Pippa shivered as she met Steph coming in the door to the nurses' home.

'Mmm, yes, I'll be glad to get out of my uniform and put some warmer clothes on. Warm enough on the wards, but as soon as you come outside . . .'

'Well, it is nearly Christmas, so it's what we should expect. Meet you down in the kitchen when you've changed, and we'll have a nice hot cuppa.'

'Sounds like heaven,' Steph agreed.

Pippa hurried upstairs to her room and changed into a thick jumper and woollen slacks. Oo, it was good to take off her shoes, give her feet a good rub and wriggle them into her cosy slippers. She'd take her hot-water bottle down to fill in the kitchen, too. She didn't fancy getting into a cold bed!

'Have you only just finished in Theatre?' Steph asked five minutes later as they waited for the kettle to boil on the gas. 'That's late, isn't it? Or have you been helping out on a ward?'

'No, it was an op,' Pippa informed her. 'An old lady fell in the snow and ice this morning and broke her ankle. Compound fracture so it needed surgery, but we had to wait for her to have been nil-by-mouth long enough before the anaesthetic. As luck would have it, she'd only had a cup of tea and a biscuit first thing. Otherwise she might've had to wait until tomorrow, and you can imagine, she was in a lot of pain.'

'Poor soul,' Steph sympathised. 'So she's likely to be in over Christmas.'

'Without doubt. But she lives alone, so she'll probably have a far better time in hospital. Kettle's boiled.' Pippa carefully measured a spoon of tea into the pot and poured in just enough hot water for two cups. It was half what you'd normally use and the tea would be weak, but it was all you were allowed.

'Always try to make Christmas special for the patients,' Steph agreed, 'especially on the children's wards. We're devising as many games as we can for those who are able. We've made a pin the tail on the donkey, only it's pin the moustache on Hitler. And there'll be singing and storytelling, and probably better food than they'd have at home.'

'They say there's a glut of carrots and it's amazing what you can with them. Apparently you can cut them into strips and make them into candy.'

Steph pulled a face as she took the cup from Pippa. 'Not sure I'd fancy that. But I'm looking forward to seeing the kiddies' faces when they get some normal sweets — courtesy of the American camp — and I'm sure you know the whole town has been collecting old toys to give as presents.'

'Duncan's made a whole boxful of little animals carved from odd bits of leftover wood he found in one of the outhouses. Going to bring them down tomorrow.'

'Oh, how wonderful! They'll love those!'

Pippa could see Steph's face was lit with enthusiasm. It really was a delight to see the old Steph beginning to return. 'Is that why you volunteered to work over Christmas?' she asked gently, knowing there was another reason.

'Mainly.' Steph's face was serious now. 'Some of the long-term tackers are almost like family now. But it's also an excuse not to go home to Mum and Dad. If I had the time off, they'd want me to be with them, and I'd rather not. Besides, you know...' She broke off, her voice faltering, and Pippa laid a comforting hand on her arm.

'Yes. Boxing Day. The first anniversary,' she said in a low voice that rang with compassion. 'I'll be going to the Chollacotts' on Christmas Day and Boxing Day. But I'll be there for you first thing in the morning and again in the evening. I won't stay late so we can spend some time together.'

Steph nodded, and gave her a watery smile. 'I know. And you're the best friend I could ever have had.'

Pippa smiled back. 'I do my best. And then don't forget we've got the nurses' Christmas dinner a few days later,' she reminded her, her tone brightening, 'when the doctors serve us. They say it used to be fabulous afore the war, but now with rationing it'll just be basic, but fun all the same. Just like the hospital dance! Apparently, they used to put on a fantastic meal for the doctors and their wives afore the dancing and party bit, but that part's been temporarily abandoned because of rationing. I'm quite looking forward to that, especially now I've persuaded Duncan to come as my partner.'

She watched as Steph's expression twisted awkwardly, and a faint flush blossomed on her cheeks. 'Did I tell you Lance... I mean Dr Whitelock, has asked me to accompany him? I mean... I didn't know what to say.'

'Well, I hope you said yes.'

'Oh, Pip.' Steph's sigh was heart-wrenching. 'I didn't really give him an answer. And he was so kind and understanding. He knows about... So he said to let me think about it. He's so nice and I want to say yes. But... Don't you think it's too soon?'

Pippa studied the anguish on her friend's face, and her heart tore. She could imagine what Steph was going through. She only had to think how she'd feel if anything happened to Duncan. But...

'What I think,' she began tentatively, 'is that if you like Dr Whitelock and you'd like to go with him, then say yes.

It's only a dance and a bit of fun, and it would help you get to know him better. But as for it being too soon, just think what Rusty would be saying if he were looking down on you now. I know he wasn't as happy-go-lucky as Jack, but I'm sure he'd be saying *go for it, girl*. You can't put your life on hold forever. Rusty will always be in your heart, but I know he'd have wanted you to look forward. Dr Whitelock strikes me as really nice. Don't let him slip through your fingers.'

She saw Steph raise her bowed head, tears glistening in her eyes. It must be so, *so* hard for her, but she had to move on.

'Oh, Pip, you're absolutely right,' Steph gulped. 'That's exactly what Rusty would've said. Thank you. When I see Lance next, I'll tell him yes.'

'Good,' Pippa smiled back. 'Now, I don't know about you, but I'm worn out, and the idea of bed feels like bliss. We've got a full list tomorrow, and I'm sure you'll have your hands full, too.'

'Yes. But I wouldn't have it any other way. And no Sister Pudifoot breathing down my neck!'

The two girls laughed at the memory. How far they'd come since those early days! But just now, a good night's sleep was what they both needed. Filling their hot-water bottles, they said goodnight and went to their separate rooms, both feeling that life had taken a step forward.

* * *

'You'd think we were going on a flaming arctic expedition rather than to a dance!' Steph observed as they stepped out into Spring Hill.

Christmas itself was over. Despite increased rationing, it had been a truly festive occasion, especially as it was at the back of everyone's mind that, with the progress the Allies were making, it could well be the last Christmas of the war. But then the news had filtered through that on Boxing Day evening, a massive V2 flying bomb had fallen on Islington,

London, killing over seventy people and injuring very many more. The appalling news put a damper on everyone's buoyant mood. The war wasn't over yet.

Now, though, all the nursing staff from the cottage hospital were setting out for Tavistock Town Hall and the hospital's Christmas dance. Everyone, that is, apart from those who'd volunteered for night duty to care for the patients who hadn't been ready for discharge. A snowstorm had raged on Christmas Day, and now the town was hushed beneath a blanket of white. The evening was still, and the air tangy with the sharpness of crispy cold that comes with snow. But with so many mainly young women in high spirits, they made a jolly crowd as they made their way down West Street to the town's square.

Pippa had to laugh at Steph's words. The old Steph was beginning to shine through. They certainly all did look a sight. With the deep snow, wellington boots were the order of the day, lined with thick socks if anyone had any sense, to be changed on arrival. Shoes for the dance were either held in a bag or tied on to the cord of the ubiquitous gas-mask box. Most still carried them, even if they were convinced there'd be no gas attacks now, and the boxes were useful for carrying combs and lipstick! To top it all, anyone lucky enough to possess a long evening gown had to hold the hem up around their knees to stop it dragging in the snow and getting soaked. A most fashionable combination with rubber boots, Pippa considered with a chuckle.

'You're right there!' she grinned back as they all trudged along in their wellies. 'But I'm really looking forward to it. Especially as Duncan will be there.'

'Leg's a lot better now, isn't it?'

'Yes, it is. He won't be able to jitterbug or jive, but then I can't do those either.'

In the reflection given off by the full moon shining on the snow, Pippa saw Steph's eyes swivel cheekily towards her. 'As long as he can do a slow, sensuous waltz,' she teased.

'Trust you!' Pippa giggled. 'And maybe you'll be dancing the last waltz with the lovely Dr Whitelock, too. And if you are, there'll be plenty an envious eye on you.'

'Touché!' Steph laughed as they arrived in the extensive square with the impressive, stone-built Victorian town hall.

Everyone traipsed through the arched wooden doors and up the stairs, leaving a wet trail. All was chaos inside as the guests found room to hang up their coats and change from their boots into shoes. Excitement simmered in Pippa's heart. She'd heard what a fun evening it usually was, and she couldn't wait to spend it with Duncan. She felt her insides do a little dance as she spied him waiting patiently for her. She'd never seen him in a suit, and it made him appear more handsome than ever. He looked a little lost and overwhelmed, which was somehow even more endearing. A dance among strangers and so many of them female was as far away as you could get from the open sea and the male-dominated world he was used to.

Pippa saw his face light up with relief as she came up to him. They exchanged broad smiles, and a thrill shot through her as he kissed her on the cheek. Not a full, deep kiss like the many they'd enjoyed. It was hardly appropriate. But to Pippa it said that there was no need to demonstrate their feelings in public. It was *accepted* that they were together, and that meant the world.

'You got down the hill all right?' she asked anxiously.

'I came down earlier, before it got dark,' he reassured her, 'and went to Walter's to change. He's such a good soul. I'm staying there overnight.'

'Are you? Oh, good. I'm so pleased Mum and Walter got together. She's the sort who needs someone to look after her, and Walter's so kind.'

'Ah, there you are!' Steph appeared at Pippa's shoulder. 'Duncan, this is Doctor Whitelock.'

'Oh, Lance, please. We're not on the wards now.' Lance held out his hand and Duncan shook it firmly, looking relieved, Pippa thought, to be properly introduced to at least one stranger among so many. 'Ex-Navy, I believe?'

'Merchant, yes,' Duncan replied, sounding more confident. 'Formerly Second Officer. Invalided out, so dancing's not my strong point.'

'No problem,' Lance grinned. 'We have fun and games here as well. A bit childish really, but it's a chance for everyone to let their hair down. Shall we go in? I can hear the band tuning up. Let's grab a table while we can.'

'Oh, I believe the Doctors Franfield were going to reserve one for us next to theirs, like,' Pippa informed him.

'Let's see if we can find them, then.' And with that, Lance propelled Steph in through the doors.

Pippa stifled a gasp as they stepped through into the hall. She'd heard it was beautiful in design. Built in Victorian times on the wealth of local copper mining, but in Tudor style. What she knew from the outside were massive, tall windows on the upper storey were hidden behind heavy blackout curtains. The ornate windows might be obscured from view, but the wood panelling around the walls and the stunning ceiling definitely weren't. What Pippa believed were called hammerbeams like the ones she'd seen in photographs of the Great Hall at Hampton Court Palace arched magnificently overhead. With a huge Christmas tree, twinkling with tinsel and tiny electric lights, standing to one side of the stage, it was all quite magical.

'Impressive, isn't it?' Lance grinned as they moved through the gathering throng, and found Elliott and his wife, Ling, and William with his wife, Deborah, already seated at a table. A fur stole and a shawl were indeed spread over the four chairs around the adjacent table, reserving it for them. Duncan only had to be introduced to Ling and Deborah as he'd met Elliott and William before, and then he and Lance went off to find drinks for them all.

'Not much choice, of course,' William said gloomily. 'Beer that I swear has been watered down, lemonade, and some bourbon gifted by the Americans, bless them. Did you hear, nearly three hundred wounded soldiers arrived by train on Christmas Day, poor sods? With the snow, the ambulances they were transferred into couldn't get up the hill to get them to the hospital at the Plaster Down Camp. So all the local women came out of their houses with buckets of fire ashes to throw under the wheels to help them get a grip. Warm's your heart, the way everyone clubs together.'

'That's the war for you,' Deborah put in. 'I hope that sort of community spirit lasts once it's over.'

There was no chance for anyone to reply as just then, the band struck up with 'In the Mood', and William pulled Deborah to her feet. Gosh, they were proper good dancers, Pippa thought as she watched them. A moment later, Lance invited Steph on to the floor, and she could see he was an accomplished dancer and all. She'd have loved to be up there with Duncan, but she'd just have to be patient and wait for a slower number. She tried to chat to Elliott and Ling, but the music was too loud. But she was perfectly content to sit and hold Duncan's hand, watching the few doctors present dancing either with their partner, or being much in demand with the unaccompanied nursing staff. Many of the nurses partnered each other for lack of men, and crikey, Pippa noticed a lot of envious glances at Steph who was tripping the light fantastic with Lance as he led her expertly around the dance floor. Pippa was filled with joy to see the happy grin on Steph's face.

At last, the band changed tempo. Pippa was disappointed to see Lance ask another staff nurse to partner him in a slow waltz. Oh, no. Poor Steph. But Pippa had no time to console her as Duncan got to his feet and, with an apologetic smile, held out his hand. They stepped on to the floor to join other couples moving slowly about the hall. Pippa noticed Elliott and Ling shuffle up beside them. Several years the younger, Ling was still light on her feet, but Elliott was clearly showing his age. Pippa felt a twinge of sadness at the thought that these two people who'd shown her such kindness were facing their twilight years.

But all was forgotten as Duncan held her close, his hand resting against her back as they progressed around the floor. It didn't matter that she was aware of his limp at every third beat of the waltz. She could feel him against her, his body pressed next to hers as she drank in the male scent of him, could feel the strength in his arms. The room, the people around them dropped away as intoxication streamed through her, and she jolted back to reality as Duncan came to a halt and she realised the music had stopped.

'It's another slow one,' Duncan whispered into her hair as the band began to play 'I'll be with you in Apple Blossom Time'.

'Is your leg okay for another dance?' Pippa asked.

'Hang my leg,' he murmured. 'I can put up with a bit of an ache if it means I can hold you like this a bit longer.'

They moved off again, and Pippa was delighted to see that Lance was back dancing with Steph. She relaxed against Duncan less self-consciously now, a gentle excitement rippling out from his hand in the small of her back. Her entire being was lost in deep contentment as they ambled around the hall, waltz steps almost forgotten as one tune followed another so that it took her by surprise when the last notes of the recent hit, 'Long Ago and Far Away', died away and the bandleader announced it was time for the games.

Pippa reluctantly pulled away from Duncan as everyone obediently divided themselves into teams. As Lance had said, it was all a bit silly. There were dressing up races, Blindman's Buff, and as balloons were unavailable, passing a loofah down the line, using only one's knees. Pippa was amazed to see Matron, usually so prim and proper, kick off her heeled shoes to be more agile in the games, and several other nurses followed suit.

Then it was back to the dancing, and Pippa felt honoured when William asked to whisk her around the dance floor in a quickstep. Sitting down to catch her breath afterwards, she watched, impressed, as Lance led Steph in a frantic jive to 'Boogie Woogie Bugle Boy', Steph following his lead as he spun her round in circles. At last, the band turned once again to slower, romantic tunes, the singer's melancholic voice heralding the end of the evening. Duncan took Pippa in his arms again, crushing her to him and forgetting all about proper steps. Pippa felt his love pouring into her and she welcomed the overwhelming emotion that filled her breast.

'Well, ladies and gentlemen, the time has come!' the bandleader announced. 'Please take your partners for the last waltz.'

Disappointed mutterings ricocheted about the hall as the singer began to croon 'Goodnight, Sweetheart'. Almost everyone found a partner, and Pippa and Duncan shuffled on one final time, Pippa feeling so close to him, drenched in the elation of the evening and sorry it was coming to a close.

'Darling Pippa,' she heard Duncan whisper against her cheek. 'Will you marry me?'

Pippa jerked to a standstill. Had she heard right? Surely she'd imagined it? But then as Duncan gently directed her into the dance again, her heartbeat quickened.

'I don't mean straight away,' she heard Duncan go on bashfully now, his voice low and tender. 'I know your career means so much to you, and I fully understand that. But . . . maybe in six or seven years' time. I can wait to have the most wonderful girl in the world as my wife. But . . . I'd love for us to be promised. To show the world that I love you and that you're mine.'

The room, the lights on the Christmas tree, the bright colours of the nurses' dresses, spun in Pippa's head like a blurred merry-go-round. When the music stopped and they finally came to a halt, she realised Duncan was gazing down at her, his eyes anxious and expectant. *Marry him?* The old dilemma tore at her soul, followed by a volcano of pure delight flowing out of her heart.

'You . . . really mean you'd be prepared to wait?' she stammered. 'I mean, not forever, but a few years?'

'Of course.' His face was utterly serious. 'And then maybe you could find other nursing work somehow. I just want to know that one day, you'll be mine. After all, who else would take on this old peg-leg?'

'Let them just try,' she answered fiercely.

Duncan started, and Pippa looked up to see tentative joy blossoming on his face.

'Do I take that as a yes?' he muttered.

She nodded as her mouth spread into a grin. 'I guess it does!'

'Then . . . if I thought I could do so without falling over and making a fool of myself, I'd pick you up and spin you round.'

'I'd rather you didn't, anyway,' Pippa giggled as a fountain of happiness sprang up inside her. 'I feel giddy enough as it is. And everyone would look at us as if we were mad.'

'Let them look. I want to tell the world!'

'Well, shush!' Laughing, she placed a finger on his lips. 'We should keep it a secret for now. We ought to tell my mum and your family first.'

Duncan's expression stilled. 'You're right, of course. Thank goodness it's only a few days till Sunday. But I'm going to find it hard keeping it a secret until then.'

'Just as well this evening's over, then. Now let's see if I can find the right wellies,' Pippa laughed as they filed out into the chaos of the lobby.

She hugged the joyous secret to her breast as they all said their goodbyes and were supervised out into the town square in batches so as to keep to the blackout rules. The war wasn't over yet. Outside, it was bitingly cold, everyone's breath billowing about them in the frosty air. Pippa lifted her face to Duncan, ready to receive a goodnight kiss.

'I'll walk my fiancée home,' he whispered in her ear.

'No, you get off to Walter's,' she told him gently. 'It's on the flat, and if you came with me, you'd have to walk back down the hill. I'll be perfectly safe with Steph, and there's a whole gang of us walking back to the nurses' home, if you hadn't noticed,' she teased.

'Well, if you're sure. But I'm not sure I can trust you not to tell Steph.'

'Then you don't know me as well as you think, Mr Chollacott!' she giggled.

'Until Sunday, then,' he said, giving her a peck on the cheek. 'I love you.' And then he turned reluctantly in the opposite direction towards Duke Street and Walter's shop.

'Proper grand, wasn't it?' Steph chortled, suddenly at her side.

'Certainly was!' Pippa agreed, and, her heart full, she linked her arm through her friend's and they set out with all their colleagues on the tramp back through the snowy, slippery town.

CHAPTER THIRTY-THREE

'Oh, that's master grand news!'

In an instant, Pippa was lost in Bea's crushing embrace, all the other cries of congratulation echoing over her head.

'Hey, Mum, don't hug her to death before I have a chance to marry her!'

'Oh, sorry, my lovers!' Bea released Pippa and held her arms open towards her eldest son instead. 'I be just that pleased for you!'

'Mum.' Pippa turned to Adeline and saw the glint of a tear in her eyes.

'I'm so happy for you,' Adeline said quietly, her voice almost a croak. 'Your dad would've been so proud, too.'

Pippa's heart contracted. Yes, her dad should have been there to share this precious moment. But the pang of sadness was dispelled as Duncan, having escaped Bea's hug, came to stand beside her.

'I know I don't need your permission as Pippa's over twenty-one, Mrs Luscombe,' he said solemnly, 'but I hope we have your blessing.'

'Indeed, you have both my blessing and my permission!' Adeline beamed, the tearful moment passed. 'But please call me Adeline. Mrs Luscombe is far too formal. Now come and sit by me, Pippa, my flower. Such wonderful news to herald in the new year.'

'Let's hope 1945 brings good news for the whole world,' Sylvie said, handing Pippa a cup of tea as she sat down on the sofa next to her mum. 'At least young Joanna, you know, Elliott's granddaughter who got friendly with that GI, has just had a letter from him. He's in France helping to drive back the Nazis, and not a scratch on him so far.'

'Let's hope it stays that way.'

'Yes, poor cheel's only just turned fifteen. It'd break her little heart if anything happened to him.'

'How are they all?' Pippa asked. 'It was so noisy at the dance, it was impossible to talk to them properly.'

'They'm all proper clever,' Bea answered. 'That young Edwin's turning into a lovely lad. Still mortal keen to follow in his dad's and granfer's footsteps and be a doctor.'

'Good for him,' Pippa nodded. 'We must pop round later to tell them our news. After all, if Elliott and William hadn't pulled a few strings to get me the post at the cottage hospital, like, Duncan and I wouldn't have had the chance to get to know each other better, and we wouldn't be celebrating today.'

'They're sure to be in. Deborah's preparing a little new year's Eve party for this evening,' Don put in. 'They've said to pop round. Sylvie's making some fish paste sandwiches to take.'

'Oh, that'll be nice. We can tell them our news, then. But I can't stay late. Monday tomorrow, and we've got a full afternoon list.'

'I wish my Len and Ernie had been able to get this evening off,' Bea grumbled. 'But they trains are still running, and they don't do so theyselves.'

Pippa nodded politely, and was relieved as various conversations broke out in different groups in the room. Personally, she wasn't sure she could live with so many people in one household. Beside her, she felt her mum squeeze her hand, drawing her attention.

'Actually,' Adeline said in a low voice, 'Walter and I have got some news, too.' Pippa saw her glance questioningly across at Walter, and he nodded his head in reply. 'We're also getting married,' Adeline continued after a short pause. 'You're the first to know. The first banns are being read next Sunday. We were just going to have a quiet wedding. Just everyone here and the Franfields with a little tea afterwards. But perhaps we should have a double wedding?'

Her mum getting married to Walter? Pippa stifled a little gasp. She was surprised, but her heart filled with happiness for them.

'Oh, Mum, that's wonderful! I'm delighted for you both! But . . .' She shot Duncan a look that sought reassurance. 'As for a double wedding . . .'

'The thing is, Mrs Luscombe, I mean Adeline,' Duncan explained in a level tone, 'we won't actually be getting married for some while. Pippa has her dream job. I won't take that away from her. She's worked so hard to get where she is, and I want her to enjoy it for some years before she has to give it up to marry me.'

'Oh, I see,' Adeline nodded with a smile. 'That's extremely understanding. And makes me respect you even more. And I know . . . I know her father would've appreciated that sentiment, too. Dear Neil . . . Pippa, love.' Her forehead folded into a tiny frown. 'You don't think it's too soon for Walter and me . . . ?'

'No, Mum, not at all. Just think, it's what Dad would've wanted. For you to be happy and move on with your life. It's been four years. Even Steph's got a new man in her life. The lovely Doctor Whitelock, and it's only been a year since Rusty died.'

'Well . . . if you're sure.'

'Of course I am, Mum. And presumably you'll go to live over the shop?'

'We will, indeed,' Walter beamed, joining in the conversation. 'I'm going to make your mum so happy, I promise.'

'And Arthur can have the box room back when he comes home.'

'*If* he comes home,' Adeline said sadly. 'He said he'd write, but he only did so twice. We don't know if he's alive or dead. His parents were his next of kin to be informed, of course. He said he'd ask them to let us know any bad news, but . . .' She let out a weighty sigh. 'We've heard nothing and we don't know where his parents are. So we can only assume he didn't make it.'

Pippa felt a lump rising in her throat. 'Oh, how sad.' She could remember his young face so clearly. So many young lives lost. But they must thrust such melancholy thoughts aside. 'So, you haven't told anyone else your news yet?' she whispered conspiratorially. 'Perhaps it's time you did?'

She watched as a loving, excited glance bounced back and forth between Walter and her mum. Adeline flushed a charming pink, while Walter's eyes were sparkling as he stood up and coughed to draw everyone's attention.

'Ladies and gentlemen,' he began, rising to his feet. 'Dear Adeline and I have some news, too,' he announced.

And Pippa's heart rejoiced as a sea of surprised, expectant faces turned towards them.

***

'You wanted to see me, Matron?' Pippa smiled expectantly as she entered Matron's office. In fact, except for when she was working in the theatre or elsewhere in the hospital, a broad grin hadn't left her face since the evening of the dance two weeks previously when Duncan had proposed.

Matron looked up, her face wearing its usual efficient expression. Goodness, she was sometimes hard to judge, was Matron. She seemed to glide effortlessly around the hospital, and yet arrived before anyone else. She could also accomplish any task in the hospital as well and as quickly as any of her staff. She ruled the hospital with a rod of iron, and yet there was deep compassion in her soul, and she'd defend any of her nurses like a mother hen. And then there'd been the night of the party when she'd completely let her hair down and had been full of fun.

Now Pippa found her expression utterly unfathomable, and her own pulse began to pound.

'Yes. Do sit down, Sister Luscombe.' And Pippa was hardly seated before she began, 'I hear congratulations are in order.'

Pippa's heart sank to her boots, her mind racing. How on earth had Matron found out? 'Yes, thank you, Matron,' she murmured.

Matron steepled her fingers and rested them against her chin, considering Pippa with piercing blue eyes and making sweat break out under Pippa's collar.

'You are considered very highly,' Matron began slowly. 'Both our own doctors and our visiting surgeons are most impressed with the efficient way you run the theatre, and when you help out on other wards, you just seem to slip in as if you were full-time on them. Both patients and staff think very highly of you, and we should be sorry to lose you.'

Pippa felt herself crumble. She was going to have to defend herself, explain . . . 'Oh, but we're not planning on actually getting married for—'

Matron appeared to ignore her, but went on regardless, leaving Pippa to gird up her courage. She'd have to interrupt before Matron could dismiss her.

'We had a board meeting yesterday, and discussed your case,' Matron continued. 'Doctor Franfield told us of your news. Now, heaven knows, we're short-staffed enough as it is, without losing valuable nurses like you. The thing is . . .'

Pippa's mind was giddy with the thoughts rushing about inside her head. Was Matron going to try and persuade her to break off the engagement? Surely she wasn't going to be forced to choose between Duncan and her career at this stage? She clenched her fists, forcing herself to allow Matron's words to percolate into her brain.

'We like to think we're a progressive hospital, and we *are* independent. Now, it is the policy of nearly every hospital in the country to dismiss nurses once they marry. It's thought that a young woman cannot be a proper wife and dedicate herself to nursing at the same time. But it isn't actual law. Now tell me, Sister Luscombe, where would you plan to live once you're married?'

Pippa wasn't expecting that. Why on earth . . . ? 'My fiancé is the caretaker at Mount House School,' she replied warily. 'He has separate quarters there, with two bedrooms. The previous caretaker was married, so we assumed—'

'Within walking distance, then? Or a short bike ride?'

'I should say so, yes, Matron,' Pippa frowned. What did that have to do with it?

'You're a very accomplished young woman, Sister Luscombe. Logical, organised. We value you highly. There was a lot of discussion around the board table yesterday, and we see no reason why someone of your calibre shouldn't continue to nurse once she's married.'

Matron sat back, eyes boring into Pippa's as she waited for the news to sink in. Pippa was dumbstruck, barely able to speak.

'Y-you mean . . . ?' she stuttered.

Matron's face now stretched into a smile. 'If you wish to marry and continue your nursing career, then you have the board's full approval. I must say, it would be a huge relief to me. We need good nurses like you.'

For a moment, Pippa could hardly believe what she'd heard. She and Duncan wouldn't need to wait to get married, and she could still continue nursing!

'Of course, I'm not quite sure what'll happen if and when this proposed new national health service comes into being,' she realised Matron was saying. 'But that could be years, and if all was working well, we'd fight tooth and nail to keep our good married nurses, provided their work was still up to scratch. You'll be our first, of course, but others may well follow in your wake.'

The mist of surprise was slowly clearing from Pippa's brain. 'Oh, Matron, I can't thank you enough!'

'Don't thank me. It was the whole board. Our country has learnt a lot from this war. Once it's over, we need to move forward. Now, I believe we both have work to do.'

'Yes, of course, Matron. And thank you again.'

Pippa got to her feet and quietly let herself out of the room. As she walked away down the corridor, her heart was singing.

***

'Well, Mrs Luscombe, Sister Luscombe.' Don smiled down at mother and daughter, one on each side of him, their arms linked into his. 'That's the last time I'll be able to call either of you that. So, are we ready?'

Pippa glanced across at her mother, and saw the look of pride mixed with emotion and excitement on her face. Marriage was a huge step for anyone, but for Adeline it was tinged with sadness. Pippa knew her mum would be thinking of her darling Neil, but Walter was a good man. And for Pippa, it should have been her dad giving her away. She lifted her eyes to Don, his back straight and looking so proud. He was the best substitute anyone could have wished for.

They entered St Eustachius' Church, and the organ music at once changed to 'Morning has Broken', that for a spring wedding, had seemed an appropriate choice. They'd decided they could hardly have 'Here comes the Bride' with there being two of them! Once the hospital had given Pippa permission to marry, a double wedding had been everyone's wish.

It was Easter, Saturday 31 March. Daffodils swayed in the churchyard, and with other flowers being difficult to get hold of, both brides carried a bunch of daffs from Don's front garden. Adeline wore a simple, calf-length dress in beige wool she'd found in the clothes exchange, with a fur stole Deborah had lent her to keep her warm, and a jaunty little hat. Understandably, she'd wanted her daughter to be the star of the day. Miss Polly and Miss Primrose had dug out an old, ivory silk gown of their mother's from back in the previous century. There'd been such a lot of material in it that they'd fashioned Pippa the most glorious full length wedding dress, and they'd spent hours embroidering the hem with silver thread. A head-dress and long veil, again borrowed from Deborah who'd kept hers from her own wedding, completed the picture, and Pippa felt like a queen as she progressed down the aisle.

Adeline and Walter were to make their vows first. It was usual for a second bride to wait outside for her turn, but there was no way Pippa was going to miss witnessing her mum's wedding, so half way down the aisle, she unlaced her arm from Don's, and took her place in a pew, as arranged. She could just see Duncan's back, shoulders tall and straight, beside Walter's shorter figure at the front of the church. Tears welled up inside her as she listened to her mum and Walter's voices. It was so moving to know her mum had found happiness again.

Then it was her turn as Don came back down the aisle to collect her. A multitude of emotions threatened to choke her, but the moment they began walking towards the altar and so many smiling faces turned towards her, the butterflies in her stomach ceased and she was swamped by overwhelming joy. The breath caught in her throat as Duncan stepped into the aisle and turned to wait for her. His naval dress uniform had been sent on to him when his ship had returned to Blighty, and he'd been given permission by the company to wear it for his wedding. Pippa had never seen it, and he looked so handsome, the usual rogue lock of hair brushed back from his face, that her heart leapt into her mouth.

Their eyes met, Duncan's gentle look sending her a message of unspoken love and devotion. She came up to his side, a flame glowing deep inside her. Time seemed to stop. This was the man she loved with a burning passion, and they would be together for ever.

After the service, her mum and Walter led the procession back down the aisle to the rousing tune of Mendelssohn's 'Wedding March'. Pippa and Duncan followed at a distance, with Steph and the Chollacott girls following on as bridesmaids. They paused while the first happy couple stepped outside to be greeted by well-wishers. Then as they emerged themselves, Pippa gasped aloud and then burst out laughing as several nurses in uniform appeared from nowhere to form an archway of bedpans for them to walk beneath.

Everyone trouped across the town square to the Town Hall, strangers calling out their best wishes as they did so. With the Chollacott and Franfield families, Steph and Lance, the other residents of the Chollacott household, various staff from the hospital, Walter's sister and husband and a few of his friends, they made a varied and happy gathering. Sylvie, Bea and Deborah between them had made sure the extra rations allowed for a wedding had been put to best advantage, while William had carried over Deborah's precious gramophone so that there was to be music and dancing after the food. There were two wedding cakes, fairly pathetic affairs, but hidden under ornate cardboard cases made to look like icing fit for royalty.

'That, my darling, was truly the best day of my life,' Duncan declared as he carried Pippa over the threshold of his converted outbuilding at the school later that evening.

'Well, I'm planning on making every day the best of our lives from now on,' she answered cheekily as he set her on her feet.

'And how, Mrs Chollacott,' a pause as he kissed her nose, 'd'you intend to do that?' Another tender kiss on her lips before his mouth moved down to her throat.

'Wouldn't you like to know?' she teased, raising her eyebrows. 'I always like a man in uniform, but maybe you'd look better without it?'

'You brazen hussy,' Duncan chuckled. 'I believe the bedroom's this way.'

He took her hand, his smile overwhelming her with happiness. An enchanted thread weaved itself about them as he led her to the half-open door.

* * *

Pippa stopped dead in her tracks as she walked down Spring Hill on her way home. Archie Yelland. Again. What the hell did he want with her? Irritation seethed inside her as he halted in front of her.

'Archie, what on earth are you doing here?' she demanded.

'I came to see you,' he answered levelly.

'Well, I don't want to see you,' she retorted. 'I told you afore, I'm not interested. And I'm a happily married woman now.'

'Congratulations,' he said, his voice so genuine, it made Pippa hesitate. 'But I still need to talk to you.'

'Just go away and leave me alone, will you?' she bristled, briskly continuing on her way. But he grasped her arm and dragged her round to face him.

'Philippa, listen to me. I've come to warn you. I could've written to you at the nurses' home, but I was worried you wouldn't get it.'

His tone was agitated, his brow folded in concern. Pippa gazed at him doubtfully, but her instincts told her she should listen. She tipped her head, a questioning expression on her face.

'It's Ruby,' he told her, eyes boring into hers. 'She's on the war path. She's only stationed in Plymouth now, so she's not far away. The thing is, I've got a new lady friend. We met in the autumn, soon after I saw you last. And it's turning out quite serious. Ruby comes home to visit often, and when she found out, she almost threw a fit. And then Edith, my new girl, had an accident. She fell down some steps and broke her ankle. Only she was sure she didn't fall. She's convinced she was pushed. By an ATS girl. She described her to me. And it was Ruby.'

A cold shiver ran through Pippa's veins. Remembering what Ruby had done at the hospital to get her into trouble, even putting an innocent patient's life at risk, she could imagine that what Archie was telling her was true. She met his anxious gaze, and bit her lip.

'Thank you for the warning. But surely she wouldn't know where I am?'

'Don't forget, I found you easily enough. Ruby could do the same. So, I'm just warning you to be on your guard. You and your husband. I believe Ruby's unstable, and I wouldn't want anything to happen to my butterfly girl. Edith's fall was bad enough, but it could've been worse. So,' Archie sighed, 'I'm glad I found you. But just be careful, eh?'

'Yes, I will. And thanks for coming all this way. And you take care, too. And your Edith.'

'And if you need to contact me about it ever, we're the saddlers on the edge of Ivybridge. Anyone in the town will tell you where we are.'

Pippa nodded. 'Bye, then. And good luck.'

'You, too. Must go now. If I hurry, I'll catch the next train.'

He spun round and began to walk down the hill before turning to give a small wave of acknowledgement and hurrying on. Pippa didn't say she was going in the same direction and could walk with him. Instead, she stood quietly for a moment, waiting for Archie's warning to sink in. It seemed unreal. Could Ruby really be that vindictive? But surely her own involvement with Archie, if you could call it that, was all in the past? This Edith, poor soul, she was the one who needed to be careful.

Pippa set off slowly down the hill. It had been good of Archie to come all that way to speak to her, but she was sure it wasn't necessary. She would put it to the back of her mind, forget about the bizarre conversation. Nevertheless, as she walked through the town, the hairs on the back of her neck bristled uncomfortably. It was ridiculous, but she had the creeping sensation that she was being followed. She shook her head dismissively. In a quarter of an hour, she'd be home, up the hill to the school and in Duncan's safe embrace, all thoughts of Ruby dissipated to the four winds.

And yet . . .

CHAPTER THIRTY-FOUR

A loving smile passed between them as Duncan handed Pippa a steaming mug. It was the end of April and a month since they'd been joined together in holy matrimony. Pippa couldn't have been happier, curled up on the sofa in their own home, however humble, listening to the radio and snuggling against the man she loved with all her soul. She was supremely content, and the strange meeting with Archie Yelland had faded to the back of her memory.

'Afraid it's only half and half,' Duncan apologised, sitting down beside her. 'I didn't want to use up all our milk ration.'

'Good thinking, but it's not bad.' Pippa took a sip of her Horlicks. 'With the war looking very much as if it's coming to an end, I think we'll all be glad to see the back of rationing.'

'Huh, I don't think rationing will end that quickly. Could be a few years before everything gets back to normal, I reckon. Talking of which, I called in at Gran and Gramps today. Mum was busy packing. She's moving back home at last. It'll be grand to see her and Dad living a normal life again. And the house won't be so crowded, what with Ernie tying the knot in the summer, and Susie staying on here.'

'Moved into my mum's old room, hasn't she, Susie?'

'Yes. And when Mum leaves at the weekend, it'll free up one of the large bedrooms and the old dining room. I thought Gran and Gramps would just want new tenants for the bedroom, but with the housing shortages, they're going to keep the dining room as another bedroom, for now at least, bless them. They put an ad in the paper at the weekend, and they've had several replies. They've got people coming to view later in the week.'

'It'll mean a lot of extra work for them, especially without Bea and my mum to help.'

'I'm sure Susie will step into the breach. If the British Restaurants close once the war's over, she'll be looking for work. But I'm not going to worry about it just now. I've got to pick up some supplies from the hardware shop in the morning, so I'll drop you off in town. Save you walking.'

'Mmm, that'll be nice. An extra ten minutes in bed. Talking of which,' Pippa yawned loudly, 'I'm turning in. I'm whacked.'

'I won't be long behind. Leave your mug there. I'll wash them up.'

'What a wonderful husband you are!'

Standing up, Pippa dropped a kiss on his forehead and went off to use the little bathroom. A few minutes later, she was curled up in bed, leaving on the side lamp for Duncan to see his way. Eyes tightly closed and almost drifted off to sleep, she was shaken by a whoop of delight from the sitting room and Duncan appeared at the door.

'Hitler's dead!' he exclaimed.

'What?' Pippa sat up in bed.

'Just been announced on the radio.'

'You sure?'

'Yes! *German Radio has just announced that Hitler is dead.* That's what he said, that Stuart Hibberd. Then he repeated it. It must be true.'

'Oh, my God. So it's over.'

'Bar the shouting, yes. Oh!'

An instant later, Pippa was wrapped in his arms, delighting in the news, hugging him tightly. 'I never thought we'd see this day,' she croaked into his shoulder, tears streaming down her cheeks. 'All those poor people who died, people's lives torn apart. All those poor babies in the maternity block. And then all the fighting still going on in the Far East.'

'Try not to think about that now,' Duncan soothed. 'Just think of the future. *Our* future.'

'Yes, you're right,' she gulped. 'But I'm so happy, I'm not sure I'll sleep.'

'Well, you must. Busy day tomorrow. I'll be in in a minute and I'll cuddle you to sleep.'

'That sounds nice,' Pippa smiled, and snuggled down again, wrapped in happiness.

***

'You in?' Duncan asked the next morning.

Pippa pulled shut the passenger door of the van. 'Yup. Off we go.'

The engine spluttered into life. Duncan put the van into gear and they moved slowly forward along the drive. A number of boys who were boarded out were coming in through the gates from the road, walking up the steep incline towards the old mansion that housed the school. At the top of the slope in front of the main building, the grass had been dug up to make two huge vegetable plots, but beyond them, the land dropped steeply away down over wild grass with trees forming a copse at the bottom. You couldn't really see the town from there, but as the van moved down the drive and the view began to flash past, Pippa reflected for the umpteenth time how beautiful the grounds were and how lucky they were to be living there.

'Aren't we going a bit fast?' she gasped.

She glanced across at Duncan. His face was set rigid. As the vehicle was gaining speed, she could see his right foot pumping up and down on one of the pedals.

'God, the brakes have gone,' he muttered, pumping furiously.

Pippa froze. Terrified as they were going even faster down the hill, boys leaping out of their way. She saw Duncan reach for what she knew was the handbrake and yank it up. They careered onwards.

'Hang on tight!' he yelled. 'I'm going to try . . .'

Pippa knew enough to realise he was fighting with the gearstick. Was he trying to slam it into reverse? Her heart clenched with fear. There was an ear-splitting grinding sound. Stunned with horror, she watched helplessly as they hurtled towards the parapet of the bridge at the bottom of the incline, its solid stones looming towards them. She clung desperately with both hands on to the door handle. They were going to hit . . . Could she hold on? Duncan?

He yanked the steering wheel round. The van slewed sideways and came to an abrupt halt as it crashed into the bridge. Pippa was catapulted forwards, but felt something across her chest, trying to restrain her. A split second later, she was thrown backwards in her seat. For a moment, her vision was dotted with black stars and she realised she'd hit her head but she was still conscious. She was safe, but a whimper of terror fluttered from her lungs.

Oh, dear God. Duncan. He was lying half across her. She realised as she clawed her way through a cloud of shock that he must have leant across to try and protect her. Now he was half slumped across the steering wheel. Utterly still.

Panic rose inside her. Instinctively she felt below his jaw for a pulse. Thank God. She turned in the seat, wincing as she realised she'd pulled her shoulder. But she must hold Duncan's head still. What if . . . ? Oh, no! It didn't bear thinking about.

It seemed an age but could only have been seconds before horrified faces were peering in at the windows.

'Get help!' she yelled.

'Simon's already gone,' an older boy told her, pulling open the driver's door. 'Should we get Mr Chollacott out?'

'No, not till we've got proper help. We need an ambulance, but the cottage hospital doesn't have one.'

'The Yanks do,' the boy said. 'We should contact them.'

'Good boy. Then go!'

He raced off, and almost at once, the headmaster and another teacher appeared in his place.

'I've sent young Fisher to the office to get Mrs Dixon to ring for help. Anything we can do here?'

'Just help me keep his neck and back straight.'

'Of course.' The headmaster opened the door as wide as it would go and grasped Duncan's shoulders in a strong hold. 'What on earth happened?'

'The brakes failed,' Pippa almost squealed in frustration. 'The footbrake and the handbrake. Duncan tried to stop but—'

'The footbrake *and* the handbrake? But that's . . . Evans, run up to the office and tell Mrs Dixon to ring the police once she's organised help for Mr Chollacott. Footbrakes and handbrakes don't both fail unless . . .'

Pippa's eyes opened wide with horror as his words sunk in. Archie's warning exploded in her head. Surely . . . ?

A tiny, strangled sound gurgled in her throat. 'If someone did this, I know who,' she managed to force out the words. 'Her name's Ruby Saundercock. She's in the ATS and would've known what to do. She must've done it overnight.'

'Ruby Saundercock? I'll remember the name and tell the police. Ah, here comes a car. I think it must be . . .'

Still holding Duncan's head firmly, Pippa turned to look out of the passenger window. A car she recognised had turned in at the gates and halted at the other side of the bridge. Her heart collapsed with relief as William Franfield leapt out and ran towards them.

* * *

'Oh, Pippa, I'm so sorry. I came as soon as I could get a break. Oh, Lord, it's just like when Rusty . . .'

Pippa rose up from her seat by Duncan's bedside and at once found herself wrapped in her friend's embrace. Oh, poor Steph. This must be bringing back such awful memories for her.

'No, no it's not,' she assured her, drawing away. 'He's had loads of X-rays and there's nothing broken. Well, apart from a couple of cracked ribs, but non-displaced. He's going to be pretty sore for a bit, but it's just a bad concussion. Probably no worse than I had myself in the bombing.'

'But . . . you're sure?'

'Yes, absolutely. Rusty's skull was badly fractured, wasn't it? But there's no reason why Duncan won't be as right as rain. We've an operating list this afternoon, so I should be in Theatre, but they won't let me. Shelley, Sister Eastercott, is always happy to step out of retirement on the odd occasion, so she's coming in.'

'Oh, that's good, then. And are you okay?'

'Shaken up, of course. I'll feel happier once Duncan's regained consciousness. I jarred my shoulder a bit, but that's all. Might've been worse if Duncan hadn't reached across to try and protect me. But if he hadn't done that, he might've been able to brace himself against the steering wheel instead of cracking his ribs on it.'

'You can't blame yourself for that.'

'I don't. But he was quite my hero.' Pippa turned back to the bed and stroked the back of Duncan's hand. 'If he hadn't tried to put the van into reverse and swung on the steering wheel, we might've hit the bridge head on rather than sideways, and it could've been an awful lot worse.'

'Yes, well, thank goodness it wasn't. And what about Bea and the family?'

'Dear Bea.' Pippa's lips curved in a wistful smile. 'She was taking a couple of suitcases back to their home in Plymouth today, and then bringing them back empty, ready to make the final move home at the weekend. Poor soul ended up coming to see Duncan in here instead. She's usually so buoyant and jolly, it was heartbreaking to see her so cut up. But she's got Sylvie and Don to support her. They're coming to visit tonight. I just hope he'll have come round by then.'

Her gaze travelled back to Duncan's pale face and the bump on the side of his forehead. It was starting to colour. She knew it could be a while before he opened his eyes. She remembered that twilight world she herself had existed in before she became fully awake. Her heart just yearned for him to show some signs of consciousness.

'I'd better get back to the ward. Lance'll be doing his rounds later.'

Pippa beamed at her friend. 'And . . . everything good there?'

She couldn't help noticing the gentle flush on Steph's cheeks. She didn't need an answer as Steph grinned and then left the room. Pippa took a deep breath to calm herself. Despite the brave face she'd put on for Steph's sake, her insides were clenched with anxiety. Steph knew as well as she did that there could be serious complications to a bad concussion. Until Duncan woke up and spoke to her, she'd be worried sick.

A knock on the door distracted her. She was grateful that William had arranged for Duncan to be in a side ward. He was sure peace and quiet would help Duncan recover more quickly, but the silence was overwhelming and Pippa was glad of the distraction. A moment later, the door opened and in walked a man she didn't recognise.

'Ah, Mrs . . . erm, Sister Chollacott, I believe,' he said, eyeing her uniform. 'Inspector Barker. May I have a word?'

Pippa's brow pleated. What would he have to say? Reluctantly, she left Duncan's side.

'Better to talk outside,' she answered. 'If Duncan can hear anything, it could cause him distress.'

'Of course.' The inspector nodded, holding the door open for her as they stepped into the corridor. 'I have some news. D'you need to sit down?'

'No, I'm fine,' she told him, though her stomach was churning. 'What have you found out?'

'Well, you were right. We inspected the van, and both the brake-fluid pipe and the handbrake cable had been cut. We checked where the van is normally parked, and there was indeed a pool of brake fluid on the ground. We also found a return train ticket to Plymouth. Must've been dropped by whoever did it. In the meantime, the headmaster immediately called an assembly and asked the boys if they'd seen anyone unusual hanging around in the last day or two. Two younger ones said they'd spoken to a woman in ATS uniform down in the spinney yesterday afternoon. She said she'd come to visit her nephew at the school, so they'd not thought anything of it. But she matched the brief description you'd given us of this Ruby Saundercock you told us about. Then another boy said he thought he'd seen the figure of a woman prowling around when he went to the lavatory in the night, but thought he must've dreamt it.

'So, we went to both Tavistock stations, knowing the woman would need to buy another ticket, and indeed a woman answering your description of her did buy a one-way ticket to Plymouth at Tavistock South. We rang Plymouth police and they sent two officers to Plymouth North Road to intercept her. In case we were too late, we also rang the station, and she was detained by Sub-station Master Chollacott. Any relation by any chance?'

'Yes. Duncan's father!' Pippa was amazed.

'Ah, I did wonder. He held her until the local officers were able to get there and arrest her. With due respect to him, he treated her with great restraint.'

'Yes, he would. So you believe it was Ruby who did it? She certainly would've had the training in the ATS. Archie, Mr Yelland, said she was doing very well as a driver.'

'That's right. We'll be talking to Mr Yelland.'

'Oh, I'm sure he had nothing to do with it. It was he who warned me about her.'

'No, well, we wanted to speak to him about this other incident with his girlfriend. And also about Miss Saundercock's state of mind. We'll be interviewing her superior officer in the ATS and also the matron at the City Hospital after what you told us about her putting a patient's life at risk just to get you into trouble. We're also seeing if we can lift any fingerprints from the van just to confirm. But Miss Saundercock has confessed. She seemed almost deranged when she did so, I have to say.'

Pippa gave a slight shake of her head. It was almost unbelievable. 'So what'll happen to her now?'

'She'll be charged with attempted murder and so forth, but she might not be seen fit to go to trial. She'll likely be held in a psychiatric prison for years, maybe for life.'

Pippa released a weighty sigh. She couldn't help feeling relieved but all the same . . .

'Don't feel sorry for her,' the inspector advised. 'You and your husband could've been killed. He could've lost control of the van because of what she did and mown down some pupils at the school. You just look after your husband now. And take care of yourself.'

'Yes, thank you, Inspector.'

She watched as he walked away down the corridor, and then went back to sit by Duncan's side. It was all so much to take in that her head was spinning. She couldn't believe that someone who'd trained as a nurse could be so callous. But then who knew what the strains of the war could do to someone's mind?

Her gaze travelled over Duncan's beloved face, and a black depression weighed down on her like a storm-cloud. Oh, God, what if there was some damage going on inside his brain that they couldn't see? Please, Duncan, wake up! And suddenly the strength emptied out of her and she burst into tears.

***

'Archie!' Pippa looked up from her position in the chair as the door opened.

'Oh, Philippa, I'm so sorry about all this!' Archie's face was screwed up in anguish. 'The police came and told me everything yesterday, so I told them all that I could. And this is . . . ?'

'Yes, Duncan, my husband.' There was a catch in her throat. She could hardly bear to take her eyes off Duncan in case there was any sign of him coming round.

'He's still . . . ?' Archie's voice was low with emotion.

'Yes,' Pippa gulped. 'It's been more than twenty-four hours. Yesterday morning we were so happy, what with the news that Hitler's dead. Like everyone, we were thinking what the future would be like once the war's over. And then this.'

Archie closed his eyes and shook his head. 'I feel this is all my fault. After what Ruby did to Edith, I should've known.'

'But you did try to warn me.'

'And in doing so, I led her straight to you. She came to see me that day. To pester me again, no doubt. My father told her I'd gone to visit an old friend. He didn't mention it to me because he knew I was fed up with her and he didn't want to upset me. But in her confession, she said she put two and two together and followed me here. Then after I spoke to you, she followed you to the school, and worked out exactly how she could try to do you harm. Or more particularly, Duncan. The police told me she said she wanted you to know what it was like to have the man you love taken away.'

'Really? Well, she certainly did that,' Pippa spat. 'I can only pray that Duncan will be all right.' She took in a deep breath, then let her shoulders fall. 'I don't blame you, Archie. So please don't blame yourself.'

'But if I'd never fallen for you, never written that stupid poem—'

'But it was really lovely, Archie. I hope you've written something like that for Edith.'

She gave a secret smile as she saw him blush. 'Yes, I have. She adored it.'

'Good. I'm very happy for you.'

'Thank you. She really is something very special. But you know I'd never do anything to hurt you. But I'll leave you for now. We might have to meet again because of all this. But in the meantime, my fingers are absolutely crossed for you.'

'Thanks, Archie, and thanks for coming.'

He nodded, and quietly let himself out of the room. Pippa turned back to Duncan, watching his chest gently rise and fall. A tide of grief streamed through her. What if he never woke up? The salty pools in her eyes suddenly overflowed in a torrent again, pouring her grief into the dreadful aching emptiness inside her.

* * *

Early that evening, there was a gentle knock on the door and Steph's head peeped around it before the rest of her came into the room.

'Any change?' she whispered.

Pippa's heart took comfort from her friend's concern. 'No, not yet. Oh, Steph, I'm so worried . . .'

'Remember, you were unconscious for a long time and you were fine,' she said encouragingly. 'But here's something to cheer you up. It's been on the radio. The German Army in Italy surrendered a couple of days ago, and this afternoon, Berlin fell to the Russians and the German Army there surrendered at three o'clock. And I expect you'd heard that Mussolini was shot dead a few days ago?'

'So, it's almost over.' Pippa's voice was flat. Right now, there was only one thing that mattered to her. 'Did you hear that, Duncan, my love?' She forced brightness into her words. 'The Germans have surrendered. It's virtually over.'

She waited, her face taut with longing. But nothing. She turned to Steph with a sigh. 'Well, that's good news anyway—'

'Pippa, look!' Steph cried. 'He moved his hand! Look, he did it again!'

Hope jangled in Pippa's heart. Yes! Steph was right! She slipped her hand into Duncan's and felt the pressure of his fingers in her palm.

'P-Pippa.' The sound rasped in his throat.

Joy erupted inside her like a fountain. 'Oh, Duncan, my darling! Please! Can you open your eyes?'

She watched as his eyelids flickered and she saw those lovely hazel orbs gazing at her as his lips lifted into a weak smile.

'Oh, thank God, my darling!' She dropped the lightest kiss on his forehead as euphoria fizzed inside her. 'You're back with us!'

'Did you . . . ever doubt it?' he croaked. 'I had to . . . come back to my lovely wife. And did I hear . . . the Germans have surrendered?'

'Yes, it's true! Surely it can only be a few days before it's all official! Oh, my love!' She couldn't help but try and hug him.

'Ouch!' He drew in a seething breath. 'Ow, that hurts.'

'Oo, sorry. You've got a couple of cracked ribs as well as a lump the size of an egg on your head. But . . . Oh, I love you so much!'

She bent over and kissed him again, this time on the lips. Behind her, Steph quietly backed out of the room.

***

'Are you sure you're all right?' Pippa glanced up anxiously at Duncan as they stepped out of the hospital doors. 'They wanted you stay a couple more days.'

But Duncan grinned down at her. 'A week in hospital's enough for anyone, especially when I've spent so long in hospital before. Besides, I wouldn't miss this for the world. VE Day! Never thought it'd come, did we?'

'Promise me you won't overdo it?'

'How could I, with you clucking over me like a mother hen? And Mum'll be even worse. Really good of William to give us a lift down into town, mind.'

'He had a couple of patients to visit here anyway. He'll be here any second. That's his car over there. And at least it's brightening up. It was a bit drizzly at first.'

'That's because Mum put in her order with the Almighty for the street party, and even He wouldn't mess with her. Put off her move back home especially so all the family could be together. Dad can't be here till later, mind. Trains still have to run. Even more important on a day like this.'

'All we need is the war in the Far East to be over and the world can breathe again.'

'The Japs are pretty fanatical,' Duncan said glumly. 'It'll take some huge victory somewhere for them to surrender. But that's not going to spoil today.'

'Sorry to keep you waiting.' Pippa was glad when William hurried up behind them and interrupted the gloomy turn of the conversation. 'Let's get you in, Duncan.'

A minute later, William was driving them down into the town. People were out in the streets, bunting strung across from one side to the other, preparations for street parties in full swing as tables and chairs, even a piano or two, were being brought out on to the pavements. William had to drive slowly and carefully, sometimes waiting for people to move out of the way to let them past. Children, especially, with an unexpected two days off school, were racing round like maniacs, the adults too occupied with preparations and too full of joy to reprimand them. Union Jacks and Stars and Stripes fluttered everywhere. American jeeps had reappeared on the streets, delivering boxes of goodies to strangers setting up tables outside their houses. Children clustered around them, hoping for a candy bar or slab of chocolate.

Driving along the wide avenue of Plymouth Road was easier. With the Meadows most of the way along and so with houses only on the one side, tables were only being set up in front of the terraces of Victorian villas, so there was plenty of room for William's car to pass.

'Mum'll be in her element,' Duncan chuckled, getting out of the car.

'Believe me, Deborah's been on cloud nine,' William grimaced. 'You know how she loves organising a party. I've got to carry out her precious gramophone later, and apparently I'm going to be the one to guard it with my life.'

'Duncan!'

Norman careered up to his big brother, ready to lock him in a hug, and Pippa grabbed him by the arm before he could do so.

'Hey, Norman, don't knock him over! You've got to be careful! He's got a couple of broken ribs, you know.'

'Oh, sorry.' Norman looked crestfallen but then grinned as Duncan ruffled his hair. 'At least you'm out of the hospital for today, and that's the best thing ever!' And a second later, he'd raced off again.

Bea hurried up, then, her face beaming so that her cheeks shone like two rosy apples. 'Come and sit down, son, afore they tackers knock you over. Us've brought out an armchair for you, special like.'

'No need to fuss, Mum.'

'Course there is. Special day this is, and you'm just out of hospital in time.'

Duncan threw Pippa a desperate look, then meekly let Bea direct him to the chair. Pippa had to admit that she, too, felt happier once Duncan was safely settled for the day, and was able to relax and enjoy the proceedings. Everyone had made a huge effort with whatever food they could lay their hands on, and Walter had produced a few luxuries from his shop.

As the day progressed and she'd helped as much as she could, Pippa sat beside Duncan, holding his hand, their eyes locking in soft enchantment. She felt so rocked in love and contentment, a happiness so deep twinkling through her. This was her extended family now, her mum and Walter, all the Chollacotts, Miss Polly and Miss Primrose, Mr and Mrs

Robbins, Elliott, William and the entire Franfield family, and the neighbours in the house between, not to mention Steph and Lance who'd joined them part way through the day. She let her mind wander back over the years of the war. She'd lost her dad, and she'd give anything to have him back. So many others had died, too, and the loss of the babies at the maternity unit would haunt her for ever. But without the war, she'd never have met all these dear people who meant the world to her now. And she'd never have met Duncan.

That evening, William drove them back up to the school. He dropped them off in front of the main building where the boys were still outside enjoying themselves, even though it was turning cooler. The headmaster and some of the staff came up to greet them and welcome Duncan back, and many of the boys did the same.

'Good to see you back, Mr Chollacott!' several of them called.

'Thanks, Simon, David. And thanks for the get-well cards!' Duncan took Pippa's hand. 'Great kids. I'm so lucky to have this job. The school've been very good. They understand that I won't be able to do any heavy jobs for a while. And it looks as if the school is going to stay here permanently, so I've got a job for as long as I want. But,' he said, glancing down fondly at Pippa, 'whatever the future holds, we'll be together.'

'Yes, of course.' she grinned up at him, linking her arm through his. 'But just now I think you've had enough excitement for one day. I think we could do with a little bit of time together on our own.'

'Yes, I think you're right,' Duncan agreed as they turned away. 'But tell me, d'you still have that poem that's caused so much trouble?'

Pippa frowned. '"The Butterfly Girl"? Yes, I do as it happens. It was really very good.'

'So, do I need to be jealous?'

Pippa's heart thumped. 'No, of course not!' she answered fiercely. 'Why should you think that? It's you I love!' She gazed up anxiously into his face. And saw the teasing light in his eyes. 'Oh, you!'

They were both laughing now, and a whirlwind of joy spiralled up inside Pippa as, arm in arm, they made their way around the back of the mansion house to their home.

THE END

ACKNOWLEDGEMENTS

A huge thank you to the fantastic team at my publishers, Joffe Books. Grateful thanks also to my wonderful agent, Broo Doherty, for all her help and her faith in my work. And as ever, to my amazing husband, for being the springboard for all my ideas, for putting up with the hours I spend creating my novels, and above all, for his love.

Others who have helped with research to a greater or lesser degree: the archive team at the Royal College of Nursing, Plymouth historian Chris Robinson for pointing me in the right direction, my dear friend, Sir Michael Willats, for his input on vintage vehicles, and Dartmoor guide and historian and another good friend, Paul Rendell, for his continuing support.

Last, but not least, to you, my faithful readers. I do hope you have enjoyed this, the eleventh saga in my Devon series. If you can spare a moment, a review, however short, on Amazon or your preferred platform would be greatly appreciated. Don't forget, you can find further details of all my books on my website www.tania-crosse.co.uk and you can follow me on my Amazon Author Page, X/Twitter @TaniaCrosse or on Facebook @Tania Crosse Author.

AUTHOR'S NOTES

Researching Plymouth's City Hospital proved not an easy task. Up until the NHS was founded in 1948, Plymouth's hospitals were independent of each other. With the coming of the NHS, they were all amalgamated and the City Hospital became known as Freedom Fields. After the new mother hospital, Derriford, was opened in 1981, services from Freedom Fields were gradually transferred until it finally closed in 1998, and the site has largely been redeveloped for housing. This chequered history made detailed research all but impossible, so I have created a general picture of what it would have been like to be a nurse during the Second World War, having read many volumes of collated memoirs. However, the horrific event on one of the worst nights of the Plymouth Blitz when the brand-new maternity unit at the City Hospital received a direct hit killing nineteen babies, one new mother and several nursing staff, tragically is true, and this book is dedicated to them.

My late mother trained as a nurse during the war, although in London. Some of the stories she told me inspired some of the scenes depicted in the novel. I also have her old nursing textbooks, which proved invaluable for research. A patient wrote her a poem called 'Nurse Blue Eyes' which gave me the idea for *The Butterfly Girl*. Sadly, my mother never achieved her dream of becoming a theatre sister as she had to leave nursing when she married. Incidentally, my father was engaged to someone else when they met, inspiring the relationship in the book between Philippa, Archie and Ruby, but broke off the engagement to marry my mother. Thank goodness he did, as I wouldn't be here now!

THE JOFFE BOOKS STORY

We began in 2014 when Jasper agreed to publish his mum's much-rejected romance novel and it became a bestseller.

Since then we've grown into the largest independent publisher in the UK. We're extremely proud to publish some of the very best writers in the world, including Joy Ellis, Faith Martin, Caro Ramsay, Helen Forrester, Simon Brett and Robert Goddard. Everyone at Joffe Books loves reading and we never forget that it all begins with the magic of an author telling a story.

We are proud to publish talented first-time authors, as well as established writers whose books we love introducing to a new generation of readers.

We won Trade Publisher of the Year at the Independent Publishing Awards in 2023 and Best Publisher Award in 2024 at the People's Book Prize. We have been shortlisted for Independent Publisher of the Year at the British Book Awards for the last five years, and were shortlisted for the Diversity and Inclusivity Award at the 2022 Independent Publishing Awards. In 2023 we were shortlisted for Publisher of the Year at the RNA Industry Awards, and in 2024 we were shortlisted at the CWA Daggers for the Best Crime and Mystery Publisher.

We built this company with your help, and we love to hear from you, so please email us about absolutely anything bookish at feedback@joffebooks.com.

If you want to receive free books every Friday and hear about all our new releases, join our mailing list here: www.joffebooks.com/freebooks.

And when you tell your friends about us, just remember: it's pronounced Joffe as in coffee or toffee!

www.ingramcontent.com/pod-product-compliance
Lightning Source LLC
LaVergne TN
LVHW030843220125
801763LV00026B/678